NADEŽDA OBRADOVIĆ

The Anchor Book of
Modern African Stories

Nadežda Obradović is a critic and scholar of African literature at the University of Belgrade. Her book reviews have appeared in *World Literature Today* and *Pen International*. She is also the editor of *Looking for a Rain God* and *The Prince of Fire*, a collection of contemporary Serbian short stories.

The Anchor Book of
Modern African Stories

The Anchor Book of
Modern African Stories

Edited by
Nadežda Obradović
with a foreword by
Chinua Achebe

ANCHOR BOOKS
A DIVISION OF RANDOM HOUSE, INC.
NEW YORK

AN ANCHOR BOOKS ORIGINAL, DECEMBER 2002

Copyright © 1994, 2002 by Nadežda Obradović
Foreword copyright © 1994 by Chinua Achebe

All rights reserved under International
and Pan-American Copyright Conventions.
Published in the United States by Anchor Books,
a division of Random House, Inc., New York,
and simultaneously in Canada by Random House
of Canada Limited, Toronto.
Previously published, in slightly different form,
as *African Rhapsody: Short Stories from*
the Contemporary African Experience,
in 1994 by Anchor Books.

Anchor Books and colophon
are registered trademarks of Random House, Inc.

Library of Congress Cataloging-in-Publication Data
The Anchor book of modern African stories / edited by Nadezda Obradovic ; with a
foreword by Chinua Achebe.
p.   cm.
ISBN 978-0-385-72240-7 (pbk.)
1. Short stories, African (English) 2. Short stories, African—Translations into English.
3. Africa—Social life and customs—Fiction. I. Title: Modern African stories.
II. Obradovic, Nadezda.
PR9348 .A53 2002
823'.0108896—dc21
2002074441

Book design by Oksana Kushnir

www.anchorbooks.com

Printed in the United States of America
10   9

CONTENTS

An abundance of books by African writers have been published in Africa, North America, and Europe since the first edition of this collection appeared in 1994. With so much rich and varied material at our disposal, it was difficult to select only nine additional stories for this expanded new edition. I opted for prize-winning stories and authors from countries that were not represented in the first: Namibia, Botswana, Ethiopia, and Cameroon.

Among the best known of these writers is Booker Prize winner Ben Okri, who began receiving accolades for his work when he was only nineteen. With the first sentence of his fairytale-like story "What the Tapster Saw," he draws us into the phantasmagoric world of a dream, where life and death, humans and animals, earthen paths and starry alleys intersect, and mythological characters walk amongst the realities of the modern world.

Another story comes to us via the first annual Caine Prize for African Writing. Established in 2000 to recognize English-language short stories from Africa, it was presented to a Sudanese author, Leila Aboulela. Her story "The Museum" describes with artistry and sincerity the clash of cultures in Sudan and the misconceptions of other countries that prevail there.

The first story that I ever read in English was a poignant tale by a Namibian writer named Milly Jafta, and I am delighted to offer it here to American readers.

Also included is Ethiopia's Hama Tuma's impressive and topical story about the difficult political situation in his country. It tells of the tragic destiny of a father who, disgusted by his son's cooperation with a brutal police force and the crimes he has committed against innocent people, betrays him, and has him killed.

We discover in the Nigerian story "The One-Handed Hero" that there are still remote villages in Africa where people care about nothing except business: that is, cacao. In this setting a good-for-nothing thief, branded for life by having had his offending hand cut off according to the judgment of a *sharia* court, deceives the naive villagers by claiming that he was a war hero, and expects a medal for his valor. The author, Funso Aiyejina, is a new and satirical voice on the literary scene and his stories are most welcome.

The vicissitudes of life under apartheid in South Africa force the protagonist of "The Woman in Green" to assume a false identity. She is the offspring of a mixed marriage. White-skinned, but having been raised in a black milieu, she marries a conservative, high-ranking political official. Facing profound hatred, the odium of her husband, sons, and the black people of her acquaintance, her mental health collapses and her life ends tragically.

The heroine of Salwa Bakr's story is also facing a bleak future. The rigid rules of Egyptian society, especially those regarding women, suffocate her. She begins to question them, gathers the courage to defy them, and follows her own impulses. But whether at home or in the office, people find her behavior strange and unruly.

But the heroine of "Smile of Fortune," by Botswanian writer Gaele Sobott-Mogwe, is more intelligent and adroit in her relations to society. She pretends to be stupid and uninterested in her husband's criminal political machinations, and ignorant of his unfaithfulness. But when he is killed, she finds herself rich and free. The story ends with the words: "As the plane took off she smiled a secret Mona Lisa half smile."

The subject of Makuchi's story, set in Cameroon, is one of both local and international concern. The protagonist is a womanizer who is afraid of contracting AIDS, so he only goes out with women who have plump, Rubenesque figures. But that does not save him.

What unites these stories? They were written over the last fifteen years. With the exception of Okri's story, they are realistic. And they are written in English (with the exception of Salwa Bakr's story, which was translated from the Arabic by Denys Johnson-Davies). Most important, all of them reflect the political situation in the authors' respective countries.

It is my hope that this second edition will be met with as much interest as the first.

—The Editor

Literary historians tell us that the English novel preceded the short story by a hundred years or thereabouts. In modern African literature events happened differently. The short story came first—a far more logical development, if one may presume to say so. And we did not, of course, have centuries but decades to play with.

In 1951 F. J. Pedler, a respected British civil servant with considerable experience of West African affairs, published a little book titled, simply, *West Africa* in Home Study Books, a prestigious series that enlisted the expertise of Britain's leaders in science, the arts, and public affairs to present in a lucid, nontechnical style recent advances in knowledge in their various fields. I suppose West Africa earned a position in the company of such topics as Russian literature, modern psychology, and organic chemistry, etc., on account of its accelerating pace of change from colonial dependency toward self-rule, a process which would change the face of the whole continent in one short decade and even encourage Prime Minister Harold Macmillan to tell South Africans of all people about "a wind of change."

Although Pedler's book was not altogether free of the stereotypes of European colonial literature, it was in some ways remarkably advanced for its time. For example, he told his readers the startling news that African men did not buy their wives. "It is misleading," he wrote, "when Europeans talk of Africans buying a wife,"* and thus assailed a pet notion which Europeans had invented and cherished and recycled again and again in popular as well as serious literature. The well-known British writer Joyce Cary had exploited this very notion in the crudest manner imaginable a few years earlier in one of the "great" novels of African denigration, called *Mister Johnson*.

* F. J. Pedler, *West Africa* (London: Methuen & Co., Ltd., 1951), p. 32.

I am recalling Pedler's book, however, for a different reason. It offered, as it were in passing, one literary comment which I find extraordinarily shrewd and even prophetic:

> A country's novels reveal its social condition. West Africa has no full-length novels, but a few short stories may serve the purpose. We quote from two recent publications which show how educated West Africans themselves describe some of the features of social life in their own country.

Pedler then proceeded to quote from and to summarize two stories published in 1945 in the Gold Coast. Having taken almost three pages to deal with this matter, he concluded as follows:

> Here is a dramatic treatment of a contemporary social phenomenon which leaves one with the hope that more West Africans may enter the field of authorship and give us authentic stories of the lives of their own people.*

These brief quotations from Pedler speak volumes on the issue of people and their stories. Note his phrases: *West Africans themselves; their own country; authentic stories; of their own people*. Without saying so in so many words, he seemed to be engaged in a running argument against the age-old practice of the colonization of a people's story by others.

It is inconceivable that Pedler was unaware of Joyce Cary's *Mister Johnson*, which was celebrated in England and America then as now, to say nothing of British expatriate circles in Africa. He must also have been aware of Cary's three earlier "African novels." And yet he sidestepped them and scores of others of their kind and went to two unassuming short stories written by two completely unknown West Africans whose names did not, and do not, ring any bells. He sought out these lowly witnesses for authenticity about "the lives of their own people."

Pedler was certainly ahead of his time, and probably of ours as well. But be that as it may, one year after his book, Amos Tutuola startled the

* Ibid., p. 51.

literary world with a strange "novel" called *Palm Wine Drunkard* that sent Dylan Thomas into raptures. Two years after that Cyprian Ekwensi published *People of the City*. Then followed Camara Laye's *L'Enfant Noir* in 1956 and my *Things Fall Apart* in 1958. For good or ill nobody could say thereafter that West Africa had no full-length novels. Indeed, a major literary development of the twentieth century was under way.

Short stories gave us a convenient bridge from oral to written literature. Amos Tutuola's episodic "novels" attest to this as does the fact that Cyprian Ekwensi preceded his novel with short fiction in traditional·settings. But short stories are not choosy about who writes them or how. They are versatile and will consort with all manner of people, especially with those caught in tight and nervous conditions and desiring to quickly unburden themselves. I recall one of my colleagues from South Africa saying sometime in the sixties that their political situation did not permit them the luxury of novels like us West Africans but had pressed them into the guerrilla, hit-and-run practice of the short story. At the time, I thought to myself: Yeah, right! Later, when I was embroiled in the Biafran catastrophe, I began slowly to understand the predicament I had been so smug about. My next novel took twenty years to come. And we are not out of the woods yet.

In the 1980s the early hopes for Africa which Nkrumah's Ghana had launched in 1957 had been throttled everywhere by a grim combination of causes: military regimes, corrupt leadership, debt bondage to Western banks, drought, and famine. If we are not pushed into despair by all of this we may earn a harvest of stories.

Last year the British newspaper *The Guardian*, as its own contribution to the thirtieth anniversary of the African Writers Series, announced a short-story contest with a one thousand–pound prize. They were literally deluged by stories from all over the world. Apparently even in China, African nationals will write short stories in English! Which reminded me of the copious response I received when, at the end of the Biafran War, I had decided to edit and publish a literary magazine called *Okike* in the war-torn territory. The journal's success as a magnet for short stories is exemplified by this present anthology where I was flattered to see that as many as six of its twenty-five stories were originally published in *Okike*. And these six stories came to us not only from Nigeria, but also Tanzania, Zimbabwe, and the French-speaking

Benin Republic. Clearly, African writers seem to find the short-story form quite appealing.

There may be many reasons for this appeal. But one of them surely must be the ease of re-creation it affords for movement from different varieties of storytelling found in oral traditions. I believe I actually saw this process taking place in the smithy of an Igbo epic recital just over a decade ago. A seventy-five-year-old epic poet from the culturally fertile Anambra River basin was performing on the invitation of *Okike* magazine and its associated Igbo journal *Uwa ndi Igbo*, on the campus of the University of Nigeria. In his rendering of an old epic, "Emeka Okoye," the poet inserted what must surely have been a new dimension in telling an ancient tale of tyranny. In this version the sky-dwelling tyrant, Enunyilimba, rains down on the world below a decree written on flying sheets of paper declaring a feast in the sky and prohibiting any food or water for twenty-eight days in the world.

The license the poet takes with his material, which is actually an infringement no less of traditional canon, can be the despair of museum-minded purists. But artists have never allowed that to trouble them unduly in Africa. We only need to take a look at the *mbari* display which the Igbo people put on in appeasement of an offended divinity to see how immemorial motifs, say the royal python, could jostle for space with the white district officer, a new icon, smoking his pipe. You might even find Amadioha, god of thunder himself, wearing a hat and tie! This is art celebrating the total world of its community, the probable and the incongruous. What the old, illiterate poet did on our university campus was to recognize and acknowledge the presence of paper and literacy in our new world. And in doing so he also challenged us to apply our new gifts and talents to the enrichment of our ancient celebration.

The short stories assembled here resemble the art of an *mbari* display in the great variety and frank energy of their styles and practices. We are not expected, or indeed intended, to experience every offering with impartial, even-handed enthusiasm. But we will do well as we embark on the journey they promise through the African terrain and cultural panorama to leave at home our baggage of pet notions and stereotypes. And we will encounter new forms and new contents and new relationships between them. If we refuse to make our journey, or if we travel lugging along heavy loads of excess baggage, we will be like the young man whom the Igbo say never left home and went on thinking his mother made the best soup in the world.

We seem to have more problem accepting unfamiliar forms than content. The reason perhaps is that the raw material of human experience does not vary that much, while the forms our art can impose on it are infinite, which should make us happy but doesn't seem to do so. When I began thinking of this foreword my mind went back to my first romance with short-story writing. It happened during that euphoric decade of the fifties when F. J. Pedler was expressing his thoughts and hopes about novels and short stories in West Africa. I was a student at the newly founded University College, Ibadan, preparing for an arts degree of London University. The department of English had just announced a short-story competition and prize. We were given the whole long vacation to think it over. A short story; I decided to write one. In due course the results were published on the departmental notice board. No story, alas, was up to the standard for a departmental prize. But wait, my story was given honorable mention! And there was the helpful information that its weakness was that of form.

I was madly excited by my partial success. The English department at Ibadan was a stern and severe place that did not encourage you to believe too much in your chances. One fellow student who later became an outstanding novelist took one look at the department and fled into the warm embrace of Latin and Greek. No, our English department was not, as my people might say, a dance you got into carrying snuff in one hand. So I was elated to be mentioned in dispatches. And then there were the prospects for learning about form, for the future!

I approached the lecturer whose name was on the notice and asked if she could enlighten me on form. *Yes, of course*, she said, *but not today. Sometime.* And she went away to play tennis. I went to her a couple of times more with no greater success. And then one day, after a whole term had passed, she said to me, *I looked at that story of yours again, and actually I don't think there is much wrong with its form.*

And so I never learned the secret about short-story forms that I could pass on to anybody today. Except perhaps what Duke Ellington taught us: If it sounds good, it *is* good!

This anthology is not a happy recital any more than Africa today is a happy continent. In a prefatory essay Joyce Cary wrote for a new edition of *Mister Johnson* in 1952, he speaks about "the warmheartedness of the African; his readiness for friendship on the smallest encouragement" and a little later adds, "I can't forget their grins (and laughter—an African will laugh loudly with pleasure at any surprise)."

Stereotypes are not necessary malicious. They may be well meaning and even friendly. But in every case they show a carelessness or laziness or indifference of attitude that implies that the object of your categorization is not worth the trouble of individual assessment.

In any event you will not encounter the famed African laughter in these pages. The twenty-five authors gathered under one roof here did not hold a meeting beforehand to banish laughter from their recital. They are responding to an overwhelming reality of their lives. Together they seem to be saying to us that the person who is laughing has not heard the news.

The decision of the editor to arrange the stories in order from birth to death is a good one. It reveals with painful poignancy how young we do hear the news. "The Advance" by Henri Lopès of the Congo is a heartrending story of a little boy who dies from disease, hunger, and neglect, trapped in his mother's hovel while she must spend the whole day in faraway suburbia minding the children of the well-to-do, coaxing food into them, and then singing them to sleep.

Tayeb Salih from Sudan is a well-known writer. His story "A Handful of Dates" is the work of a master craftsman: no fuss, no tool marks.

> I must have been very young at the time. While I don't remember exactly how old I was, I do remember that when people saw me with my grandfather they would pat me on the head and give my cheek a pinch—things they didn't do to my grandfather. The strange thing was that I never used to go out with my father, rather it was my grandfather who would take me with him wherever he went, except for the mornings when I would go to the mosque to learn the Koran. The mosque, the river, and the fields—these were the landmarks in our life.

In this lucid and compact tale we see how a sensitive little boy's love and admiration for his impressive grandfather crumbles quickly in revulsion as the old man reveals callous self-righteousness and lack of humanity.

This anthology brings together names already widely recognized—such as the Senegalese filmmaker and writer Sembène Ousmane, Njabulo Ndebele, Charles Mungoshi, Alifa Rifaat, Luis Honwana, Bloke Modisane, and the brilliant and tragic Dambudzo Marechera—with others not so well-known and with some new discoveries, especially the writers from North Africa whose work in Arabic was specially translated for this book.

Sindiwe Magona is one of the new voices. Her very powerful story tells of the blighted life of a mere fourteen-year-old on whom the cruelties of apartheid on a victim who is black and female are embellished further by the terror of incest.

There are many good things in this anthology. The betrayal of innocence comes up again and again in different configurations and circumstances. Ossie Enekwe's "The Last Battle," a story of the Biafran War, presents in stark and simple lines how a hero is betrayed by the cause he fights for and is turned by that very cause into a traitor.

The common factor in all the stories is a pervasive atmosphere of pain and life's injustice—an atmosphere so powerful that even when the actors think they are having a good time with alcohol and sex and card games in Charles Mungoshi's Zimbabwean story "The Brother," they could just as well be at a funeral.

Chinua Achebe
Bard College
Annandale-on-Hudson, NY

PREFACE

We have gone beyond the era when the African writer stated, much as Chinua Achebe did, "I would be perfectly satisfied if my work, particularly when I speak of the past, was to teach my readers—at least my compatriots—that their past, with all its imperfections, was not a long dark night for society, from which the Europeans delivered them." Or as Bernth Lindfors later wrote, "Instead of representing Africa as a barbarous wilderness where savages lived in a permanent state of anarchy until the white man came bringing peace, law, order, religion, and a 'higher' form of civilization, Achebe showed how Africans led decent, moral lives in well-regulated societies that placed strict legal and religious constraints on human behavior. Indeed, according to Achebe, things did not fall apart in Africa until Europe intruded and set everything off balance by introducing alien codes which Africans were then told to live by. Europe did not bring light and peace to the Dark Continent: it brought chaos and confusion."*

The new generation of writers is more determined, theirs is a loftier goal.

"The African writer cannot and must not take pen in hand merely to offer pretty expressions and phrases. As the product of a society that has its problems, he can and must help in their presentation so that each person becomes completely aware of them, so that people think of them, and look for their solution. If that is what it means to be a committed writer, then that is what I am," said Aminata Sow Fall, the prominent Senegalese author, in an interview, adding, "Our literature must raise issues that summon men to devise solutions to problems that are specifically ours, problems which, although existing in other places, take on a special dimension in our country."

* Bernth Lindfors, "New Trends in West and East African Fiction," *Black Africa* 15 (1971).

These specific problems, related to their inherited past or to conflicts brought by the new era, are reflected in almost all the works originating in this large, heterogeneous continent with its countless different peoples, religions, languages, and customs. These shared situations of conflict include making the transition from childhood to maturity, moving from a rural to an urban environment, the encounter and collision with foreign or Western cultures, rebellion against colonial exploitation, and—themes that often prevail in the most recent works—disappointment with the new movement and merciless criticism of corruption, unemployment and dishonor, exploitation, and adopting others' (Western) values. All these conflicts rightfully find their place in African prose.

Achieving national independence brought with it liberation from the linguistic domination of the colonizer, and a retreat from Western writing models in order to reach original solutions, regardless of the fact that the colonizer's language is often still used. The problem of which language to write in is a frequent dilemma of African authors and has been ever-present since the Negritude movement (1934) when Senghor wondered whether the "music, melody and rhythm comprising the essence of poetry could be written in another's language." After fifty years, these words still resound in the statement by Congolese Labou Tansi, "We must attempt to shatter the frigid French language . . . trying to lend it the opulence, the twinkle of our tropic temperament, the breathiness of our languages." This dilemma has still not been resolved. Writing in one's own language means a small reading public—due to the enormous number of languages spoken in Africa and due to illiteracy. Writing in another language means a large international reading public and the possibility of world fame. Each writer finds his own answer: some write in their own language and then translate their own works into English (Ngugi Wa Thiong'o) and French, or try the new African English (Gabriel Okara) or French (A. Kourouma), while others turn to film (Sembène Ousmane), considering the silver screen to have replaced the traditional African tree where villagers used to gather to hear the griot—the oral storyteller.

The emphasis in this collection, apart from literary merit, is on the diversity of topics from the variety of countries involved—ranging from the North African areas, Algeria, Morocco, Tunisia, and Egypt, to the southern, Mozambique and South Africa. The everyday ways of life, culture, tradition, superstition, religion, marital customs, politics, interpersonal and interfamily relations, and the behavior of men and women in crisis situations such as war all permeate the pages of these thirty-four stories from twenty countries. Their plots span the colonial period (Henri Lopès's story "The Advance," L. Honwana's "Papa, Snake & I") to the troubled years of the Biafran War (O. O. Enekwe's "The Last Battle" and A. Maja-Pearce's "Civil War I–VII") and religious riots (Abdulrazak Gurnah's "Bossy").

The greatest number of stories are from Nigeria. No wonder: Nigeria is not only a mammoth country with over 100 million inhabitants, it is also the country that produced *The Palm Wine Drunkard* by Amos Tutuola in 1952, the first book to earn worldwide acclaim and hint to the large international public something of the unknown creativity of this continent. An entire galaxy of talented writers followed. Chinua Achebe's books sold millions of copies and became mandatory texts in African schools and European, American, and Australian universities. Wole Soyinka received the Nobel Prize; Ben Okri was recently awarded the Booker Prize. Such greatness nurtured other creators of similar merit.

Many of the stories in this collection were originally written in English; others were translated from French, Arabic, and Portuguese. This fact further contributes to the variety of plots and literary expressions.

The wellsprings of these stories include the collections of individual writers and anthologies of African stories published by European publishing houses such as Heinemann Educational Books, Longman (Great Britain); Malawi Writers Series (Malawi); Mambo Press, Zimbabwe Publishing House (Zimbabwe); Enterprise Nationale du Livre (Algeria); literary journals such as the Nigerian periodicals *Okike* and *Lotus*, the journal of the Association of African and Asian Writers; South African publisher David Philip; and Saros International, Nigeria. Several tales were translated especially for this collection and appear for the first time in English ("The Wicked Tongue" by Mohammed Moulessehoul from Algeria, for example).

The stories could have been arranged in several ways: alphabetically by author for example, or by geographical region. I have adopted another approach, however, arranging the stories by plot. The beginning of the collection presents stories with children as protagonists ("The Prophetess," "A Handful of Dates"), and the end stories of war, destruction, and death ("The Last Battle," "Civil War"). The middle presents tales of everyday life and customs. Thus, I have attempted to portray a large spectrum of African life.

This collection mosaic may serve as a window on the present and future development and abundance of literary creations on African soil, where new literary names emerge almost daily and continue to provide their valuable contributions to the body of African literature.

Nadežda Obradović
February 1994

The Anchor Book of
Modern African Stories

TAYEB SALIH

Tayeb Salih was born in 1929 in Sudan. He attended university
in England before working at the BBC as Head of Drama in the
Arabic Service. He later worked as Director-General of Infor-
mation in Qatar in the Persian Gulf, and with UNESCO in
Paris. He is the author of *The Wedding of Zein and Other Stories*,
Bandarshah, and the widely acclaimed *Seasons of Migration to the
North*.

A Handful of Dates

Translated by Denys Johnson-Davies

I must have been very young at the time. While I don't remember
exactly how old I was, I do remember that when people saw me
with my grandfather they would pat me on the head and give my cheek a
pinch—things they didn't do to my grandfather. The strange thing was
that I never used to go out with my father, rather it was my grandfather
who would take me with him wherever he went, except for the mornings when I would go to the mosque to learn the Koran. The mosque,
the river, and the fields—these were the landmarks in our life. While
most of the children of my age grumbled at having to go to the mosque
to learn the Koran, I used to love it. The reason was, no doubt, that I was
quick at learning by heart and the Sheikh always asked me to stand up
and recite the Chapter of the Merciful whenever we had visitors, who
would pat me on my head and cheek just as people did when they saw
me with my grandfather.

Yes, I used to love the mosque, and I loved the river too. Directly after
we finished our Koran reading in the morning I would throw down my
wooden slate and dart off, quick as a genie, to my mother, hurriedly swallow down my breakfast, and run off for a plunge in the river. When tired
of swimming about I would sit on the bank and gaze at the strip of water
that wound away eastward and hid behind a thick wood of acacia trees. I

loved to give rein to my imagination and picture to myself a tribe of giants living behind that wood, a people tall and thin with white beards and sharp noses, like my grandfather. Before my grandfather ever replied to my many questions he would rub the tip of his nose with his forefinger; as for his beard, it was soft and luxuriant and as white as cottonwool—never in my life have I seen anything of a purer whiteness or greater beauty. My grandfather must also have been extremely tall, for I never saw anyone in the whole area address him without having to look up at him, nor did I see him enter a house without having to bend so low that I was put in mind of the way the river wound round behind the wood of acacia trees. I loved him and would imagine myself, when I grew to be a man, tall and slender like him, walking along with great strides.

I believe I was his favorite grandchild: no wonder, for my cousins were a stupid bunch and I—so they say—was an intelligent child. I used to know when my grandfather wanted me to laugh, when to be silent; also I would remember the times for his prayers and would bring him his prayer rug and fill the ewer for his ablutions without his having to ask me. When he had nothing else to do he enjoyed listening to me reciting to him from the Koran in a lilting voice, and I could tell from his face that he was moved.

One day I asked him about our neighbor Masood. I said to my grandfather: "I fancy you don't like our neighbor Masood?"

To which he answered, having rubbed the tip of his nose: "He's an indolent man and I don't like such people."

I said to him: "What's an indolent man?"

My grandfather lowered his head for a moment, then looking across at the wide expanse of field, he said: "Do you see it stretching out from the edge of the desert up to the Nile bank? A hundred feddans. Do you see all those date palms? And those trees—sant, acacia and sayal? All this fell into Masood's lap, was inherited by him from his father."

Taking advantage of the silence that had descended upon my grandfather, I turned my gaze from him to the vast area defined by his words. "I don't care," I told myself, "who owns those date palms, those trees or this black, cracked earth—all I know is that it's the arena for my dreams and my playground."

My grandfather then continued: "Yes, my boy, forty years ago all this belonged to Masood—two-thirds of it is now mine."

This was news to me for I had imagined that the land had belonged to my grandfather ever since God's Creation.

"I didn't own a single feddan when I first set foot in this village. Masood was then the owner of all these riches. The position has changed now, though, and I think that before Allah calls to him I shall have bought the remaining third as well."

I do not know why it was I felt fear at my grandfather's words—and pity for our neighbor Masood. How I wished my grandfather wouldn't do what he'd said! I remembered Masood's singing, his beautiful voice and powerful laugh that resembled the gurgling of water. My grandfather never used to laugh.

I asked my grandfather why Masood had sold his land.

"Women," and from the way my grandfather pronounced the word I felt that "women" was something terrible. "Masood, my boy, was a much-married man. Each time he married he sold me a feddan or two." I made the quick calculation that Masood must have married some ninety women. Then I remembered his three wives, his shabby appearance, his lame donkey and its dilapidated saddle, his djellaba with the torn sleeves. I had all but rid my mind of the thoughts that jostled in it when I saw the man approaching us, and my grandfather and I exchanged glances.

"We'll be harvesting the dates today," said Masood. "Don't you want to be there?"

I felt, though, that he did not really want my grandfather to attend. My grandfather, however, jumped to his feet and I saw that his eyes sparkled momentarily with an intense brightness. He pulled me by the hand and we went off to the harvesting of Masood's dates.

Someone brought my grandfather a stool covered with an ox hide, while I remained standing. There was a vast number of people there, but though I knew them all, I found myself for some reason watching Masood: aloof from the great gathering of people he stood as though it were no concern of his, despite the fact that the date palms to be harvested were his own. Sometimes his attention would be caught by the sound of a huge clump of dates crashing down from on high. Once he shouted up at the boy perched on the very summit of the date palm who had begun hacking at a clump with his long, sharp sickle: "Be careful you don't cut the heart of the palm."

No one paid any attention to what he said and the boy seated at the very summit of the date palm continued, quickly and energetically, to work away at the branch with his sickle till the clump of dates began to drop like something descending from the heavens.

I, however, had begun to think about Masood's phrase "the heart of the palm." I pictured the palm tree as something with feeling, something possessed of a heart that throbbed. I remembered Masood's remark to me when he had once seen me playing about with the branch of a young palm tree: "Palm trees, my boy, like humans, experience joy and suffering." And I had felt an inward and unreasoned embarrassment.

When I again looked at the expanse of ground stretching before me I saw my young companions swarming like ants around the trunks of the palm trees, gathering up dates and eating most of them. The dates were collected into high mounds. I saw people coming along and weighing them into measuring bins and pouring them into sacks, of which I counted thirty. The crowd of people broke up, except for Hussein the merchant, Mousa the owner of the field next to ours on the east and two men I'd never seen before.

I heard a low whistling sound and saw that my grandfather had fallen asleep. Then I noticed that Masood had not changed his stance, except that he had placed a stalk in his mouth and was munching at it like someone surfeited with food who doesn't know what to do with the mouthful he still has.

Suddenly my grandfather woke up, jumped to his feet and walked toward the sacks of dates. He was followed by Hussein the merchant, Mousa the owner of the field next to ours and the two strangers. I glanced at Masood and saw that he was making his way toward us with extreme slowness, like a man who wants to retreat but whose feet insist on going forward. They formed a circle round the sacks of dates and began examining them, some taking a date or two to eat. My grandfather gave me a fistful, which I began munching. I saw Masood filling the palms of both hands with dates and bringing them up close to his nose, then returning them.

Then I saw them dividing up the sacks between them. Hussein the merchant took ten; each of the strangers took five. Mousa the owner of the field next to ours on the eastern side took five, and my grandfather took five. Understanding nothing, I looked at Masood and saw that his eyes were darting about to left and right like two mice that have lost their way home.

"You're still fifty pounds in debt to me," said my grandfather to Masood. "We'll talk about it later."

Hussein called his assistants and they brought along donkeys, the two strangers produced camels, and the sacks of dates were loaded onto them. One of the donkeys let out a braying which set the camels frothing at the mouth and complaining noisily. I felt myself drawing close to Masood, felt my hand stretch out toward him as though I wanted to touch the hem of his garment. I heard him make a noise in his throat like the rasping of a lamb being slaughtered. For some unknown reason, I experienced a sharp sensation of pain in my chest.

I ran off into the distance. Hearing my grandfather call after me, I hesitated a little, then continued on my way. I felt at that moment that I hated him. Quickening my pace, it was as though I carried within me a secret I wanted to rid myself of. I reached the riverbank near the bend it made behind the wood of acacia trees. Then, without knowing why, I put my finger into my throat and spewed up the dates I'd eaten.

Henri Lopès was born in the Congo in 1937. In 1971 he published his first collection of stories, *Tribaliks*, and was awarded the Grand Prix Littéraire de l'Afrique Noire the following year. He followed this with the novels *The Laughing Cry* and *The Lily and the Coral Tree*. Also active in political office, he has served in the Congo as Minister of Education, Minister of Finances, and as Prime Minister. He is currently the Congolese Ambassador to France and England.

The Advance

Translated by Andrea Leskes

"No good," the little girl said, screwing up her face.

"Yes it is, Francoise. Look." Carmen herself swallowed a mandarin section, then closed her eyes. The little girl looked at her, impassively.

"Eat it all up."

Like a priest proffering the host, Carmen offered her the orange quarter. Haughtily, the little girl turned her head away. It was already seven o'clock. Carmen was eager to finish up her work, especially since she had not yet asked the mistress . . .

She spoke more sharply and looked stern.

"If you don't eat, Francoise, I'm going to tell your mother." Still the little girl did not relent.

The mistress of the house was in the living room, together with her husband, entertaining friends they had invited over for bridge. She had already warned Carmen several times not to bother her when she was, as she said, "with company." Did Carmen dare to interrupt the happy group anyway? She did not fear being yelled at. People raise their voices mostly to relieve their own tensions. And since, according to Ferdinand the watchman, Madam's husband beat her, she took her revenge out on the servants. Why feel resentful? It was far better to just accept it philosoph-ically. But to be taken to task in front of others, strangers, that was worse than being slapped. So Carmen preferred to wait.

Also, Madam had the annoying habit of speaking to her daughter as if she were an adult.

"Francoise, sweetheart, what did you have to eat?" And little Fran-coise, while reciting for her mother, would delight in explaining that she had not eaten any dessert because the mandarins Carmen wanted to give her were rotten. And Madam would admonish Carmen for not hav-ing told her about it. Especially since she had already explained that without dessert the child might not get a well-balanced meal, and so on and so forth. Carmen would usually listen to it all, seriously. In her vil-lage, and over in Makélékélé, what mattered was that a child had a full belly and did not go hungry. If, in addition, they had to worry about a balanced diet, there would never be an end to it. Besides, Carmen must not forget to ask her mistress . . .

There was only one solution. Do as her own mother had done to get her to eat. With one hand she opened the child's mouth and with the other shoved in the piece of fruit. As expected, Francoise howled. She cried and choked with rage. From the hallway came hammerlike sounds on the tile floor—the footsteps of Madam who came running. Carmen had won.

"What's going on in here?"

"She doesn't want to eat, Madam."

"Oh, don't force her, poor little thing. Get her some grapes from the refrigerator. She likes grapes."

Madam took the little girl's head in her hands and kissed her several times. Carmen went to get the European-style dessert. As she was returning, she crossed Madam in the hall and almost broached the sub-ject that was on her mind. But it did not seem like quite the right moment.

Francoise ate the grapes with relish. They must be good because instead of being her usual, talkative self, she remained calm and quiet as she ate the fruit. One day Carmen would have to swipe some of them and see what they tasted like.

While the little girl ate, Carmen wiped the tears from her cheeks. In her heart she cared a great deal for this child. Carmen had been with her since she was two months old and had practically brought her up. Francoise was as much her daughter as Madam's. Even if she quit her job, or Madam fired her, she would not be able to resist returning from time to time to see how Francoise had grown.

Then Carmen took the little girl to spend a penny, changed her, and put her to bed. By then it was 7:30. Night had fallen and she would still have to walk two hours to reach Makélékélé. But Francoise did not want her maid to leave. She clung to her annoying routine of wanting Carmen to sing her to sleep with a song.

> Nguè kélé mwana ya mboté,
> Sleep baby sleep,
> Sleep baby sleep.

After that she had to sing another. Usually the child would fall asleep during the second song but that evening it took three. While Carmen sang, her thoughts were elsewhere. She thought about Francoise whom she loved as much as her son, a child of the same age yet so different. Francoise was the picture of health, while her son had come close to death several times already. Nothing intimidated Francoise, she was comfortable speaking with grown-ups, ordered about the servants and already showed a certain fussiness in her choice of clothes. Her Hector did not dare to speak. He was shy and withdrawn with strangers. His unhappiness already showed in his eyes. Yet both children were of the same generation. They spoke the same language but would they be able to understand each other? Carmen did not think this jealously. No, she would like Hector to be "well brought up," but how could that possibly be? Society and human nature would have to change.

That morning she had been very tempted to stay home from work. All night long the poor little fellow had cried. He complained of a stomachache. He had diarrhea and vomited at least three times. The first time seemed to relieve him, but the last brought something greenish up from his little stomach. Then his stomach continued to contract spasmodically and nothing more came up. The child was clearly in pain. His breathing was labored, his forehead covered with sweat. She was very frightened and thought of the two children she had already lost. She even panicked. She had almost awakened her mother, asleep in the same compound. But she restrained herself. Her mother would have taken him immediately to the fetishist. That was how it happened with the other two. And they died. Yet each time she paid the equivalent of her own earnings. And after their deaths it was worse. The fetishist concluded she kept losing her children because for five years she had been refusing to marry the man her parents had chosen for her. And, in addition to her grief, she was obliged to suffer the nonsense of a relentless succession of old hags who harped on the subject, and tried to pressure her into yielding and giving in to either the will of God, the ancestors, the spirits, or her poor children. She should marry Kitonga Flavien and then everything would be all right again. Wasn't he a good catch? Besides his job as a government chauffeur, he was his own boss after work. He owned four taxis, a shop and a bar in Ouenze-Indochina. Kitonga would support her, she wouldn't have to work any longer. Besides, he already had two wives. One at Bacongo and the other who ran the bar at Ouenze.

While she contemplated all this, her son called. He wanted to sleep on her mat. He was afraid to be alone. Would he last until morning? When some children are sick their parents can immediately pick up the phone, dial a number and go straight to the doctor who does whatever is needed, or reassures them. But not poor people! The closest dispensaries are closed at night. And at the hospital we are received by a nurse who is rude and makes a fuss because we dared to wake him. As for going to a doctor, well, folks who live in the better parts of town won't open their doors at night to just anyone. Besides, she is letting her imagination run wild. A visit to a private doctor costs money.

Finally, at dawn, the child fell asleep. As for Carmen, she had to get up and go to work. Every day she must walk two hours from Makélékélé to Mipla. Since her mistress wants her to be there before 7:30, it's easy to calculate . . .

Despite her exhaustion she did not want to stay in bed. But neither did she want to go to work that morning. She would have preferred to go to the hospital and find out exactly what was wrong with Hector. Whenever he was ill, Carmen did not like to leave him alone. Her heart was not at ease. Once she tried to take him along to work, but Madam had made it plain that she was not being paid to care for her own son but for Francoise. Carmen knew that her mother and the other female relatives would take him to see a doctor. The tribal family is large and a child, no matter what happens, is never alone. But nonetheless, she believed that a child is best off being brought up by its mother. And those we have brought into the world need us most of all when they are sick.

But if she had devoted the day to her son, she would have been fired and then how would they manage? She had already missed work twice that month. The first time she really had been sick and had spent two feverish days on her mat. The second time was for a funeral. Madam was very angry.

"Carmen, I have had just about enough! Each time I need you, you aren't here. It almost seems as if you do it on purpose. You choose to stay home the very days I've made plans. My dear woman, I'm warning you now. If you miss one more day this month, you'll have to look for work elsewhere."

How could she explain? Carmen tried her best. But white people, they think that whenever we don't come to work, it's because we're lazy.

And today she came to work despite Hector being so ill. At noon her sister sent word that the doctor had prescribed some medicine. It was always the same old story. How would she pay for it? Yet Hector must be cured.

And that evening, there she was, singing for a little girl who had everything, and whose parents were playing cards with other ladies and gentlemen.

When Francoise had fallen asleep, Carmen went to wait in the kitchen until the guests had finished their game of bridge. She spent the time talking to Ferdinand, the old watchman. Those were moments she generally enjoyed. It lightened her spirits, eased her worry. They exchanged gossip on the shortcomings of their employers. Usually when Ferdinand described things he had seen, he would mimic them and Carmen would laugh. That evening, however, she remained serious and Ferdinand remarked on it.

Finally Madam came into the kitchen.

"Haven't you left yet, Carmen?"

It was the most difficult moment. "Madam, I need some money."

"Again? But I paid you only ten days ago."

"My son is sick. He needs medicine."

"Listen to that, just listen to that! So I am now the public welfare fund. They have children without a husband and then they can't manage to take care of them!"

"Madam, white people say that . . ."

"So your child is sick? Well, it's because you don't listen to me. I've told you again and again that you must feed him properly. Did you do it?"

"No, Madam."

"No, of course not. It's easier to fill his stomach with your rotten old *manioc*."

What could Carmen answer? That she had tried the diet Madam suggested but it was beyond her means. It seemed that Madam did not realize how in one week she spent three times Carmen's monthly salary just to feed her husband, her daughter, herself and their cat. If the maid had reminded her of that, she would have been fired for insolence.

"But anyway, I don't have any cash at home this evening. When will you natives understand that money doesn't grow on trees? When will you learn to put money aside and save?"

And Madam continued speaking like that for a long time. Carmen did not understand all she said. When people speak French too rapidly, she doesn't have time to translate it all in her mind, so she just tunes out and nods her head, as she did at that moment. Had that perhaps softened Madam? In any case, she gave her some aspirin and promised her 500 francs the following day.

So finally black Carmen left. She walked all the way back to Makélékélé. It was far from Mipla to Makélékélé. As far as from her native village to where she was sent to school. It left plenty of time for thought.

Carmen wanted to run, she felt so strongly that Hector needed her. But after not having slept the whole night, and eating nothing but a slice of *manioc* for lunch, she could not run. Suddenly she felt that Hector was calling her.

Poor little thing. "When he grows up, will he love me? To support us both I must leave him alone all day long. Maybe he'll resent it. I regret having left him without medical care so long. But I had faith in the white man's medicine and in his goodwill. If Mamma suggests I take him to the fetishist tonight, I won't be able to refuse any longer."

And she thought about all Madam had said. They would never really understand each other. Carmen spent more time with her mistress than with her own son. Madam entrusted her daughter to Carmen in complete confidence. And yet Carmen could not understand Madam's reactions nor could Madam imagine what was going on in her maid's head, or the difficulties of her world. She considered Carmen an irresponsible and frivolous girl.

How does she expect me to save money on 5,000 francs a month? Last month she only paid me 4,000. For six months now she has been keeping back 500 francs a month to help repay the cost of the watch I bought. It was my only extravagance. Then I had to give 1,000 francs to the *tontine** of our community, 1,000 francs to my mother, 1,000 francs to pay for the trip home of my aunt and cousins who had moved in with us for a month. I had only 1,000 francs left. And what is 1,000 francs? Madam spends that much on food every day.

Cars passed by in the poorly lit streets. Those that came toward Carmen blinded her with their headlights. Those that arrived from behind barely missed hitting her. And no one stopped to give her a lift. Yet she knew that at least half of the cars were driven by blacks like herself. In today's world, each to his own.

Oh, if only Madam would remember to give her money for the medicine tomorrow.

As she approached Biza Street, the cry of women's voices raised in the night reached her:

Mwana mounou mê kouenda hé!
Hector hé,
Mwana mounou mê kouenda hé.

She understood that medicine or fetishist, it was too late.

Oh, my son has gone away!
Oh, my Hector,
Oh, my son has gone away.

---

* Community-based method of saving. Every month, each participant contributes a fixed sum. The entire amount is handed over monthly, in turns, to one of the members.

Luis Bernardo Honwana was born in 1942 in Mozambique. He was imprisoned from 1964–67 for his political activities. Upon his release, he moved to Portugal, and has since lived in Switzerland, Algeria, and Tanzania. He has made several documentary films, was awarded a prize at the Leipzig Film Festival, and is the author of *We Killed Mangy Dog*, translated from the Portuguese and published in English in 1969. He lives in Mozambique, where he is Chief of Staff to the President.

Papa, Snake & I

Translated by Dorothy Guedes

As soon as Papa left the table to read the newspaper in the sitting room, I got up as well. I knew that Mama and the others would take a while longer, but I didn't feel like staying with them at all.

When I stood up, Mama looked at me and said, "Come here, let me look at your eyes."

I went toward her slowly, because when Mama calls us we never know whether she's cross or not. After she had lifted my lids with the index finger of her left hand to make a thorough examination, she looked down at her plate and I stood waiting for her to send me away or to say something. She finished chewing, swallowed, and picked up the bone in her fingers to peep through the cavity, shutting one eye. Then she turned to me suddenly with a bewildered look on her face.

"Your eyes are bloodshot; you're weak and you've lost your appetite."

The way she spoke made me feel obliged to say that none of this was my fault or else that I didn't do it on purpose. All the others looked on very curiously to see what was going to happen.

Mama peered down the middle of the bone again. Then she began to suck it, shutting her eyes, and only stopped for a moment to say, "Tomorrow you're going to take a laxative."

As soon as the others heard this, they began eating again very quickly and noisily. Mama didn't seem to have anything else to say, so I went out into the yard.

It was hot everywhere, and I could see no one on the road. Over the back wall three oxen gazed at me. They must have come back from the water trough at the Administration and stayed to rest in the shade. Far away, over the oxen's horns, the gray tufts of the dusty thorn trees trembled like flames. Everything vibrated in the distance, and heat waves could even be seen rising from the stones in the road. Sartina was sitting on a straw mat in the shade of the house, eating her lunch. Chewing slowly, she looked around, and from time to time, with a careless gesture, she shooed away the fowls who came close to her hoping for crumbs. Even so, every now and then one of the bolder ones would jump onto the edge of the plate and run off with a lump of mealie meal in its beak, only to be pursued by the others. In their wild dispute, the lump would become so broken up that in the end even the smallest chicken would get its bit to peck.

When she saw me coming near, Sartina pulled her *capulana* down over her legs, and even then kept her hand spread out in front of her knees, firmly convinced that I wanted to peep at something. When I looked away she still didn't move her hand.

Toto came walking along slowly with his tongue hanging out, and went to the place where Sartina was sitting. He sniffed the plate from afar and turned away, taking himself off to the shade of the wall where he looked for a soft place to lie down. When he found one, he curled round with his nose almost on his tail, and only lay still when his stomach touched the ground. He gave a long yawn, and dropped his head between his paws. He wriggled a little, making sure that he was in the most comfortable position, then covered his ears with his paws.

When she had finished eating, Sartina looked at me insistently before removing her hand which covered the space between her knees, and only when she was sure I was not looking did she spring to her feet with a jump. The plate was so clean that it shone, but after darting a last suspicious glance at me, she took it to the trough. She moved languidly, swaying from the waist as her hips rose and fell under her *capulana*. She bent over the trough, but the back of her legs was exposed in this position, so she went to the other side for me not to see.

Mama appeared at the kitchen door, still holding the bone in her hand, and before calling Sartina to clear the table, she looked around to see if everything was in order. "Don't forget to give Toto his food," she said in Ronga.

Sartina went inside, drying her hands on her *capulana*, and afterward came out with a huge pile of plates. When she came out the second time she brought the tablecloth and shook it on the stairs. While the fowls were skirmishing for the crumbs, pecking and squawking at each other, she folded it in two, four, and eight, and then went back inside. When she came out again she brought the aluminum plate with Toto's food, and put it on the cement cover of the water meter. Toto didn't have to be called to eat and even before the plate was put down, he threw himself on his food. He burrowed into the pile of rice with his nose, searching for the bits of meat which he gulped up greedily as he found them. When no meat was left, he pushed the bones aside and ate some rice. The fowls were all around him, but they didn't dare to come nearer because they knew very well what Toto was like when he was eating.

When he had swallowed the rice, Toto pretended he didn't want any more and went to sit in the shade of the sugarcane, waiting to see what the fowls would do. They came nervously toward his food, and risked a peck or two, very apprehensively. Toto watched this without making a single movement. Encouraged by the passivity of the dog, the fowls converged on the rice with great enthusiasm, creating an awful uproar. It was then that Toto threw himself on the heap, pawing wildly in all directions and growling like an angry lion. When the fowls disappeared, fleeing to all corners of the yard, Toto went back to the shade of the sugarcane, waiting for them to gather together again.

Before going to work Papa went to look at the chicken run with Mama. They both appeared at the kitchen door, Mama already wearing her apron and Papa with a toothpick in his mouth and his newspaper under his arm. When they passed me Papa was saying, "It's impossible, it's impossible, things can't go on like this."

I went after them, and when we entered the chicken run Mama turned to me as if she wanted to say something, but then she changed her mind and went toward the wire netting. There were all sorts of things piled up behind the chicken run: pipes left over from the building of the windmill on the farm, blocks which were bought when Papa was still thinking of making outhouses of cement, boxes, pieces of wood, and who knows what else. The fowls sometimes crept in among these things and laid their eggs where Mama couldn't reach them. On one side of the run lay a dead fowl, and Mama pointed to it and said, "Now there's this one, and I don't know how many others have just died from one day to the next. The chickens simply disappear, and the eggs too. I had this one left here for you to see. I'm tired of talking to you about this, and you still don't take any notice."

"All right, all right, but what do you want me to do about it?"

"Listen, the fowls die suddenly, and the chickens disappear. No one goes into the chicken run at night, and we've never heard any strange noise. You must find out what's killing the fowls and chickens."

"What do you think it is?"

"The fowls are bitten and the chickens are eaten. It can only be the one thing you think it is—if there are any thoughts in your head."

"All right, tomorrow I'll get the snake killed. It's Sunday, and it will be easy to get people to do it. Tomorrow."

Papa was already going out of the chicken run when Mama said, now in Portuguese, "But tomorrow without fail, because I don't want any of my children bitten by a snake."

Papa had already disappeared behind the corner of the house on his way to work when Mama turned to me and said, "Haven't you ever been taught that when your father and mother are talking you shouldn't stay and listen! My children aren't usually so bad-mannered. Who do you take after?"

She turned to Sartina, who was leaning against the wire netting and listening. "What do you want? Did anyone call you? I'm talking to my son and it's none of your business."

Sartina couldn't have grasped all that because she didn't understand Portuguese very well, but she drew away from the netting, looking very embarrassed, and went to the trough again. Mama went on talking to me, "If you think you'll fool me and take the gun to go hunting you're making a big mistake. Heaven help you if you try to do a thing like that! I'll tan your backside for you! And if you think you'll stay here in the chicken run you're also mistaken. I don't feel like putting up with any of your nonsense, d'you hear?"

Mama must have been very cross, because for the whole day I hadn't heard her laugh as she usually did. After talking to me she went out of the chicken run and I followed her. When she passed Sartina, she asked her in Ronga, "Is it very hot under your *capulana?* Who told you to come here and show your legs to everybody?"

Sartina said nothing, walked round the trough, and went on washing the plates, bending over the other side.

Mama went away and I went to sit where I had been before. When Sartina saw me she turned on me resentfully, threw me a furious glance, and went round the trough again. She began to sing a monotonous song, one of those songs of hers that she sometimes spent the whole afternoon singing over and over again when she was angry.

Toto was bored with playing with the fowls, and had already finished eating his rice. He was sleeping again with his paws over his ears. Now and then he rolled himself in the dust and lay on his back with his legs folded in the air.

It was stiflingly hot, and I didn't know whether I'd go hunting as I usually did every Saturday, or if I'd go to the chicken run to see the snake.

Madunana came into the yard with a pile of firewood on his back, and went to put it away in the corner where Sartina was washing the plates. When she saw him, she stopped singing and tried to manage an awkward smile.

After looking all around, Madunana pinched Sartina's bottom, and she gave an embarrassed giggle and responded with a sonorous slap on his arm. The two of them laughed happily together without looking at each other.

Just then, Nandito, Joãozinho, Nelita, and Gita ran out after a ball, and started kicking it around the yard with great enjoyment.

Mama came to the kitchen door, dressed up to go out. As soon as she appeared, Madunana bent down quickly to the ground, pretending to look for something, and Sartina bent over the trough.

"Sartina, see if you can manage not to break any plates before you finish. Hurry up. You, Madunana, leave Sartina alone and mind your own business. I don't want any of that nonsense here. If you carry on like this I'll tell the boss.

"You, Ginho," (now she spoke in Portuguese) "look after the house and remember you're not a child anymore. Don't hit anybody and don't let the children go out of the yard. Tina and Lolota are inside clearing up—don't let them get up to mischief.

"Sartina," (in Ronga) "when you've finished with that put the kettle on for the children's tea and tell Madunana to go and buy bread. Don't let the children finish the whole packet of butter.

"Ginho," (now in Portuguese) "look after everything—I'm coming back just now. I'm going along to Aunty Lucia's for a little chat."

Mama straightened her dress and looked around to see if everything was in order, then went away.

Senhor Castro's dog, Wolf, was watching Toto from the street. As soon as he saw Wolf, Toto ran toward him and they started to bark at each other.

All the dogs of the village were frightened of Toto, and even the biggest of them ran away when he showed his temper. Toto was small, but he had long white hair which bristled up like a cat's when he was angry, and this is what must have terrified the other dogs.

Usually he kept away from them, preferring to entertain himself with the fowls—even bitches he only tolerated at certain times. For me he was a dog with a "pedigree," or at least "pedigree" could only mean the qualities he possessed. He had an air of authority, and the only person he feared was Mama, although she had never hit him. Just to take him off a chair we had to call her because he snarled and showed his teeth even at Papa.

The two dogs were face-to-face, and Wolf had already started to retreat, full of fear. At this moment Dr. Reis's dog, Kiss, passed by, and Toto started to bark at him too. Kiss fled at once, and Wolf pursued him, snapping at his hindquarters, only leaving him when he was whining with pain. When Wolf came back to Toto they immediately made friends and began playing together.

Nandito came and sat down next to me, and told me, without my asking, that he was tired of playing ball.

"So why have you come here?"

"Don't you want me to?"

"I didn't say that."

"Then I'll stay."

"Stay if you like."

I got up and he followed me. "Where are you going? Are you going hunting?"

"No."

"Well, then?"

"Stop pestering me. I don't like talking to kids."

"You're also a kid. Mama still hits you."

"Say that again and I'll bash your face in."

"All right, I won't say it again."

I went into the chicken run, and he came after me. The pipes were hot, and I had to move them with a cloth. The dust that rose was dense and suffocating.

"What are you looking for? Shall I help you?"

I began to move the blocks one by one and Nandito did the same. "Get away!"

He went to the other end of the run and began to cry.

When I had removed the last block of the pile I saw the snake. It was a mamba, very dark in color. When it realized it had been discovered it wound itself up more tightly and lifted its triangular head. Its eyes shone vigilantly and its black forked tongue quivered menacingly.

I drew back against the fence, then sat down on the ground. "Don't cry, Nandito."

"You're nasty. You don't want to play with me."

"Don't cry anymore. I'll play with you just now. Don't cry."

We both sat quietly. The little head of the snake came slowly to rest on the topmost coil, and the rest of its body stopped trembling. But it continued to watch me attentively.

"Nandito, say something, talk to me."

"What do you want me to say?"

"Anything you like."

"I don't feel like saying anything."

Nandito was still rubbing his eyes and feeling resentful toward me.

"Have you ever seen a snake? Do you like snakes? Are you scared of them? Answer me!"

"Where are the snakes?" Nandito jumped up in terror, and looked around.

"In the bush. Sit down and talk."

"Aren't there any snakes here?"

"No. Talk. Talk to me about snakes."

Nandito sat down very close to me.

"I'm very frightened of snakes. Mama says it's dangerous to go out in the bush because of them. When we're walking in the grass we can step on one by mistake and get bitten. When a snake bites us we die. Sartina says that if a snake bites us and we don't want to die we must kill it, burn it till it's dry, then eat it. She says she's already eaten a snake, so she won't die even if she gets bitten."

"Have you ever seen a snake?"

"Yes, in Chico's house. The servant killed it in the chicken run."

"What was it like?"

"It was big and red, and it had a mouth like a frog."

"Would you like to see a snake now?"

Nandito got up and leaned against me fearfully. "Is there a snake in the chicken run? I'm scared—let's get out."

"If you want to get out, go away. I didn't call you to come in here."

"I'm frightened to go alone."

"Then sit here until I feel like going out."

The two of us stayed very quietly for a while.

Toto and Wolf were playing outside the fence. They were running from one post to another, going all the way round and starting again. At every post they raised a leg and urinated.

Then they came inside the chicken run and lay on their stomachs to rest. Wolf saw the snake immediately and began to bark. Toto barked as well, although he had his back turned toward it.

"Brother, are there always snakes in every chicken run?"

"No."

"Is there one in here?"

"Yes."

"Well then, why don't we go out. I'm scared!"

"Go out if you want to—go on!"

Wolf advanced toward the snake, barking more and more frenziedly. Toto turned his head, but still did not realize what was wrong.

Wolf's legs were trembling and he pawed the ground in anguish. Now and again he looked at me uncomprehendingly, unable to understand why I did not react to his hysterical alarm. His almost human eyes were filled with panic.

"Why is he barking like that?"

"Because he's seen the snake."

The mamba was curled up in the hollow between some blocks, and it unwound its body to give itself the most solid support possible. Its head and the raised neck remained poised in the air, unaffected by the movement of the rest of its body. Its eyes shone like fires.

Wolf's appeals were now horribly piercing, and his hair was standing up around his neck.

Leaning against the fence, Tina and Lolota and Madunana looked on curiously.

"Why don't you kill the snake?" Nandito's voice was very tearful and he was clutching me around the neck.

"Because I don't feel like it."

The distance between the snake and the dog was about five feet. However, the snake had inserted its tail in the angle formed between a block and the ground, and had raised its coils one by one, preparing for the strike. The triangular head drew back imperceptibly, and the base of the lifted neck came forward. Seeming to be aware of the proximity of his end, the dog began to bark even more frantically, without, however, trying to get away from the snake. From a little way behind, Toto, now on his feet as well, joined in the barking.

For a fraction of a second the neck of the snake curved while the head leaned back. Then, as if the tension of its pliant body had snapped a cord that fastened its head to the ground, it shot forward in a lightning movement impossible to follow. Although the dog had raised himself on his hind legs like a goat, the snake struck him full on the chest. Free of support, the tail of the snake whipped through the air, reverberating with the movement of the last coil.

Wolf fell on his back with a suppressed whine, pawing convulsively. The mamba abandoned him immediately, and with a spring disappeared between the pipes.

"A *nhoka!*"* screamed Sartina.

* "A *snake!*"

Nandito threw me aside and ran out of the chicken run with a yell, collapsing into the arms of Madunana. As soon as he felt free of the snake, Wolf vanished in half a dozen leaps in the direction of Senhor Castro's house.

The children all started to cry without having understood what had happened. Sartina took Nandito to the house, carrying him in her arms. Only when the children disappeared behind Sartina did I call Madunana to help me kill the snake.

Madunana waited with a cloth held up high while I moved the pipes with the aid of a broomstick. As soon as the snake appeared Madunana threw the cloth over it, and I set to beating the heap with my stick.

When Papa came back from work Nandito had come round from the shock, and was weeping copiously. Mama, who had not yet been to see the snake, went with Papa to the chicken run. When I went there as well, I saw Papa turn the snake over onto its back with a stick.

"I don't like to think of what a snake like this could have done to one of my children." Papa smiled. "Or to anyone else. It was better this way. What hurts me is to think that these six feet of snake were attained at the expense of my chickens. . . ."

At this point Senhor Castro's car drew up in front of our house. Papa walked up to him, and Mama went to talk to Sartina. I followed after Papa.

"Good afternoon, Senhor Castro. . . ."

"Listen, Tchembene, I've just found out that my pointer is dead, and his chest's all swollen. My natives tell me that he came howling from your house before he died. I don't want any back chat, and I'm just telling you—either you pay compensation or I'll make a complaint at the Administration. He was the best pointer I ever had."

"I've just come back from work—I don't know anything. . . ."

"I don't care a damn about that. Don't argue. Are you going to pay or aren't you?"

"But, Senhor Castro . . ."

"Senhor Castro nothing. It's 700 paus.* And it's better if the matter rests here."

---

* 700 "paus"—slang for 700 shillings (about 8 pounds).

"As you like, Senhor Castro, but I don't have the money now. . . ."

"We'll see about that later. I'll wait until the end of the month, and if you don't pay then there'll be a row."

"Senhor Castro, we've known each other such a long time, and there's never . . ."

"Don't try that with me. I know what you all need—a bloody good hiding is the only thing. . . ."

Senhor Castro climbed into his car and pulled away. Papa stayed watching while the car drove off. "Son of a bitch. . . ."

I went up to him and tugged at the sleeve of his coat.

"Papa, why didn't you say that to his face?"

He didn't answer.

We had hardly finished supper when Papa said, "Mother, tell Sartina to clear the table quickly. My children, let us pray. Today we are not going to read the Bible. We will simply pray."

Papa talked in Ronga, and for this reason I regretted having asked him that question a while ago.

When Sartina finished clearing away the plates and folded the cloth, Papa began, "*Tatana, ha ku dumba hosi ya tilo misaba. . . .*"*

When he finished, his eyes were red.

"Amen!"

"Amen!"

Mama got up, and asked, as if it meant nothing, "But what did Senhor Castro want, after all?"

"It's nothing important."

"All right, tell me about it in our room. I'll go and set out the children's things. You, Ginho, wake up early tomorrow and take a laxative. . . ."

When they had all gone away, I asked Papa, "Papa, why do you always pray when you are very angry?"

"Because He is the best counsellor."

"And what counsel does He give you?"

"He gives me no counsel. He gives me strength to continue."

* Father, we put our trust in Thee, Lord of Heaven and earth.

"Papa, do you believe a lot in Him?"

Papa looked at me as if he were seeing me for the first time, and then exploded. "My son, one must have a hope. When one comes to the end of a day, and one knows that tomorrow will be another day just like it, and that things will always be the same, we have got to find the strength to keep on smiling, and keep on saying, 'This is not important!' We ourselves have to allot our own reward for the heroism of every day. We have to establish a date for this reward, even if it's the day of our death! Even today you saw Senhor Castro humiliate me: this formed only part of today's portion, because there were many things that happened that you didn't see. No, my son, there must be hope! It must exist! Even if all this only denies Him, He must exist!"

Papa stopped suddenly, and forced himself to smile. Then he added, "Even a poor man has to have something. Even if it is only a hope! Even if it's a false hope!"

"Papa, I could have prevented the snake from biting Senhor Castro's dog. . . ."

Papa looked at me with his eyes full of tenderness, and said under his breath, "It doesn't matter. It's a good thing that he got bitten."

Mama appeared at the door. "Are you going to let the child go to sleep or not?"

I looked at Papa, and we remembered Senhor Castro and both of us burst out laughing. Mama didn't understand.

"Are you two going crazy?!"

"Yes, and it's about time we went crazy," said Papa with a smile.

Papa was already on the way to his room, but I must have talked too loudly. Anyway, it was better that he heard, "Papa, I sometimes . . . I don't really know . . . but for some time . . . I have been thinking that I didn't love you all. I'm sorry. . . ."

Mama didn't understand what we had been saying, so she became angry. "Stop all this, or else. . . ."

"Do you know, my son," Papa spoke ponderously, and gesticulated a lot before every word. "The most difficult thing to bear is that feeling of complete emptiness . . . and one suffers very much . . . very, very, very much. One grows with so much bottled up inside, but afterward it is difficult to scream, you know."

"Papa, and when Senhor Castro comes . . . ?"

Mama was going to object, but Papa clutched her shoulder firmly. "It's nothing, Mother, but, you know, our son believes that people don't mount wild horses, and that they only make use of the hungry, docile ones. Yet when a horse goes wild it gets shot down, and it's all finished. But tame horses die every day. Every day, d'you hear? Day after day after day—as long as they can stand on their feet."

Mama looked at him with her eyes popping out.

"Do you know, Mother, I'm afraid to believe that this is true, but I also can't bring myself to tell him that it's a lie. . . . He sees, even today he saw. . . . I only wish for the strength to make sure that my children know how to recognize other things. . . ."

Papa and Mama were already in their room, so I couldn't hear anymore, but even from there Mama yelled, "Tomorrow you'll take a laxative, that'll show you. I'm not like your father who lets himself get taken in. . . ."

My bed was flooded in yellow moonlight, and it was pleasant to feel my naked skin quiver with its cold caress. For some unknown reason the warm sensation of Sartina's body flowed through my senses. I managed to cling to her almost physical presence for a few minutes, and I wanted to fall asleep with her so as not to dream of dogs and snakes.

Njabulo S. Ndebele was born in Johannesburg in 1948. He has a master's degree from Cambridge University and a Ph.D. from the University of Denver. His poetry has appeared in numerous anthologies, and his works of fiction include *Bonolo and the Peach Tree*, *Fools and Other Stories*, and *Sarah, Rings and I*. He is also the author of several critical essays published in a collection called *South African Literature and Culture: Rediscovery of the Ordinary*. Professor Ndebele has served as president of the Congress of South African Writers and is currently a resident scholar at the Ford Foundation.

The Prophetess

The boy knocked timidly on the door, while a big fluffy dog sniffed at his ankles. That dog made him uneasy; he was afraid of strange dogs and this fear made him anxious to go into the house as soon as possible. But there was no answer to his knock. Should he simply turn the doorknob and get in? What would the prophetess say? Would she curse him? He was not sure now which he feared more: the prophetess or the dog. If he stood longer there at the door, the dog might soon decide that he was up to some mischief after all. If he left, the dog might decide he was running away. And the prophetess! What would she say when she eventually opened the door to find no one there? She might decide someone had been fooling, and would surely send lightning after the boy. But then, leaving would also bring the boy another problem: he would have to leave without the holy water for which his sick mother had sent him to the prophetess.

There was something strangely intriguing about the prophetess and holy water. All that one was to do, the boy had so many times heard in the streets of the township, was fill a bottle with water and take it to the prophetess. She would then lay her hands on the bottle and pray. And the water would be holy. And the water would have curing powers. That's what his mother had said too.

The boy knocked again, this time with more urgency. But he had to be careful not to annoy the prophetess. It was getting darker and the dog continued to sniff at his ankles. The boy tightened his grip round the neck of the bottle he had just filled with water from the street tap on the other side of the street, just opposite the prophetess's house. He would hit the dog with this bottle. What's more, if the bottle broke he would stab the dog with the sharp glass. But what would the prophetess say? She would probably curse him. The boy knocked again, but this time he heard the faint voice of a woman.

"*Kena!*" the voice said.

The boy quickly turned the knob and pushed. The door did not yield. And the dog growled. The boy turned the knob again and pushed. This time the dog gave a sharp bark, and the boy knocked frantically. Then he heard the bolt shoot back, and saw the door open to reveal darkness. Half the door seemed to have disappeared into the dark. The boy felt fur brush past his leg as the dog scurried into the house.

"*Voetsek!*" the woman cursed suddenly.

The boy wondered whether the woman was the prophetess. But as he was wondering, the dog brushed past him again, slowly this time. In spite of himself, the boy felt a pleasant, tickling sensation and a slight warmth where the fur of the dog had touched him. The warmth did not last, but the tickling sensation lingered, going up to the back of his neck and seeming to caress it. Then he shivered and the sensation disappeared, shaken off in the brief involuntary tremor.

"Dogs stay out!" shouted the woman, adding, "This is not at the white man's."

The boy heard a slow shuffle of soft leather shoes receding into the dark room. The woman must be moving away from the door, the boy thought. He followed into the house.

"Close the door," ordered the woman who was still moving somewhere in the dark. But the boy had already done so.

Although it was getting dark outside, the room was much darker and the fading day threw some of its waning light into the room through the windows. The curtains had not yet been drawn. Was it an effort to save candles, the boy wondered. His mother had scolded him many times for lighting up before it was completely dark.

The boy looked instinctively toward the dull light coming in through the window. He was anxious, though, about where the woman was now, in the dark. Would she think he was afraid when she caught him looking out to the light? But the thick, dark green leaves of vine outside, lapping lazily against the window, attracted and held him like a spell. There was no comfort in that light; it merely reminded the boy of his fear, only a few minutes ago, when he walked under that dark tunnel of vine which arched over the path from the gate to the door. He had dared not touch that vine and its countless velvety, black, and juicy grapes that hung temptingly within reach, or rested lusciously on forked branches. Silhouetted against the darkening summer sky, the bunches of grapes had each looked like a cluster of small cones narrowing down to a point.

"Don't touch that vine!" was the warning almost everyone in Charterston township knew. It was said that the vine was all coated with thick, invisible glue. And that was how the prophetess caught all those who stole out in the night to steal her grapes. They would be glued there to the vine, and would be moaning for forgiveness throughout the cold night, until the morning, when the prophetess would come out of the house with the first rays of the sun, raise her arms into the sky, and say: "Away, away, sinful man; go and sin no more!" Suddenly, the thief would be free, and would walk away feeling a great release that turned him into a new man. That vine; it was on the lips of everyone in the township every summer.

One day when the boy had played truant with three of his friends, and they were coming back from town by bus, some grown-ups in the bus were arguing about the prophetess's vine. The bus was so full that it was hard for anyone to move. The three truant friends, having given their seats to grown-ups, pressed against each other in a line in the middle of the bus and could see most of the passengers.

"Not even a cow can tear away from that glue," said a tall, dark man who had high cheekbones. His balaclava was a careless heap on his head. His mustache, which had been finely rolled into two semicircular horns, made him look fierce. And when he gesticulated with his tin lunch box, he looked fiercer still.

"My question is only one," said a big woman whose big arms rested thickly on a bundle of washing on her lap. "Have you ever seen a person caught there? Just answer that one question." She spoke with finality, and threw her defiant skepticism outside at the receding scene of men cycling home from work in single file. The bus moved so close to them that the boy had feared the men might get hit.

"I have heard of one silly chap that got caught!" declared a young man. He was sitting with others on the long seat at the rear of the bus. They had all along been laughing and exchanging ribald jokes. The young man had thick lips and red eyes. As he spoke he applied the final touches of saliva with his tongue to brown paper rolled up with tobacco.

"When?" asked the big woman. "Exactly when, I say? Who was that person?"

"These things really happen!" said a general chorus of women.

"That's what I know," endorsed the man with the balaclava, and then added, "You see, the problem with some women is that they will not listen; they have to oppose a man. They just have to."

"What is that man saying now?" asked another woman. "This matter started off very well, but this road you are now taking will get us lost."

"That's what I'm saying too," said the big woman, adjusting her bundle of washing somewhat unnecessarily. She continued: "A person shouldn't look this way or that, or take a corner here or there. Just face me straight: I asked a question."

"These things really happen," said the chorus again.

"That's it, good ladies, make your point: push very strongly," shouted the young man at the back. "Love is having women like you," he added, much to the enjoyment of his friends. He was now smoking, and his rolled-up cigarette looked small between his thick fingers.

"Although you have no respect," said the big woman, "I will let you know that this matter is no joke."

"Of course this is not a joke!" shouted a new contributor. He spoke firmly and in English. His eyes seemed to burn with anger. He was young and immaculately dressed, his white shirt collar resting neatly on the collar of his jacket. A young nurse in a white uniform sat next to him. "The mother there," he continued, "asks you very clearly whether you have ever seen a person caught by the supposed prophetess's supposed trap. Have you?"

"She didn't say that, man," said the young man at the back, passing the roll to one of his friends. "She only asked when this person was caught and who it was." The boys at the back laughed. There was a lot of smoke now at the back of the bus.

"My question was," said the big woman, turning her head to glare at the young man, "have you ever seen a person caught there? That's all." Then she looked outside. She seemed angry now.

"Don't be angry, mother," said the young man at the back. There was more laughter. "I was only trying to understand," he added.

"And that's our problem," said the immaculately dressed man, addressing the bus. His voice was sure and strong. "We laugh at everything; just stopping short of seriousness. Is it any wonder that the white man is still sitting on us? The mother there asked a very straightforward question, but she is answered vaguely about things happening. Then there is disrespectful laughter at the back there. The truth is you have no proof. None of you. Have you ever seen anybody caught by this prophetess? Never. It's all superstition. And so much about this prophetess also. Some of us are tired of her stories."

There was a stunned silence in the bus. Only the heavy drone of an engine struggling with an overloaded bus could be heard. It was the man with the balaclava who broke the silence.

"Young man," he said, "by the look of things you must be a clever, educated person, but you just note one thing. The prophetess might just be hearing all this, so don't be surprised when a bolt of lightning strikes you on a hot sunny day. And we shall be there at your funeral, young man, to say how you brought misfortune upon your head."

Thus had the discussion ended. But the boy had remembered how, every summer, bottles of all sizes filled with liquids of all kinds of colors would dangle from vines and peach and apricot trees in many yards in the township. No one dared steal fruit from those trees. Who wanted to be glued in shame to a fruit tree? Strangely, though, only the prophetess's trees had no bottles hanging from their branches.

The boy turned his eyes away from the window and focused into the dark room. His eyes had adjusted slowly to the darkness, and he saw the dark form of the woman shuffling away from him. She probably wore those slippers that had a fluff on top. Old women seem to love them. Then a white receding object came into focus. The woman wore a white *doek* on her head. The boy's eyes followed the *doek*. It took a right-angled turn—probably round the table. And then the dark form of a table came into focus. The *doek* stopped, and the boy heard the screech of a chair being pulled; and the *doek* descended somewhat and was still. There was silence in the room. The boy wondered what to do. Should he grope for a chair? Or should he squat on the floor respectfully? Should he greet or wait to be greeted? One never knew with the prophetess. Why did his mother have to send him to this place? The fascinating stories about the prophetess, to which the boy would add graphic details as if he had also met her, were one thing; but being in her actual presence was another. The boy then became conscious of the smell of camphor. His mother always used camphor whenever she complained of pains in her joints. Was the prophetess ill then? Did she pray for her own water? Suddenly, the boy felt at ease, as if the discovery that a prophetess could also feel pain somehow made her explainable.

"*Lumela 'me*," he greeted. Then he cleared his throat.

"*Eea ngoanaka*," she responded. After a little while she asked: "Is there something you want, little man?" It was a very thin voice. It would have been completely detached had it not been for a hint of tiredness in it. She breathed somewhat heavily. Then she coughed, cleared her throat, and coughed again. A mixture of rough discordant sounds filled the dark room as if everything was coming out of her insides, for she seemed to breathe out her cough from deep within her. And the boy wondered: If she coughed too long, what would happen? Would something come out? A lung? The boy saw the form of the woman clearly now: she had bent forward somewhat. Did anything come out of her onto the floor? The cough subsided. The woman sat up and her hands fumbled with something around her breasts. A white cloth emerged. She leaned forward again, cupped her hands, and spat into the cloth. Then she stood up and shuffled away into further darkness away from the boy. A door creaked, and the white *doek* disappeared. The boy wondered what to do because the prophetess had disappeared before he could say what he had come for. He waited.

More objects came into focus. Three white spots on the table

emerged. They were placed diagonally across the table. Table mats.
There was a small round black patch on the middle one. Because the
prophetess was not in the room, the boy was bold enough to move near
the table and touch the mats. They were crocheted mats. The boy
remembered the huge lacing that his mother had crocheted for the
church altar. ALL SAINTS CHURCH was crocheted all over the lacing. There were a number of designs of chalices that carried the Blood of
Our Lord.

Then the boy heard the sound of a match being struck. There were
many attempts before the match finally caught fire. Soon, the dull
orange light of a candle came into the living room where the boy was,
through a half-closed door. More light flushed the living room as the
woman came in carrying a candle. She looked round as if she was wondering where to put the candle. Then she saw the ashtray on the middle
mat, pulled it toward her, sat down, and turned the candle over into the
ashtray. Hot wax dropped onto the ashtray. Then the prophetess turned
the candle upright and pressed its bottom onto the wax. The candle held.

The prophetess now peered through the light of the candle at the
boy. Her thick lips protruded, pulling the wrinkled skin and caving in
the cheeks to form a kind of lip circle. She seemed always ready to kiss.
There was a line tattooed from the forehead to the ridge of a nose that
separated small eyes that were half closed by large, drooping eyelids. The
white *doek* on her head was so huge that it made her face look small. She
wore a green dress and a starched green cape that had many white
crosses embroidered on it. Behind her, leaning against the wall, was a
long bamboo cross.

The prophetess stood up again, and shuffled toward the window which
was behind the boy. She closed the curtains and walked back to her chair.
The boy saw another big cross embroidered on the back of her cape. Before
she sat down she picked up the bamboo cross and held it in front of her.

"What did you say you wanted, little man?" she asked slowly.

"My mother sent me to ask for water," said the boy, putting the bottle
of water on the table.

"To ask for water?" she asked with mild exclamation, looking up at
the bamboo cross. "That is very strange. You came all the way from
home to ask for water?"

"I mean," said the boy, "holy water."

"Ahh!" exclaimed the prophetess, "you did not say what you meant, little man." She coughed, just once. "Sit down, little man," she said, and continued, "You see, you should learn to say what you mean. Words, little man, are a gift from the Almighty, the Eternal Wisdom. He gave us all a little pinch of his mind and called on us to think. That is why it is folly to misuse words or not to know how to use them well. Now, who is your mother?"

"My mother?" asked the boy, confused by the sudden transition. "My mother is staff nurse Masemola."

"Ao!" exclaimed the prophetess, "you are the son of the nurse? Does she have such a big man now?" She smiled a little and the lip circle opened. She smiled like a pretty woman who did not want to expose her cavities.

The boy relaxed somewhat, vaguely feeling safe because the prophetess knew his mother. This made him look away from the prophetess for a while, and he saw that there was a huge mask on the wall just opposite her. It was shining and black. It grinned all the time showing two canine teeth pointing upward. About ten feet away at the other side of the wall was a picture of Jesus in which His chest was open, revealing His heart which had many shafts of light radiating from it.

"Your mother has a heart of gold, my son," continued the prophetess. "You are very fortunate, indeed, to have such a parent. Remember, when she says, 'My boy, take this message to that house,' go. When she says, 'My boy, let me send you to the shop,' go. And when she says, 'My boy, pick up a book and read,' pick up a book and read. In all this she is actually saying to you, learn and serve. Those two things, little man, are the greatest inheritance."

Then the prophetess looked up at the bamboo cross as if she saw something in it that the boy could not see. She seemed to lose her breath for a while. She coughed deeply again, after which she went silent, her cheeks moving as if she was chewing.

"Bring the bottle nearer," she said finally. She put one hand on the bottle while with the other she held the bamboo cross. Her eyes closed, she turned her face toward the ceiling. The boy saw that her face seemed to have contracted into an intense concentration in such a way that the wrinkles seemed to have become deep gorges. Then she began to speak.

"You will not know this hymn, boy, so listen. Always listen to new

things. Then try to create too. Just as I have learned never to page
through the dead leaves of hymn books." And she began to sing.

> *If the fish in a river*
> *boiled by the midday sun*
> *can wait for the coming of evening,*
> *we too can wait*
> *in this wind-frosted land,*
> *the spring will come,*
> *the spring will come.*
> *If the reeds in winter*
> *can dry up and seem dead*
> *and then rise*
> *in the spring,*
> *we too will survive the fire that is coming*
> *the fire that is coming,*
> *we too will survive the fire that is coming.*

It was a long, slow song. Slowly, the prophetess began to pray.

"God, the All Powerful! When called upon, You always listen. We
direct our hearts and thoughts to You. How else could it be? There is so
much evil in the world; so much emptiness in our hearts; so much
debasement of the mind. But You, God of all power, are the wind that
sweeps away evil and fills our hearts and minds with renewed strength
and hope. Remember Samson? Of course You do, O Lord. You created
him, You, maker of all things. You brought him out of a barren woman's
womb, and since then, we have known that out of the desert things will
grow, and that what grows out of the barren wastes has a strength that
can never be destroyed."

Suddenly, the candle flame went down. The light seemed to have
gone into retreat as the darkness loomed out, seemingly out of the very
light itself, and bore down upon it, until there was a tiny blue flame on
the table looking so vulnerable and so strong at the same time. The boy
shuddered and felt the coldness of the floor going up his bare feet.

Then out of the dark came the prophetess's laugh. It began as a giggle,
the kind the girls would make when the boy and his friends chased them
down the street for a little kiss. The giggle broke into the kind of laugh-

ter that produced tears when one was very happy. There was a kind of strange pleasurable rhythm to it that gave the boy a momentary enjoyment of the dark, but the laugh gave way to a long shriek. The boy wanted to rush out of the house. But something strong, yet intangible, held him fast to where he was. It was probably the shriek itself that had filled the dark room and now seemed to come out of the mask on the wall. The boy felt like throwing himself on the floor to wriggle and roll like a snake until he became tired and fell into a long sleep at the end of which would be the kind of bliss the boy would feel when he was happy and his mother was happy and she embraced him, so closely.

But the giggle, the laugh, the shriek, all ended as abruptly as they had started as the darkness swiftly receded from the candle like the way ripples run away from where a stone has been thrown in the water. And there was light. On the wall, the mask smiled silently, and the heart of Jesus sent out yellow light.

"Lord, Lord, Lord," said the prophetess slowly in a quiet, surprisingly full voice which carried the same kind of contentment that had been in the voice of the boy's mother when one day he had come home from playing in the street, and she was seated on the chair close to the kitchen door, just opposite the warm stove. And as soon as she saw him come in, she embraced him all the while saying: "I've been so ill; for so long, but I've got you. You're my son. You're my son. You're my son."

And the boy had smelled the faint smell of camphor on her, and he too embraced her, holding her firmly although his arms could not go beyond his mother's armpits. He remembered how warm his hands had become in her armpits.

"Lord, Lord, Lord," continued the prophetess, "have mercy on the desert in our hearts and in our thoughts. Have mercy. Bless this water; fill it with your power; and may it bring rebirth. Let her and all others who will drink of it feel the flower of newness spring alive in them; let those who drink it break the chains of despair, and may they realize that the desert wastes are really not barren, but that the vast sands that stretch into the horizon are the measure of the seed in us."

As the prophetess stopped speaking, she slowly lowered the bamboo cross until it rested on the floor. The boy wondered if it was all over now. Should he stand up and get the blessed water and leave? But the prophetess soon gave him direction.

"Come here, my son," she said, "and kneel before me here." The boy stood up and walked slowly toward the prophetess. He knelt on the floor, his hands hanging at his sides. The prophetess placed her hands on his head. They were warm, and the warmth seemed to go through his hair, penetrating deep through his scalp into the very center of his head. Perhaps, he thought, that was the soul of the prophetess going into him. Wasn't it said that when the prophetess placed her hands on a person's head, she was seeing with her soul deep into that person; that, as a result, the prophetess could never be deceived? And the boy wondered how his lungs looked to her. Did she see the water that he had drunk from the tap just across the street? Where was the water now? In the stomach? In the kidneys?

Then the hands of the prophetess moved all over the boy's head, seeming to feel for something. They went down the neck. They seemed cooler now, and the coolness seemed to tickle the boy for his neck was colder than those hands. Now they covered his face, and he saw, just before he closed his eyes, the skin folds on the hands so close to his eyes that they looked like many mountains. Those hands smelled of blue soap and candle wax. But there was no smell of snuff. The boy wondered. Perhaps the prophetess did not use snuff after all. But the boy's grandmother did, and her hands always smelled of snuff. Then the prophetess spoke.

"My son," she said, "we are made of all that is in the world. Go. Go and heal your mother." When she removed her hands from the boy's face, he felt his face grow cold, and there was a slight sensation of his skin shrinking. He rose from the floor, lifted the bottle with its snout, and backed away from the prophetess. He then turned and walked toward the door. As he closed it, he saw the prophetess shuffling away to the bedroom carrying the candle with her. He wondered when she would return the ashtray to the table. When he finally closed the door, the living room was dark, and there was light in the bedroom.

It was night outside. The boy stood on the veranda for a while, wanting his eyes to adjust to the darkness. He wondered also about the dog. But it did not seem to be around. And there was that vine archway with its forbidden fruit and the multicolored worms that always crawled all over the vine. As the boy walked under the tunnel of vine, he tensed his neck, lowering his head as people do when walking in the rain. He was anticipating the reflex action of shaking off a falling worm. Those worms were disgustingly huge, he thought. And there was also something terrifying about their bright colors.

In the middle of the tunnel, the boy broke into a run and was out of the gate: free. He thought of his mother waiting for the holy water; and he broke into a sprint, running west up Thipe Street toward home. As he got to the end of the street, he heard the hum of the noise that came from the ever-crowded barbershops and the huge beer hall just behind those shops. After the brief retreat in the house of the prophetess, the noise, the people, the shops, the streetlights, the buses, and the taxis all seemed new. Yet, somehow, he wanted to avoid any contact with all this activity. If he turned left at the corner, he would have to go past the shops into the lit Moshoeshoe Street and its Friday night crowds. If he went right, he would have to go past the now dark, ghostly Bantu-Batho post office, and then down through the huge gum trees behind the Charterston Clinic, and then past the quiet golf course. The latter way would be faster, but too dark and dangerous for a mere boy, even with the spirit of the prophetess in him. And were not dead bodies found there sometimes? The boy turned left.

At the shops, the boy slowed down to maneuver through the crowds. He lifted the bottle to his chest and supported it from below with the other hand. He must hold on to the bottle. He was going to heal his mother. He tightened the bottle cap. Not a drop was to be lost. The boy passed the shops.

Under a street lamp just a few feet from the gate into the beer hall was a gang of boys standing in a tight circle. The boy slowed down to an anxious stroll. Who were they, he wondered. He would have to run past them quickly. No, there would be no need. He recognized Timi and Bubu. They were with the rest of the gang from the boy's neighborhood. Those were the bigger boys who were either in Standard Six or were already in secondary school or were now working in town.

Timi recognized the boy.

"Ja, sonny boy," greeted Timi. "What's a picaninny like you doing alone in the streets at night?"

"Heit, bra Timi," said the boy, returning the greeting. "Just from the shops, bra Timi," he lied, not wanting to reveal his real mission. Somehow that would not have been appropriate.

"Come on, you!" yelled another member of the gang, glaring at Timi. It was Biza. Most of the times when the boy had seen Biza, the latter was stopping a girl and talking to her. Sometimes the girl would laugh. Sometimes Biza would twist her arm until she "agreed." In broad daylight!

"You don't believe me," continued Biza to Timi, "and when I try to show you some proof you turn away to greet an ant."

"Okay then," said another, "what proof do you have? Everybody knows that Sonto is a hard girl to get."

"Come closer then," said Biza, "and I'll show you." The boy was closed out of the circle as the gang closed in toward Biza, who was at the center. The boy became curious and got closer. The wall was impenetrable. But he could clearly hear Biza.

"You see? You can all see. I've just come from that girl. Look! See? The liquid? See? When I touch it with my finger and then leave it, it follows like a spider's web."

"Well, my man," said someone, "you can't deceive anybody with that. It's the usual trick. A fellow just blows his nose and then applies the mucus there, and then emerges out of the dark saying he has just had a girl."

"Let's look again closely," said another, "before we decide one way or the other." And the gang pressed close again.

"You see? You see?" Biza kept saying.

"I think Biza has had that girl," said someone.

"It's mucus, man, and nothing else," said another.

"But you know Biza's record in these matters, gents."

"Another thing, how do we know it's Sonto and not some other girl. Where is it written on Biza's cigar that he has just had Sonto? Show me where it's written 'Sonto' there."

"You're jealous, you guys, that's your problem," said Biza. The circle went loose and there was just enough time for the boy to see Biza's penis disappear into his trousers. A thick little thing, thought the boy. It looked sad. It had first been squeezed in retreat against the fly like a concertina, before it finally disappeared. Then Biza, with a twitch of alarm across his face, saw the boy.

"What did you see, you?" screamed Biza. "Fuck off!"

The boy took to his heels wondering what Biza could have been doing with his penis under the streetlamp. It was funny, whatever it was.

It was silly too. Sinful. The boy was glad that he had got the holy water away from those boys and that none of them had touched the bottle.

And the teachers were right, thought the boy. Silliness was all those boys knew. And then they would go to school and fail test after test. Silliness and school did not go together.

The boy felt strangely superior. He had the power of the prophetess in him. And he was going to pass that power to his mother, and heal her. Those boys were not healing their mothers. They just left their mothers alone at home. The boy increased his speed. He had to get home quickly. He turned right at the charge office and sped toward the clinic. He crossed the road that went to town and entered Mayaba Street. Mayaba Street was dark and the boy could not see. But he did not lower his speed. Home was near now, instinct would take him there. His eyes would adjust to the darkness as he raced along. He lowered the bottle from his chest and let it hang at his side, like a pendulum that was not moving. He looked up at the sky as if light would come from the stars high up to lead him home. But when he lowered his face, he saw something suddenly loom before him, and, almost simultaneously, felt a dull yet painful impact against his thigh. Then there was a grating of metal seeming to scoop up sand from the street. The boy did not remember how he fell but, on the ground, he lay clutching at his painful thigh. A few feet away, a man groaned and cursed.

"Blasted child!" he shouted. "Shouldn't I kick you? Just running in the street as if you owned it. Shit of a child, you don't even pay tax. Fuck off home before I do more damage to you!" The man lifted his bicycle, and the boy saw him straightening the handles. And the man rode away.

The boy raised himself from the ground and began to limp home, conscious of nothing but the pain in his thigh. But it was not long before he felt a jab of pain at the center of his chest and his heart beating faster. He was thinking of the broken bottle and the spilt holy water and his mother waiting for him and the water that would help to cure her. What would his mother say? If only he had not stopped to see those silly boys he might not have been run over by a bicycle. Should he go back to the prophetess? No. There was the dog, there was the vine, there were the worms. There was the prophetess herself. She would not let anyone who wasted her prayers get away without punishment. Would it be lightning?

Would it be the fire of hell? What would it be? The boy limped home to face his mother. He would walk in to his doom. He would walk into his mother's bedroom, carrying no cure, and face the pain in her sad eyes.

But as the boy entered the yard of his home, he heard the sound of bottles coming from where his dog had its kennel. Rex had jumped over the bottles, knocking some stones against them in his rush to meet the boy. And the boy remembered the pile of bottles next to the kennel. He felt grateful as he embraced the dog. He selected a bottle from the heap. Calmly, as if he had known all the time what he would do in such a situation, the boy walked out of the yard again, toward the street tap on Mayaba Street. And there, almost mechanically, he cleaned the bottle, shaking it many times with clean water. Finally, he filled it with water and wiped its outside clean against his trousers. He tightened the cap, and limped home.

As soon as he opened the door, he heard his mother's voice in the bedroom. It seemed some visitors had come while he was away.

"I'm telling you, *Sisi*," his mother was saying, "and take it from me, a trained nurse. Pills, medicines, and all those injections are not enough. I take herbs too, and then think of the wonders of the universe as our people have always done. Son, is that you?"

"Yes, Ma," said the boy, who had just closed the door with a deliberate bang.

"And did you bring the water?"

"Yes, Ma."

"Good. I knew you would. Bring the water and three cups. MaShange and MaMokoena are here."

The boy's eyes misted with tears. His mother's trust in him: would he repay it with such dishonesty? He would have to be calm. He wiped his eyes with the back of his hand, and then put the bottle and three cups on a tray. He would have to walk straight. He would have to hide the pain in his thigh. He would have to smile at his mother. He would have to smile at the visitors. He picked up the tray; but just before he entered the passage leading to the bedroom, he stopped, trying to muster courage. The voices of the women in the bedroom reached him clearly.

"I hear you very well, Nurse," said one of the women. "It is that kind of sense I was trying to spread before the minds of these people. You see, the two children are first cousins. The same blood runs through them."

"That close!" exclaimed the boy's mother.

"Yes, that close. MaMokoena here can bear me out; I told them in her presence. Tell the nurse, you were there."

"I have never seen such people in all my life," affirmed MaMokoena.

"So I say to them, my voice reaching up to the ceiling, 'Hey, you people, I have seen many years. If these two children really want to marry each other, then a beast *has* to be slaughtered to cancel the ties of blood. . . .'"

"And do you want to hear what they said?" interrupted MaMokoena.

"I'm listening with both ears," said the boy's mother.

"Tell her, child of Shange," said MaMokoena.

"They said that was old, crusted foolishness. So I said to myself, 'Daughter of Shange, shut your mouth, sit back, open your eyes, and watch.' And that's what I did.

"Two weeks before the marriage, the ancestors struck. Just as I had thought. The girl had to be rushed to hospital, her legs swollen like trousers full of air on the washing line. Then I got my chance, and opened my mouth, pointing my finger at them, and said, 'Did you ask the ancestors' permission for this unacceptable marriage?' You should have seen their necks becoming as flexible as a goose's. They looked this way, and looked that way, but never at me. But my words had sunk. And before the sun went down, we were eating the insides of a goat. A week later, the children walked up to the altar. And the priest said to them, 'You are such beautiful children!'"

"Isn't it terrible that some people just let misfortune fall upon them?" remarked the boy's mother.

"Only those who ignore the words of the world speaking to them," said MaShange.

"Where is this boy now?" said the boy's mother. "Son! Is the water coming?"

Instinctively the boy looked down at his legs. Would the pain in his thigh lead to the swelling of his legs? Or would it be because of his deception? A tremor of fear went through him; but he had to control it, and be steady, or the bottle of water would topple over. He stepped forward into the passage. There was his mother! Her bed faced the passage, and he had seen her as soon as he turned into the passage. She had propped herself up with many pillows. Their eyes met, and she smiled, showing the gap in her upper front teeth that she liked to poke her tongue into. She wore a fawn chiffon *doek* which had slanted into a care-less heap on one side of her head. This exposed her undone hair on the other side of her head.

As the boy entered the bedroom, he smelled camphor. He greeted the two visitors and noticed that, although it was warm in the bedroom, MaShange, whom he knew, wore her huge, heavy, black, and shining overcoat. MaMokoena had a blanket over her shoulders. Their *doeks* were more orderly than the boy's mother's. The boy placed the tray on the dressing chest close to his mother's bed. He stepped back and watched his mother, not sure whether he should go back to the kitchen, or wait to meet his doom.

"I don't know what I would do without this boy," said the mother as she leaned on an elbow, lifted the bottle with the other hand, and turned the cap rather laboriously with the hand on whose elbow she was resting. The boy wanted to help, but he felt he couldn't move. The mother poured water into one cup, drank from it briefly, turned her face toward the ceiling, and closed her eyes. "Such cool water!" she sighed deeply, and added, "Now I can pour for you," as she poured water into the other two cups.

There was such a glow of warmth in the boy as he watched his mother, so much gladness in him that he forgave himself. What had the prophetess seen in him? Did she still feel him in her hands? Did she know what he had just done? Did holy water taste any different from ordinary water? His mother didn't seem to find any difference. Would she be healed?

"As we drink the prophetess's water," said MaShange, "we want to say how grateful we are that we came to see for ourselves how you are."

"I think I feel better already. This water, and you . . . I can feel a soothing coolness deep down."

As the boy slowly went out of the bedroom, he felt the pain in his leg, and felt grateful. He had healed his mother. He would heal her tomor-row, and always with all the water in the world. He had healed her.

Olympe Bhely-Quenum was born in 1928 in Benin. He moved to France at the age of twenty and studied at the Sorbonne. In addition to teaching courses in Greek and Latin, he later worked as a journalist and founded, with his wife, the French-English bilingual magazine *L'Afrique Actuelle*. In 1968 he joined UNESCO Headquarters in Paris as an African issues specialist. His books include *Snares Without End*, *The Song of the Lake*, *The Initiate*, *Thousand Axes*, and *The Calls of Voodoo*.

A Child in the Bush of Ghosts*

Translated by Willifried F. Feuser

When I was eleven years old, one of my uncles one day took me along with him to his farm. His name was Akpoto. He was a handsome man with large black eyes, sturdy and distinguished-looking.

We had set out early, and yet the African morning sun had beaten us to it. We had covered more than thirteen kilometers on the district council road; then we had taken the pathway that led to Houêto. A small river, fordable at any time of the day, cut across the path of fine golden sand which meandered through a high and dense forest.

We had crossed the river and continued walking on sand. I loved the softness of that sandy earth; its velvety surface pleasantly caressed the soles of my bare feet. But the joy I felt in walking on that path gradually gave way to fear as we penetrated ever more deeply into the forest.

When we left the path for a sodden trail, I suddenly had the feeling that the humidity pervaded my whole body, and the sense of fear became intolerable.

---

* To Andre Breton to whom I first told this story; to the College Littre in Avranches and my former schoolmates in that establishment where I wrote this story; but also to the city of Avranches where I learned a great deal.

I therefore started pestering my uncle with little questions which were as irritating as they were foolish. I kept knocking against him, clung to his hand, or moved clumsily in front of him and thus almost succeeded several times in making him fall . . .

We were crossing a kind of clearing where the sky above remained invisible as in most of our forests. We had already walked too much. For how long? I can't say. I was not yet going to school and, naturally, did not know any French, to the utter indignation of my father, the respectable primary schoolteacher who always saw me sickly and unable to stand the hustle and bustle of a school in session. As far as my uncle was concerned, he was able to determine the time of day from the position of the sun through a special kind of sensory perception, or other intuition. Therefore, after having raised his eyes in vain toward the arches of the towering trees hiding the sky from our eyes, he said to me in his gentle voice which I can still hear: "Wait for me here, I'll be back in a short while."

He left me, plunging with big steps into the bush that stretched out as far as the eye could see. He had put a big orange and four guavas into my hands.

Suddenly I felt dead tired. I was gripped by the urge to cry but controlled myself. I've never had much use for crybabies. There is nothing I detest so much as giving unbridled expression to our sorrows. And I waited. Oh, I certainly waited more than I shall ever be able to wait again, but my uncle did not return. There was plenty of time for me to eat two guavas, then my orange, and then I waited again a very long time before munching my remaining two guavas.

Worn out by the anxiety brought about by seeing nothing but the bush with its frightening calm around me, I sat down on the black forest earth and buried my face in my hands as if I never wanted to see any more of the place where I was. But as the humidity caught hold of me I had to rise again and started walking without really having any idea of where I was going.

I ought to have searched for the path we had followed until then but all my senses were gripped by panic and I marched like an automaton. I would have wished to be able to give out a single scream, to whistle, sing or talk loudly, or only just to mutter something—anything to assuage the effect of the fear in me, anything to make me feel aware of my person or simply to give me the illusion that I still was myself a human being, alive, finding myself there by chance, but I could not say anything . . . True to God, it is the only time I remember ever having felt fear.

I walked on relentlessly, unable to rediscover the path covered with sand; neither did I see the river again, its waters rolling with a sweet music, but I suddenly noticed in front of me a big woman wrapped in a white lappa that concealed her face and covered her feet. She advanced toward me; my heart started pounding precipitately; I felt as if I were receiving heavy blows from a ram inside me that did not quite succeed in splitting my chest wide open. I started shouting, no, I would have liked to shout; I felt I was shouting but did not hear myself shouting.

I wished to see the earth opening under my feet but the humus refused to do my bidding. Only then did I concede defeat and stretched out my arms to the lady like a baby to its mother.

To my surprise the woman passed me by in mute indifference. I looked backward. She too had turned her head and before I found the time to avert my eyes, she had already uncovered her face. I then saw something frightful: an emaciated face, the face of a fleshless skull, which made a horrid and repugnant grimace at me.

I started running head over heels but glanced backward from time to time. It was to no avail, for I constantly saw the person at a distance of twenty paces behind me, although she was not running. But my mad gallop did not last very long, for a few moments after that encounter I found myself right in front of the railway tracks. My heart was thumping so violently that it seemed to be about to burst in my chest. I looked back again and saw my uncle.

"Where have you been? Why did you forsake me in the forest?" I asked, staring at him in bleak reproach.

He looked at me with pity because he read the anguish in my eyes; he told me, however, that he had not wasted any time at Houêto:

"I ordered my farm laborers at once to catch the chickens you see here, and I went to dig out cassava tubers for your grandmother and grand-aunt myself. As soon as the job was finished, I returned to the clearing and was greatly surprised not to find you. I then continued my return journey, looking everywhere. All of a sudden I heard a rustle in the bush to my left; first I thought it was a deer but I changed my mind afterward when I saw a human shape running helter-skelter; it was you. I could have called you but I preferred to follow you with my eyes, for we

were moving along parallel lines. A single step, but a big one, separated
me from you, my boy. And then, I had nothing to fear for you, for the
bush is not dangerous."

I felt sad at having brought him to the point where he thought he
owed me an explanation. But on the other hand, my heart was still
throbbing with anger and subdued sobs when I asked him in a trembling
voice whether he had seen the river again.

"Yes, of course. It was there even before our ancestors were born, and
will certainly remain after we're dead and gone."

"You may be right, but I did not recross it."

"What are you telling me there? You must have forded it without
noticing."

"But it's true, uncle! I didn't see the slightest trace of the river; just
look at my legs and feet, they aren't soaked like yours."

"You surprise me, Codjo!"

"Let's return to the clearing by the path that has brought me here, if
you don't believe me!" I said with an assurance that today I find astounding on the part of the child I was.

My uncle tucked his baskets with cassava and chickens under a
thicket, put me astraddle his shoulders and we took the path on which I
had come, or rather the trail which perhaps would never have come into
existence if I had not been the first human being who in his terrorized
gallop had savagely flattened the grass along that line.

We had arrived at the clearing, then at the farm much more quickly
than we could have managed by walking on the sand-covered pathway.

Akpoto was dumbfounded not to be compelled to pass the river he
had been crossing for more than thirty-five years, the source of which he
imagined to be somewhat in the forest.

He put me down, my mouth felt dry. I quenched my thirst by drinking
from a gourd, and this made me feel the freshness of the water and the
pleasure of drinking it more keenly. Then we set out on the return journey, taking once more the kind of game track I had discovered and
which had become the fastest way to go to Houêto and back.

"*A walking skeleton, that sort of thing doesn't exist. No dead man comes
back to stay among the living: my paternal grandmother and great-grandfather
followed one another into death at a month's interval; nobody ever told me that
he has met them during the three years since they stopped coddling me.*" So

went my train of thought, and I was convinced that my encounter with
the skeleton was merely the result of a hallucination.

Still I wanted to make sure it was only an illusion, and taking advantage of a moment when my parents' watchfulness had flagged, I fled from
our compound where I was getting bored. I liked the open air, the solitude at the seaside or in the bush, and likewise the company of human
beings who made no impositions on me but allowed me to make myself
useful without feeling duty-bound to do so.

In my parents' house everything was offered to me on a golden plat-
ter; I was pampered and idle and felt my uselessness to the full.

I reached the clearing again through the game track and started
searching for the source of the river. My mind was totally absorbed in
the operation, perhaps because I was what my parents called "a self-
willed child," or perhaps also because I had an ulterior motive: to surprise my uncle by discovering the truth I wanted to find out.

I therefore headed into the bush, slipping over pebbles, sinking into
the spongy suction of the soft ground; skipping over creepers, crawling
among thorns. In front of me appeared a big chameleon. We looked at
each other for a good second and its skin visibly, and gradually, took on
the color of the indigo cloth tied around my neck, which I was wearing
over my khaki shorts. At that moment I thought of my revered great-
grandfather who in telling tales did not hide his predilection for the
chameleon: "It rarely misses its destination because it knows how to adjust
itself to its surroundings and never looks backward."

What did that mean? I hadn't the slightest idea. I was a spoiled,
demanding child whom a too indulgent grandfather had perhaps wanted
to convert to patience and gentleness by lecturing him on moral philos-
ophy. But he had reasoned through the use of symbols that remained a
mystery to the child. Still, it was of that venerable aged man that I
thought on that day, and seeing the chameleon take on the color of my
cloth, I not only decided not to look back but also to adapt myself to the
bush, to understand its language, to bow to its laws, without however
forgetting that I was a human being, the only creature who would not be
forgiven voluntary subservience. I was born to grow big and to live even
beyond death . . .

A small noise startled me; I did not pay any heed and continued
slinking through the thorns that tore my cloth. A long snake carelessly

passed between my legs, a boa rolled itself around a tree toward which I was heading. I was unafraid, beyond caring. My only concern was to discover the source of the river. I had met the chameleon that perhaps still retained the color of my garment in memory of our chance encounter or had swapped it for that of some of the distinctly green or red leaves I remembered seeing.

From among creepers and thorns I emerged into another clearing. In its immobility, the canopy of leaves above my head sealed off the place in tragic solitude. I felt the void within me as if I were nothing thenceforth but a wretched carcass draped with black skin. At that moment, the skeleton appeared a few steps away from me, wrapped in its big white *lappa* which covered its head. I felt no emotion, or more precisely, I was not afraid since I considered it like something I was used to. Still I rubbed my eyes as if to rid myself of an optical illusion, to make sure of what I was seeing. It drew closer; I did not rush toward it as in our first encounter, for I had to preserve my dignity. In my view, it represented nothing. It was nothingness in motion, and I was a man. This certainty, due to the realization of the difference between us, fortified me not with courage—that I didn't care about—but with cockiness, and I saw my body rising to its level. This was not the time for any more concessions. I felt that the bush was not supposed to be the abode of the dead but of the living. Wasn't I one of them? We converged as on a one-way track where no provision has been made for people to cross each other. I did nothing to let it pass when we were face-to-face. Then it stretched out its hand to me. At that moment I would have liked to cross my arms, to sport a scornful countenance since last time it too had snubbed me; but I decided to let bygones be bygones and gathered its bony hand in mine.

Instead of forcing me to retrace my steps it did the opposite, still holding my hand. I thus followed it, eager to discover where it was taking me. We wended our way side by side without my feeling the slightest apprehension. After all, what was there to be afraid of? Holding in my hand that of a human skeleton? Human. That was just the word I needed. Was I not with something human? Was I not sure now that my first encounter was not simply the effect of a delusion?

No, really, I was no longer afraid. I was eight years old when my grandmother and great-grandfather stopped living. I remember having cried a great deal by their bodies seated beside the mortal remains of these old people in their barely gnarled tallness during my vigil, despite my parents' vain effort to spare me what they called too violent shocks. Yes, I still remember: I hurled myself on my grandmother when they wanted to put her in the bier; I took her hand and squeezed it very hard so as to communicate all my warmth to her. Oh, the piercing coldness she left in my hands and which is still there, evermore! It was her that I felt again all along, while the skeleton kept my hand in its own. It did not hold it in a tight grip, did not apply any pressure, and we just wandered like two friends.

Still I did not forget that I was a man, a human being, a child barely twelve years old, while it was a skeleton. Had it been a man or a woman? I never found out. Besides, this was of no importance. With wide open eyes I stared at the bush in front of me. Not a single time did it occur to me to have a look at my fellow traveler. And why should I have looked at its skeletal visage since I was feeling its hand in mine? Had it suddenly vanished I would most assuredly not have worried about its disappearance but would have continued on my way amid the trees, the thorns and the beasts.

But I have to admit today that I had realized that from the moment we walked together the thorns no longer tore my cloth; everything slipped smoothly off me as it did off the skeleton. A wild boar and his mate emerging from their lair took to flight on seeing us. My uncle had told me that the bush was not dangerous; all the same, we saw more than one pair of lions and panthers: they had passed us by with something approaching indifference. To be precise they had invariably passed on my side; they had all sniffed at me and then walked away in haughty grandeur. Why? I wouldn't know. I may have appeared vile-smelling and undesirable to them, unless they just happened not to be hungry just then.

We had been walking like that for a time that seemed reasonably long to me but I was not tired. I did not feel any sign of fatigue. I paid attention to everything. Then, to my great surprise, I stopped seeing the bush around me and realized that we were in an underground tunnel hung with tree roots. The walls were oozing moisture but the ground was dry. The ear perceived the gentle distant murmur of a stream. I thought of the river while striding along with my queer companion.

At certain places the walls of the long gallery through which we were proceeding had been discreetly adorned with symbolic graffiti: snakes biting their own tails; arms cut off and placed on top of each other in the form of an X; sexual organs; copulation scenes; skin-bones; human skulls; mouths that were either laughing or distorted in an agony of suffering; horses without heads but galloping at full speed, tails and manes flying in the wind; fire shaped like an open lily blossom flaring from a pit; coffins; people performing a ritual dance; a clumsily drawn rectangle representing a mirror.

We turned to the left and I had the impression that we were changing our direction from north to sunrise. A light entering the place from heaven knows where gently lit up the underground passage sloping downward in front of me. We walked unceasingly descending the slope, and arrived at a kind of crypt where human skeletons without the tiniest bone missing were stretched out side by side.

My guide stopped in front of one of them, uncovering his cavity-riddled face. I looked straight at him. He bowed slightly to one of the skeletons which sat up, crossed its legs, then its arms; he continued his homage and each one of his fellow skeletons took the same posture as the preceding one. And I saw seventy-seven skeletons thus sitting up and leaning their backs against the wall of the crypt.

Did they want to impress me? I had experienced fear before but fear held no more meaning for me. I had heard people talk a lot about death, but since the death of my grandparents I no longer feared it. Death had become for me such a familiar companion that I gave it no more thought. But looking at the skeletons attentively, I had a feeling that each one of them represented a human being I had known, and to which I had perhaps been close. It was good to see them again but I had not come here for them.

"Where is the source of the river?" I suddenly cried in a tragic voice which struck the walls in a zigzag line, provoking a long and sonorous echo.

And again I perceived murmurings of the water, then a groan followed by the sound of a torrent rushing away.

The skulls all seemed to have been raised again to look me straight in the face.

"You see that I have come to visit you without misgivings. I'm not afraid of you because you used to be men; for me you still are, and I don't believe in death!"

I heard my voice reecho. It ricocheted away from me along the underground passage.

"Why don't you answer? Should you really be so useless?" All I received for an answer was my own voice and its echo which gabbled any utterance.

"You hear me?"

"You hear me?"

"—ear me?"

"—me?"

"—e?"

"Why did you bring me here?"

"—bring me here?"

"—me here?"

"—ere?"

I looked around me and noticed that my guide had disappeared; maybe he had quietly slipped back to his little niche among his peers. So I thought of setting out on my return journey but as the passage stretched out farther before me, I preferred not to retrace my steps; hence I moved ahead. Thus I continued marching at a normal walking pace, looking all the while at the walls covered with graffiti fraught with symbolism. Despite my casual and almost leisurely gait I was feeling tired. I later realized that the way was sloping upward. Moreover, the certainty that I was advancing toward the sun became more and more acute.

As if in a fog I saw a shadow passing before my eyes; then the shadow became a reality: a majestic skeleton without any garment, his right hand clutched to his heart and his left holding a shinbone with a skull on top.

I stopped short in front of him. He made to let me pass and the moment I was going to continue on my way he slightly stroked my head with the skull resting on the shinbone. I did not react, did not look back. The light entering the cavern was becoming more and more intense. I inhaled the air charged with a thousand smells from the fields ... Abruptly I felt carried off into a long sleep and saw myself in a place, the name of which someone seemed to murmur into my ear.

"Wassai."

O Wassai! Wassai! disturbing, exciting paradise of entwined bodies.

Here was a pathway sundered into five branches, each leading to clearly defined places. On the one side of the main path stood a hedge of hibiscus, bougainvillea and campeachy separating the path from a vast ground planted with kola-nut trees dwarfed by iroko and silk-cotton trees. In the hollows of those giant trees nested birds; their lugubrious shrieks did not frighten me. Wisps of white smoke rose from the foot of the trees. Little did I care about their origin and meaning! Let the sorcerers abandon themselves to their orgies, let them devour the souls of their victims. I was in Wassai.

On the other side of the road was Wassai, little house of joy without a keeper. I entered. Ravishing young beauties with sturdy breasts, black skin, athletic bodies. And their nimble legs with prettily proportioned muscles, readily intertwining, pushed me gently into voluptuous depths. At Wassai I experienced unforgettable little tremors brought about by girls I did not know; their names have remained unspoken, I've forgotten their seductive faces; but the form of their lithe and supple bodies remains in my arms, the freshness of their jet-black skin still vibrates through my nerves. In their midst I underwent my sexual initiation till all the flowers of the world blossomed within me, till the hard egg was hatched whose unwonted presence I had felt deep within. No outburst of rebellious sex will ever surprise me. I have explored all its domains in Wassai, fearsome black slowly unfolding in the deep nights of a dwelling without a master.

When I came to myself, I went my way without slowing down my pace and thus came out into the open air.

Let it be said in passing that I did not for a single moment feel like a prisoner in that underground gallery. But instead of finding myself on even ground, at the skirt of the forest as I expected, perhaps because I had scented the wind and the sun, I realized that I was perched high up on a mountainside studded with shrubbery.

A little farther down, beneath my feet, a spring, gushing out from this imposing height I had not known before, flowed into the plain before me with a murmur. And the glittering reflections of light, a vast imaginary ocean, seemed to undulate on the surface of the stream.

I climbed on all fours up to the summit, stood erect and saw the top of the forest covering the villages all around.

Far away thin columns of smoke rose above the trees. Coming from another world I discovered the immensity of space above the earth; then I descended from the mountain as if gently impelled and held back at the same time by a protecting hand.

I had not succeeded in seeing what I was searching for: the source of the river. Disappointed, I had to rest content with following the stream which flowed into a natural canal, the banks of which were hemmed in by aquatic plants; and I saw the river again which here to my great surprise almost flowed alongside the railway line.

My cloth was in shreds. I followed the railway line, then the habitual way to go to town. I arrived there at nightfall. In front of the door of my parents' house, I was stunned to see on either side an earthenware pot containing a decoration such as our custom prescribes for funeral ceremonies; I also heard a dirge gently syncopated by calabash rattles.

I entered and saw a gathering of sad people. The women, including my mother, had untied their hair as a token of mourning. The gathering noticed my presence and started up. Some took to their heels, others, paralyzed by fear, just looked at me. I stepped forward to my mother who had been quickly joined by my father.

"What happened? Who has died?"

Dead silence.

"You have to forgive me for leaving without telling you about it."

"Where are you coming from? Are you a dead or a living person in our midst?" my father asked.

"I'm alive."

"What, alive?" my mother said, weeping.

"Nobody's dead. Death doesn't exist and if it does, no dead man will ever return," I replied firmly but with my most casual expression.

The people had come back, more numerous now than when I first had set foot in the house.

"Where are you coming from?"

"Where've you been?"

"For us you were dead."

"For the past three days we've been sure about it."

"The diviners have confirmed it."

I was somewhat depressed by these comments and asked if the funeral ceremonies had anything to do with me. They said yes.

"The diviners have all been telling you lies. I went for a walk, and

I've come back with flesh and blood, body and soul, cured from the fear of death. I apologize for having given you so much worry."

"My son, tell me honestly where you're coming from," my father said.

"From a simple walk. I didn't realize that it lasted three days."

"What did you eat?" asked my mother.

"Nothing."

"Whom did you stay with?"

"Nobody."

"I don't understand you."

"I've nothing to explain."

"Why?"

"Such things can't be explained. I am alive and life goes on."

"Oh, this child!" my mother murmured.

"I'm hungry, Mother. You see I'm alive and kicking since I'm hungry and thirsty."

"May you never again disappear like that."

"I promise, but don't you ever ask me for an explanation," I said. And everything was all right again.

How long did this dream last? I shall never know.

Sindiwe Magona was born in the Transkei in 1943 and grew up in Cape Town's black townships. She attended the University of London, earned her bachelor's degree in psychology and history from the University of South Africa, and a master's degree in Organizational Social Work from Columbia University. Her books include two autobiographies, *To My Children's Children* and *Forced to Grow*; the short story collection *Living, Loving, and Lying Awake at Night*; and the novel *Mother to Mother*. She lives in New York and works at the United Nations.

It Was Easter Sunday the Day I Went to Netreg

Brakes grinding in protest, the bloodred Volkswagen lurched to an uncertain, shuddering stop outside our gate. All cars lurch drunkenly in Guguletu, for what passes for streets are nothing but pitted, dirt-covered trails pockmarked with ditches, and potholes so big a full-grown man could drown in one. Stock-still I stood, looking out of the window opening of the one-room shack I shared with Makhulu, my mother's mother.

A full five minutes I'd been waiting for the car; alerted of its arrival by the chorus "Imoto! Imoto!" Shouts that painted a clear picture in my mind: barefooted children panting alongside the car; galloping as I had done so many times. And not that long ago.

Until the car leapt right into my eyes, I'd been standing on the coir mattress on the floor staring out unseeingly. In the harsh glare of the unafraid early afternoon autumn sun, the opening was not unlike a gouged eye. Blindly, it stared out. And I, behind it, like some deadened nerve, mimicked. Now, the smell of the old blanket with which we stuffed the window opening at night assaulted my nose and its weight glued my feet onto the mattress.

A small, compact woman, not yet thirty, scrambled out of the car:
Mother, a bright yellow-and-black plastic shopping bag suspended from
each hand. Food and clothing. The invariable badge of her *medem*'s
bounty; things Mrs. Wilkins had given her out of the kindness of her big
heart. Too bad she had the body of an elephant in the family way; only
Makhulu wore the clothes Mrs. Wilkins gave Mama. Makhulu didn't
mind folding, pleating, and wrapping the voluminous garments around
her own far from substantial frame. Mother, stooped under the weight of
her employer's goodness, walked slowly from the car toward our shack. I
watched her, and knew that the fact that today Mrs. Wilkins's benefi-
cence stretched to include even me, personally, weighed heavily on my
mother's heart. The same knowledge paralyzed me.

'Khulu, who had as usual been hovering around it, opened the door
for Mother.

It was Easter Sunday. Three days before, Mother had said, "Mrs.
Wilkins will come with me on my next day off, Sunday." I was ready long
before they came. They were taking me to Netreg. Netreg (which means
just right) is a colored residential area not far from Guguletu where I live.
Guguletu is an African township.

"Are you ready, Linda?" I knew she had not put the bags down. I
would have heard the "table," a plank nearly a meter long, sighing. The
"table" sighed each time it had to find a new way of balancing itself on
the empty paraffin tins on which it rested. I understood its disgust. I, too,
had my sighs; but I kept them to myself.

"Is that how you greet these days?" asked Makhulu, clearly piqued.

First, the rustle of plastic as bags exchanged hands hit me. A few seconds later, the smell of fried fish enveloped me, blocking my air passage;
I gagged.

"Oh, I'm in such a hurry. I'm sorry, Mama," replied Mother. She had
come nearer where I stood, I could tell from her voice. The linoleum on
bare sand floor did not make much noise. But I knew she had come
closer. I froze.

She lifted the "curtain," a tired, discolored damask tablecloth sport-
ing interesting tears in varying shapes and sizes. It was, no doubt,
bequeathed to us by some white family for whom Mother or 'Khulu (for
she used to be in the same line of work in her younger days) worked.

Behind this was my place: the mattress on the floor, a cardboard box with all my wordly possessions, mainly schoolbooks. A thin, bare wire hanger drew a dull gray outline on the newspaper-plastered wall where it hung forlornly from a crooked, rusty nail.

"Come." And, ffwhissh! I heard the curtain fall and sensed her stalking away. I turned and looked at the spot where, I fancied, she'd stood a second ago. The dumb "curtain" stared back, and I pictured her stalking back to the car. Once more, my eyes flew to the window opening, but my feet were still cemented onto the mattress on the floor.

I did not move. But my heart jumped, forsaking its seat, and went and plonked itself up my throat making breathing difficult. A cold blanket wrapped itself tightly around all of me as it coated every inch of me inside. I was turning into Lot's wife, in ice.

There was Mother getting back into the car. Come. One word. And all the fear I had ever felt since I was born collected itself into a ball of writhing worms at the pit of my stomach. COME, said the ball turning and turning in my stomach.

I was not surprised she had said no more to me. I did not expect her to be fussing over me. But Mother's one-word command stabbed my heart and jellied my already wobbly legs. I do not know how my feet managed it, but they must have done so because I was saying "Good Afternoon, Me'm" to Mrs. Wilkins as I slid onto the seat behind her.

"Linda," scolded Mrs. Wilkins, "when will you stop calling me Medem?" She was smiling her brown teeth smile to show me she was not angry. She wanted me to call her by her name, Sue. But, to this day, I don't know how to call any white person by their name. It is not done. Besides, she was older than my mother. So, I mumbled, "I'm sorry," and just in the nick of time, stapled my tongue to the roof of my mouth. I'd nearly said "I'm sorry, Me'm."

Me'm Sue started the car and we were on our way. Unconcerned, the car grunted and tottered while a group of children, in varying states of nakedness, sprinted alongside it. Lithe mahogany limbs glistened announcing some mothers had had the Vaseline and time to scrub their offspring. One little fellow caught my eye. He was shaven so blindingly clean the sun bounced off his head as if it were a mirror or a miniature glass dome. He was clad in a torn, once-upon-a-time-white vest.

Absentmindedly, I noticed that he'd grow to be a fine-membered man one day; for beneath the torn, scant garment dangled definite promise. That, or he badly needed to wet the grass.

I forgot . . . As the wonder of the ride filled me, I swelled: I was a passenger in a real car, a moving car. Then, glonk! went my heart as I remembered why I was in that car and where it was taking me.

Netreg is about ten minutes from Guguletu, by car. On those few occasions I had traveled to Langa or Cape Town I had seen the houses of Netreg, for the train passes through the township. But I had never set foot in Netreg (or, for that matter, any colored township).

It's strange how ten minutes can be such a long time. That was easily the longest ten minutes of my life. What would it be like? Netreg itself as well as the reason I was being taken there? How could I be doing what I was about to do? And Mama? What was Mama thinking of me right now? Would things ever be right between us, ever? What would Mrs. Wilkins think of me? What would she think of poor Mama? All these questions raced through my mind robbing me of the joy that should have been mine on the occasion of my first real car ride.

Briefly, once more, the thrill of the ride seduced me. Oh, I had been inside an uncomfortable number of cars: that is, the broken bodies of cars cast off by their owners or stolen and stripped to nothing anyone in their right mind would attempt to salvage. Wrecks were a penny a dozen throughout Guguletu. But this was different. This was a living car. And not only was I in it, it was moving; going; VRROOHM! Actually taking me somewhere. My first car ride!

I was a Standard Three pupil at St. Monica's Primary School, the only Catholic school in Guguletu. The uniform—a badly cut dress the color of bile, a sickly yellow-green—was the only decent article of clothing I owned. Hence the unclad hanger I'd left behind, a grotesque shape blotting out part of a large smiling face belonging to an African woman hanging clothes washed "WHITER than WHITE—in OMO—OF COURSE!"

Any hopes of a few additions to my wardrobe had long been quashed: "That woman I work for does not only pay me better. She is a person. She knows I am a person." What did it matter to Mother that the woman she worked for had no children? That I would never get any hand-me-downs from her? Who can blame me for being so angry at Mrs.

Wilkins? All the possible castoffs she had deprived me of: dolls, shoes, dresses, jerseys, to name a few. And then she wanted to tell me we were friends, equals, "Call me Sue!" Not me; she wouldn't get any Sue from me.

During the short journey, I sat behind Mrs. Wilkins driving her red Beetle while Mama sat kitty-corner to her and the empty seat between us yawned, a *donga* neither she nor I would ever be able to ford; for that was the last day I would be a child.

It was also the day, although I didn't know that at the time, that would affect my whole life as a woman. Looking back, I am amazed at how normal a day it looked: gay, even.

Three weeks before, St. Monica's had played a game of netball with their arch rivals, Bulelani Higher Primary School. Bulelani is in Langa. And, for us therefore, this was an away from home match on two accounts: Langa was hostile territory.

For me, however, that match was to be the beginning of the new me. Or should I say the old me? The new me, whatever else she is or isn't, is very, very old: older than any living person I know.

And the day I went to Netreg is part of the birth of the me who became that day. Although, on second thought, perhaps it is not fair to blame it all on that one day.

Perhaps it all started when I was born. Or in Langa that day we played Bulelani and they clobbered us ten–zip; an unprecedented wounding. Or, perhaps it is all a bad dream.

At Netreg we had a little problem finding the address Mrs. Wilkins had been given by one of the women in her rap group, feminists. Thanks to her smattering of Afrikaans, Mrs. Wilkins was able to ask for directions and we finally made it to our destination. As we trooped out of the car, my last netball game flashed through my mind.

I played center. And, usually, I played a game both defensive and offensive: feeding my shooters and blocking the ball from getting to the wings of the opposition. I was an enthusiastic, energetic player who threw herself completely into a game. And early on in the match that was to change my life I'd done exactly that.

Now, as we walked uncertainly to the house whose number was written on a scrap of paper Me'm Sue held in her hand, the sickening feeling born in me the day of that match returned.

Fifteen minutes or so into the game, the Bulelani center shot the ball toward the wing nearest her posts. From the wing, I knew the ball could only come back to her or, with luck and skill, go straight to one of their shooters. Aiming at reinforcing our defenses, I went for the shooter positioned under the post; she had stepped out of the circle where I could not go.

Sure enough, the wing sent the ball flying to the shooter: a high, slow curve. I crouched, waiting. Then, like a spring, uncoiled as the ball began its descent, timing myself to grab it above the outstretched hands I knew would materialize. Grab it before they reached it, or bounce it right out of their fingers. That was my plan.

Three clear feet from the ground and, WHAAM! I'd made contact with a flying rhinoceros. At least, that is how I felt.

BOOM! I hit the ground. Flat on my face. I lay sprawled, certain that never again would I be able to move even a finger. Total paralysis.

Then, movement. A tumultuous, agitating protest. Inside my belly. A frightened, turbulent fluttering.

For a moment I thought the ground under me was heaving. And then, beyond doubt, suddenly and with utter searing clarity, I knew.

I was pregnant.

No one had ever told me babies move before they are born; move in their mothers' wombs. But that stirring told me all I did not want to know. After all, I was only nearly fourteen.

That was three weeks before Easter Sunday. I thought Gran would kill me. You see, she raised me from the age five when I became too old to stay with Mother at her place of employment. Mother has always worked sleep-in. That helps a little bit with accommodation.

Till every hair on my head has turned snow white, I will never forget the look Gran gave me when I told her. Naked contempt stared at me as at a monster. If a look in the mirror had shown me I'd sprouted a second head, I would not have been surprised. And then when she started wailing: the frail but piercing wail women make when someone has died. And then the insults had rained.

That day I finally learned something of the father not frequently mentioned.

"What am I crying for? Yhoo! Ma Tolo! What am I crying for?" The anguished call to her ancestors brought a swift, brutal answer through her miserable lips: "What did I expect from a she-dog's illegitimate child?"

What had happened to the hero who was felled by the heartless Boers during the 1960 riots? But the kindly old woman who had been love itself to me was not quite done. Like a venomous snake, she hissed: "Doesn't a she-dog beget another she-dog? Hee-eh?" Her face was contorted with . . . grief?

As if my own revelation had not caused enough pain, my grandmother could not seem to stop herself from dishing out further enlightenment. For my benefit: my death. Or, hers? Her face was a hideous mask of moving emotions. Hate, fear, and dire misery chased one another; flitting across the kaleidoscopic landscape. Her eyes, florets of pain that had looked into her grave and seen the bones of the fruit of her womb, generations to come. In a voice I did not recognize she went on: "Your mother was a child herself when she went and spread herself at the zones. I never even got any payment for damages from that man. Indeed, I do not know his face because as soon as he knew that the she-dog was riding with his pup, he did what all these men from the zones do. Went back to his village and made sure he never again took a contract to Cape Town."

The zones, euphemistically called Single Men's Quarters, are barracks used to house African men forced to leave their wives and children in the village when they get "permission" to come and work in the cities. That most of these "migrant" laborers were very much married bothered government policy makers not at all. It could not. The white, highly specialized, and learned officials had yet to grasp the simple fact of these men being human too.

The father of the child I was carrying was such a man. But that did not worry me. He had assured me that he wanted to meet my parents and not only pay damages but pay *lobola*, the bride price. When I'd told him about my father he was all concern. "Your poor mother," he said, "all alone, bringing you up by herself." He wanted to make me his wife. We had talked about this the night of the netball match. But, with Gran's ranting, I decided to wait until Mother's next day off.

That Sunday, my world did a crazy higgledy-piggledy and has not righted itself since. I doubt it ever will.

Mother had arrived a little after lunch. The kettle had not boiled before Gran gave her the bad news. But, although I knew I had done wrong and hurt Mother a lot, I was convinced when I told her of the willingness of my man to shoulder full responsibility she would feel a little less hurt; grateful I would not become an unmarried mother.

As is the custom when things of this nature happen, several male relatives were summoned. These would be men of the Tolo and Bhele clans; Makhulu's and Mama's clans. The clan ensures our survival. Everyone belongs to a clan and because of that, no one can ever be without kin. When we introduce ourselves, the clan name is of more importance to us than the surname, for marriage within the clan is taboo. A complete stranger becomes a brother or sister when it is found that he or she is of the same clan. I was being brought up as a Bhele since my own father had died before I was born and I had had no connection with his people. Now, our relatives had come to assist kin in distress. It was decided to waste no time but go, that very same day, to discuss *lobola* with the culprit. I would accompany the party, for that too is the custom.

Mother, either not trusting these men to represent her capably or at Gran's instigation, I never found out which, decided to come too. Up to this point, everything seemed to be going according to plan.

"And these white people don't listen to us when we tell them it is not right to put all these 'single men' so close to our families." This came from the most senior of the men on realizing that the zones were where we were headed for. Fearing repercussions, I had not volunteered this information earlier on: there is a name for women who frequent the zones.

I had warned Mteteleli we were coming; so he was expecting us. He was not a boy by any reckoning. But he was also not old. We had never discussed things like age but I knew he was "proud to be with such a young, unspoilt, sweet thing." And I liked his being proud of my tender age. It meant he would never leave me, I thought. Oh, yes, young I may have been, but I'd seen and heard enough of life to know that men did tire of women. Therefore, I saw it as advantageous that I was young enough for him to like it.

The visit to Netreg is vivid in some respects, dull in others. All I remember of the face of the woman who opened the door to our knock are the crow's feet etched around her eyes. Her hair, streaked with gray, is pulled harshly back into a matronly bun at the nape of her neck. I remember being taken to an inside room, a bedroom I think, although

what makes me think that, I do not know. I dimly recall seeing some furniture in the room but when I close my eyes now and try to see then, the
room is blurred, empty except for the thickset woman whose flesh sags
every which way, like an aged wrestler's.

Neither do I recall whether she spoke to me in English or in
Afrikaans. Indeed, did she say anything at all or did she make gestures;
point and show me what to do? Did she smile? frown? or was her face
barren of all expression? For whatever reason, all this has been banished
from my mind.

What I do remember has never left my recall. On the other hand,
what I have forgotten, I forgot with amazing swiftness: inside a week,
and it was all gone. Moreover, it has remained safely tucked away. It
doesn't haunt me. And for that, I am truly grateful.

What has stayed obstinately with me, like plaque to rotting teeth, are
the sensations grooved into my heart, deep, deep inside my heart.

She had spread the newspapers on the floor. We were alone in the
room, my mother and her *medem* had remained in the outer room. I
remember a bowl of innocent-looking water, soapy water. She dipped
her hands in it. Then she made me open my legs. Wide.

A wet hand touches me. Warm. I remember thinking, Oh, that water
in the bowl must be warm, because of that. She forces a cold, smooth,
slippery object into me. Although it is much smaller than a little boy's
penis it snags, only for a second, however. Then coldly and stiffly it
glides into me. Deep into me. I arch my back; expecting pain. My eyes
are closed tight as a spoiled clam. I hear the grinding of my teeth. An
elusive smell wafts softly up my nostrils.

Is this all? I begin to wonder. I begin to relax; the anticipated pain has
not come. I start thinking this is one of those cases, where collective
memory multiplies the experience. I must have heard exaggerated tales,
I tell myself, stories far from the truth. Correction comes swift, hard, and
scorching; jogging the memory of my race.

This is what it must feel to swallow petrol and set a match into the
mouth. My intestines are on fire. A raging fire that pushes and swells
everything inside of me, puffing it up until I feel my tummy burst. I
writhe, groaning. Tears wash my face. I am hot all over. Flames liquify my
insides, filling me as they spread ever upward and outward and downward.

A terror-filled scream pierces my burning ears. A mad woman's scream? Or, a dying woman's?

The woman gives me a tablet. Thereafter, she calls the two people who'd brought me. While Mother helps me out of the house and toward the car, her kind employer reaches for her purse. Whether the money she gives the woman will be deducted from my mother's pay, I do not know. And I do not care. At that moment, I doubt I will ever care about anything at all again. I am convinced I am about to die. My legs confirm this; they have already died. I can't feel them. But the ton of lead they weigh slows me; that, I do feel. The awful heaviness makes the distance, a mere twelve meters at most, a torturous trek. I feel as if some powerful evil force has come to dwell inside my body and now, for each step I take, drags me back double the ground I've gained. A century later, we reach the car.

I am alone in the back. Ma is sitting in front with Mrs. Wilkins. I'm sprawled across the whole back seat, wide enough for three. My spine, too, has died. I can't sit up. My tummy, my thighs, and every other part of me, everything is on fire.

Soon, we are home. It is not quite dark yet. "Stand up straight and walk upright." We live in dread of our neighbors' vigorous tongues. Mother does not want to give them any encouragement. She does not want them to start any gossip. She is a member of the Catholic Mother's Guild, a prominent member. A scandal would shatter her reputation.

Late that night, an ambulance carried me to Peninsula Hospital. Later still that same night, with doctors in attendance, I lost my son, my blood.

That thieving day! My childhood gone. Forever. Gone, too, a special part of my life as a woman. Not because, years later, I would come to know that I would never bear a child. No. Not because I would never be able to have sex and enjoy it, because as a man's penis glides into me it triggers the memory of what glided out of me those many years ago. No. Nor is it the secret I carry, dark and fearful. The secret I fear will burst into full flower one day; explaining my love of washing babies—especially little boys. That is not what haunts me.

My friends know they can rely on me to look after their babies when I am not on duty. Yes, I went back to school, later on. Thanks to Sue, the feminist. She paid for my education and today I am a qualified midwife.

But she can never really buy me what I lost that day she took me to Netreg. No one can. And nothing can bring back the innocence I'd lost by the day we went there, when Mteteleli was supposed to pay *lobola* and make me his wife.

Fifteen years before, Mteteleli, then a boy of sixteen or so years old, had come to Cape Town as a migrant laborer.

Mother too has never been the same since that Sunday we went to the zones to get *lobola* from the father of the child I was carrying, the day Mother saw Mteteleli and recognized my father.

So, three weeks later to the day, I went to Netreg. It was Easter Sunday and I was almost fourteen years old.

Charles Mungoshi was born in 1947 in a village near Chivhu, Zimbabwe (then Southern Rhodesia). Writing in both English and Shona, he published his first novel in 1970. His first collection of short stories, *Coming of the Dry Season*, was banned by the government in 1974. When the country won independence, several of Mungoshi's works became standard readings on Zimbabwean school syllabi. He has won two International P.E.N. awards, the Noma Prize for his children's book *One Day, Long Ago*, and in 1998 he won the African region Commonwealth Writers Prize for *Walking Still*. His book *The Setting Sun and the Rolling World* was a *New York Times* Notable Book of the Year in 1989. He lives in Harare with his wife and family.

The Brother

Tendai felt very excited as he knocked on the door. He was going to a secondary boarding school and he would be spending the last three days before schools opened with his eldest brother in the city. He knocked again. In his left hand he carried a paper bag full of food from the farm. There were two tins of peanut butter, one for him to take to school, and the other for his brother. There were cobs of green maize, some cucumbers and mangos. In the inside pocket of his jacket were his identity card and traveling papers, a list of the things that his brother would buy him for school, and a letter to his brother from his wife. The brother had just married and the wife would be expecting soon. She was at home helping with the farm work. They had taken her too early from her husband and she was worried that her husband would not be there when she went into labor.

At the third knock, the door opened. Magufu, Tendai's brother, stood in the doorway.

"Oh, it's you," he said. He didn't seem at all happy to see Tendai.

"Yes," Tendai answered, slightly put off.

"Come in."

They went into the house.

"I wasn't expecting you today. I thought you'd be coming tomorrow. Today isn't Sunday, is it?"

"No. Today is Saturday."

They sat on the sofas in the living room. There were some magazine pictures of naked women hung on the walls. For some reason, Tendai had expected to see some pictures of his brother's recent wedding. There were just those naked women pictures, a big portrait of his brother in dark glasses, like a black pop star, and some out-of-date calendars displaying more naked women.

It didn't feel like his brother's house at all. Not the brother who would drive the whole family to church every Sunday he was on leave.

Vaguely, Tendai expected some explanation.

"So?" Magufu was looking at him.

"So?" Tendai was startled. "What?"

"I thought you said you'd be coming on Sunday—tomorrow."

"Oh. Mother thought I should come today."

"So it's Mother, is it?"

Tendai didn't understand.

Magufu looked at his watch. "Look. I am going out to meet some people right now. I was just about to leave when you came in."

He pulled out a dollar. "You know where the shops are, don't you? Right where you dropped off the bus here. Get yourself something to eat. Everything you need—pots, pans, salt—is right in the kitchen. I won't be long." He was moving toward the door.

"I have brought some things—a letter from your wife—and . . ."

"I won't be long."

Magufu went out and Tendai heard his car driving away. All of a sudden Tendai felt he missed home very much.

Magufu didn't come back until Tendai was fast asleep, after midnight: with a woman.

Tendai had to get off the bed and spread out on the floor. He had not quite heard his brother's coming in and shaking him and telling him to take some blankets off the bed and spread out on the floor because he had been confused by having to be awakened in the middle of a dream into the nightmare of a glaringly lit room. Now, as he lay himself down and his head cleared, he realized that it was not his dream that had spilled into reality: the house *was* really full of people. There seemed to be a drinking party out there in the living room.

Tendai turned thrice before finding a comfortable position.

There were voices of men and women in the living room and they all seemed very happy because they were laughing and shouting and singing and now and then Tendai heard the noise of breaking glass.

His brother's voice seemed the loudest. Troubled by something he couldn't understand, Tendai drifted off into that uncharted world between sleep and wakefulness.

Later he woke up to the presence of someone in the room. He opened his eyes and saw his brother swaying in the doorway to the living room. There were still some low voices all over the house, otherwise there was a kind of tired quietness.

Tendai smelt perfume.

He looked round.

She was sitting on the bed. Magufu was swaying in the doorway, half turned, as if he was giving last orders to someone in the living room. Then he turned, switched on the light.

"Please," the woman pleaded, shielding her face with her hands. She was fully dressed, Tendai saw.

"Afraid of the light, huh?" Magufu laughed.

The woman didn't say anything. She kept her face in her hands. She wasn't a big woman. And she wasn't old either. From what he saw of her, sitting on the bed, her face covered and her head lowered, Tendai felt that she was younger than his brother's wife.

"A night mover, heh?" Magufu was laughing. He began to sing and shuffle on the floor, singing something about women of the night who shun the light, and shuffling in a drunkard's dance.

"Please. The light is killing my eyes," the woman pleaded. She had a girl's voice, an abused girl's voice.

"The light kills their eyes," Magufu danced toward the switch. The room flipped into darkness.

"Feel better? Feel safe?" Magufu asked, already half turning the words into song.

He shut the door and shuffled toward the bed.

There was the sound of the outside door opening and someone with good-humored drunken violence came in shouting.

"Magufu! Hey, Magufu!"

The whole house woke up—laughing and shouting.

"Who's that?" Magufu shouted, swaying near the bed. He stroked the girl's head.

"It's Sam!" called a voice from the sitting room.

"Oh, Sammy boy!"

"Wake up you louts! Wake up! Where's Magufu? I say—what's this? A hotel or brothel? My! My! My! Hey, Magufu! Wake up and tell me what you think you have got here!"

"Get out, idiot!" Magufu shouted.

"Who is calling me idiot? Huh? Where is the unnamable obscenity that's calling me . . ."

"Oh, Sam! Watch out. There're broken bottles on the floor."

"Sam. Oh, Sam."

"Where have you been, Sam?"

"Good old Sam."

"One of these days they are going to drag you out of Mukuvisi with a long knife in your back!"

"Hey, Magufu!"

"Sam's here, Magufu."

"Where's that black fart Magufu? Asleep is he? I'll teach him to . . . hey, Magufu!"

"Magufu your mother! Can't you fellows have respect for an honest, tired, hardworking man?" Magufu shouted.

"Won't you please tell them to keep quiet?" the girl said.

"Hey, Sam! Sam! The missus says you oafs shut up!" Magufu laughed.

"So you are there, are you? I'll teach you to leave a brother . . ." Sam was banging on the door. "Open up!"

"Please, Magufu . . ." the girl pleaded.

"Sam's all right. Hey, Sam, you are all right, aren't you?"

"Open up in there or I'll . . ."

"Respect, Sam! Respect!" Magufu shouted, laughing.

The banging stopped. In a semisober voice Sam said, "Respect, eh? You said respect, did you, Mag?"

"You heard me, idiot!"

"But look," Sam hissed, "you can't do this to me, you know. It's not fair."

"What's not fair?"

"Where the hell did you go? You nearly got me killed, you know."

"Killed?"

"Damnit, Magufu. They are right out here in the van! And do they want to see you! Oh boy, oh boy, oh boy."

"What are you talking about?"

"You know what I am talking about, you black this-and-that. And you know damn well that there isn't going to be any peace if you-know-who finds out that you have been knowing-what an unknown-who . . ."

Magufu sat up. "You mean . . . ?"

"Yes. I mean she is here and you know what that means." Magufu whistled.

"Sam."

"Yes, ass?"

"Do our skin a favor?"

"And my reputation?"

"You know what your reputation is worth you this-and-that. Now, listen. Do us a real big favor."

"You mean she is that you-know-what?"

"I wouldn't be asking you if she weren't, would I?"

Sam whistled. "You know, Mag."

"Come on."

"You'll get us all killed one of these days. You-know-who is really in one of her foul weather moods."

"Sam?"

"Yes, ass?"

"We are tired. We want to sleep."

Sam whistled. "Mag?"

"Uh-huh?"

"Is it worth breakfast with . . ."

There was a loud car horn blast outside.

"Get going, Sam, before . . ."

"I am on my way. See you at farting time!"

Sam went out shouting, "So all you I-don't-know-what-to-call-you don't know where that idiot Magufu is, huh?"

"Go on, Sam. We told you he isn't here, didn't we?" a voice in the sitting room shouted after Sam.

A minute later they all heard the sound of a car angrily starting and driving off with three short blasts of the horn.

"Good old Sam," Magufu said.

There was the sound of a bolt being shot home.

"You seem to have very good friends," the girl said. She was still sitting on the bed.

"Come on. You aren't going to spend all night sitting there, are you?" Magufu was undressing in the dark.

Dimly, Tendai saw the girl standing up and beginning to take off her dress. Tendai looked away.

The bed creaked as Magufu got into the blankets.

"Come on. What are you standing there for?"

"Who is this on the floor?"

"He doesn't bite. Come into bed."

"My things."

"What about them?"

"Where shall I put them?"

"Oh, damnit! Hang them on your nose and come right into bed."

"I can't put them on the floor—it's the only pair I have."

"You want me to take you right back where I took you from?"

"Please, I just . . ."

"You want me to take you back there?"

"Please, Magufu," she giggled and threw her things on top of Tendai. Tendai heard her climbing into bed.

"I said take off *everything!*"

"Oh, please. I can't go to bed completely naked, you know." She gave a short nervous laugh. "It's only my pants."

"Take the damn stink off!"

The girl gasped. She got out of bed.

"All right. If that's how you like it. All right. If—there!"

The thing landed in Tendai's face. A smell of sweat and very strong perfume. Tendai quickly removed it.

"Good. Now come into bed."

She didn't move.

"Sheila! Sheila!"

The girl didn't answer.

"Do you hear me, Sheila?" Magufu's voice was thickening with anger.

Then slowly, terribly, Tendai realized that the girl was crying, trying hard to suppress violent sobs.

"Sheila, what's wrong?"

She didn't answer.

"Sheila! Sheila!"

"Yes?" Her voice was broken because of the crying.

"Don't you want?"

"I—I—don't . . ." She sobbed.

"Come on, Sheila. Tell me, what's wrong?"

"Nothing."

"Nothing?"

She didn't answer.

"I don't understand. I just don't understand." Magufu half rose in bed and leaned toward Sheila. He put his arm round her shoulders. She stiffened, caught her breath: "Don't."

"But why?" Magufu's voice was menacing.

"I didn't want to drink," Sheila said.

"Are you ill or something?"

"No."

"But . . ."

"Please, Magufu. You won't beat me, will you?"

"Why would I want to do that?"

"If you find out that I am a big disappointment."

"What do you mean?" Magufu's voice was very dark with suspicion.

Sheila didn't answer.

"Look, Sheila. I am not playing games anymore. What's bothering you?"

The girl seemed to think for a long time, then said, "All right then. I don't care. All right. Oh, it's all right."

She crawled into bed beside Magufu.

"Hell, you're so small," Magufu whispered.

The girl didn't answer. She seemed to be crying.

"What's wrong, Sheila? You ill or something?"

"I am all right."

"No. You are not all right at all. You are shivering like a kitten out of water."

Sheila didn't answer.

There was a long silence, then later on, as if she were being smothered, Sheila protested. "Please, Magufu. No. Please. No. No. No."

"Why?"

"I—just—can't—"

"Why?"

She didn't answer.

"Why, Sheila? I thought you loved me."

"It's not that."

"What is it then?"

She was quiet for some time, then said, "Promise me you won't be angry."

"Oh, come on, Sheila."

She thought for some time, then asked, "You are married, aren't you?"

"No."

"True?"

"What the hell."

"I have got to know, you know."

"And if I am?"

"But *are* you?"

"Look. I don't see where this is getting us."

"You are getting angry."

"What's all this mystery talk about? I thought you understood when we left that place together."

"Understood what?"

"That you were coming home with me."

"I was drunk. You got me drunk."

"So what?"

"I haven't been drunk before."

"You would have had to start someday."

"No. I don't think so. You tricked me."

"Oh, come on, Sheila."

"You tricked me and now you say you love me but you won't tell me whether you have got a wife or not."

"I don't see what my wife has got to do with this."

"So you *are* married?"

"Oh, hell."

"Where is your wife?"

"Come on, Sheila."

"Does she know you trick people and when they don't know who they are and what they are doing anymore you drag them home to bed and tell them to strip to the skin?"

"Look, Sheila . . ."

"And who is that Sam?"

"A friend."

"What was he talking about?"

"Look, Sheila . . ."

"What was he talking about?"

"Look. If you're going to spend all night talking I am going to sleep, okay?"

"Why have you brought me here, Magufu?"

"You came on your own."

"Did I?"

Magufu didn't answer.

"Where are my sisters, Magufu? You brought me here together with my sisters, didn't you? Where are they?"

Magufu didn't answer.

"Where are they, Magufu?"

"Look. Your sisters went out with some men and now shut up and let me go to sleep, will you?"

"They went with some men . . . did they say where they were going?"

"Sheila, you want me to take you back?"

"Where did they go?"

"I don't know."

"How did I come to be here without my sisters? You have got a wife haven't you? And you let my sisters go away without me. Do you always do this?"

"Do what?"

"Drug people's drinks and when they . . ."

The slap was like the sharp crack of close thunder.

Sheila didn't scream. She held her breath as if someone had pushed her head underwater, then she gasped.

"Take me home," she said, gasping. "I want to go back home. Please

THE BROTHER

77

take me back home." She was quickly getting out of bed and Magufu was holding her back and then she began to shout and scream and Magufu was telling her to shut up and there were two more short, sharp slaps and Tendai realized they were fighting. They were now both on the floor and rolling toward him.

Tendai quickly got dressed and opened the door into the sitting room. In the dim light from the street Tendai could make out shapes of people sleeping on the sofas. There was deep guttural snoring. The place reeked with the stench of beer. The whole room seemed full of sleeping people.

Tendai opened the door and went out into the street. He leaned his head against a lamppost.

Then slowly, all the bile he had been resisting gathered into a tight burning knot inside his chest.

He hit the pole again and again till his knuckles were sore. He hit the pole again and again till he was sweating.

Then he began to walk along the street.

There was the sharp smell of flowers from the trees lining the street. The leaves reflected the yellow light. The location was sunk in a drunken stupor, with the slightest hint of the stench of urine, stale vomit and human sweat. There was a low hum which told Tendai that even in sleep the township was very much alive, dangerously alive, but he didn't care.

There was a little hill at the end of the street. There was a church on the hill.

He found the heavy dark doors of the church closed. Through a window he saw that it was very dark inside the church.

He walked round the church into the trees at the back.

He lay down on a flat rock under the trees and looked at the lights of the town on the other side of the hill. He found the garish brilliance of the city hurting his eyes and he looked into the deep moving darkness of the leaves of the trees above him. He closed his eyes and soon lost himself in the smell of the flowers and the darkness of the leaves. Something warm and comfortable moved into the center of his belly and he felt very safe. He didn't care for the stories they told about township thugs and *tsotsis*.

He heard the sound of the leaves calmly soughing in the slight wind on the hill, and he slept, carrying with him the play of dull light and deep shadow in the leaves above him.

He woke up at the milkman's bell just a little before sunrise. His body was stiff and numb from sleeping on the hard rock. He stretched and yawned and felt his muscles and joints cracking. The city lights and streetlights looked very weak in the eye of the coming sun.

His brother's house wasn't in his mind as he got down from the hill, so he walked round the location which at this early Sunday hour seemed to belong to children armed with loaves of bread wrapped in newspaper and the morning's paper.

When the streets began to fill up with older people looking sick and threatening from the heavy night, Tendai made his way to his brother's house.

There was a VW van parked in front of the house. Through the window Tendai saw a man lying between two women on a blanket on the floor of the van. They were fast asleep in their clothes. Tendai quickly looked away and passed on.

He tried the door and found it unlocked. He entered. There were two couples sleeping on the sofas in the sitting room. Empty beer bottles were scattered all over the floor. There were broken bottles and cigarette ends and ash swimming in dark splotches and puddles of beer. The air was heavy with the smell of beer, tobacco smoke and something else that could have only come from the sleepers.

Tendai went into the kitchen where he found two women sleeping in each other's arms, their mouths wide open and saliva trickling from the corners. They lay on a dirty tarpaulin without blankets. A black pot lay on its side in a puddle of dirty water and there were lumps of *sadza* at their feet. Close to it was a plate with the remains of a meal in it. On a little stand at the women's heads, right below the kitchen window, was a paraffin stove with a dirty pan on it. There were onion skins and pink stains in the pan. The lower end of the curtain had been burnt.

Tendai felt sick from the complex smell in the kitchen. He went out. He hadn't realized that women could outsnore men.

The door to his brother's bedroom was closed. Tendai didn't bother to find out whether it was locked or not. No one had stirred since he came in, and as he was about to go out one of the women stirred and sleepily said, "Turn your lavatory mouth the other side." The man didn't hear and the woman turned away from the man and went back to sleep with slight sleepy moans and groans.

Tendai walked to the back of the house where he began to shoot imaginary villains and prodigal brothers with a shotgun as he had seen in Western films. The villains were too many for one man. They crawled out of holes and dropped down from trees and he was glad to forget them as he watched the breathtaking thing that was the sun rising: so close, so big, weak and vulnerable and glowing without hurting his eyes. Tendai felt that the sun was very friendly and lovely as it rose, it only got angry as it grew older and climbed higher in the sky. He felt sorry for it. It couldn't help it.

He was so lost in himself, getting restless and angrier as the sun got higher and forbade him to look it in the face, that he didn't realize that they were all up in the house behind him.

A man came round the back and startled him with his "Oh." Tendai looked at him. The man's eyes were puffed up and bloodshot, his lips very thick with scales of skin and corn beer. He winked and grinned, shook his head and, as he passed water against the wall of the house, said, "What a night" in a voice that sounded like gravel being unloaded.

There was a girl washing pots and plates at an outside sink at the next house. Tendai saw her giggling and pretending to be busy with the washing.

"Ohiyo—oughh! What a drunken terrible fanta—stic night," the man said, stretching and rubbing his eyes and trying to stop the yawn.

"Your fly," Tendai said, worried, looking quickly at the girl across at the other house.

"Oh, thanks," the man said zipping it up, then: "Hey!" The girl looked up at them. The man made come-here signs with his finger, making exaggerated motions of opening and closing his fly.

The girl stared.

"Want a sausage?" the man called in a loud whisper.

The girl giggled and went back to her pots.

"Good tail end, eh?" the man said to Tendai, winking and nodding to the girl.

Tendai left him and went round to the front of the house.

When he entered the sitting room all eyes turned toward him, including his brother's. But no one said anything. They were playing cards at a long low coffee table in the center of the room.

There were three men and two women playing and two more women who were sitting close together, sometimes watching the game, sometimes talking to themselves. They looked as if they didn't belong to the group, Tendai felt. They talked in very low voices, between themselves. Tendai recognized them as the women who had been sleeping in the kitchen.

There was an empty chair at the other end of the room. Tendai took it and went to sit by the window. He looked out.

They were playing seriously, tiredly but good-humoredly, like people who have been together for such a long time that they need not discuss it. Except the two women who were not playing. One was tall and thin in a used sort of way and the other one was ugly, plump and pouting. They seemed to be disagreeing in a secret sort of way.

"Where have you been, Tendai?"

It was like a gunshot in a quiet room. Tendai looked round from the window. His brother was not looking at him. He had the pack in his hands and was dealing the cards. All the others had their heads turned toward Tendai.

"Haven't you got a mouth?" Magufu said loudly.

"I have been out."

"Where?"

"Just around."

"Don't give me the lip."

"Oh, leave him alone," one of the playing women said. She was pretty and brightly brittle. She said, "Is that your little brother?"

Tendai didn't like her voice. It was too high and brittle. Magufu didn't answer her.

"I said don't give me the lip, do you hear?"

"Yes."

"You can do that sort of thing to Mother and Father but I am paying your fees and responsible for you from now on. Do you hear me?"

"Kick it under, Magufu," one of the men said. He wore dark glasses and a thick beard. He didn't look as if he had been part of last night.

"I said do you hear me, Tendai?" Magufu wasn't looking at him.

"Yes," Tendai said in a small voice.

"Come on, Magufu," the bearded man said. "Talk to him later."

"I bloody well can talk to him anytime I damn well want and if it's now, it is now and who the hell is going to tell me not to?"

There was a terrible silence. Magufu had the cards in his hands. He slapped them hard on the table.

Everyone was looking down at the table.

"I said who the hell is going to tell me not to?"

No one answered.

"Magufu," the bearded man touched Magufu's shoulder. Magufu violently shook the man's hand off. The man shrugged his shoulders. He looked round at the others. They lowered their eyes.

"Let's go, Dan," one of the playing women said. She was small but hard and old. She had her hand on the knee of the third man, short, nervous-looking and frightened.

They stood up and left without saying good-bye.

The two women who were not playing looked at each other, said something to each other and stared at the men.

"Don't frighten the child," the woman with the brittle voice said. She looked at Tendai, smiled, then looked round the room and suddenly shouted: "Where is Sam? Did any of you see where Sam's gone?" She stood up.

"Sit down, Martha," the bearded man said. The two women by themselves giggled to themselves.

"Where is Sam?"

Martha's voice was shrill. "Did either of you see where Sam has gone?" She looked at the two women giggling between themselves. They didn't answer her.

"Am I talking to . . ."

"What's the trouble, Martha?" Sam entered. He came up to Martha and put his hands round her waist and pecked her on both cheeks. Martha closed her eyes and sighed, sinking back into her seat.

The two women laughed.

Martha looked at them hard and they shut up.

The bearded man smiled at Sam and Martha, absently taking the cards up. He began to shuffle them.

Magufu put his face in his hands and planted his elbows on the table.

"Where have you been, darling?" Martha asked Sam, picking at something invisible on his chin.

"Selling sausages, darling." Sam kissed her but she quickly pulled away.

"Selling what?"

"Sausages," Sam said lazily and tried to kiss her again. She slapped him hard on the cheek: "I don't like that, ever! Do you hear me Sam? Don't ever bring the sausage joke with me!"

"Oh dear, oh dear," Sam said. "But they are in great demand." He winked at the giggling women. They squealed brightly and clapped their right hands together in a popular greeting gesture.

"Oh, Sam!" said the tall one.

"You kill me!" said the plump one.

Martha swiveled round and glared at them. "Get out!" She hissed. "Get out right now and don't ever let me see your dirty little tails again!"

Sam put his hand round her shoulders. She put her left hand round his neck. Sam winked at the two women. And they laughed into their hands, their heads down on their knees.

The bearded man smiled.

"Sam is my man and if either of you think you can repeat last night's scene with him you are getting out of town right now!"

"Oh, shut up, Martha!" Magufu roared, pulling his face out of his hands and glaring at her. Everyone looked at him, surprised, except the bearded man who was quietly shuffling the cards as if he wasn't there.

Sam looked at Magufu, suddenly very concerned and worried, then, just as suddenly, his face dissolved into its mischievous hangover.

Martha had stiffened, looking into Sam's face, hanging from his neck as if she were going to drown. Now, Sam looked down into her eyes and kissed them shut. They began to play, whimpering like ecstatic puppies. The two women looked elsewhere, very serious.

Magufu returned his face into the cave of his hands.

The bearded man began to play a game they called solo.

"Tendai," Magufu called, quietly, without taking his face out of his hands.

"Yes?"

"Did you see my letter?"

"Your letter?"

"I wrote a letter to Father. Didn't he say anything to you about it?"

"No."

"Are you sure?"

"Did it concern me?"

"Yes."

"He might have decided to keep it to himself. Was it about anything you wanted me to do?"

"It was about money."

"Money?"

"Your fees—damnit—haven't you got ears?"

Tendai said nothing. The others were careful not to look at Magufu.

"Didn't your father give you money for this term's fees?"

"No. He just gave me bus fare to town, some pocket money and told me you'd fix the rest."

"Including school uniform, toothpaste, soap, towels—and—?"

"Yes."

There was a silence.

The bearded man was trying very very hard to concentrate on his cards.

The two women kept whispering into each other's ear now and again, looking away from each other, apparently disappointed, and constantly watching the closed door into Magufu's bedroom.

Sam had leaned back in his seat, his face turned up to the roof, his right hand absentmindedly tap-tapping Martha's right shoulder as if he were trying to put her to sleep. Martha had gathered all her upper self on Sam's chest, eyes closed, left hand round Sam's neck and the right moving up and down, across his back and chest, inside his open shirt.

It was a tense moment.

The bearded man quietly reached inside his jacket and pulled out a bottle of brandy. He put it on the table and pushed it across to Magufu, and went to his cards without looking or talking to Magufu.

Suddenly Sam brightened and leaned across Martha: "Aaah! The little blighter that's going to kill us all. And I thought we didn't have a single sip round the place. Good old Sando. How do you manage to pull out these wonders when everyone has begun to think the world is dead?"

Martha opened her eyes and said, "What is it?" She followed Sam's eyes and saw the bottle. She sat up suddenly. "Salvation at last!" She tried to reach for it but Sando held back her hand. She looked surprised. "But why?"

"No," Sando said quietly, firmly.

"Why not?" Martha shrilled.

"Because no," Sando said.

"Oh, come on, Sando. Don't be hard on your poor old friends. We'll soon be dead anyway, why the Censorship Board?"

Magufu was looking at the bottle from above his fingers with only his eyes, the rest of the face still covered.

The two women nudged each other and looked at the bottle and then at the others. They looked as if they were watching the opening moves in a boxing match.

"Huh—Brother Sando?" Sam pleaded.

Sando was back at his cards. Whenever he turned round, the dark glasses were in Tendai's way. He would have liked to see the man's eyes. The man's firm calmness was beginning to frighten Tendai a little, in an exciting kind of way.

"Brother Sando? Do you hear me? It's your wee little brother Sam out here. There is dry dust in my throat and a chill in my belly, Brother Sando?"

Sando went on playing solo.

"Brother Sando, please!" Martha croaked. She was licking her lips and there was a big cordlike vein bulging out from below her ear down across her neck into the little cavity where the neck disappeared into the chest.

Magufu was still looking at the bottle.

The women were waiting, excitedly, a little afraid perhaps.

"Brother Sando!" Sam and Martha said together.

Sando quietly laid down a card on top of another and said, "You vultures are a real hard boil in the innermost softest part of my ass's heart, you hear that?" He was very motionless, looking at the cards, but not playing. There was a slight tremor in the hands that held the cards.

Martha wriggled into some impossibly warmer and hidden place on Sam's chest moaning to herself. Sam swallowed and said, "No harm meant, Brother Sando," and his eyes suddenly dropped out of his face into some inner cave inside his arid belly.

The women waited.

Slowly Sando turned toward Magufu.

He looked at him hard and long from behind his dark glasses.

"Oh, damn you, Sando! To hell with you, Sando! Do you hear me, Sando? I said to hell with you and keep going don't you ever turn back because—" his hand trembling, reaching for the bottle. Suddenly Sando's hand flashed out and locked round Magufu's wrist in a grip that made both their arms shake.

Sweat broke over Magufu's face.

"All right, Sando," he whispered hoarsely. Sando let go Magufu's hand.

"Get us a jar of water, Sonnybig," Sando called over his shoulder to Tendai.

Tendai went out to get the water.

"It's all your fault, Sando," Magufu was saying, his face hidden in his hands again. "I told you I don't want to touch the stuff anymore. What are you doing to me, Sando?"

"Nothing that you aren't doing to yourself."

"Oh no!" Magufu was sobbing.

The plump woman whispered, "Let's go, auntie."

"And Sheila? We just can't leave her here alone with—with—"

Sando was looking at them. Their eyes clashed on the closed door to Magufu's bedroom.

Tendai brought in the jug of water.

"Get us some glasses, Sonnyboy."

Tendai went into the kitchen to fetch the glasses.

"Your brother is very sick, Sonnybig," Sando told Tendai as he handed him the glasses. "Every Sunday morning I have to come here very early to keep him company." Sando was pouring little measures into four glasses. "Tell you a secret, Sonnyboy? Without me your brother would have killed himself. You saw me hold back his hand there? He would have taken that stuff straight and dry without a blink."

Sando was adding water into the glasses. "Don't you every try it, Sonnyboy. This stuff is a killer. And don't ever try it alone. Share it with friends. Don't transfer your troubles to it thinking it will burn them. It will only create more trouble."

Sando was handing the glasses round to the others. "It's a real chariot of fire that takes you—in the opposite direction. Ever read the Bible, Sonnyboy?"

"Yes."

"So you know about the Chariot of Fire?"

"Yes."

"Here is one but harnessed to the devil's horses."

Sando was screwing the lid back onto the bottle. He didn't give the two women any of the brandy.

"I am trying very hard to make your brother stop taking this stuff. It is bad for his health, and lately it's been very very bad for his work."

Sando sipped from his glass.

Sam and Martha did the same.

Magufu stared at his as if he didn't want to drink. His fingers were tightly curled in his face.

"You see, Sonnybig. This stuff is very bad for your brother. In the beginning it gave him a name and earned him admirers right and left in the drinking community. But now it's losing him friends fast, money faster and his health and sanity fastest. You understand all this, don't you?"

"Yes."

"No, you don't. Not now, later maybe, but not today. This stuff, my friend, taken dry and straight at the rate you drink water in a day, completely wipes out any sense of self, shame, pride or dignity, wrong or right out of some people's minds. It also causes blackouts, the shaking of hands, sleepiness, loss of memory and a queer hating and avoiding of people, especially those dearest to one's heart. Conversely it breaks the loved ones' hearts into so many tiny pieces and throws them as far apart as heaven and hell."

Magufu stealthily reached for his glass.

"Easy, Magufu, easy on it. Just a tiny wee sip to wet your tongue . . . that's right. Now, put it back . . . good.

"It is very important that you understand what's happening to your brother right now. It's a secret between you and me. Don't tell your father or mother. You still have an expanding heart. You can accommodate almost anything if you try hard enough.

"Parents are a different thing altogether. They think they have seen the worst and now their hearts are built into little concrete squares that have no more room for expansion. If you tell them what I have told you about your brother you will only kill them. They haven't been taught to break the little concrete squares and make more room for emergencies like these."

"Aren't we going to have something to eat here?" Martha asked. Her glass was empty.

"So, Sonnybig brother, don't let me ever hear that you have been playing over this song to Ma and Pa back home or I'll break your neck, right?"

"Yes."

"It's not fair on your brother here and all of us his friends, right?"

"Yes."

"One day, if you live long enough, you will learn that in this life you can only talk of certain things and leave out certain others about other people."

Magufu put his glass down on the table. It was empty.

"Tendai," he said. His fingers were now locked together between his knees with the elbows resting on the knees.

"Yes."

"I am going to give you a letter to Father."

"Yes."

"When are you wanted at school?"

"On Wednesday."

"Today is Sunday morning. If you take the three p.m. bus you will be home before six. You will put up at home tonight and take the early morning bus back to town tomorrow—so around eleven you should be here. Tuesday I'll take a day off to do your shopping and you will take the Tuesday afternoon bus to school . . ."

"Aah, Sheila!"

"Sheila!"

The two women shouted together. Everyone looked up.

Sheila closed the door to Magufu's bedroom and came to sit between the two women.

"Hallo Sheila babe!" Sam shouted. His glass, too, was now empty. Only Sando seemed not to be drinking. He was concentrating on the game of solo.

Martha kept dangerously quiet but looking at Sheila with such a bright brittle look that one expected to hear the sharp breaking of glass anytime.

"And how is our Sheila?" Sam said.

"Let's go, Sam," Martha stood up.

"Come on, Martha."

"Come on yourself. What are we hanging round here for anyway? No food, no beer, no music. Come on, let's go." She was tugging at Sam's shirt sleeve.

Sam looked up at her, narrowed his eyes and said, "You know something, Martha?"

"No? What? Come on, let's get out of here."

"One of these very lovely days, Martha . . ."

"What is it?"

"Aren't you interested?"

"I am but hurry it up."

"Sit down first," Sam was smiling brightly at Martha.

Sando was looking at them.

Magufu was staring at his empty glass.

The two women were looking at Martha with open contempt. Sheila was looking for something in her handbag. She hadn't smiled or said anything since she came in.

"What is it, Sam?" Martha said, putting her hand round Sam's neck and kissing him on the mouth with a bright brittle look at Sheila.

Sheila wasn't looking at them at all.

"Oh, I forgot to say hello, Sheila," Martha said. "Hello, Sheila!" she shrilled across the room and began to titter hysterically.

"Hello, Martha," Sheila said, looking up and smiling sadly at Martha and going back to searching for what she could never seem to find in her handbag.

"Isn't Sheila beautiful, darling?" Martha told Sam, kissing him on the mouth again.

"Not as beautiful as you are, my own dearest darling," Sam said, turning his mouth away from Martha's kisses, "and listen, darling. Remember what I said?"

"Yes. You said one of these lovely days . . . isn't that what you said?"

"Yes, exactly. You know you are very intelligent, Martha."

"Come on, Sam," Magufu said. He wasn't looking at them. "Not in front of the . . ."

". . . and you are very very bright and I love you so much that . . ."

"Cut it, Sam!" Magufu shouted.

Sando was looking at them and not playing solo anymore.

". . . one of these fine lovely days I'll tan your hide so black and ram your teeth right back your mouth so they will be smiling north when you are going south!"

"Sam!"

Magufu's shout was too late. Martha was lying back on the sofa, her mouth looking as if she were eating raw liver. She looked too surprised to say anything.

Tendai saw Martha's lips swelling. He looked out through the window, his eyes filled with tears.

Martha didn't get up where she lay. She was very still. She turned over on her belly to hide her fast-swelling lips.

"Don't mess up that seat. Go and wash!" Sam told her roughly, yanking her up by the scruff of the neck.

"Leave her now, Sam," Sando said. "She is all right now."

Sam dropped her and she lay without a sound or making the slightest movement.

Sando poured brandy into three glasses. He added water and gave Sam and Magufu theirs. He emptied his in one gulp. Sheila and the two women were looking at them.

Sam downed his and winked at the women. "Hi, Sheila!" He smiled. Sheila looked away and the women giggled and then burst into loud laughter.

Magufu was studying his glass, not yet touched, in both his hands.

Suddenly, Sheila spoke.

Her voice was very different from last night, Tendai felt. It was soft, low and lost, and it was worse than Martha's lips suddenly changing into overblown lungs.

"I had forgotten," she said to her two friends, her sisters of last night—"I had forgotten that it's my birthday today."

They all stared at her.

"How old are you now, Sheila?" Sam asked.

"Fifteen."

Suddenly the room was very quiet, everyone listening to but not looking at her.

"I had promised Connie and Rudo a party at our house. Now they will come and find I am not there."

Silence.

"You drank too much last night," the tall woman said unkindly.

"I was tricked. And you encouraged it." She searched in her bag. "I had never tasted a drop of beer or spirits all my life until last night. And you sat there while they poured that—what do you call it?—hot stuff into my Coke." She pulled her woman's things out of the bag. "Now, if only I can get those aspirins I hope by the time I get home nobody won't notice a thing." She turned her bag upside down and shook it. Nothing dropped. "Will just have to keep a mile's distance away from Father, though. No toothpaste will ever get this stink out of my mouth." She stuffed her things back into the bag. She looked up straight at Magufu. "No aspirins or anything for a headache in this house heh? Magufu?" She was smiling at him. Sam looked at her, at Magufu, then back at her and lowered his head, hiding something behind a forced cough.

"No. Nothing." Magufu shook his head and quickly brought his hand to his mouth, tilted his head far back and knocked out the drink without making a single sound down his throat. The two women looked at each other in amazement. He banged the glass on the table and shivered throughout his whole body.

Sando was now very involved in his game.

"I am hungry. Is there anything to eat in here?" Sheila asked.

Magufu shook his head.

The women giggled.

"Or milk," Sheila said. "Haven't you got any milk—fresh milk?"

"Get her a bottle of milk, Sonnybig," Sando said, tossing a coin toward Tendai.

"Thank you very much," Sheila said. "And—and Sonnybig—is that your real name? Anyway, no matter—Sonnybig—you are Magufu's brother, aren't you? You are the one who was sleeping on the floor in there last night, aren't you? I remember that part—what I can't remember is the earlier part after everything was reeling and the lights were

killing my eyes—anyway you, Sonnybig, please get me some aspirin if
there is any change. Is that all right, mister—if there is any change?"

"Get her some aspirins and a bottle of milk, Sonnyboy," Sando said.

Sheila giggled, "Sonnybig, Sonnyboy. Can't ever trust boys with too
many names." She put her head on her knees and was still.

Everyone looked at her.

"Let's have a game of Crazy Eight," Sam suggested.

Sando dealt the cards and they began to play.

"Let's go, auntie," the plump woman said.

"Let's wait for Sheila's milk and pills."

After drinking the milk Sheila rushed outside and was violently sick.
She came back and rinsed her mouth thoroughly with water, then
she swallowed her aspirins.

"You promised to take us back to Hartley, remember?" She was talking to Magufu.

"Oh, did I?"

"Yes. And you promised me four dollars last night after you hit me
and I agreed to do what you wanted me to do."

Sam looked up. His mouth dropped. Magufu looked at the cards that
were becoming smudged in his sweaty hands.

"Your turn, Magufu. Play," Sando said. Magufu played.

"I think you have forgotten what I said," he told Sheila.

"No. I haven't. Didn't he say that he would bring us back when we
refused to drive out here with him last evening, auntie?"

"You promised," the tall woman said.

"You have to get us back," the plump one said.

"Please, Magufu," Sheila said. "Forget the four dollars for last night
but please take us back to Hartley."

Magufu scratched his chin.

"Well—petrol. I haven't got any petrol. Have you got any petrol in
the van, Sam?"

"Not enough to get us to Hartley and back."

"You can buy petrol, can't you?" Sheila asked.

"Yes—but—"

"Forget it, girls," Sando said, "we are all broke."

The women looked at each other.

Sheila put her head in her hands. When she looked up there were tears in her eyes.

"Look, Magufu. I said forget the four dollars you promised me when you thought I wouldn't give you what you wanted. Forget about driving and get us a lift home."

"Well—let me see. One dollar? Sorry. Can't help you."

"But, Magufu—just a dollar?"

"Honestly I don't—"

"Borrow from your friends then."

"These are my friends and they too are broke."

"Please."

She was trying very hard not to spill any tears. "One night is all right. I can always tell Father we stayed up late at Rudo's place and her parents asked me to spend the night—but two nights? Have heart, heh, Magufu?"

Then she did a terrible thing. She went down on her knees and, her hands on Magufu's knees, looked directly into his eyes.

"Have heart, huh? I did what you wanted. Came all the way from Hartley with you, let you put brandy in my Coke, danced with you, came here and spent the night with you—my first night ever—and you can't do a little thing like giving me a dollar to see me home to my folks, huh, Magufu?"

There was a silence. One of the calendars flapped against the wall.

"Sonnybig?" Sando said.

"Yes?"

"You said Father gave you some pocket money, didn't he?"

"Yes."

"You still have it?"

"Yes."

"Could I borrow a dollar? You got more than a dollar haven't you?"

"Yes."

"Can you get home and back on the remainder?"

"Not quite."

"Well—you can use part of the fees Father will give you—"

"The fees? But I am supposed to get fees from brother Magufu here."

"Your brother hasn't got any money. That's why you are going back home today. You are going to collect school fees and money for your school clothing from Father. Now, lend us that dollar and I shall give it and any money you will have used on the way back to you tomorrow evening."

Tendai handed Sheila the dollar.

"Thank you very much again," Sheila said. "Well bye, Magufu."

She didn't even say good-bye to her "sisters" as she went out. The men went back to their game and later the two women also left without saying good-bye to anyone. Only a funeral party could break up this way.

Tendai went into his brother's bedroom to collect his jacket. The bed hadn't been made and there were some bloodstains on the crumpled sheets and right on the floor was a ball of crumpled newspaper with more blood on it. Tendai saw the letter from his brother's wife on the bedside stand where he had put it the day before, still unopened. He grabbed his jacket and went out.

"I am going now," he told his brother without breaking his stride toward the door to the street.

"Hey, Tendai!" Magufu called.

Tendai turned his head. Magufu was smiling. "If you have just a little surplus of the money you really need—you see—we haven't got anything to eat here and—"

"I just have enough to get home on," and he turned on his heel and fled from that house. He felt very desolate.

Later on he would forget some details of those people in his brother's house that day but he would always remember that something very violent had been done to him, and that is when he had begun not to care very much for his brother Magufu . . . except that they had the same parents.

William Modisane was born in Johannesburg in 1924. For years
he worked on the editorial staff of *Drum* magazine and as a jazz
critic for the *Golden City Post*. He left South Africa in 1959,
spent a brief stint in Germany, and then settled in England. His
autobiographical account of growing up in the slums of Sophiatown, *Blame Me on History*, was published in 1963 and immediately banned in his native South Africa. He died in 1986.

The Dignity of Begging

The Magistrate raises his eyes above the documents and plunges
them like daggers into my heart. His blue eyes are keen: my heart
pounds like the bass of a boogie-woogie.

"I'm sick to death of you . . . heartily sick. There's not a native beggar
on the streets whose full story I don't know," the Magistrate says. "I've
watched some of you grow up. There isn't one I haven't tried to rehabilitate many times. Some I was forced to send to jail, but they always come
back . . . they come back to the goose that lays the golden egg."

These are fighting words. The Magistrate sounds as though he's going
to put us away for a few weeks. My only regret is that Richard Serurubele
has to share my fate. If only the Magistrate knew that he is not a parasite
like the rest of us, that he's what is called an exploited beggar. He was
crippled by an automobile accident, and since then his parents have
made capital out of it. They use him to beg so they can balance the family budget. They never show him the comfort of love. Relentlessly they
drive him, like an animal that has to work for its keep and feed. He is
twenty-one. Dragging one foot along, he is an abject sight who has all
the sadness of the world in his face. He looks many times older than my
mother-in-law.

"You beggars make it difficult for me to do my duty, and in spite of my failure to rehabilitate you, I always believe in giving you another chance . . . A fresh start, you might call it.

"But I'm almost certain that you'll be back here in a few days."

The Magistrate is getting soft; I can see my freedom at a distance of an arm's stretch. Here is my chance to put on my act. A look of deep compunction and a few well-chosen words can do the trick. I clear my throat and squeeze out a tear or two.

"Your Honor, most of us beg because we've been ostracized by our families; they treat us as though we were lepers," I say, wiping off a tear. "They want us to look up to them for all the things we need. They never encourage us to earn our own keep. Nobody wants to employ us, people are more willing to offer us alms, rather than give us jobs. All they do is show us pity . . . We don't want to be pitied, we want to be given a chance to prove that we're as good as anybody else."

I can see from the silence in the court that everybody is deceived . . . Everybody is filled with a sense of self-reproach. The Magistrate is as mute as the undertaker's parlor. I can read pity on the faces of all the people in the court; perhaps the most pathetic is my own. I am magnificent . . . an answer to every film director's dream. I know I have said enough . . . enough to let us out, that is.

"I understand you have matriculated, your name is Nathaniel, isn't it?" He turns a page of the report prepared by a worker in the Non-European Affairs Department. "Yes, here we are, Nathaniel Mokgomare, the department recommends that you be sent to a place where you will be taught some useful trade. I want you to report to Room 14 at the department's building tomorrow morning."

This is not what I had bargained for; my brilliant idea has boomeranged. Why must I take a job when I can earn twice a normal wage begging? After all, what will horses do if I take a job? I *must* uphold the dignity of begging. Professional ethics forbid all beggars from working.

"As for you, Richard Serurubele, I'll let you go this time, but mark my words: the next time you appear before me, I'll have you sent to the Bantu Refuge. Now get out of here, both of you."

If the Magistrate had seen the big grin on my face as we leave the court, he would have thrown my deformed carcass in jail and deliberately lost the key. He does not see it though.

With the exception of a few loose ends everything has gone accord-

ing to schedule, but my friend Serurubele is just about the most miserable man on earth. The trouble with him is he lacks imagination, but
then of course, not everybody is as bright as I am. He always seems to be
looking at the dull side of life, a vice coupled with an appalling brand of
honesty most bishops would swear didn't exist.

"One of these days, I'm going to kill myself," Serurubele says. "I can't
go on like this; I'm tired of living off other people. Why did this have to
happen to me? Tell me, Nathan. Why?"

How this man expects me to answer a question like this is beyond me.
For one unguarded moment I almost tell him to send his Maker a
telegram and ask Him all about it, but my gentler nature sees the harm
such an answer might do.

"I don't know," I say, abruptly. "Things like this just happen; it's not
in us to question why. Nature has a way of doing things, but even then
she gives something in return . . . at least I think so . . . But how should I
know, anyway?"

This is the one time I cannot find something concrete to say; I want
to show him that there is compensation for his disability, but I just cannot lay my hands on it. This, I remember, is what made me leave home.

I left because my parents did not understand. They almost made a
neurotic out of me; but today I wonder if it wasn't my own sensitivity
which gave their actions then their seemingly absurd proportions. They
seemed afraid to walk about freely; everybody sat down as if the house
were full of cripples. I was treated like a babe in arms. All the things I
wanted were brought to me, I was not even allowed to get myself water
to drink. This excessive kindness gradually began to irritate me . . . It
became a constant reminder that I didn't belong, that I was an invalid. It
then became apparent that they would soon put the food into my mouth
which they had already chewed for me, and push it down my throat.
These thoughts of inadequacy drove me from home.

A new life opened for me. I got myself a wife, two bouncing boys and
a property at Pampoenfontein, also a room at Sophiatown complete
with piano. Within two years I had begged well over a few hundred
pounds. The money had been used wisely. Only one problem confronts
me now, I want enough money to provide for my old age . . . The two
boys are also to be considered.

"For Christ's sake, Nathaniel," Serurubele says, "what's wrong with you? Why are you always so wrapped up in your thoughts . . . this is where I stay, remember?"

I say good-bye to him and go to my room. After having something to eat I settle down to some hard thinking. There are all sorts of insurances and societies, unions and what have you, which protect workers. Why not a beggars' union? I could rally all the beggars of the city into one union with some professional name like The United Beggars' Union, into whose funds every beggar would contribute ten shillings a week. In the city of Johannesburg alone, there are over a hundred beggars and if they could all be talked over, a capital of about two thousand four hundred pounds could be realized in one year.

What a brilliant idea . . . an inspiration of genius. Sometimes I feel depressed that the world has not had the vision to realize the potentialities of my genius . . . possibly it cannot accommodate Einstein and myself in the same generation. Anyway, so much for that.

I could promise to offer each a bonus of ten pounds a year. That would be smart . . . No beggar could resist such an offer. Maybe I should promise to buy each a property somewhere cheap, say, buy one property a year for the needy ones like Serurubele, equip him with third-rate tools and interest him in turning out junk that nobody will care to give a second look at. The scheme would be costly, but at least it would go far in enlisting their confidence. Only one would get the property; the others would wait patiently until I get religion.

The following morning I'm at Room 14 bright and early. A white man with a bored expression on his face is sitting behind a big mahogany desk. I tell him my name. He takes some paper and writes on it. He tells me to go to the address written on the paper.

The faint showers that were falling outside have become heavier, and as I go out I say something nasty about the weather. A brilliant idea strikes me as a well-dressed lady is walking toward me. She looks like a mobile gold mine ready to be tapped . . . in fact, I can almost see the gold nuggets in her teeth. I put on a gloomy face, bend lower than usual and let my deformed carcass shiver. She stops and looks at me as if she's responsible for my deformity.

"Why, you poor boy, you're freezing to death," she says, with melodrama. "Here, go buy yourself something to eat."

I feel the half-crown piece in my hand and give her the usual line of how the good Lord will bless her, and send her tons and tons of luck: but from the way she's dressed, she appears to have had more than her share of luck.

I play this trick all the way to the address I'm given, and by the time I get there, I count well over ten half-crowns. Not bad, I say to myself; at this rate I can become the richest and most famous beggar in the city. To think the department wants to pin me behind a desk! The idea is criminal, to say the least.

One of these days when I'm on my annual leave, I hope to write a book on begging, something like a treatise on the subject. It will be written with sensitivity and charm, brimful with sketches from life, and profusely illustrated with colored photographs, with easy-to-follow rules on the noblest and oldest occupation in the world: begging! It will be a textbook for all aspiring beggars, young and old, who will reap a wealth of knowledge from my personal experience and genius. In fact, it will be the only one of its kind in world literature. Even millionaires will take up begging as a pastime to color their humdrum existence.

It will naturally begin with a history of the art from its ancient crudity of maiming children as a preparation in their education, right up to the contemporary age of beggars who are driven to the city in the latest American cars . . . beggars with a bank balance big enough to impress the Receiver of Revenue. I can almost see it on the best-seller list for several months. This reverie almost causes me to lose my way.

I find the place and go in. My heart just misses a beat when I see the large number of people inside. Some, if not most, are deformed monstrosities like myself. What could be sweeter? I can see my plan taking shape.

The man in charge starts explaining the elementary principles of the typewriter. I pretend to be interested and ask many unnecessary questions, but intelligent enough to impress him. By five o'clock I'm running over the keyboard like a brilliant amateur.

On my way home I go via Serurubele's corner. He is still there and looking as miserable as ever. I suggest that we go home. I lure him to my room and when we get there I begin playing a certain tarantella like Rubinstein, only my rendering is in A flat Major. Either my piano recital is good or my friend just loves bad sounds.

"You can have a house like this and everything that goes with it; it's yours for the taking. Why beg for other people when you can do it for yourself?"

"I've got to help with the rent and the food," he says. "How do you think I'm going to get a house like this? I can't just wish for it."

"You don't have to, you must plan and work for it like I did. I have a plan that will give it to you in less than a year . . . Listen."

I then start explaining to him about the society with particular emphasis on the good it will do to all beggars. I see his teeth sparkling behind thick lips. I put him in charge of organizing them for our first meeting.

Last night I dreamt I was at the race course and I saw the winning double as plain as I see my twisted leg. I raid my savings in the room and make my way to Turfontein. When I get there I start scouting around for policemen. None are about and a soothing satisfaction comes with the realization that I shall not bother myself with police badges. I put a pound win on two and seven, a double in the first leg. As I'm making my bet, a man with eyes as big and lethargic as an owl's is standing next to me and beaming like a blushing groom.

I'm too nervous to watch the race, so I decide to walk about and appreciate the scenery. Suddenly I feel as though someone is staring at me. I turn round and look straight at Miss Gallovidian, a welfare worker, who has the uncanny habit of showing up at the most unexpected places. I don't need a fortune-teller to tell me I'm in trouble. She has a notorious record of having safely deposited more than twelve beggars in the Refuge. My only chance is to get out of here before she can find a beefy policeman. I'm walking to the gate when I hear people talking about two and seven. I even forget the trouble Miss Gallovidian is going to bring me. I run as fast as a man with a twisted leg can to the Bookie. Only six tickets were sold, the loudspeaker was saying, only I'm not interested.

As the Bookie is handing me the money Blushing Groom seems even happier than I am. His crooked teeth, which are dulled by tobacco, click every time the Bookie counts a hundred. His greasy lips are watering while a pair of bloodshot eyes are blinking with a dull brilliance. It hurts my eyes to look at him. I have hardly put the money in my pocket, when Gruesome pats me on the back and says, nice and loud: "We make it!"

I must have been a fool not to have been wise as to why Blushing Groom was acting the perfect chaperon.

"That's fine," I say. "What have *we* made?"

"Don't be bashful," he says, "we caught the richest double. Come, this calls for a celebration." He extends a hand, and all the time he's smiling as if his wife has given birth to quadruplets.

"Look, pal," I say. "It's a good try. I couldn't have done better myself. This is the perfect setup, isn't it? Well, I've got news for you: I caught that double alone, I don't know you and I don't care to. Go get yourself another piece of cheese . . . I'm not that easy."

This ape suddenly stops smiling and looks at me like I had the plague. His broad, flat nose starts puffing out steam like an angry Spanish bull (only I'm not in the mood to make fancy passes like a toreador). All in all, he looks positively fierce, like the animal in the simile.

"Six hundred and seventy pounds is a lot of money," he shouts. "Nobody's going to cheat me out of my share. You being a cripple . . ."

"Shut up!" I yell. "Never call me that again, you . . . You!" I swing a right cross to his face, but this ape is smart. He blocks it and lands a hard one on my chin. I rock back and land flat on my sitters, while jungle tom-toms beat out a solid conga in my head. After a while my head clears and I get up, burning with rage. If I only had the strength, I would tear this ape apart.

Blushing Groom has put on quite a show; we have a good audience. Some white folk are threatening to beat his brains out . . . I sincerely hope they do.

Suddenly I see a police badge jostling its way through. This is no place for me! I dash and start zigzagging through the people. A junior confusion starts, with everybody trying to give way. I run a few minutes, stumble and fall on my face. The policeman bends down and grabs me firmly by the arm and whispers: "Look, John, let's not have trouble. Come along quietly and everything will be just fine."

Under these circumstances I have no choice but to submit. My mother always told me never to resist arrest, let alone striking a uniformed officer of the law. Me and my money part company after Blushing Groom had proferred charges. My submission causes me to spend a not-so-glorious weekend at the Bantu Refuge. My transfer there being arranged by the thoughtful sergeant in the charge office, who out of pure love could not have me thrown in with hardened criminals . . . what with the place filled with housebreakers, extortioners, professional pick-pockets and a generous assortment of other unsavory characters. Frankly, I hoped he would mind his own business. I might even have started a craps game and made me some money.

"I am almost certain that you will be back here in a few days," the Magistrate had said. Somebody ought to tell him he has a great future . . . reading palms. He looks at me and a grin spreads over his pancakelike face. This place must be short of Magistrates; why has it got to be the same one all the time?

"Beggars who play the horses are a dangerous nuisance. They misuse kindness that is shown to them."

Just my luck: now I have to listen to a lecture on morals. The Magistrate looks pleased with himself, and I don't like it. Miss Gallovidian looks at me and smiles like a proud victress. She probably expects a promotion for this. I'm called onto the stand.

Some man with a thin face asks me to raise my right hand and swear to tell the truth. After saying my piece, the prosecutor starts questioning me as if he's promised thirty percent of Blushing Groom's cut. After his session with me, he calls Blushing Groom to the stand.

"Do you know this man?" the prosecutor says.

"No, sir."

"How was it then you put up ten shillings to bet the horses with him?"

"I was losing all morning when I decided to try somebody's guesses. I met him and we started talking."

"Did anybody see you talking to him?"

"I don't know, but somebody must have."

"Then what happened?"

"I asked him if he had a tip. He said he had one straight from the horse's mouth . . . A sure thing, he said. I then asked him if I could put up ten shillings. He agreed. I was afraid to make the bet, so I gave him the money and walked over to the Bookie's stand with him where he placed a pound win on two and seven."

"Why were you afraid to make the bet?"

"I thought he was luckier than I was . . . besides, I had been losing all morning."

"Why did you strike him?"

"He was trying to cheat me out of my share, and tried to hit me when he couldn't."

The Magistrate looks at me with something like contempt in his eyes. I won't have to put on a show for him this time. I might just as well kiss half my money good-bye. Blushing Groom's story is watertight.

"I'm thoroughly disappointed with you," the Magistrate says. "I didn't know you were a thief too. I don't believe you could have made that bet alone; beggars haven't got so much money. I believe his story, things like this do happen. The money will be shared equally between the two of you."

"I don't believe you could have made that bet alone." What a cheek! I'll have that hobo know I make more money in one week than he does in a month. I don't believe you . . . Good God!

I feel like committing mass murder as the court hands Blushing Groom three hundred and thirty-five pounds of my money. This prehistoric beast has a swell racket. A few more jobs like this and he can retire and buy himself a villa on the Riviera.

Blushing Groom is magnificent, inspiring awe. He is completely uncompromising, thoroughly unscrupulous, without qualms or a conscience. He has wholly realized the separateness of good and evil and attained a purity in evil worthy of honest appraisal. He would not allow himself to be swayed from cheating me by my being a cripple. If I were allowed to choose a brother, he would be my only choice.

I take my share of the money and clear out before the Magistrate and Miss Gallovidian cook up another charge against me. On my way home I find it difficult to resist the temptation of stopping at some busy corner and doing my stuff. I might make up for some of the money, but I just happen to be wearing my best and have been a beggar long enough to know that people don't give money away to beggars who are dressed better than they. People who give alms to beggars do so to establish their superiority over the receiver, and like I said: I'm not an apprentice beggar.

When I get home I find a letter from my wife.

Our son Tommy is sick. Please come home . . .

I become afraid and anxious for my Tommy, and even the kind words of my outsize landlady fail to move me.

I had to wait for something like this to show me the folly of my ways. A man's place is next to his wife and family. I had hoped that someday I would be able to provide my boys with a decent education, to grow them like normal boys, not just sons of a helpless cripple . . . to find a place for them in the sun. I might be a big shot beggar but as a husband and father, I stink.

"If I should not see my friend Serurubele, will you . . ."

"Yes, I'll explain to him. I'll always have your room for you if you should ever want it again."

Deep down I know that I will want it again. I have three hundred and thirty-five reasons why I should. Blushing Groom and the gullible public of Johannesburg will live in my mind forever . . . I have to come back. I owe it to the profession.

WILLIAM SAIDI

William Saidi, though a Zambian, was born and educated in Southern Rhodesia, now Zimbabwe. In 1964 he founded the New Writers Group of Zambia, the first organization for creative writers in the country. He is currently assistant editor of Zimbabwe's only independent daily newspaper, the *Daily News*. His books include *The Old Bricks Lives*, *Day of the Baboons*, and *Gwebede's Wars*.

THE GARDEN OF EVIL

Mr. Parker said, "*Wena skelem, wena,*"* speaking in kitchen kaffir.

Old Mwanza smiled his ancient smile. He surmised that Mr. Parker was complimenting him. His withered chest filled with pride. Mr. Parker was not generous with his praise. He was an inspector in the Northern Rhodesia Police.

"*Ya, wena skelem wena* Mwanza," Mr. Parker said again.

He was surveying with a lordly contentment the garden of vegetables. The dark rich greenness of the cabbages and the bright luscious greenness of the lettuce were mouth-watering. Everything exuded a health, a vitality and a delicious aliveness which rejuvenated Old Mwanza's tired faith in life.

Mr. Parker smiled at Old Mwanza. That too was a rarity and a bonus. Mr. Parker had false teeth. They were unnaturally, almost obscenely white. To most Africans, they constituted an unfathomable curiosity, to be ogled at until the mystery was unraveled. Mr. Parker hated the experience.

Old Mwanza had discovered Mr. Parker's toothlessness on a day that was to prove portentous for both men.

* "You are dangerous, you."

Mr. Parker's wife and three children had flown to Durban, Natal, in the Union of South Africa. They had gone for a weekend holiday with Mr. Parker's parents who lived there in the luxury of seaside retirement. Mr. Parker saw them off at Lusaka airport that morning and returned to the house with an evil, vengeful glint in his eye.

Mwanza worked steadily in the garden, wondering idly when his daughter would visit him from her home in Chilenje African township. Her last visit had been an elixir for Old Mwanza. She had brought her firstborn child, two weeks old, his first grandchild. Old Mwanza gazed in lachrymose gratitude and amazement at the little cherubic face, its eyes closed softly and its fresh lips parted slightly. His daughter kept reminding him how much like him the little boy looked.

"Let your husband hear you say that and you will be sorry," he admonished her gently.

As he worked, with one ear cocked for outlandish noises from the huge house, he waited for the explosion. It was uncanny, he thought. Mr. Parker's wife and children were away. The cook had taken the day off and so had the South African–born nanny. Mr. Parker and Old Mwanza had the entire house and the vast garden and orchard to themselves. There was a tranquility about the place, a tranquility which Old Mwanza knew to be unnatural and transient.

It came two hours later.

"Mwanza, you *skelem! Buya lapa!* You *bobojan!*"*

He heard the shout clearly from behind the huge closed windows of the bedroom. Mr. Parker had a stentorian voice to match his police inspector's physique.

In his weak, reedy voice, Mwanza replied, "*Mina buya, Bwana!*"†

He could feel the tendons in his neck standing out with the exertion. "*Mina buya, Bwana!*" He quickened his normally lugubrious, tortured pace. You are not a young man anymore and remember that stupid foot of yours, he reminded himself unnecessarily, as he hurried into the house.

In the bedroom, with its luxurious white furniture and expensive lace curtains, he found Mr. Parker lying cadaverously in the massive double

* "Mwanza, you dangerous animal! Come here! Come here! You Baboon!"
† "I am coming, Master!"

bed with the snow-white eiderdown. His face was a bizarre study in drunken idiocy. The lips were slack and there were no teeth. The skin on the face was a flaming pink and the eyes appeared opaque and wild. Mr. Parker had no clothes on except a pair of white tennis shorts.

Old Mwanza walked fretfully into the room, his bare feet sinking dangerously into the thick pile of the carpet. He waited. At last Mr. Parker stirred.

"Yes, *Bwana? Mina buyile."** Old Mwanza spoke in a tremulous whisper.

"Mwanza, *wena yazi lo skelem ena kona lapa* township? *Lapa Matelo, na lapa Chilenje? Wena yazi lo skelem?* Those little bastards, those little half-educated bastards! *Ena fun bulala lo Mazungu, wena yazi? Ena funa bulala lo Mazungu.†* The stupid idiots!"

Old Mwanza had the weird sensation that this was a monologue. He kept his peace. Most white people in Northern Rhodesia spoke thus at this time. In Southern Rhodesia and Nyasaland, on the borders, the Africans were reported to be speaking of getting rid of the white people too. Mr. Parker had himself spoken like this before, even when he was sober. So Old Mwanza concluded benevolently that the viciousness came from the drink.

His discovery of Mr. Parker's toothlessness was a secret triumph for Old Mwanza. He was older and had all his teeth. It was true that he could not chew with the same efficiency as before, but he still had his teeth. Mr. Parker's misfortune (to Old Mwanza it was something to be utterly ashamed of, like losing your toes in a war) made him—Mr. Parker—vulnerable, mortal, weak and susceptible to all human frailties. For Old Mwanza, it was an astounding revelation.

Mr. Parker's speech had not been entirely shorn of its military thunder. Yet to Old Mwanza there was something comical about it. He concluded sagely that people with false teeth had no business trying to speak without them.

"Where are my teeth, Mwanza? *Upi lo* teeth *kamina? Upi Upi!*" Old Mwanza cast his tired eyes around the opulently furnished bedroom and

---

* "Yes, sir? I have come."
† "Mwanza, you know those dangerous animals in Matero and Chilenje African townships? They want to kill all white people."

wondered mischievously what would happen if the teeth, by some miracle, disappeared forever. His amusement was short-lived. The family had two cars and three servants, including the nanny, whom Old Mwanza had wooed in vain. The family always ate well, their dinner table invariably replete with fresh fruit, apart from the other victuals. To Old Mwanza, any European family which could afford fresh apples and oranges (not even from their own orchard) for dessert had to be rich.

The teeth were in a glass of water on a small table next to the bed. Old Mwanza cleared his throat to suppress laughter.

Loudly, he exclaimed dramatically, *"Bwana Bwana!"* With a shaking finger, he pointed to the glass, in which the dentures floated calmly.

Mr. Parker looked at the glass in amazement and laughed with exaggerated gusto, his rubbery lips stretched taut to reveal the barren pink gums in the darkened cave of his mouth. Old Mwanza felt laughter bubbling in his throat, but experience restrained him. To laugh with your master presumed equality. It could spell the end of a good job.

Mr. Parker walked regally along the smooth paths which separated the symmetrically arranged beds. Haughtily polite cauliflower looked with tolerant disdain at the lowly, peasant-looking cabbage. That perennial garden vegetable, the asparagus, looked with suspicion at the green virility of the spinach, while the juicy tomato, its eyes closed coyly, pleaded not to be bothered by the ungainly beet.

Old Mwanza thought Mr. Parker had at last begun to recognize the incredible beauty and aliveness of the garden. For years, he and the garden had lived a separate existence from the rest of the household. Even the cook, who marched neatly into the garden to cut vegetables for the pot, was an alien here. Mrs. Parker and the children? For all the attention they paid to the garden, it was nothing but a plaything for the eccentric, senile African gardener. It was Old Mwanza's kingdom, his own little garden of Eden. He knew every plant like the master of a castle knows his servants. Sometimes he would speak to them and a strange sensation would assail him, that they responded familiarly. Mr. Parker had not bought a hose or sprinkler for watering the garden. By tacit arrangement, Old Mwanza had devised his own ingenious irrigation system. This consisted of two cans fashioned crudely from two discarded four-gallon paraffin tins. These were suspended on a thick wooden pole placed horizontally on his shoulders. Old Mwanza did not know the pesticides by name. He could read or write after a fashion and only in his mother tongue, Nsenga, a derivative of the more widely spoken Nyamja of the Eastern Province. He approached both writing and reading with acute trepidation and performed them only when his life or job depended on it.

Today, Mr. Parker walked in the garden as if he too wanted to be close to the plants. The prospect filled Old Mwanza with foreboding. He treasured his attachment to the garden to the point of being insanely possessive and jealous.

"There is no garden boy like you, my boy. You are . . . how old . . . about sixty? Yes, you are . . . you are just fantastic."

When Mr. Parker spoke to him in straight English, Old Mwanza felt humbled. It signified Mr. Parker's profound depth of feeling in what he was saying. That he believed that Old Mwanza had only a vague notion of what he was saying probably made him feel a martyr in the cause of better understanding between Europeans and Africans in the three troubled territories which constituted the ill-fated federation of Rhodesia and Nyasaland at the time.

Mr. Parker walked back into his house, leaving Old Mwanza to speculate anxiously on whether his daughter would visit him again. He lived in the servants' quarters which were concealed from general view by a high wall between it and the big house. He had a bedroom and a kitchen to himself. The other half of the semidetached house was occupied by the cook, who was married.

Old Mwanza rarely ventured into the townships now. He had lived there all his life, raising his children with the same haphazard devotion that any other African paterfamilias raised their offspring in that detribalized maze.

During those sprightly days, Old Mwanza had worked as an office messenger, flitting from office building to office building on his bicycle, delivering letters, buying sandwiches and cold drinks and performing other menial errands for the Europeans. He enjoyed the social life too. Even his wife had enjoyed it, though she always went to the local church on Sundays. They lived in Matero, the African township on the outskirts of Lusaka. At weekends, he and his wife joined friends and neighbors in orgies of senseless drinking and singing. His wife recounted the events to the Catholic priest every Sunday. Old Mwanza became something of a local bon vivant until his wife clipped his wings. His ardor for the hedonistic life evaporated quite suddenly when she threatened to leave him unless he reformed. Abruptly, maturity came and without ever consciously acknowledging the fact, he recognized the essential truth that life did not finally constitute a series of liaisons with women of easy virtue. Then he joined friends who had boasted that there was adventure, fame and fortune to be made in the army. He went to Malaya and spent most of his time cooking. For all his relative security among the foul-smelling cabbages and beans, the Japanese had almost blown off his foot. It ended up with three toes, happily for Old Mwanza, including the big one. When he returned, wiser but frightened of life, they gave him a medal and he gravitated almost inevitably to a night watchman's job. The foot gave him frightening moments and he changed to gardening. He had almost no hope and soon after his discovery that he and Nature wanted the same things he was more or less settled spiritually. His war experiences helped. They earned him the kind of respect that acted as a powerful talisman. He had fought on the side of RIGHT. In truth, he had only a hazy recollection of his days in the jungle of Malaya. After the Japanese had nearly blown off his foot, the whole experience became something of a living, waking nightmare.

As a gardener, he developed a liaison with Nature, an affinity which his first employer suspected had something to do with primitive witchcraft. In Mr. Parker's garden, Old Mwanza found his métier.

Often, he would sit up in bed, unable to sleep. Memories of his wife, memories of his halcyon days in Matero, memories of the cordite-filled days in Malaya would come flooding into his mind. His head would throb and reverberate and there would be explosions of a thousand cannons, their roar deafening. He would get up and walk into the quiet darkness of the night. In the distance he would hear the noise of barking dogs. In Chilenje township, they would be barking, not here in the European suburb of Woodlands, where the dogs were trained to bark only when there was an intruder. Mr. Parker had a basenji dog, which Old Mwanza had been told never barked. He had never heard it bark and had been told by Mrs. Parker that the basenji was a rare dog. It was so intelligent that it was almost human, she said. It was probably the only one of its kind in Northern Rhodesia, she claimed breathlessly. Old Mwanza, who had been raised entirely in the city where respect for dogs was only incidental, did not believe her. A dog was a dog.

In the darkness, knowing that the barkless dog would be watching his every move from its kennel near the house, Old Mwanza would walk into the garden, his nostrils distending as he savored the fresh smell of the vegetables. He would close his eyes and try to think of the object of all his love, past and present. He would see the image of his wife. He would think of his wife and the garden, the garden and his wife, his wife and the garden, until the two would blend into one individual unity. He would return to his bed, his disturbed soul somehow satiated. On the periphery of his consciousness, he would hear the cook and his wife trying once more to explore the chemical impurity which was preventing them from having a child.

His daughter came the following Saturday afternoon. Old Mwanza was ecstatic. She brought him a cooked chicken swimming in curry soup. As she warmed it on his primus stove in the little kitchen, he cradled the boy in his lap. His daughter was a short, chubby woman who had the cheeks and watery smile of her mother. She smiled often, a sexy smile, which Old Mwanza knew to have been one of the attributes which had drawn him, mothlike, to her mother. She was a healthy woman and he hoped fervently that her husband, a young man who worked for the government, was her equal. There was love between father and daughter.

Old Mwanza held the boy in his arm and watched with tenderness as his daughter prepared the chicken. She worked with the same effortless dexterity that he had loved in his wife. When she had cooked the nshima, they sat down to eat, talking quietly with familiar laughter and smiles, about their lives and about the boys.

"Jeremiah was at our house yesterday."

The daughter spoke with an imperceptible shake of her head, a nascent choke in her voice.

"What is it this time?" Old Mwanza squeaked with accustomed fright.

"He said you should not go on working. He says Mr. Parker is an evil man. He says things are going to be different soon. He says you fought for nothing in Malaya, now you are growing vegetables for nothing. He says you should be ashamed of yourself."

"This is an old story. An old story. He is young. How is Obadiah? He is older. He understands how these things are. Have you seen him recently?"

"No, Father, I have not seen him recently. He lives in Chibolya. You know what type of people live there. Criminals and prostitutes."

"Is he a criminal too? He was always very quiet. How does he feel? Mr. Parker says I am nearly sixty years old now. I cannot return to the village. I would not survive. My people have forgotten me. I have forgotten them too."

Father and daughter were silent. Old Mwanza enjoyed the chicken with much licking of the fingers. He wished they could leave some of it for the next day. He would hold a small party and invite the South African nanny. It could be the catalyst.

"Father, you know that something terrible is going to happen. Not to you. Something terrible is going to happen in the country. In the townships, they are talking wildly."

"Of what, my dear child?"

"Of things. Obadiah and Jeremiah, they may be different. But they say you should go to the village. They are always talking wildly."

"Of what?"

"Of the white people."

"What of the white people?"

The woman placed the plates softly into a dish of water. Her face was impassive, her voice steady and her demeanor unhurried. Only the wet smile was missing.

"They say they are evil. They say we should get rid of the evil."

Old Mwanza laughed nervously, trying to put derision to the laughter. His daughter turned abruptly to look at him in exasperation. The expression touched her face briefly, like a passing shadow. She was still his daughter.

"This is what Obadiah and Jeremiah are saying? My own children. They are mad." He laughed again, reflectively. "No they are just little children. Just children. The white man is evil? Who gave us Light? Who gave us God? Obadiah, he was a prophet. He called upon doom on Edom and predicted triumph for Israel in the Judgment. Jeremiah. He was a prophet too. A great prophet who was imprisoned for warning of doom. Your mother chose those names. She also chose yours. Esther. She loved God, your mother. All these things, who brought them?"

The woman was silent, sitting cross-legged on the floor, one big breast's dark teat in the mouth of her sleeping infant.

In a sudden, querulous voice, Old Mwanza exploded. "I am not a village boy. My people have forgotten me. We are strangers. You understand?"

The woman looked at her baby, serenely sucking on the teat. She nodded noncommittally. Old Mwanza was perplexed. "You understand, don't you? You are the oldest. You understand."

"Yes," she said, not looking at him. Old Mwanza shook his head in uncomprehending despair.

"No, Father. They are just wild, Obadiah and Jeremiah. They are just wild. They are wild to talk of driving out the white people. Forget about them, Father."

She rose, her practiced arms transferring the baby from her lap to back in one swift, fluid movement. Her breast, the milk dripping slowly from it, hung in embarrassment from her bosom. Old Mwanza did not look at her, his gaze examining in dawning consternation to the uneven floor of the little room. He was a man to whom the Truth had been dramatically exposed as something less than pure, something foul and filthy, something he now looked at with deepening suspicion and mounting revulsion.

They talked on about known innocents, about truths that could be perceived, fathomed, and comprehended at one uncomplicated glance. She talked about her husband, the great job he was doing for the government. He talked briefly about his garden, about his wife, her mother, and soon they lapsed into an embarrassed, tense silence, as each remembered the tender moments with the departed woman. Old Mwanza shook his head, as if to acknowledge his senile failure to grasp the true meaning of the new life.

That evening, after his daughter had left, he strolled through his kingdom, speaking quietly to his subjects, questioning them about Life and its lost meaning. He had asked his daughter to prevail on the two boys to visit him the next weekend. He loved the garden. Mr. Parker's relevance was receding. Neither he nor his family cared much for it. It was the only thing that mattered now, not Mr. Parker, not his wife, not his children.

He stood still and closed his eyes. His two sons came into focus. They were there, two short, powerfully built, younger replicas of himself, with the chubby smile of their mother and the primitive physique of their father during his heyday. They were dark, with short kinky hair which never seemed to grow to its natural length. Hard to comb. They were two good, good-looking boys. They were unmarried.

He smiled. Probably still sowing their wild oats. He remembered his predilection for the company of girls, many girls, different girls. If his wife had not threatened him so earnestly, if he had not grown up so suddenly, he would still be as wild. They were good boys, considerate and loving. When he returned from the war and found his wife sick, they cared for her while he searched for a new niche in a changed society.

They hadn't berated him for his purposeless absence. They should have, he realized with new insight. It had been a waste of manhood. He did not fight for anything that he knew or understood. The people of Malaya were small, but they had not called him to help their jungle war. He had always done what the white man asked of him. Even in the garden? Not the garden. He loved the garden. He did what he and Nature wanted done. Not Mr. Parker. He hoped fervently that his children would understand.

"Mwanza? *Wena kono lo skopo. Wena yazi lo Mazungu en kona skopo maningi.*"*

Old Mwanza knew that the white people were more than just ordinarily clever. People who could invent the airplane had to be extra clever. He did not need reminding. He did not need reminders of their unhuman cleverness. Mr. Parker said he, Old Mwanza, was also clever. That was because he did not believe, as did those fools in the townships, that he had even an iota of the cleverness of the white man, that he could conceivably devise anything, ANYTHING at all, that could rival anything that the white man had already created. The knowledge that he was clever because of his recognition of the white man's superior cleverness warmed him.

They were walking in the garden. Most of their conversations, most of their intimate exchanges, took place here. It was their common denominator. In the garden, Mwanza thought he was king. Mr. Parker did not, could not know it, but Old Mwanza watched his every move, lest he stepped on the vegetables. Old Mwanza did not know how he would react if he had.

Mr. Parker talked on in kitchen kaffir, reminding Old Mwanza that

* "Mwanza? You have brains. You know that the white people have a lot of brains."

those stupid agitators in the townships were going to be punished most severely. It was explained that the authorities were preparing for the rascals. They had guns which spat smoke and some which spat real bullets. Did not Old Mwanza remember those guns? Hadn't he used such guns in the war in Malaya, when he fought for justice and freedom? Oh, yes, Old Mwanza remembered them. Yes, didn't that mean that they would kill some of the Africans?

Of course, it did, but didn't Old Mwanza realize that if the authorities did not kill the agitators, they (the agitators) would kill innocent white people and perhaps innocent Africans, good Africans as well, such as Old Mwanza himself? Oh, was that the problem. The assurance gave him a real sense of security. Yes, people like Old Mwanza and himself, Mr. Parker, had to protect themselves (with the aid of the authorities) against the agitators who were nightly preparing to kill them.

In his bed that night, Old Mwanza trembled in indescribable terror. It hurt his atrophying limbs to know that death—his, Mr. Parker's or his children's—was in the air, that it could visit any of them now. People who walked innocently during the day, even the cook and the nanny, were plotting to kill, or had someone else plotting to kill them. There was a war on. It was nothing like the terrible business in Malaya, but it was there.

The next morning, Old Mwanza sought out the cook. They rarely spoke, the cook believing that his status precluded any obligation to speak politely to the gardener and the nanny. He was a thin, mustachioed young man who kept himself scrupulously clean, in a strange narcissistic way. The smell of an anti-B.O. soap floated above him like an invisible halo. He took a bath two times a day, forcing his naturally slovenly wife to do the same. Old Mwanza had long wondered why he suspected that the man's fastidious care of his body explained more easily than any witchcraft the couple's childlessness.

The kitchen window was high above the ground. Old Mwanza walked slowly from his garden and stood some distance from the window, speaking loudly and looking up at the cook, who was busy rinsing something in the sink.

"What do you make of all this wild talk in the townships?"

"What wild talk, old one?" he asked crossly.

"About what they are going to do to the white people, like Mr. Parker and his family?"

"Oh, that." The Oracle in him, flattered, opened up with haughty condescension. "It is much stupid talk. It is these people, who think they are educated. They want to chase away the white people. I laugh at them. No, I spit on them."

"So you think they are wild too?"

"Of course, they are wild." He leaned toward the window and spoke in a conspiratorial tone. "Can you imagine anyone being cleverer than the white man, than Mr. Parker?"

"I am happy that you think it is all wild talk."

"It is wild talk. You know, it is the hyenas, making all that noise when they cannot fight." They laughed. Old Mwanza walked back to his kingdom, his crooked step firm and confident.

"You are my children. I have always taught you the right way to behave. I want to teach you again today."

The two boys, casting furtive glances at the door, listened. Their eyes were impatient, darting from the door to the old man, from the uneven floor to the corrugated iron roof and back to the old man. Old Mwanza spoke with paternal authority and the assurance of one who is conscious of the infallibility of his advance. He sat in the one chair in the room and they sat cross-legged on the floor. They had arrived after he had retired. He had not heard their footsteps or any sound. He had not even heard the gate opening and wondered how they could come into the yard without alerting the deadly, silent basenji. They could only have been allowed in by Mr. Parker himself. After all, they were his children.

"This foolishness must stop. I told your sister. It is impossible for me to return home. I am too old. There is nothing for me there. Mr. Parker is not an evil man. All white people are not evil. What do you know about evil?"

Obadiah spoke. He was only slightly taller than his brother, though they appeared to be identical twins. They were dressed in uniformly threadbare nondescript clothes and the odor of stale sweat filled the room.

"Father, if Mr. Parker were not here, what would you do?" he asked nonchalantly, already preparing his follow-up question.

"Well . . . I . . . would . . . what do you mean, if Mr. Parker were not here?"

"What he means is, if we are able to arrange for Mr. Parker's removal, would you go home, even to confront strangers?" Jeremiah spoke with the same sangfroid.

Old Mwanza laughed, his spirit buoyed by Mr. Parker's assurances.

"I have heard the wild talk in the townships. It is like hyenas. Just loud talk. Your people think you are cleverer than the white people? Ha ha ha ha! You wait. They are preparing to deal with you. They have guns that spit smoke and fire."

"We know all about that, Father. We are also prepared. The point is, would you like us to remove Mr. Parker so that you can go home?"

"Now listen. Go back to the townships and talk to your sister. She knows these things. More than you do. She will advise you. Stop all the nonsense."

"Father," Obadiah said as they stood up languidly, their eyes still searching the room, catlike, "she is with us. Her husband is helping us. She told us to urge you to leave. She said she could not say so to you herself."

Old Mwanza wept when they had gone. Again, he saw his Truth being soiled, abused, dirtied, and muddied. He walked silently into his garden, enveloped in a stygian darkness of uncertainty. He spoke to the vegetables, and discovered with shame that no one, not his daughter, not his sons, not his vegetables, listened to him anymore. In the far-off distance, he heard raucous, derisive laughter. He walked back to his house, his aching shoulders hunched, his head bowed, his mouth slack. People who appeared vaguely familiar seemed to be laughing at him.

In the night, he heard little that he could later associate with the bloody violence to which he was to be introduced. It was three days after his sons' visit, Old Mwanza could not reconcile himself to the truth, which was that his Truth had been mutilated and trampled underfoot by creepy, crawling monsters who said they were his progeny and bore no resemblance to him. He gazed for long minutes at Mr. Parker, even as he spoke while they strolled leisurely in his garden. He had forgotten his tragic toothlessness. Mr. Parker was a pitiable man. All the truth that Old Mwanza had gleaned from him, which Old Mwanza had embraced as universal truth, was being challenged. Old Mwanza tried to cling to his belief in Mr. Parker's invincibility.

Indeed, until the very last moment, until that apocalyptic moment, when his eyes saw what had to be seen, he still retained a residual faith in the power of Mr. Parker, in his cleverness and the cleverness of his race.

Absently, Old Mwanza wondered once more how the boys had neutralized the great basenji. He had felt the sleep creeping slowly upon him, like a thief for he had not wanted to sleep, being possessed of a presentiment once more.

They came to the door of his house, called him out in whispers and shepherded him to the main house respectfully, two sons taking their doubting father to a scene that would furnish incontrovertible testimony of their maturity.

The three children and Mrs. Parker were tied with pieces of torn bedsheets. They were tied so tightly that a uniform dull and deadly purpleness was spreading slowly up to their faces, as the flow of blood appeared to be slowly down. They were all on the huge four-poster double bed with the white eiderdown. They stared with long-glazed eyes at Mr. Parker who was on the carpet. Old Mwanza saw Mr. Parker's head split neatly in half, the short, sharp-bladed ax up to its hilt in the crown of his head. Mr. Parker was in his white tennis shorts. He was on his back and stared with blank, terrified, unbelieving eyes at the ceiling.

Old Mwanza looked from the inert body to his sons. He screamed a meaningless scream. He was screaming incoherently at his sons. Then he started to scream his wife's name. There was terror, disbelief and supplication in the voice. It was the mendicant wail of a recalcitrant child, begging its mother for forgiveness.

"You will return home now?" Jeremiah did not boast. He spoke with emotion.

"No! No! No! What about the garden? What about the garden? Will you give me a garden?"

He rushed at them, his fingers talons, tearing at their faces, wanting to obliterate their existence, as he had brought it into being.

They grabbed him easily and led him out of the house.

As they approached the gate, the old man's meager belongings fashioned into a crude bundle on the shoulders of Obadiah, powerful searchlights lit up the house and the whole yard. The basenji stood victoriously in front of the lights. They heard the familiar, commandingly insolent voice of a white police officer: "*Wena, funa ifa? Kabanga wena kumbuka tina dhlala kupela? Tina kona lo makulu gun. Makulu steleki.*"*

* "You want to die? Perhaps you think we are just playing? We have very big guns. Very big."

There was a white man in pajamas whom Old Mwanza recognized as the man who lived at the next house. His eyes returned to the barkless dog, which Mrs. Parker had said was incredibly intelligent.

His two sons released him and retreated into the darkness behind them. He heard the roar of the powerful guns. He hit the ground as they had taught him in Malaya. He thought of the garden.

He wondered if the white police officer would shoot a man who spoke to vegetables in the dead of night.

Abdulrazak Gurnah was born in 1948 in Zanzibar. His novel *Paradise* was short-listed for both the Booker and the Whitbread Prizes in 1994. He is also the author of *Memory of Departure, Pilgrims Way, Dottie, Admiring Silence,* and *By the Sea.* He teaches at the University of Kent in England.

Bossy

A long time ago that was, sitting on the barnacled pier, swinging our legs through the air. Princess Margaret pier in the long shadow of the afternoon, watching the sea beneath us frothing with arms and legs and flashing teeth. A long story I told him, urbane and wise, a fabric of lies. I told him of a man who stood by the sea and peed, and how his pee was continuous without end. Like the tongue of infinite length, all coiled up in a man's insides. On Princess Margaret pier we watched Ferej eat up the water like a shark. The water choppy and bright on the day he won the schools championship. On Princess Margaret pier after a day in 1956 when the good princess laid foot on our humble land. On the other side were four guns, riveted into the concrete and facing the sea. Ceremonial firecrackers to bid the princess welcome.

The letter had arrived that morning, a dirty scrap to shatter my self-inflicted peace. Karim's name was written clearly on the back of the air mail form, and all the remaining space was covered with handwritten HAPPY NEW YEAR wishes.

31st December 73.

Dear Haji,

(O Pilgrim to the Promised Land)

I am sitting inside our office, or to be more precise our storeroom, being entertained by the sounds of the sawing, planing, sanding and drilling machines. Together with the rhythmic tapping of hammers on nails, all this combines to form a unique masterpiece at the eleventh hour of the year. The prevailing atmosphere has nothing to do with my writing to you, but just to deliver that presently I am indentured to a cyclops by name Rahman whose cave this Wood-Works is. I guess you will be surprised to hear that I am also concubined to his daughter.

You may also be surprised to hear that today I am celebrating my first "Go West Young Man" anniversary. It is only twenty miles west, but you know how big that distance really is. Exactly a year ago, on a Sunday afternoon, myself along with some other freedom lovers were preparing to act and follow that great genius, master and generator of electricity, the organizer and pilot of our expedition, Captain General Jabir Dumas (also well-known as Hamlet of ST 9 fame). Between you and me, I learned the identity of the mastermind too late to retreat, just when the sail was being hoisted in fact. But before we could wave fond good-bye to the dear homeland, forever verdant and green, we were tackled by a wandering varantia. It needed a hefty bribe to fix him. We had a hazardous journey, during which it was apparent that our Hamlet did not know southerly from a handsaw. However, we landed on a beach which turned out to be some eighty miles north of our destination. Once we'd landed, the journey was smooth and easy, and I shall remain content to say that we arrived here tired but in one piece. So much for the forced adventure.

What has been happening to you over the last year? Your silence seems to grow deeper with time. Your last letter contained only one line, and I did not even understand it. Are you still working or have you found a University place yet? Write and tell me how you are doing, buddy. I want to hear about all those females who are keeping you busy. Send me a snapshot if you can. I want to see if you have got any fatter.

I have been continuing with my studies in evening classes. It's damned hard work getting back from the mill and going straight to college. As you might guess, I am not doing very well. I have to attend every evening. I start work at seven in the morning which doesn't leave much time for studying at home. Still, nothing ventured: I have become very interested in the poetry of the French Symbolists, but as you know it's not easy to get books here. If you see anything along those lines, I would be very grateful if you would send it to me. Refund by pigeon-post. You know, I miss all those conversations we used to have. There's no one here to talk to, not seriously anyway. People just want to talk about who has been caught fiddling with govern-ment funds.

A lot of the pals from home are here now. Hassan was caught trying to escape with some Goan girls in a ngarawa. They were kept for a few days, then released, nobody knows why. Hassan somehow managed to find another way of escaping and he too is here now. The Barrister has gone to a University in Boston to do Intentional Chemistry. Don't ask me, that's what he said. I met his brother recently and he told me that our Barrister is paid a lot of dollars by the American government, who are also paying his fees. So I am thinking of applying to Uncle Sam too.

Did you have a nice Christmas? It was very quiet here except Bachu got drunk and started calling our island leader "ham-neck." Poor fellow got kicked out of his office for calling his boss a donkey. Incidentally, do you remember Amina Mare-hemu Rashid's sister? She must have been about ten when you left. She is now a prostitute. No more room. Write soon and don't forget the snap. Regards from all the pals.

Yours,
Karim.

Gleeful tally sheet of past misdeeds. A time there was . . . but we ended it all with a careless selfishness. Now a fool with a poor style can make fun of your sister. He wants me to send him books of the French Symbolists because he can't get them out there. You missed the worst, Rashid. You missed the worst, my Bossy. Your sister appears as a footnote and not a tear shed for her. You too, you and I, we would have watched while a neighbor turned beggar and sold his daughter for shark meat.

And we too would have laughed. All they taught us was how to be meek while they rode roughshod. You and I, we had something . . . In this cold and often hostile place I often think of you. It was a morning in December that I first wept for you. But by then that heartless land had turned your blood to dust.

It was a beautiful morning in December, bone dry and hot. We went to borrow a boat to go sailing because we were bored with being on holiday with nothing to do. He went one way, I went the other. He got a boat. I didn't.

—This is your captain speaking, he said, assuming command.

When he saw that I wasn't going to argue, he suggested that we go and find somebody else to go with us. At that very minute a fellow called Yunis appeared and we struggled into the outrigger and pushed off before he could come and talk to us. Yunis was nicknamed Wire because it was quite obvious that he had some wires disconnected in his head. He was harmless enough but he had allowed this idiocy of his to go to his head. A little guiltily I watched him standing on Ras Matengo looking our way. He was probably used to people running away from him.

Before I got to know Rashid well, Wire and I used to spend a lot of time together. He told me about his crazy projects and I told him about mine. He was going to build a ship and sail it himself. He possessed several manuals on shipbuilding and navigation. The people at the shipping control office knew him well and called him captain to please him. Wire never seemed to listen when you talked to him and even little children could bully him. I saw a little boy of six pee in his mouth once while he was lying in the shade of a tree. Without saying a word, Wire had stood up and left. The adults watching had laughed and patted the boy on the back. I have seen Wire walking past a group of youths lathering at the mouth with fear. But under the line of trees by the dockside, very few people bothered us. We started a club the two of us. It was really a prisoner of war camp. I was a major and he was, of course, a captain. I boasted to him about how well I was doing at school and he lied to me about his father's estates in India.

His father lived in one of the houses my father owned. It was supposed to be a shop and apparently was at one time a thriving shop. But as far as I can remember, all it ever had were boxes of rusty nails and showcases with old fishing hooks and twine. If anybody stopped to buy any-

thing from the shop, Wire's father would ask them to lend him some money. He went to the mosque every day, five times a day, and always asked somebody for money. He did the rounds of his neighbors and asked them for money. He went to the welfare office and asked them for money. I don't know if he made any money from all this, but I know he never paid my father any rent. He was thin and small and the skin on his cheeks was leathery and flabby. His jaw was sunken because he had no teeth left. Wire told me that he had large estates in India but he did not have enough money for the journey back home. Wire would build a ship and take his family back home. In the meantime his father tried to persuade him to take a job, but Wire always refused on the grounds that then he would not be able to continue with his maritime studies.

I watched him standing at the water's edge on Ras Matengo and remembered the times we used to sit under the line of trees and eat rotten fruit and stolen biscuits. My parents were worried then, they thought I too had a screw missing. I watched the idiot standing at the brink, watching us sailing to his father's estates in India.

Rashid was laughing, saying what a close call that was. In full sight of the beach Rashid began to imitate Wire's mad mannerisms. He folded his legs under him and rocked his trunk backward and forward in a steady rhythm. Wire used to do that when he was young, for hours on end. He was watching us with a smile. He smiled and waved and turned to go.

—What did you do that for? I said to Rashid.

He ignored me and peeled his shirt off. I think he was ashamed of my former friendship with Wire.

—Let's get cracking, he said, if you want to get to the island and back in time for dinner.

Bossy was in his element. I knew nothing about boats and he was an expert. He was also a champion swimmer, a national record holder over 400 meters. He was a footballer with a future and a very useful slow left-arm bowler. He was fair-skinned and handsome and wore a wristwatch with a silver strap. It was given to him by the English Club for taking seven of their wickets for twenty-three runs. To begin with I was proud to be his friend, but over the years we have got to know each other and he has stopped bossing me around.

My God, it hurts to talk like this, as if what had happened has not happened. Bossy and I walked the streets in tandem. We wrote love letters to Hakim and signed them "Carol" and watched him strut and preen and boast of a secret admirer. We even arranged meetings between him and "Carol" and always canceled them at the last minute. Bossy and I spent many dark hours by the cricket ground talking about the future and the past.

On that day in December we set off for Prison Island. The island had been used briefly by the British as a jail. There was now only the perimeter of the camp left. It was a beautiful island, with gently rolling hills and underground springs bubbling into streams. It was off bounds to visitors but nobody took any notice.

The sail on the outrigger caught the breeze and we slipped over the water with only a faint tearing sound. The sea was calm and blue under the morning light, and Rashid started to sing. He sang very badly and did it to provoke laughter more than anything else. He turned to look back toward land. I remember that because then he turned round to me and said didn't it look beautiful from here. It was calm and peaceful and the breeze was just enough to keep the boat moving and us cool. But there was something else. You felt that somehow you had got away from a suffocating room and you were now running free in an open field. The water was cool, as you might imagine water to be, not like the lukewarm water out of a tap. It was the town that looked unreal, like a quaint model in a builder's office. Out here it did not matter that the trousers did not fit, that your skin was fair or dark. There were no smelly alleys to walk through, no slippery ditches to cross, no fanatical and self-righteous elders to humiliate you. There were not even women to taunt you with their bodies beyond your reach.

—I can't just leave Mama and Amina, said Rashid.

His father had died a couple of years previously. In the Msikiti Mdogo I had stood at a distance and watched him calmly performing the duties of a bereaved son. He walked around among the mourners, accepting the condolences of neighbors and strangers with a dry face. I wished he would shed a few tears, for his own sake. It doesn't look good when a sixteen-year-old can go to his father's funeral with a dry face. Afterward he said that he did not cry because he had felt nothing inside. He had wanted to feel sad that his father had died but instead has felt only responsibility. He said his father had been cruel and distant to him ever

since he could remember. And now he was really quite relieved that the
old bastard had died. I said you can't hold that sort of thing against a
dead man. So he smiled his tolerant big brother smile at me and asked
who he should hold it against then. I told him that a dead man needed
our prayers and he said that prayers would not do that old fucker any
good at all. He said the angels of hell must be rubbing their hands at the
prospect of his arrival. I said it didn't seem right to talk about your father
like that. He said I did not understand because I had a kind father who
cared about me and took an interest in me. I said it still didn't seem right
to want him to go to hell. He was silent for a long while, then told me
that there was no hell. And here I told him that he was wrong.

—I can't just leave them on their own, he said. What will they do?
What will they do on their own?

—You won't be gone forever, I said. You'll be back to care for them.

—Mama is getting old, he said. What's the use of me going away
somewhere for five or six years to become a forestry officer only to come
back and find that my mother is dead and my sister is a whore?

—Don't bullshit, Bossy, I said.

—Okay, he said, maybe I'm not painting it too bright.

I told him that his tone reminded me of Mundhir's painting of the
Black Sea.

Ancient perambulator of a seaward elitat. Velvet blue waistcoats and
dark green metal rims waving from the steamer. Buibui on a waterborne
outing with a crowd of ragamuffins to serve the sweetmeat. Out for the
day with muscular chaperones and camera-clicking siblings.

At the island.

Improvised louver in the bush for temporary lordosis with bent knees.

Hasty dunking on the treacherously sandbanked beach to wash the
crumbs away and depart for the crumbling fortress of a bygone empire.

Bygone by name.

Over the remains Bossy read the Psalm of Life and lingered meaning-
fully over dust to dust and sang "Rule Brittania" with an emotional
choke. Lest there be any mistaking his intention, he waved two fingers
in benediction.

Deadwood remnants at the camp of the trivial offender against the
crown. At the word of command the salvo blew the cheeks apart. That
will teach the silly bugger to pay his taxes next time.

Deadwood remnants of pillar post contumelia in thatchwood alcoves in Indonesian plan.

Over the water turned to dust and a musical lyre was found by the British Archaeological Expedition to the Eastern Coast of Africa in 1929 to clinch the theory of an Indonesian invasion plan. Fragments of skull found by Blunt KCMG at the lip of the gully to suggest human life before the beginning of time. As counted from the eighth millennium B.C. Before that do not apply.

In Blunt Gully Bossy louvered again and nearly choked from the smell.

In a grotto of palms choked with weeds and wild tomatoes we discovered an underground town. We were not welcome and hurried from fierce mandibles until weakened by fatigue and hunger we collapsed under a mango tree which we immediately named Out of Town.

Pungent leaf mold and rotting humus and ripe mangoes oozing on the ground. Bossy bigboots was voted upstairs to wheedle bounty for the starving vanguard of a civilizing race. Mangoes on the ground in torpid contentment, oozing like dysentery in harmony with the flies. The captain returned with phosphates in his eyes, the bounty of a discordant piebald crow. We sank to our knees in humiliating penance and fought for mangoes with the flies. God was on our side.

Bossy bigboots brushed the dirt off his booty while hygiene rang through my skull.

I held Hunger in Abeyance and warned Bossy that by Avarice he was undone.

O Mummy in my heart, I prayed, if ever I needed you it is now. Tell me truly, O Fount of Hygiene, will I sooner die of Hunger or of Dysentery. O Wiper of my Arse, I have heeded your word through Thick and Thin generally speaking, but now a Text sirens through my guts to throw Caution to the winds. Could it be the Serpent, viper vile, that so flatters me to eat against your word? To a thicket I slunk and guilty rash gorged of the forbidden fruit. Earth trembled from her entrails but I took no thought content to eat my fill.

Faint rumble pinpoint umbilical cord, distant flutter in the heart. I knelt down waiting for the thunder to strike, and Bossy looked on with pagan amazement. Mother Hygiene restrained her hand. We left that pernicious grotto myself restrained and chastened, Bossy exultant and full.

To the waterfall.

It seemed then that there ought to be a watermill as a sign of progress and evidence of an ancient Indonesian culture. Feet in the pool at the bottom, kicking the water in adolescent delight. We drank the water at our feet, walked to the slimy rocks midpool like rising crustaceans covered with slime. We posed for a photo to show the folks back home hand on hip. This rock we named Bygone My Arse.

As we sat under that rippling fall, I gazed in wonder at what the old voyagers must have seen. In this same place an Indonesian sultan must have stood with the power of the human gaze to tear holes through nature's incomprehensible veil. Bear thee up Bossy and trust the power of thy unflinching gaze. How many men had stood where you and I then stood and saw nothing of what we saw? We were God's chosen few . . . and we sat by the brimming pool and saw world without end in our humble reflections . . . in foolish daydream pretense. The words of dead past masters ringing anvils to stiffen our self-esteem.

But soon it was time to leave the haven of that waterfall encampment for the final leg of our journey. Bossy took the lead while I patrolled the rear. As I watched him cut his way through the thicket I wondered again at the destiny that the Almighty had arranged for us. But come what may, I knew that we had done our share in fulfilling the burden of our race. Notwithstanding. Around.

We got back to the beach where we had left the outrigger and went in for a swim. At least Bossy did while I stood in water waist deep and washed the grime off my body.

—Don't show off, I shouted to him.

He waved back, turned to face the beach and came in at a sprint. I told him he was a bighead and he just grinned contentedly. We sat on the beach to dry off and he told me that he could swim back to town quicker than I could sail the boat back. He was always boasting like that and I just said yeah.

—You don't believe me? He asked.

—I believe you, Bossy, I said. Now stop mucking around.

It was getting late in the afternoon and I suggested that we make our way back. We turned the boat round and pushed it out to sea. I jumped into it first and helped Bossy in. As soon as we'd hoisted the sail, Bossy stood up, said good-bye and jumped overboard.

—See you in town, he said, grinning in the water.

I shouted to him not to be stupid but he was already on his way.

Suddenly a fierce squall filled out the sail and I struggled for the tiller. The wind was blowing the boat across the island and away from the town. I tried to turn the tiller and nearly overturned. I sat horrified while the boat sped along like a frenzied animal. I thought of lowering the sail but as soon as I let go of the tiller, the sail flapped savagely and I had to grab the tiller to steady the boat again. I cursed that bloody fool and his showing off. He would have known what to do. We were still going across the island and I could see me being blown out to sea and dying a violent death at the jaws of a shark or something. We passed the island, the boat and I, and we were still going in the wrong direction. Then just as suddenly as it had started the wind died away. I rushed for the sail and lowered it.

I could not find him. I called for him, yelled out for him, screamed for him. I tried to turn the boat round to go back to the island, but as soon as I put up the sail the wind filled it out and took me in the opposite direction. I didn't know what to do.

You left me, Bossy. You played your games once too often.

Bossy, what happened to you?

Bossy, you left me.

Bossy, what happened to you?

Bossy, I sat in that boat frightened to death that you might be in trouble but there was nothing I could do. The boat was too big for me, the water was too deep for me and you were nowhere in sight, Bossy. I called for you and all the time, Bossy, I was moving away from you. Bossy O Bossy, my Bossy, you wanted to make me feel a fool while you swam to land and I felt like a fool but where did you go, Bossy? I did all I could with that boat but I could not turn it back to you. You would have admired its power, Bossy, you would have admired its power, even while you laughed at me you would have admired its power. I tried all I could . . . What else is there to say? I turned the boat round once but I lost control and had to lower the sail. When I put it up the wind took me away from you again.

Bossy, what happened to you?

I tried all I could.

I stayed there and called out for you and called and cried out for you. Then I thought that maybe I was just being a fool, that you were safe and well and on your way back to the town. Then I thought that maybe I would never make it back to the town myself and I was angry at what you had done, Bossy, and I stood up in the boat and called you names for running off and leaving me like that.

And all the time I was sailing farther away from you.

And all the time I knew that I had lost you.

I called you a bastard for making me feel such pain. And all the time I knew that you had left me.

I made it back to land. I don't know how.

You missed the worst, Bossy.

That night I landed at Mbweni and walked the three miles to town. I did not get past the golf course. I was beaten by men with sticks and stones and they told me the day had come. They beat me and said this was the day when all Arabs would get theirs. They beat me and the blood was pouring off my face and I don't remember. I came to on the beach by the golf course. There was the sound of gunfire in the air. I did not recognize it at first, it sounded like children playing with pop guns. I struggled along the beach bleeding and weak. I got as far as Shangani before I was stopped by some wild men with *pangas* and guns and they said I was *askari* from the barracks and they wanted to shoot me. They said they had overrun the barracks and the Prime Minister had surrendered and they had beaten the fuck out of him. They said the day had come and all the Arabs would get theirs. They said the sultan had already run away to the ship off the harbor and if they were to get hold of him they would whip his *kikoi* off and fuck his arse before stuffing it full of dynamite. They said I deserved to die for being an Arab, they said anybody who was no good must be an Arab. They said where did you get those cuts if you weren't at the barracks? They said it was all over and what was I shaking like that about. They said this fellow is a weakling; shall we fuck him first before we put a bullet in him? They said we have not time and they said kill him now before the others get to the rich houses. They said if we don't hurry all the best stuff will be gone and all the good women will be ruined. They said don't waste a bullet on him, here let me show him my steel. Here they said, hold this . . . but I was too tired and weak and they beat me and urinated on me and left me lying senseless on the beach.

You missed the worst, Bossy.

T O L O L W A   M A R T I   M O L L E L

Tololwa Marti Mollel was born in Tanzania. His stories have
appeared in the Nigerian literary journal *Okike* and have been
broadcast on the BBC. He is the author of several books for
children, including *Subira Subira*, *The Princess Who Lost Her
Hair*, *Dume's Roar*, and *Rhinos for Lunch and Elephants for Supper! A Maasai Tale*.

A Night Out

For a long moment, Mika sat awkwardly, without his usual self-
assurance, despite the alcohol singing in his veins. But suddenly
feeling a fool for his unease, he cleared his throat, a trifle too loudly, and
ventured: "What's your name?"

"Mama Tumaini." (Mother of Tumaini)

She did not lift her eyes but went on busying herself with putting the
child to sleep on the mat on the floor. Quite unexpectedly, the child
began to cough, a violent, racking outburst that threw his little body
into spasms.

Mika leaned forward and felt the child. His brow was damp and hot
with fever. "Has he had treatment?" he asked, relieved to find something
neutral to say.

She replied, "There isn't an aspirin to be had at the dispensary."

Under the mother's soothing, the child Tumaini eventually lay still,
asleep, his breath rasping in and out. Mama Tumaini wrapped herself in
a *khanga*, then lit a mosquito coil. Smoke rose in spiral, spreading over
to the mat. The child stirred and sneezed. The mother, squatting, gently
patted him to sleep.

"God grant you health, my little one," she murmured, "God grant you
health and strength, good little mama's soldier!"

"Why soldier . . . ?" Mika asked, rather pointlessly.

"Yes, soldiers don't starve, or get sick." She spoke with such toneless simplicity, it could have been a child talking.

"Yes, they don't starve," Mika said, "they get killed!"

"Better to die than this nameless misery of ours," she shot back. "Better a quick clean bullet in the head than this slow dying and burning from hunger and disease!"

"Oh, soldiers starve too, you know, when there is nothing to eat . . ." Mika said hard-heartedly.

But she was sunk deep in her thoughts, she might not have heard. Then, as if to herself, alone in the room, she said, "Tumaini's father was a soldier . . ."

"Was . . . ?" went Mika.

". . . a real bull of a man he was, with none to equal him. Life was easier then, with him around. He was like a father to me, to my mother, to all of us. Now living has become such a task. You have to struggle for each small thing. Everything, everything, you have to pay for in blood, if you can find it! If Tumaini's father were around still . . ." She seemed almost on the point of bursting into tears, but she didn't.

"Why, is he dead?" Mika asked, but purely out of curiosity, his voice too loud and untouched by the woman's dull sorrow.

"I don't want to talk, don't ask me, please . . ." she pleaded, then she began to cry and said through her tears, "He went off to Uganda, to war. He might be alive, he might be dead . . ."

Mika said nothing. The child Tumaini was still again, his mother's hand on him, still patting, absently. At last Mama Tumaini straightened up and turned off the small tin lamp in the room. In the dark, she submitted herself, silently, dutifully, and professionally. But, afterward, when Mika rolled his body off her, there wasn't the usual feeling of having conquered; though fully sated, he lay back less than happy, vaguely unsettled, the labored breathing from the mat adding to his sense of deflation.

He did not know when he finally fell asleep and woke up with the panic of one who does not know where he is. It was not until he felt Mama Tumaini's body by his side that he remembered where he was.

He got out of bed and lit a cigarette. The coil had burnt out and mosquitoes buzzed angrily. He sat frowning in the dark, something troubling him, though he didn't know what. Suddenly he was aware of the silence in the room.

Mouth dry and head faintly throbbing, he got up putting out his cigarette, and went to the mat. There was no sound from the child and in the darkness he could only make out a mute, still haze, but he dared not strike a match to light the lamp. He put his hand out toward the child, and his eyes, gradually used to the dark, gazed down fascinated at the little body, lifeless and cold to his touch, its form now becoming distinct under the first stabs of dawnlight.

Mama Tumaini stirred, mumbled something, then went back to sleep. Mika waited until her breathing grew deep and even again before he sat on the bed, gingerly, and lit another cigarette, his mind busy.

Then, moving softly, he picked up his clothes from the floor where he had dumped them in a drunken pile. Dressed, he paused awhile, his eyes involuntarily seeking the child's body. No, he must leave immediately, he urged himself. It wouldn't do to get caught in the mourning and the funeral ceremonies. There was no point and it would delay him further. And anyway, he found himself thinking, what was the child to him, or the mother for that matter? Mechanically, he took out his wallet, peeled off several notes, and with no attempts to make out the amount, placed the money on a stool by the bed, and set the lamp on it as weight.

The door squeaked as he unbolted it. He paused, his heart pounding, his ear strained toward the bed.

Mama Tumaini stirred. "You're going already?" she asked him.

"Yes," he answered.

"This early?"

"You know that transport is a problem, and I have to travel today."

Come what may, he just had to get out today, and try and make it to Dar es Salaam by nightfall. For two days now, he had been sunk in this dreary little town, because petrol shortage had crippled transportation and inundated the small town with stranded travelers. It was to get away from the sweating hordes hopelessly milling all over the town in search of transport that on the previous day he had decided on an evening of entertainment and action. Drink had appealed to him as just the antidote he needed for his despondence. But the search for beer, which he preferred, was doomed from the start. There had been no beer in town, he was told at the first bar he stopped in, since the day the beer truck went crashing over a bridge leading into town. The truck was still there, a useless wreck of scrap metal. Mika did not want to believe this although he suspected it was probably the truth. He would have given his little finger for a drop of beer, and he went all over town, which didn't take long as there was little of it besides the bus stop.

A couple of depressing, dusty, narrow lanes made up the backbone of the town and beyond that was only a patchwork of slums. But he had no luck whatever in his search and had to make do with the local pombe which was in abundance. He had little stomach for local stuff, but even though he imbibed it slowly and grudgingly, gradually the booze took hold and he felt some of his despair lift. He even felt cheerful enough to join a group of local drinkers at a nearby table. But just as the evening seemed to be taking off, he suddenly found himself abandoned, his fellow drinkers having left for other bars or their homes. He had left too, and gone stumbling through the night. He would never remember how he ended up in Mama Tumaini's place, or why he decided he could not spend the night alone in his bed in the room he had rented at the lodging house. Funny, he thought aimlessly, paying for a room then sleeping elsewhere; wasteful, he concluded grimly.

Mama Tumaini was talking. "Even so," she said, "won't you wait for me to make you a cup of tea at least, to start you off?" That was the last thing he wanted, her getting up and finding out about the baby. He had to get away first. "No, no," he said quickly, "my things are at the lodging house, I have to get ready. I'll eat somewhere."

"Suit yourself," she said, turning over. Then faintly, almost inaudibly, as if it was an afterthought, she wished him a safe journey.

He thanked her, then limply, guiltily, he mumbled, "Your money . . . I've put the money . . . your money . . . on the stool." But she might have gone back to sleep or she might have had enough of him, as she made no response.

Mika opened the door and walked away in quick, tense steps, as light broke out over the rooftops and wisps of smoke from the early morning cooking lazed over the slums, announcing the start of another day.

N N A D O Z I E   F.   I N Y A M A

Nnadozie F. Inyama was born in Nigeria in 1946. He graduated
with a degree in English in 1974, and went on to England for
his Ph.D. Since 1980 he has published numerous critical essays
and short stories in a variety of literary and academic journals.
He is currently a senior lecturer in English at the University of
Nigeria.

Hot Days, Long Nights

From sunup in the great city of Akassa, a central noise would hit
the visitor's ears, no matter where he stood. In the mornings, a
person standing a mile away from the source of this noise could break it
into different notes, some rising high, others trailing off. In the afternoon, as the heat intensified and breathed down in waves on people, the
noise and the varying notes would acquire a rhythmic harmony, no
longer high, or low, but coming in waves like wind, as if some force had
finally fused the noise into one heavy, almost hypnotizing blanket of
sound.

If one walked toward the source of this noise, ever present, ever constant in its pattern of development, he would discover it to be the great
Akassa City Market, where men and spirits alike meet, and where all
things imaginable, from trinkets to human spare parts, are sold. In the
morning, when the market has many different voices, the traders would
be opening their sheds and setting up their goods. From the countryside
lorries laden with food, and bearing the hardy producers of these goods,
would be arriving, powerful engines revving as the drivers maneuvered
for parking space. The noise of the morning would also be that of market
mammies, arguing and quarreling as they bid and outbid each other for
goods. "Dis woman, why you always coming for something I price? You
no see another place?" they would ask in the central dialect of the city.

And, "Customer, if you no sell this thing to me today I no-go happy. Okay, I go put two shillings on what I price, if you no 'gree, fin' anoder person."

And the men who pull handcarts and wheelbarrows, by no means pleased by these delays, would stand and wait for the haggling to end and the goods to be lifted into their carts and barrows and wheeled, with great curses, into various parts of the market. Their impatience is understandable. The morning is boom time in Akassa market.

In the mornings, the traders, especially the mammies, usually stood out behind their wares, because the sun would not be high and hot yet, and called on everyone who passed to take a look at their goods. They knew that anyone who came to the market in the morning had not come for mere sight-seeing. The traders would watch out particularly for the up-country people. They were easy to spot. They clutched their handbags to themselves and frowned sternly at any person who so much as involuntarily rubbed his body against theirs. They knew the city to be full of notorious pickpockets and bag snatchers.

If a trader talked one such up-country man into his stall, his day had started off well. He could keep the up-country man there and fetch for him all the things he wanted to buy that morning, making great profits in the process.

There were also budding merchants, carrying penny-grouped wares, mostly groundnuts, kola nuts and akara, and screaming these goods at people, so that even if one didn't buy they had the satisfaction of giving him a little displeasure with their shrill voices.

The Tinkers Row, an all-male zone, was distinctive for many reasons. The men worked always with their shirts off because they sweated easily, even in the morning. The Tinkers Row contributed powerfully to the noise from Akassa city market as hammer went resolutely against metal. It was not often that sophisticated city wives came there. But up-country wives did, and when they concluded a deal they would step aside and dip their hands into their loincloths to extract the money from some secret receptacle, paying almost the same amount of money for the tin pot as it would have cost them to buy the shiny *English-made* ones they left somewhere else, suspecting that they would cost very much more. The men would look discreetly away when this operation was on, and wink at each other, knowing that a good sale had been made.

The Tinkers Row was never a quiet zone. Even in the midday when the sun had forced most traders to semidazed retirement into their stalls and the mammy's temper was no longer long with late shoppers, and her voice no longer cajoling, the tinkers would go at their work with unabated vigor, noise and sweat. And it was at this time that their voices rose in song. They always sang. Songs of hard work, of joy and of sorrow. Bawdy songs too, of the young madam who did her buying on the bed hidden behind the handsome trader's goods; of maids who took madam's husband. They also would sing popular record hits, adding their own touches—salt and pepper—to suit their own humors. It was not always that they sang together. But often they did, going at a currently popular song with amazing gusto and laughing together when they hit a funny line in the song.

Abafa and Akori occupied shed 4 on the Tinkers Row, and Oga Dako occupied "Double" shed 2. Dako was the master craftsman of this trade and he was the president of the A.C.M.T.U., the Akassa City Market Tinkers Union, for every trade in the market had a union for the protection of its interests. But it was not for this only that everyone called him Oga. It was more because many of the tinkers in this place had learned their trade from him, and even those who had "freed" from his tutorship would come to him from time to time to learn some new intricate way of fashioning metal, for Oga Dako had creativity flowing through his hands. He was a rather quiet man, speaking as little as possible; and even after more than twenty years in Akassa, he still didn't know most parts of the city. He never joined in the songs, but when a song was particularly sweet he would be seen nodding his head in time to it. But that was as far as his participation went.

Abafa and Akori owned one work shed together. They were the most traveled, for, according to them, they had seen most of the world together. They had spent years in such romantic and far-off places as Accra-Ghana, Santa-Isabell and Matadi-Congo and numerous other places. Ah! They had seen the world and known happy times. They came home, they told everybody, because a man couldn't spend his life wandering all over the face of the earth. And Abafa was home also because his "brother" would soon come back from "oversea." He was learning to be a doctor. The rest of the people in the Tinkers Row would see him one day "enjoying" in his brother's car and they would open their eyes wide and ask, "Is that not Abafa who was here with us yesterday?" And he would laugh and tell them "Na so the world be." And he would elaborate so much on his coming prosperity that people would lose interest and get impatient.

Abafa and Akori did not sing with the rest of the people in the Row. They sang strange songs—songs they said they learned in the strange lands they had visited and lived in. They would wait till there was a pause in the singing of their neighbors, then they would break into their own songs. Often, there was no uniformity in the words and this discord made the songs more meaningless and pointless to their neighbors. But the two would insist that they were singing the same thing, only the hearers were unfamiliar with the language. The other men tolerated these things and would at times set them off on one or other story of great doings in far-off places, real or imagined.

Oga Dako, you remember, never took any great interest in these songs, except to nod his head like a lizard from time to time. It was, therefore, a great surprise to everyone when he asked Abafa and Akori the meaning of the song they were singing at that particular moment. The interruption from Oga Dako was so unexpected that everyone stopped work for a time. Perhaps, this particular song, new and even more meaningless to the ears, had annoyed him. But no one could tell, because his face was as calm and dignified as always, and as befitted the president of a union.

"Ah . . . em . . . Oga," said Abafa, "is song we learn for Sombrerro."

"Which country dat one dey now?"

"Ah, Oga," said Akori, "Sombrerro no be country. Is a nightclub for Saida Layout. 'E dey for Akassa here." Oga Dako was inwardly irritated by the relish with which Akori gave this piece of knowledge. He seemed to be finding great joy in exposing their ignorance of Akassa, in addition to their lack of knowledge of other lands, like Matadi-Congo and Younde . . .

"If de Sombrerro, or whatever you call it dey for dis town, why you dey sing for dat kin' language? Abi dem no fit sing for we language?"

"No be so, sir," Abafa put in. "De band is not call Sombrerro. De band is from Ghana and dem name be De Seven Aces. Dem come new for de town and na for Sombrerro dem dey."

"Is dat so?" asked Dako, a very faint note of interest in his voice. This seemed to put Abafa on the path to new great tales.

"We go dere every night to enjoy and . . ."

"Every night? Abi de thing is for free?" asked Dako in disbelief.

"No be so, Oga. You pay only four shillings at de gate . . ."

"You pay four shillings every night to learn dis kin' song?"

Oga Dako was as surprised as the other men who were listening to this conversation with almost total attention. And they wondered, how could these two be going to the nightclub every night and paying four shillings? Dako knew that they were among the least productive of the tinkers, producing more noise than finished wares. It was impossible to reconcile what they earned in a week with such a rate of spending. It would be ungenerous to say that they must be stealing, so it meant that they were lying.

But Abafa, completely insensitive to the surprise he had created, went on, "Like yonder night we been drink with Honorable Alakeda. Me I drink four bottle of beer. Is good to know de big men . . ."

"What do you mean?" asked Dako. He knew Hon. Alakeda, everybody knew Hon. Alakeda, the flamboyant member of parliament for Akassa Sough. How could these two be drinking with him at a club? His face mirrored the disgust he felt at these two storytellers.

"Nothing we no go hear for dis place!" someone exclaimed. The roars of laughter that greeted this statement in no way embarrassed Akori. "Plenty big men come dere every night. All de big politician use to come wit' dem girl frien'. Dey always buy beer for all de people inside de club. You know, de politicians always campaigning for vote."

Dako and the other people were not convinced, but they let the matter be. Abafa and Akori did not seem to care whether they were believed or not, they went at their songs with greater gusto, ignoring the laughter that was all round them.

It was Saturday evening. Oga Dako was feeling very satisfied. The Ministry of Welfare had paid him one hundred and sixty pounds for a contract. This was no small money and it would justify some kind of celebration. Apart from the mandatory two pounds he would pay the Umuachara Abroadian Union, because they had helped him win the contract, the rest of the money was his. And it was no small money! But how was he to celebrate? His social engagements in all his years in Akassa ended with monthly attendances of the Abroadian Union meetings. He was unfamiliar with places of enjoyment. Then, he remembered Sombrerro. Had not Abafa and his friend said that it was a place for enjoyment? The more he thought about it the more excited he became. Yes, he would go there and "make big man" for once. Perhaps he would meet Abafa and Akori, if what they said was true, and buy beer for them. One hundred and sixty pounds was no small money, he told himself again.

Soon he was dressed, in baggy trousers, a great John White pair of shoes, a coat he had worn only once since he bought it, being mostly unable to overcome his shy nature—and topped off with a hat of the type called "London Opinion." When he emerged in the street his confidence in his appearance as a "big man" was reinforced by the numerous "good evening sirs" he received from people.

Then he remembered that he did not know the exact location of the club, except that Abafa had said that it was at the Saida Layout. He decided to take a taxi, and was soon on his way. In ten minutes he arrived. The driver charged him one shilling above the normal fare, and Dako obligingly paid. This evening he would play big.

The club was a large house. An electric sign proclaimed its name. From inside it poured forth the sharp blare of trumpets and the thunderous beat of drums and the clash of cymbals. The people inside cheered uproariously. Outside, on the paved front of the building there was a crowd of Akassa's less affluent class, made up mostly of youths who had run to the city from the villages. They did odd jobs in the daytime, pushing barrows, selling hemp, carrying loads on their heads and at night seeking out places such as this and getting into mischief. Dako knew that many of them owned no rooms to sleep in and would make themselves comfortable at night in motor parks or abandoned kiosks and cars. They knew who played what songs and knew all the dance styles. A fight was often a part of the evening's fare.

Whenever a car arrived they rushed up to identify who was in it and would emit jeers or applause, depending on how they rated the man. All this was exciting, but Dako felt frightened. His confidence sank appreciably. This was a new environment, something he did not know existed in Akassa. He hesitated, and one mind asked him to call the taxi back and go back to his house. But the car was already far away. Someone from the crowd said, "You no wan' enter again?" Dako was lucky because at this time most of them were dancing. Only a few had noticed his arrival, otherwise this hesitation, brief as it was, would have earned him very cruel taunts. They would have minutely analyzed his mode of dress and made him feel like one clothed in straw. He walked to the door of the club, as solidly as he could muster courage. He was surprised when they informed him that a ticket cost six shillings. When he asked if it was not four shillings they laughed and said, "Four shillings? Who say is four shillings? Is always six shillings." This rebuke was almost making him ashamed as he fumbled in his pocket and brought out his money. They made way for him and he escaped into the room. He thought, "Abafa and Akori lied to me."

The room was large, one end of it was full of tables, the other half was the dancing area. A few people were sitting and drinking, the tables were packed with bottles, full and empty. He wondered why the empty bottles were not carried away. The dance floor was full. The couples, either because of limited space, or out of desire, held themselves in so close a manner that Dako was shocked. These people were not just dancing, he thought, seeing for the first time another side of the city.

As he stood and watched these things, a woman walked up and put her hand around Dako's shoulder.

"Dance?" she asked. He woke with a shudder. He looked at the woman, so young, and she smiled alluringly at him. Dako disengaged her hand and said, "No, I just arrive. I wan' to sit down."

"Okay," she said, and guided him to a table. He sat down and she said, "You want drink, not so? How many bottles?" Dako looked at the other tables. Filled with bottles. It would be shameful to stay without beer on his table; it would also be shameful if he did not ask for many bottles like those who were drinking on the other tables. He did not like beer, it always tasted bitter. He always drank cola when he went to Union meetings. But he would buy the beer and let the bottles be on his table. He would open one, pour some into a cup and just let it stay there.

"Bring four," he said to her. She stretched out her hand for the money. He gave it to her and she went off, turning and twisting her buttocks. Soon she was back, the four bottles in a tray. She also had two glasses. A man was following her along, a half-filled tumbler in his hand. She sat down and the man sat on the next chair. She opened the bottles and poured into the two glasses. The man who had followed her turned to Dako.

"I been watching you since you enter. I think I see you for de conference last Thursday?" Dako said he was not at any conference. He was the president of the Metal Workers' Union. He asked the man to drink. The woman smiled. She knew the man and his ways of getting free drinks.

There was no conversation between them. Dako watched them drinking away his money. If he had not come to make "big man," he would have been very bitter. He wished that Abafa and Akori would appear now; then, at least, some people he knew would be gaining from his money. Except that they had told him all those lies and he had come here. The band, for instance, sang in his own language. And, nobody was buying any free drinks for people, except perhaps himself. Everyone went and bought his own beer and sat down and kept drinking it, offering none to his neighbor. As for the big men, the few who looked like truly "big men" were the most distant. So where were the big men who turned magic beer taps for Abafa and Akori? And now these people were drinking his beer so fast, especially the woman. He had always heard of such women, but he had never been to a place like this to see one.

Then the music ended. The dancers clapped and made their way to their seats. The response from outside was a thunderous roar. They wanted more, and any break was greeted with shouts and curses for more. Then they rushed to the windows, pressing their faces on the glass panes, eager to see what was going on inside. Dako looked at the windows. At one of the windows he could see the face of Abafa staring unmistakably at him. Then when their eyes met, Abafa dodged out. Dako was sure of whom he had seen. Should he go and bring him in? That would embarrass the poor fellow, especially after all those stories at the Tinkers Row. And if he was with Akori that would drag Dako into great expenses. Dako took another look at the window as the band struck up again. This time Abafa was not alone. He was engaged in a heated argument with Akori, glancing in his direction from time to time, perhaps trying to settle whether it was him or not. He turned his face away, ignoring them and giving them no chance to know, as they could not see his face properly now. Soon they tired of their argument and went off to the crowd of dancers outside.

Dako got up and headed straight for the door. The woman was surprised at this unexpected movement. She shouted after him, "You no wan' go wit me?" He had no ears for such things. He only wanted to escape now, after discovering Abafa and Akori. He felt slightly guilty for having known their secret.

Outside, the scene was as rowdy as when he arrived. There were circles around people "demonstrating" the "latest" dance styles, and the smell of dust and cheap cigarettes and marijuana smoke produced a suffocating pungency. There was a departing taxi and Dako gratefully hailed it. Soon he was going away to where he belonged and where he felt most at home.

Monday morning, Akassa market was shouting in its many voices and the sun gave promise of a hot day. At the Tinkers Row the men had already taken off their shirts. The lorries bellowed like cattle in a wild fury. The tinkers were again beating metal with a post-weekend vigor. From his shed Dako watched Abafa and Akori. He saw that they were giving him frequent, uneasy glances.

Finally, unable to contain himself, Abafa said, "Oga, you been go to 'Sombrerro' last night?" Dako did not expect the question. But, he was also not surprised that it was asked. Should he say "yes," and cut away the foundations of their stories? Their make-believe world? He thought about it in a quick moment and said, "No. I don' know de place at all." "You see?" Akori said in apparent triumph. "Oga no go there at all. I tell you say dat person no fit be Oga his self."

Abafa, deflated, said, "People use to resemble too much. 'E get person we see dere dat night. He look like you. But we no look proper. De dance too hot dat time." But he was reassured. Nobody knew yet where they did their dancing and drinking. They wouldn't even wait for midday to come before they were again singing unintelligible songs. Dako watched them, unable to even make himself angry or spiteful. If they chose this kind of illusion to tide them over life's hardness, why should he destroy it for them?

Sembène Ousmane was born in 1923 in Senegal. He left school
at the age of fifteen after only three years of formal education.
He joined the French Army in 1939, and accompanied them to
liberated France in 1944. After the war Ousmane became a
longshoreman in Marseilles, drawing on his experiences for his
first novel, *Le Docker Noir* (The Black Docker), published in
1956.

   Believing that film had the potential to reach a wider audience than the written word, he enrolled at the Gorki Studio in
Moscow in 1961. He returned to Senegal two years later, and
since then has produced a number of feature and short subject
films. In 1966 he directed *La Noire de*. . . . The first feature ever
produced by an African filmmaker, it won a prize at the 1967
Cannes Film Festival. Beginning with *Mandabi* (The Money
Order), Ousmane has been producing films in the Wolof language, taking his work on tours throughout Senegal. His subse-
quent films have often been temporarily banned or censored for
their political commentary. Among his books are *God's Bits of
Wood*, *The Last of the Empire*, *Niiwam* and *Taaw*.

Her Three Days

Translated by Len Ortzen

She raised her haggard face, and her faraway look ranged beyond
the muddle of roofs, some tiled, others of thatch or galvanized
iron; the wide fronds of the twin coconut palms were swaying slowly in
the breeze, and in her mind she could hear their faint rustling. Noumbe
was thinking of "her three days." Three days for her alone, when she
would have her husband Mustapha to herself . . . It was a long time since
she had felt such emotion. To have Mustapha! The thought comforted
her. She had heart trouble and still felt some pain, but she had been dos-

ing herself for the past two days, taking more medicine than was prescribed. It was a nice syrup that just slipped down, and she felt the beneficial effects at once. She blinked; her eyes were like two worn buttonholes, with lashes that were like frayed thread, in little clusters of fives and threes; the whites were the color of old ivory.

"What's the matter, Noumbe?" asked Aida, her next-door neighbor, who was sitting at the door of her room.

"Nothing," she answered, and went on cutting up the slice of raw meat, helped by her youngest daughter.

"Ah, it's your three days," exclaimed Aida, whose words held a meaning that she could not elaborate on while the little girl was present. She went on: "You're looking fine enough to prevent a holy man from saying his prayers properly!"

"Aida, be careful what you say," she protested, a little annoyed.

But it was true; Noumbe had plaited her hair and put henna on her hands and feet. And that morning she had got the children up early to give her room a thorough clean. She was not old, but one pregnancy after another—and she had five children—and her heart trouble had aged her before her time.

"Go and ask Laity to give you five francs' worth of salt and twenty francs' worth of oil," Noumbe said to the girl. "Tell him I sent you. I'll pay for them as soon as your father is here, at midday." She looked disapprovingly at the cut-up meat in the bottom of the bowl.

The child went off with the empty bottle and Noumbe got to her feet. She was thin and of average height. She went into her one-room shack, which was sparsely furnished; there was a bed with a white cover, and in one corner stood a table with pieces of china on display. The walls were covered with enlargements and photos of friends and strangers framed in passe-partout.

When she came out again she took the Moorish stove and set about lighting it.

Her daughter had returned from her errand.

"He gave them to you?" asked Noumbe.

"Yes, Mother."

A woman came across the compound to her. "Noumbe, I can see that you're preparing a delicious dish."

"Yes," she replied. "It's my three days. I want to revive the feasts of the old days, so that his palate will retain the taste of the dish for many moons, and he'll forget the cooking of his other wives."

"Ah-ha! So that his palate is eager for dishes to come," said the woman, who was having a good look at the ingredients.

"I'm feeling in good form," said Noumbe, with some pride in her voice. She grasped the woman's hand and passed it over her loins.

"*Thieh, souya dome!* I hope you can say the same tomorrow morning . . ."

The woman clapped her hands; as if it were a signal of an invitation, other women came across, one with a metal jar, another with a saucepan, which they beat while the woman sang:

Sope dousa rafetail,
Sopa nala dousa rafetail
Sa yahi n'diguela.
(Worship of you is not for your beauty,
I worship you not for your beauty
But for your backbone.)

In a few moments, they improvised a wild dance to this chorus. At the end, panting and perspiring, they burst out laughing. Then one of them stepped into Noumbe's room and called the others.

"Let's take away the bed! Because tonight they'll wreck it!"

"She's right. Tomorrow this room will be . . ."

Each woman contributed an earthy comment which set them all laughing hilariously. Then they remembered they had work to do, and brought their amusement to an end; each went back to her family occupations.

Noumbe had joined in the laughter, she knew this boisterous "ragging" was the custom in the compound. No one escaped it. Besides, she was an exceptional case, as they all knew. She had a heart condition and her husband had quite openly neglected her. Mustapha had not been to see her for a fortnight. All this time she had been hoping that he would come, if only for a moment. When she went to the clinic for mothers and children she compelled her youngest daughter to stay at home, so that—thus did her mind work—if her husband turned up the child could detain him until she returned. She ought to have gone to the clinic again this day, but she had spent what little money she possessed on preparing for Mustapha. She did not want her husband to esteem her less than his other wives, or to think her meaner. She did not neglect her duty as a mother, but her wifely duty came first—at certain times.

She imagined what the next three days would be like; already her "three days" filled her whole horizon. She forgot her illness and her baby's ailments. She had thought about these three days in a thousand different ways. Mustapha would not leave before the Monday morning. In her mind she could see Mustapha and his henchmen crowding into her room, and could hear their suggestive jokes. "If she had been a perfect wife . . ." She laughed to herself. "Why shouldn't it always be like that for every woman—to have a husband of one's own?" She wondered why not.

The morning passed at its usual pace, the shadows of the coconut palms and the people growing steadily shorter. As midday approached, the housewives busied themselves with the meal. In the compound each one stood near her door, ready to welcome her man. The kids were playing around, and their mothers' calls to them crossed in the air. Noumbe gave her children a quick meal and sent them out again. She sat waiting for Mustapha to arrive at any moment . . . he wouldn't be much longer now.

An hour passed, and the men began going back to work. Soon the compound was empty of the male element; the women, after a long siesta, joined one another under the coconut palms and the sounds of their gossiping gradually increased.

Noumbe, weary of waiting, had finally given up keeping a lookout. Dressed in her mauve velvet, she had been on the watch since before midday. She had eaten no solid food, consoling herself with the thought that Mustapha would appear at any moment. Now she fought back the pangs of hunger by telling herself that in the past Mustapha had a habit of arriving late. In those days, this lateness was pleasant. Without admitting it to herself, those moments (which had hung terribly heavy) had been very sweet; they prolonged the sensual pleasure of anticipation. Although those minutes had been sometimes shot through with doubts and fears (often, very often, the thought of her coming disgrace had assailed her; for Mustapha, who had taken two wives before her, had just married another), they had not been too hard to bear. She realized that those demanding minutes were the price she had to pay for Mustapha's presence. Then she began to reckon up the score, in small ways, against the *veudieux*, the other wives. One washed his *boubous* when it was another wife's turn, or kept him long into the night; another sometimes held him in her embrace a whole day, knowing quite well that she was preventing Mustapha from carrying out his marital duty elsewhere.

She sulked as she waited; Mustapha had not been near her for a fortnight. All these bitter thoughts brought her up against reality: four months ago Mustapha had married a younger woman. This sudden realization of the facts sent a pain to her heart, a pain of anguish. The additional pain did not prevent her heart from functioning normally, rather it was like a sick person whose sleep banishes pain but who once awake again finds his suffering is as bad as ever, and pays for the relief by a redoubling of pain.

She took three spoonfuls of her medicine instead of the two prescribed, and felt a little better in herself.

She called her youngest daughter. "Tell Mactar I want him."

The girl ran off and soon returned with her eldest brother.

"Go and fetch your father," Noumbe told him.

"Where, Mother?"

"Where? Oh, on the main square or at one of your other mothers'."

"But I've been to the main square already, and he wasn't there."

"Well, go and have another look. Perhaps he's there now."

The boy looked up at his mother, then dropped his head again and reluctantly turned to go.

"When your father has finished eating, I'll give you what's left. It's meat. Now be quick, Mactar."

It was scorching hot and the clouds were riding high. Mactar was back after an hour. He had not found his father. Noumbe went and joined the group of women. They were chattering about this and that; one of them asked (just for the sake of asking), "Noumbe, has your uncle (darling) arrived?" "Not yet," she replied, then hastened to add, "Oh, he won't be long now. He knows it's my three days." She deliberately changed the conversation in order to avoid a long discussion about the other three wives. But all the time she was longing to go and find

Mustapha. She was being robbed of her three days. And the other wives knew it. Her hours alone with Mustapha were being snatched from her. The thought of his being with one of the other wives, who was feeding him and opening his waistcloth when she ought to be doing all that, who was enjoying those hours which were hers by right, so numbed Noumbe that it was impossible for her to react. The idea that Mustapha might have been admitted to hospital or taken to a police station never entered her head.

She knew how to make tasty little dishes for Mustapha which cost him nothing. She never asked him for money. Indeed, hadn't she got herself into debt so that he would be more comfortable and have better meals at her place? And in the past, when Mustapha sometimes arrived unexpectedly—this was soon after he had married her—hadn't she hastened to make succulent dishes for him? All her friends knew this.

A comforting thought coursed through her and sent these aggressive and vindictive reflections to sleep. She told herself that Mustapha was bound to come to her this evening. The certainty of his presence stripped her mind of the too cruel thought that the time of her disfavor was approaching; this thought had been as much a burden to her as a heavy weight dragging a drowning man to the bottom. When all the bad, unfavorable thoughts besetting her had been dispersed, like piles of rubbish on wasteland swept by a flood, the future seemed brighter, and she joined in the conversation of the women with childish enthusiasm, unable to hide her pleasure and her hopes. It was like something in a parcel; questioning eyes wondered what was inside, but she alone knew and enjoyed the secret, drawing an agreeable strength from it. She took an active part in the talking and brought her wit into play. All this vivacity sprang from the joyful conviction that Mustapha would arrive this evening very hungry and be hers alone.

In the far distance, high above the treetops, a long trail of dark gray clouds tinged with red was hiding the sun. The time for the *tacousane*, the afternoon prayer, was drawing near. One by one, the women withdrew to their rooms, and the shadows of the trees grew longer, wider and darker.

Night fell; a dark, starry night.

Noumbe cooked some rice for the children. They clamored in vain for some of the meat. Noumbe was stern and unyielding: "The meat is for your father. He didn't eat at midday." When she had fed the children, she washed herself again to get rid of the smell of cooking and touched up her toilette, rubbing oil on her hands, feet and legs to make the henna more brilliant. She intended to remain by her door, and sat down on the bench; the incense smelt strongly, filling the whole room. She was facing the entrance to the compound and could see the other women's husbands coming in.

But for her there was no one.

She began to feel tired again. Her heart was troubling her, and she had a fit of coughing. Her inside seemed to be on fire. Knowing that she would not be going to the dispensary during her "three days," in order to economize, she went and got some wood ash which she mixed with water and drank. It did not taste very nice, but it would make the medicine last longer, and the drink checked and soothed the burning within her for a while. She was tormenting herself with the thoughts passing through her mind. Where can he be? With the first wife? No, she's quite old. The second then? Everyone knew that she was out of favor with Mustapha. The third wife was herself. So he must be with the fourth. There were puckers of uncertainty and doubt in the answers she gave herself. She kept putting back the time to go to bed, like a lover who does not give up waiting when the time of the rendezvous is long past, but with an absurd and stupid hope waits still longer, self-torture and the heavy minutes chaining him to the spot. At each step Noumbe took, she stopped and mentally explored the town, prying into each house inhabited by one of the other wives. Eventually she went indoors.

So that she would not be caught unawares by Mustapha nor lose the advantages which her makeup and good clothes gave her, she lay down on the bed fully dressed and alert. She had turned down the lamp as far as possible, so the room was dimly lit. But she fell asleep despite exerting great strength of mind to remain awake and saying repeatedly to herself, "I shall wait for him." To make sure that she would be standing there expectantly when he crossed the threshold, she had bolted the door. Thus she would be the devoted wife, always ready to serve her husband, having got up once and appearing as elegant as if it were broad daylight. She had even thought of making a gesture as she stood there, of passing

her hands casually over her hips so that Mustapha would hear the clink-
ing of the beads she had strung round her waist and be incited to look at
her from head to foot.

Morning came, but there was no Mustapha.

When the children awoke they asked if their father had come. The
oldest of them, Mactar, a promising lad, was quick to spot that his
mother had not made the bed, that the bowl containing the stew was
still in the same place, by a dish of rice, and the loaf of bread on the table
was untouched. The children got a taste of their mother's anger. The
youngest, Amadou, took a long time over dressing. Noumbe hurried
them up and sent the youngest girl to Laity's to buy five francs' worth of
ground coffee. The children's breakfast was warmed-up rice with a meager sprinkling of gravy from the previous day's stew. Then she gave them
their wings, as the saying goes, letting them all out except the youngest
daughter. Noumbe inspected the bottle of medicine and saw that she
had taken a lot of it; there were only three spoonfuls left. She gave herself half a spoonful and made up for the rest with her mixture of ashes
and water. After that she felt calmer.

"Why, Noumbe, you must have got up bright and early this morning,
to be so dressed up. Are you going off on a long journey?"

It was Aida, her next-door neighbor, who was surprised to see her
dressed in such a manner, especially for a woman who was having "her
three days." Then Aida realized what had happened and tried to rectify
her mistake.

"Oh, I see he hasn't come yet. They're all the same, these men!"

"He'll be here this morning, Aida." Noumbe bridled, ready to defend
her man. But it was rather her own worth she was defending, wanting to
conceal what an awful time she had spent. It had been a broken night's
sleep, listening to harmless sounds which she had taken for Mustapha's
footsteps, and this had left its mark on her already haggard face.

"I'm sure he will! I'm sure he will!" exclaimed Aida, well aware of this
comedy that all the women played in turn.

"Mustapha is such a kind man, and so noble in his attitude," added
another woman, rubbing it in.

"If he weren't, he wouldn't be my master," said Noumbe, feeling flattered by this description of Mustapha.

The news soon spread round the compound that Mustapha had slept elsewhere during Noumbe's three days. The other women pitied her. It was against all the rules for Mustapha to spend a night elsewhere. Polygamy had its laws, which should be respected. A sense of decency and common dignity restrained a wife from keeping the husband day and night when his whole person and everything connected with him belonged to another wife during "her three days." The game, however, was not without its underhand tricks that one wife played on another; for instance, to wear out the man and hand him over when he was incapable of performing his conjugal duties. When women criticized the practice of polygamy they always found that the wives were to blame, especially those who openly dared to play a dirty trick. The man was whitewashed. He was a weakling who always ended by falling into the enticing traps set for him by women. Satisfied with this conclusion, Noumbe's neighbors made common cause with her and turned to abusing Mustapha's fourth wife.

Noumbe made some coffee—she never had any herself, because of her heart. She consoled herself with the thought that Mustapha would find more things at her place. The bread had gone stale; she would buy some more when he arrived.

The hours dragged by again, long hours of waiting which became harder to bear as the day progressed. She wished she knew where he was . . . The thought obsessed her, and her eyes became glazed and searching. Every time she heard a man's voice she straightened up quickly. Her heart was paining her more and more, but the physical pain was separate from the mental one; they never came together, alternating in a way that reminded her of the acrobatic feat of a man riding two speeding horses.

At about four o'clock Noumbe was surprised to see Mustapha's second wife appear at the door. She had come to see if Mustapha was there, knowing that it was Noumbe's three days. She did not tell Noumbe the reason for her wishing to see Mustapha, despite being pressed. So Noumbe concluded that it was largely due to jealousy, and was pleased that the other wife could see how clean and tidy her room was, and what a display of fine things she had, all of which could hardly fail to make the other think that Mustapha had been (and still was) very generous to her, Noumbe. During the rambling conversation her heart thumped ominously, but she bore up and held off taking any medicine.

Noumbe remembered only too well that when she was newly married she had usurped the second wife's three days. At that time she had been the youngest wife. Mustapha had not let a day pass without coming to see her. Although not completely certain, she believed she had conceived her third child during this wife's three days. The latter's presence now and remarks that she let drop made Noumbe realize that she was no longer the favorite. This revelation, and the polite, amiable tone and her visitor's eagerness to inquire after her children's health and her own, to praise her superior choice of household utensils, her taste in clothes, the cleanliness of the room and the lingering fragrance of the incense, all this was like a stab in cold blood, a cruel reminder of the perfidy of words and the hypocrisy of rivals; and all part of the world of women. This observation did not get her anywhere, except to arouse a desire to escape from the circle of polygamy and to cause her to ask herself—it was a moment of mental aberration really—"Why do we allow ourselves to be men's playthings?"

The other wife complimented her and insisted that Noumbe's children should go and spend a few days with her own children (in this she was sincere). By accepting in principle, Noumbe was weaving her own waistcloth of hypocrisy. It was all to make the most of herself, to set tongues wagging so that she would lose none of her respectability and rank. The other wife casually added—before she forgot, as she said— that she wanted to see Mustapha, and if mischief makers told Noumbe that "their" husband had been to see her during Noumbe's three days, Noumbe shouldn't think ill of her, and she would rather have seen him here to tell him what she had to say. To save face, Noumbe dared not ask her when she had last seen Mustapha. The other would have replied with a smile, "The last morning of my three days, of course. I've only come here because it's urgent." And Noumbe would have looked embarrassed and put on an air of innocence. "No, that isn't what I meant. I just wondered if you had happened to meet him by chance."

Neither of them would have lost face. It was all that remained to them. They were not lying, to their way of thinking. Each had been desired and spoilt for a time; then the man, like a gorged vulture, had left them on one side and the venom of chagrin at having been mere playthings had entered their hearts. They quite understood, it was all quite clear to them, that they could sink no lower; so they clung to what was left to them, that is to say, to saving what dignity remained to them by false words and gaining advantages at the expense of the other. They did not indulge in this game for the sake of it. This falseness contained all that remained of the flame of dignity. No one was taken in, certainly not themselves. Each knew that the other was lying, but neither could bring herself to further humiliation, for it would be the final crushing blow.

The other wife left. Noumbe almost propelled her to the door, then stood there thoughtful for a few moments. Noumbe understood the reason for the other's visit. She had come to get her own back. Noumbe felt absolutely sure that Mustapha was with his latest wife. The visit meant in fact: "You stole those days from me because I am older than you. Now a younger woman than you is avenging me. Try as you might to make everything nice and pleasant for him, you have to toe the line with the rest of us now, you old carcass. He's slept with someone else—and he will again."

The second day passed like the first, but was more dreadful. She ate no proper food, just enough to stave off the pangs of hunger.

It was Sunday morning and all the men were at home; they nosed about in one room and another, some of them cradling their youngest in their arms, others playing with the older children. The draughts players had gathered in one place, the cardplayers in another. There was a friendly atmosphere in the compound, with bursts of happy laughter and sounds of guttural voices, while the women busied themselves with the housework.

Aida went to see Noumbe to console her, and said without much conviction, "He'll probably come today. Men always seem to have something to do at the last minute. It's Sunday today, so he'll be here."

"Aida, Mustapha doesn't work," Noumbe pointed out, hard-eyed. She gave a cough. "I've been waiting for him now for two days and nights! When it's my three days I think the least he could do is to be here—at night, anyway. I might die . . ."

"Do you want me to go and look for him?"

"No."

She had thought "yes." It was the way in which Aida had made the offer that embarrassed her. Of course she would like her to! Last night, when everyone had gone to bed, she had started out and covered quite some distance before turning back. The flame of her dignity had been fanned on the way. She did not want to abase herself still further by going to claim a man who seemed to have no desire to see her. She had lain awake until dawn, thinking it all over and telling herself that her marriage to Mustapha was at an end, that she would divorce him. But this morning there was a tiny flicker of hope in her heart: "Mustapha will come, all the same. This is my last night."

She borrowed a thousand francs from Aida, who readily lent her the money. And she followed the advice to send the children off again, to Mustapha's fourth wife.

"Tell him that I must see him at once, I'm not well!"

She hurried off to the little market nearby and bought a chicken and several other things. Her eyes were feverishly, joyfully bright as she carefully added seasoning to the dish she prepared. The appetizing smell of her cooking was wafted out to the compound and its Sunday atmosphere. She swept the room again, shut the door and windows, but the heady scent of the incense escaped through the cracks between the planks.

The children returned from their errand.

"Is he ill?" she asked them.

"No, Mother. He's going to come. We found him with some of his friends at Voulimata's (the fourth wife). He asked about you."

"And that's all he said?"

"Yes, Mother."

"Don't come indoors. Here's ten francs. Go and play somewhere else."

A delicious warm feeling spread over her. "He was going to come." Ever since Friday she had been harboring spiteful words to throw in his face. He would beat her, of course . . . But never mind. Now she found it would be useless to utter those words. Instead she would do everything possible to make up for the lost days. She was happy, much too happy to bear a grudge against him, now that she knew he was coming—he might even be on the way with his henchmen. The only means of getting her own back was to cook a big meal . . . then he would stay in bed.

She finished preparing the meal, had a bath and went on to the rest of her toilette. She did her hair again, put antimony on her lower lip, eyebrows and lashes, then dressed in a white starched blouse and a hand-woven waistcloth, and inspected her hands and feet. She was quite satisfied with her appearance.

But the waiting became prolonged.

No one in the compound spoke to her for fear of hurting her feelings. She had sat down outside the door, facing the entrance to the compound, and the other inhabitants avoided meeting her sorrowful gaze. Her tears overflowed the brim of her eyes like a swollen river its banks; she tried to hold them back, but in vain. She was eating her heart out.

The sound of a distant tom-tom was being carried on the wind. Time passed over her, like the season over monuments. Twilight came and darkness fell.

On the table were three plates in a row, one for each day.

"I've come to keep you company," declared Aida as she entered the room. Noumbe was sitting on the foot of the bed—she had fled from the silence of the others. "You mustn't get worked up about it," went on Aida. "Every woman goes through it. Of course it's not nice! But I don't think he'll be long now."

Noumbe raised a moist face and bit her lips nervously. Aida saw that she had made up her mind not to say anything.

Everything was shrouded in darkness; no light came from her room. After supper, the children had refrained from playing their noisy games.

Just when adults were beginning to feel sleepy and going to bed, into the compound walked Mustapha, escorted by two of his lieutenants. He was clad entirely in white. He greeted the people still about in an oily manner, then invited his companions into Noumbe's hut.

She had not stirred.

"Wife, where's the lamp?"

"Where you left it this morning when you went out."

"How are you?" inquired Mustapha when he had lit the lamp. He went and sat down on the bed, and motioned to the two men to take the bench.

"God be praised," Noumbe replied to his polite inquiry. Her thin face seemed relaxed and the angry lines had disappeared.

"And the children?"

"They're well, praise be to God."

"Our wife isn't very talkative this evening," put in one of the men.

"I'm quite well, though."

"Your heart isn't playing you up now?" asked Mustapha, not unkindly.

"No, it's quite steady," she answered.

"God be praised! Mustapha, we'll be off," said the man, uncomfortable at Noumbe's cold manner.

"Wait," said Mustapha, and turned to Noumbe. "Wife, are we eating tonight or tomorrow?"

"Did you leave me something when you went out this morning?"

"What? That's not the way to answer."

"No, uncle (darling). I'm just asking . . . Isn't it right?"

Mustapha realized that Noumbe was mocking him and trying to humiliate him in front of his men.

"You do like your little joke. Don't you know it's your three days?"

"Oh, uncle, I'm sorry, I'd quite forgotten. What an unworthy wife I am!" she exclaimed, looking straight at Mustapha.

"You're making fun of me!"

"Oh, uncle, I shouldn't dare! What, I? And who would help me into Paradise, if not my worthy husband? Oh, I would never poke fun at you, neither in this world nor the next."

"Anyone would think so."

"Who?" she asked.

"You might have stood up when I came in, to begin with . . ."

"Oh, uncle, forgive me. I'm out of my mind with joy at seeing you again. But whose fault is that, uncle?"

"And just what are these three plates for?" said Mustapha with annoyance.

"These three plates?" She looked at him, a malicious smile on her lips. "Nothing. Or rather, my three days. Nothing that would interest you. Is there anything here that interests you . . . uncle?"

As if moved by a common impulse, the three men stood up.

Noumbe deliberately knocked over one of the plates. "Oh, uncle, forgive me . . ." Then she broke the other two plates. Her eyes had gone red; suddenly a pain stabbed at her heart, she bent double, and as she fell to the floor gave a loud groan which roused the whole compound.

Some women came hurrying in. "What's the matter with her?"

"Nothing . . . only her heart. Look what she's done, the silly woman.

One of these days her jealousy will suffocate her. I haven't been to see her—only two days, and she cries her eyes out. Give her some ash and she'll be all right," gabbled Mustapha, and went off.

"Now these hussies have got their associations, they think they're going to run the country," said one of his men.

"Have you heard that at Bamako they passed a resolution condemning polygamy?" added the other. "Heaven preserve us from having only one wife."

"They can go out to work then," pronounced Mustapha as he left the compound.

Aida and some of the women lifted Noumbe onto the bed. She was groaning. They got her to take some of her mixture of ash and water . . .

Mohammed Berrada was born in 1938 in Morocco. Primarily known as a scholar and critic, he has translated several works of literary theory, including Roland Barthes's *Le Degrée Zero de L'Ecriture* and Mikhail Bakhtin's *Le Discours Romanesque*. He is also the author of several works of fiction, including the novels *Fugitive Light*, *The Game of Forgetting*, *A Summer Never to Be Repeated*, and *Skinning*, a collection of short stories.

A Life in Detail

Translated by Alice Copple-Tošić

It is already quite late when we wake up, we stretch in bed, our body softens. This new day promises to be like the others preceding it. We rest the back of our neck on the head of the bed; our face has a troubled look. A bleak pallor spreads most indubitably over our face. We have already taken our case to the doctor, he nodded his head as he said, "You are not the only ones to experience this . . . All of those who meditate and dream, all those who are dissatisfied, are familiar with these symptoms."

We remember that a doctor (perhaps it was this very same one) has already given this same answer to one of the friends of our friends when he complained of digestion troubles and acute gastritis.

"Is there a cure for it, Doctor?"

"I will prescribe some very effective pills, but above all, I advise optimism . . . The moment you awake in the morning, rummage through your memory in search of a funny story or an amusing event, and laugh heartily, then jump out of bed and put on whatever air comes to mind (even the most disagreeable voices are allowed)."

We decide to try out the doctor's advice and rummage through the recesses of our mind in search of a story that can make us laugh before breakfast . . . Ah . . . We have found one. It is the story of our neighbor, the foreign woman, who, although she has a car of her own, amuses herself from time to time and takes a taxi home. When she reaches the door of the building, she pretends to have forgotten her wallet at home and asks the taxi driver to wait for her while she goes to fetch the fare, then she disappears . . . and does not return. The poor man honks his horn at length, all the tenants of the building rush to their windows wondering who has brought on this situation . . . Not knowing the apartment of his passenger, the taxi driver loses hope and leaves while the hussy shakes with laughter in her room. Ha, ha, ha!!! We laugh until we cry and secretly thank our malicious neighbor, then we jump out of bed and into another new day of our summer holiday.

We linger for a long time in front of the crammed shelves of our library. Most of the books have not been read, we have always put off reading them until the appropriate moment appeared. Our hand reaches toward a volume with a red binding. The author, Mohammed Ben Abdallah Al Mouakit, lived in Marrakech forty years ago: his book is entitled *Alrihla Al Marrakchiya, Aw Mirat Al Massaoui Al Waqtiya (Sojourn in Marrakech or Mirror of Fleeting Misfortunes)* or there is *Esseif Al Massloul A la Al Muridh an Sunnat Ar-Rassoul (The Sword Hanging over the Head of Those Who Turn Away from the Traditions of the Prophet)*.

". . . Then Sheikh Abdel Hadi continued: the examiner and the examinee lived in the tenth century, thus in our own epoch, as dark as the black night, whose leaders oppress their peoples, devour their flesh and drink their blood, gobble their bones and suck the marrow. They leave people neither the world nor religion; they have monopolized the world, and distorted religion. We have seen it with our own eyes and by no means imagined . . ."

Abou Zeid asked, "God help you, does he wish to live in this place in spite of his powerlessness in the face of injustice?"

Reading brings no relief, the past seems to be the present, the present seems past, reason roars at the impossible and refuses to admit that "the sun is blind." We think that the cause of all the pain could be boredom, friendships of many years, the exploration of the depths, shrinking illusions, fading dreams, an attachment to the future, lack of interest in what is established. Let us therefore exert patience; let us live the present in detail and daily routine.

Our guest at lunch is a close relative, he is pushing sixty. He learned the Koran when he was a small child, tried all different types of professions, then finally ended up as a muezzin.* A widower who lost his wife a year ago, he chose a new fiancée from among his relatives (it is hardly fitting to be an unmarried muezzin) but preferred to postpone the marriage until he returned from his *hadj*.†

Schemers made moves during his absence, the woman found another husband and left him forsaken . . . He is still in search of a spouse . . .

"Thank God, everything is going well. We praise him at any rate. How is your health, work? All right, don't ever forget to pray for us. How is our young 'El Azri,' is he a conscientious worker? Ask him, he will tell you; as far as I am concerned, I don't think he works enough. You are wrong, my son . . . If you would only follow the example of your uncle Abder-Rahmane."

And since these words reawakened a sad memory in us, we asked, "The one who drowned?"

"Yes . . . the martyr . . . for according to the Hadith‡ those who are burned, drowned and buried alive are considered to be martyrs."

Now he addresses "El Azri" who does not seem to be much concerned since he is so used to hearing all forms of advice and instruction. "At the age of eighteen your uncle Abder-Rahmane already excelled in all the sciences."

The child interrupts him with a smile. "I'm only seventeen."

A delicate intervention proves necessary.

"Your head is as empty as a jackass's skull . . . You should listen to what you're told . . . the future is yours. You will be the one to lose out if you don't follow our advice . . . Do you think all you have to do is bend down to pick up your bread . . . You shouldn't think that the moon is made of green cheese."

El Hadj continued: "Abder-Rahmane—may his God keep his soul—excelled in all the sciences . . . his handwriting was one of the loveliest. He was employed in Dar el Makhzen, he already wore the caftan and turban when still quite young . . . He was a good swimmer, a dashing young man . . . A fakir from Sousse noticed him while visiting us, he was

* The crier who calls the faithful to prayer.
† Pilgrimage to Mecca.
‡ Traditions arising from the prophet Muhammad.

fascinated by his intelligence and the extent of his knowledge, particularly when he found out that he knew el Damiti by heart. He therefore wanted to protect him from the evil eye of humans and jinni, and transcribed an amulet that he asked him to pin to his caftan."

To show our pretended interest, we feel it worth remarking, "And he drowned in spite of this amulet?"

"It was destiny. Returning to Sale from Rabat, he crossed the Bouregreg wadi in a small boat. Once he reached the other side, he took off his turban, made the ritual ablutions, said the midday prayer and then left. After several dozen steps, he felt like taking a swim, so he retraced his steps, undressed and entered the water . . ."

As the first time, the child interrupts with a smile. "Did they swim naked in those days?"

The question seems reasonable to us, but the situation requires a different demeanor, we shoot him a glance, clap our hands and make superhuman efforts not to burst out laughing.

"No, they had loincloths . . . That day he had forgotten his amulet in another caftan, his swimming skill was of no avail, the sea swallowed him up forever. Thus died Abder-Rahmane and we, we lose ourselves in the science of our world and that of the hereafter."

The discussion wears out before the end of the meal. We observe the man chewing carefully. What other subject could we take up? We try to remember the stories and tales that he has recited to us countless times . . . It would suffice to mention just one of them and he would launch once more into relating these tales that we have heard so many times. We could say perhaps: the people of that time were quite right to acclaim their king and chant, "Glory and fortune to Moulay Abdelaziz." He would then recount the maneuvers and battles led by Sultan Moulay Abdelaziz against certain tribes and, threading his way through the story, would reach the era of Bouhmara and the arrival of the French . . . But this subject is very dull and we prefer to question him about his private life. What does he do after the call to prayer? He has stopped smoking "kif" since his return from Mecca, he has still not found a new wife, so how does he spend his time? Does he imagine he is dead? His relations with his surroundings seem very limited, he receives information, swears to keep it a secret and concludes by saying, "God puts to the test and chooses."

The child eats heartily, perhaps he is not thinking about anything? He is interested in his surroundings in a purely mechanical manner. He has tasted the pleasure of smoking in secret, of running after the neighbor girls, he is crazy about soccer . . . He expresses the desire to go to Europe during his summer vacation, even on foot (making the pilgrimage all the more meritorious). And us? We think of the sheikh and the child, we try to guess what could be on their minds. We ask ourselves about their relations with their environs, but afterward? The siesta. And then? Take a stroll and breathe in a bit of fresh air, what next? Telephone a friend, meet her, chat, get fired up, let our instincts break loose, then find boredom once more and take leave of each other. Join friends, talk about everything, criticize, approve, denounce, then see our enthusiasm decline before the magnitude of our powerlessness. We rush into the street once more. Feel desire mounting once again through the bouncing of the round and curved parts of women's bodies. We asked our married friends each time if their wives replaced all those of their sex? The answer was invariably: Not at all, no one desires other men's wives more than married men, even when they claim to love their spouses. We then tried to understand and rationalize these facts: there is not a single doubt that this is due to mingling, exciting advertising, makeup, high heels and . . . what else?

We were saying this to him but he interrupted severely: "Rubbish . . . With love we can overcome the obsession with sex."

"Then where is love?"

"Ah . . . so you are one of these pessimists . . . I will tell you about my case." (Obviously the story is completely innocuous . . . They wanted to marry her to an old man, she threatened suicide, they swore to love each other until death . . . etc.).

Fine, he will never understand us, there is no use in citing Freud: "I am beginning to believe that there are four partners in every sexual act."

We exaggerate, the moment subdues us and imprisons us. Obsession with sex is not all that threatens us and fascinates us. There is also obsession with crime, with suicide, with alcohol, and with revolution. The other forms of obsession are less attractive because they do not destroy routine. And writing?

He is quiet, does not offer any reply and starts to finger his chaplet. Abdel-basset says to him, "Master, we have always known you to be endowed with a quick flair to disarm the most brilliant orators and dazzle the best minds . . . You stimulate us morning and evening with your lectures that captivate the heart and refresh the soul . . . what is therefore the matter?"

In the evening, the same sluggishness overcomes us, but the melancholy is still too somber to chase it away, we think of administering this memorable medical prescription, but we hesitate, the doctor has indicated quite precisely that it is to be taken in the morning and not the evening . . . We are going to take a stroll through the streets, scrutinize the faces, perhaps it is there that we will discover the remedy. We walk for a long time: the cafés are full, bottles of beer are emptied in the blink of an eye, laughter rises, the tapping of the flippers is continuous . . . nonetheless, our melancholy is clinging. Cars pass, the buses are packed and slow, the movie theaters display posters of their heroes . . .

It seems to us that all those around us are fleeing, we are tempted to stop them and shout in their faces, "You are running away," but the idea seems idiotic and unfounded. We therefore wonder: Is there no way out? We return home to write down this life that we are living by well-rationed portions.

Ali Deb was born in 1941 in Tunisia. In addition to a collection of poems, he has published several short stories and plays, many of which have been broadcast on Tunisian radio. He works as a high school teacher and is a member of the board of directors of the Tunisian Writers' Union.

The Three-Piece Suit

Translated by Alice Copple-Tošić

This month, for the first time, the household budget has been met and . . . even left me a little supplement . . . I don't know why, I went against my habits and bought myself an elegant three-piece suit, tailored in a magnificent English fabric of lovely sky-blue—the color of sunlit days—in which the tailor's skill was displayed so well that one would say we were born together, one for the other . . . The buttons sparkling in the sun were like stars on the shoulder of a sailor swollen with courage. The spinning sensation that its price aroused did not last long, and I said to myself as I straightened my head and shoulders, "Tell me how you dress, and I'll say who you are."

I made my way without hesitation toward the largest café on the main street. As expected, my friends made a fuss over me, touching, feeling and dusting me with their fingers. I strutted, proud as a peacock, then I took out a package of paper handkerchiefs and cigarettes and offered them to eager hands. "Usually I don't smoke, but they are truly fine, what a pleasure!" exclaimed one of them.

I murmured: "Ordinary cigarettes are infested with tar and nicotine."

Naturally I paid for the drinks and left a fat tip for the waiter who gave me his best compliments. There was glib talk of the rise in prices and the high cost of living.

At this point one of them murmured into my ear, "What kind of shirt and tie are these?" Then he led me to a shop that was celebrated for the high quality of its merchandise and for its voraciousness. His good taste and affability were such that my pockets were emptied and it was only with great difficulty that I managed to pay the ticket home.

For one whole week, I concentrated on straightening out my accounts and forced myself to exactitude and strict austerity. I was thus obliged to forgo luxury and excess such as eggs and butter. I also reduced by half my consumption of meat and cigarettes and pretended to lack the time for entertainment with my friends . . . I managed somehow or other to put my accounts back in order, while still not forgetting to trim my mustache, smooth my face with a close shave, and spray myself with aftershave.

There I was, strolling about, puffed up with pride, on the main street, taking care to pass by the women's soaks since their tastes are more refined and assured and their eyes are sharper . . . I heard as though a murmur in my ear, "The flaw is in your shoes." I turned and noticed a light blush on the face of a young girl. I counted the age of my shoes on my fingers. Goodness, how quickly the months had flown by. "Only a pair of shoes stands between me and perfection!" I chose a pair on Liberty Avenue, then returned to my friends. They directed their entire repertoire of flattering expressions my way and I was literally overcome by a delicious peace that was only troubled by the price of a cup of coffee. I almost proposed another spot in which to drink it but gave up, this café was better suited to my attire. My only recourse was a long but discreet sigh.

On the way home, the weather took a sudden turn and fine little drops fell on my oh-so-proud-nose. "Abominable sky," and I bought an umbrella that saved me, in spite of its poor quality.

On Barcelona Square, I was accosted by young beggars. Their sullen faces, extended hands and supplications surrounded me to the point of suffocation. There were three of them, I handed fifty millimes to each one and, rid of their harassment, I gave a sigh of relief, but their leader came after me, repeating, "You're worth much more," showing the coin to all the passersby. I bought his silence for double the amount . . .

I walked prudently, taking the sidewalk, avoiding the dust on carts and jostling pedestrians. I fled the crowd and buses and never forgot to polish my shoes and iron my shirts carefully, often using the fire to dry them faster. The January cold suddenly came to mind and I anticipated the need to buy a coat and change my suit when winter had passed. Should I hold out my hand for a loan or draw directly from the company's cash box? Finally, I got on the train. I breathed in the fetid breath of the passengers. I leaned on the armrest of a seat; a lady grumbled and said to her neighbor, "They're even contesting our second-class seats." So I slipped into the first class where a seat and a supplementary fee of some consequence awaited me. I went into the local supermarket. It had been quite some time since I had taken care of my shopping. Upon seeing me, a neighbor literally shrieked for joy, shook my hand and then, raising his flat voice, asked me for a loan that I would have naturally refused him if I had not been wearing my suit.

I bought several items and held them in my arms against my chest. The salesgirl greeted me and unhooked a suitable basket. I had no other alternative but to deposit my purchases inside, and since the proper sort of people, my sort, buy without consideration for the price, I did not even bother to look at the cash register total. When I had returned home, my blood pressure was at its peak, my head was literally boiling, my tongue was twisted and my chest heaving. I no longer saw where I walked or where I threw my jacket, vest and trousers. I clenched my teeth and gritted them as I cursed the traps of this century and the folly of fools. I finally went back to being my old self and since that day no one has troubled me anymore.

Mohammed Moulessehoul was born in 1955 in Algeria. He served as an officer in the Algerian army for many years, writing and publishing on the side. When the military ordered that all manuscripts be vetted by their censors, he adopted a woman's pseudonym, Yasmina Khadra. He went on to publish two more works, *The Caliphs of the Apocalypse* and *The Way Things Are*, both detailing the mounting political crisis in his country. With the help of the International Parliament of Writers, he moved to France in 2000. His other books include *The Writer, In the Name of God*, and *L'Imposture des Mots* (The Deception of Words), a short book in which he describes what happened when Yasmina Khadra revealed his identity.

The Wicked Tongue

Translated by Christina Zorić

She resembled all the women in the village.

She had neither a third eye between her brows, nor four arms. Not beautiful and not ugly, men said she was all right. In the middle of a crowd, she attracted no more attention than the neighboring women. If you didn't know her, you would never doubt her.

She seemed modest and clean. Her physiognomy gave no hint of any dark secret and betrayed nothing spiteful. She sported an affable smile that put the timid at ease.

In the beginning, she was respected.

Women called her: "Sister Mimouna."

Children: "Auntie."

Men greeted her courteously when she passed their way.

She even served as a model of behavior in her day. Husbands never stopped holding her up as an example to their wives: "You disgrace your home, can't you behave decently, like your seida Mimouna? Why do you always have to drive me out of my mind? Oh God, why have you given me this unbearable creature for my lifelong companion, when all she knows how to do is vex and exasperate me? What intolerable thing have I done to be condemned to drag around such a woman, like a convict his ball and chain?"

Mimouna took meticulous care of herself. She washed every day, wore clean dresses and could not bear the slightest stain on her veil. Her gestures, her words, her comportment, bespoke a great sense of measure, a sterling quality of reserve.

Women envied her.

Men envied her husband.

But all that was before.

Now, things had taken a different turn. Mimouna had become a different woman. People avoided her. They accorded her not even a passing glance. At the fountain, the women would move away when she approached, returning to fill their jugs only after she had departed.

Everywhere she encountered nothing but contempt and animosity.

At the *djemaa*, men fell silent when she passed by, averting their eyes. Some, unable to contain their disgust, railed against her.

"Scum!"

"If I were her, I'd go and hide my shame at the bottom of a grave."

"She'd poison the earth with her sins."

"Why don't they run her out of town? She'll finish by uprooting our trees, drying up our rivers, making our fields crack open, dispersing our neighbors and emptying our village. Our walls tremble with disgust when she touches them. Our most intrepid dogs flee from her. Even the sun in our sky is niggardly and seems to swerve widely to avoid our houses."

Mimouna hid her face behind her veil. Every word made her stumble, every sentence wrenched her heart. She fled, only to find the same hatred everywhere.

What had happened? What disgrace followed this woman?

Mimouna was the tenth child of a humble family numbering fifteen. Nine boys and six girls. The house, while not a palace, was spacious, and the food sufficient, despite the mediocrity of its quality. The father worked for a rich *kaid* who owned two hundred head of sheep and three fields of corn.

In Hassi Taha, the seasons quietly took their meandering course. Feast days were an event. Charlatans found nourishment among these small people until their next customers. Sometimes, a troubadour, surrounded by a flock of ragamuffin children, would break the monotony of the mornings, and except for the *kaid*'s occasional outbursts of rage, time passed like a slow Sunday stroll.

At the time, Mimouna was a young headstrong girl, as frisky as a gazelle. She played with girls her own age, went bathing with the most brazen and foraging with the most audacious. No one held it against her. She could also be useful. She went shopping for her mother, took care of others, collected wood for the fire, washed the dishes and, when her brothers were away, took meals to her father who worked in the distant fields.

After a few years, she succeeded, through her work and her conduct, to win over her closest neighbors.

"This little one would make a good wife for my son," some of the women murmured. Active and enterprising, wise and chaste, what else could one ask for?

Flattered, her mother smiled at the overtures made by her companions, saying: "Come, come now. She's still just a grasshopper."

Another woman would add: "My little cricket would be proud of her."

At fifteen, she was already being coveted by boys. She had only to cross her doorstep, and their eyes would be riveted on her. She was not very pretty, but her lissomeness and many other qualities were impressive. Her couscous and sweets were renowned. Moreover, she liked cleanliness and order.

Mothers homed in on her.

"Mimouna would be the joy of my house. She's an angel and my son is a lion cub. Their union would be a blessing, and their children unrivaled."

"Mimouna is capable of taming a bull. Tayeb, my nephew, is a real devil. Wine and bad company are relentlessly dragging him to bottomless depths. Your daughter could put him back on the right track."

"Sister, your virgin deserves everything because she is capable of giving everything. Give her to me and I will be more than generous. It's a happy prospect for all of you. I know lots of families that would like to be in your place. I hope you realize, my dear, the place you could hold by joining the biggest and richest family in the region: the family of the *kaid*, Othman Ben Othman. Furthermore, my son is a handsome man. He has been educated like the Roumis. He comes from the city. He still reads books as thick as this, books which talk about things that neither you nor the imam could manage to understand. I will even go so far as to say that, with his charm and his eloquence, my son has captivated Michele, Captain Desmarnes's daughter."

Some were timid, with nothing more to offer than a piece of their heart.

Others were haughty and garrulous, promising a thousand moons for one night of lies.

They were easy to recognize. The former, with their baskets of sweets and their heads bowed. The latter, with their bright scarves, little slippers, gold bracelets running up their arms and, above all, their imperial way of sizing up the poor.

The mother knew only how to listen.

She consulted the father.

He stood stunned in front of the procession passing through his house. He retreated into a corner and meditated at length. He wanted happiness for his daughter and had to consider everything before making any decision. He started by discarding the families that were too rich. He had served them all his life and knew only too well what went on behind their deceptive facades. He knew that these people were bad players: they placed too much on temporary life, the flash of gold making them forget the accounts being kept by eternity. With them, girls like Mimouna withered young and subsisted on contempt and leftovers.

He said finally: "My dear wife, we have a conscience so as to avoid the bad and seek the good. When it happens that we must choose, then we must reflect upon it. Marriage is a grave decision. It has the aftertaste of a verdict. To make a mistake would be a crime which would haunt us to our graves. If you are in agreement with me, this is what I'll tell the drunkards who see my daughter as their remedy: 'He who turns his back on the affairs of life cannot defend himself; to hide in the fog of oblivion is to risk losing one's way forever. Wine is a mirage of false promises; man can define himself only in reality. My daughter is not crazy to forgive sins or rectify wrongs. She is but a woman. And a woman is more fragile than a man . . .' I will reply to the *kaid*'s family: 'Let those who see their opulence as a magic wand know that the world can be bought, but love, never . . .' Our daughter is neither an object for sale nor a decorative piece of furniture. Boudjemaa is a simple man, a perfect Moslem. His gaze is clear and honest. He is not rich, but he is well off. His father is the imam, the renown of his faith graces every mosque. His mother is kindness itself; for her honesty has the magnitude of miracles . . . Stand up, my wife. Go see your daughter and speak to her of Boudjemaa. She will know how to understand you better than she would me."

The ululating shook the terrace.

The knife gleamed on the stone before slitting the throats of seven sheep.

The guests invaded the main house and its outbuildings.

The *ghaita* wailed and the drummers beat in rhythm.

When the bride appeared, decked out in her prettiest dress, cries of admiration rang out. Supported by her mother, who was crimson with pride, Mimouna walked slowly, her eyes lowered.

All the women sang:

Belle, belle is my gazelle
With the light of day on her cheeks,
The sparkle of the moon in each tooth.
Belle, belle is my gazelle
She is the jewel of all women
And the mad dream of all men.

Outside, the men thronged around the dishes laden with couscous, grapes, and pieces of meat. They ate, laughing. One song followed another, the crowd applauded until the palms of their hands were raw. The *berrah*, dressed with finesse and imagination, surpassed himself with taunts and scathing gibes at the expense of his audience.

On an esplanade, splendid horsemen performed a fantasia. They could be seen urging on their swift mounts in a cloud of dust, their burnooses flying in the wind of the race. The loud shot was answered by the powerful ululation of the women perched on the terraces.

Sid er-Jem did not flag. He deserved his praiseworthy nickname "The

Wind." He blew into his immense *ghaita*, the way the storm blows on the islands. He moved his head to the beat, pretending not to notice the admiration of the listeners. Beads of sweat formed on his protruding forehead, his eyes bulged with the effort and his chubby face was afire, threatening to explode when his cheeks puffed up.

He was seated on two thick pillows, surrounded by his illustrious orchestra: two rawboned men, as mysterious as fakirs, one banging his *derbouka* with zeal, the other beating his drum with dignity. Enthroned slightly in front was the most celebrated singer in the entire Grand Rif, an immense plate overflowing with honey within reach. He had one hand on his ear and his neck painfully strained by the dissonant yelling which the people, in their exultation, interpreted otherwise.

Sometimes, unable to resist the temptation, Sid er-Jem whispered to him: "Can I have a drop of that honey that smells so good?"

And the singer would reply disdainfully: "What for? I think your saliva lubricates your monstrous sound box well enough."

"I just want to taste it. It smells so good!"

"But you, you don't sing. Come on now, you can't enjoy such a privilege. Honey is for preserving the voice . . ."

"Just a little drop."

"Out of the question. Blow your *ghaita*, Sid er-Jem, and spare my ears a language that is as boring as it is insipid. Don't you see that by your deplorable conduct you are mocking the pure soul of the artist, who is such a rarity in this day and age? Listen to your *ghaita* and you will hear it reproach you for such a lack of scruples."

Thereupon, the scowling singer, not without a certain deliberateness, sucked his fingers which were dripping with the "sacred" nectar.

The festivities intensified with nightfall. The young groom arrived on his dazzling white steed, escorted by some twenty close friends. He went straight in to the virgin. Outside, the singing and dancing were relentless. The noise died down for an instant. A gunshot! Everybody looked up . . . ululation . . . The virgin had become a woman!

The celebration died down with the first light of dawn. The guests began going home. Mimouna's mother, her eyes puffy with fatigue, tried to smile at the congratulations. The father, ever arrogant, regretfully watched the rise of the sun and fall of his own reign. His sons lay sprawled out here and there, exhausted.

The band collected its instruments and prepared to move on to fresh glories. The singer deemed it necessary to have one last lick of the honey plate, smacked his lips and arranged his fez. Sid er-Jem, who twice had vomited into his *ghaita* because he had wolfed down too much, dipped his buzzing head in a basin of water, giving sound to uncontrollable "ahs."

Slowly the *haouch* was emptied of people and the father wished to lie down for a bit.

Thus passed Mimouna's marriage, in the utmost joy.

Mimouna started off her married life in happiness. Her husband pampered her. He was a traveling tradesman and never failed to bring her back a present from every trip. Harmony reigned in their home, and the neighbors tried to follow their example.

"Look at how they live, man. We're wrong to bicker, when they know how to savor every moment of life."

"Know, woman, that your bellowing penetrates the walls of our hut and know that behind these walls Boudjemaa and his wife are laughing and loving."

Mimouna cropped up in conversation all the time. She kept house like no other, was the pride of her family, and her reputation won tribute all around. And from the height of her pedestal, she raised and raised her head, losing it in the clouds. In the face of so much praise, she learned to despise first other women, and then her own circle.

"Mansourah," she told a neighbor, "is a real pest. She never stops bending our ears with her bragging. What on earth does her husband do, then?"

"Well! Her husband has no authority over her. He's ineffectual. She leads him around by the nose."

And Mimouna: "I hate men who make themselves their wives' slaves."

"Some women are terrible."

"Certainly not! There are no terrible women; there are only naive men. A slap in the face; what am I saying? A frown and the terrible tigress becomes a docile, loving cat."

The days rolled by, the weeks and the seasons, and Mimouna turned into a perfidious tongue. The ease and especially the efficacy of slander enthralled her. She thought that in it she had found the best way to pre-

serve her superiority and pitilessly crush her rivals. She came to deni-
grate the whole world. Nothing found favor in her eyes. The woman
watching a man pass by was soon drowned in Mimouna's venom. The
woman who dared to oppose her or proved to be more beautiful or intelligent than she was finished.

The treacherous tongue without end, without borders, lashed, tore,
smeared, bit, darted in every direction, like a ravaging tentacle. It sowed
doubt in families. Men became suspicious, women fearful and distrustful.
Neighbors avoided talking or lingering outside. They watched each
other like clay dogs and pointed deadly fingers at one another. The
bedouin smells were smothered under the stench of the plots. People
began to drink too much coffee, eat too little, sleep badly, mistreat their
children for no apparent reason. Everybody became increasingly short-
tempered and a catastrophe would develop out of nothing.

Mimouna glowed, burning like a torch in a night of reprisals. She
succeeded at each blow . . . In one month, four broken homes. First the
qadi's; Mimouna claimed to have surprised his wife with a stranger in
the fields. Humiliated, the *qadi* did not seek to understand. He chased
off his wife with a gun. Then Mimouna laid into the home of a peasant.
The third woman barely escaped her husband's knife. And the fourth, a
delightful creature whom everybody revered, threw herself down a well.

The village discarded its burnoose of respectability and confidence to
don the black cape of infamy. Women cloistered themselves at home to
avoid the possibility of scandal. But this was no protection against the
viper's tongue.

Mimouna babbled, talked, lied. Without drawing breath. She armed
each word with a merciless poisoned barb. She wanted to be the only
perfect woman around, the only unsullied woman . . .

The only one!

By besmirching everyone else. Even the men!

She went so far as to accuse a poor impotent old man of attempted
rape: "I was filling my jugs when he came out from behind the Big Boul-
der. I thought he was thirsty and wanted to drink some water. I stepped
aside. Without any warning, he pounced on me and tried to rip off my
clothes . . . . Thank God, I managed to slip through his grasp."

After this story, Boudjemaa saw red. He grabbed his gun and went in search of the old man. He found him in the fellow's orchard and, without asking for an explanation, fired a bullet straight at his head.

The old man's body was discovered and taken home. He was mourned for a long time. Women tore at their cheeks with their nails. Young men dispersed into the night, each to shed the tears of his sorrow in a corner where nobody would disturb him.

At sunrise, the body was moved to the mosque. The cortege accompanying Sid Ali was impressive. The deceased had spent all his life preaching the five pillars of Islam, loving his neighbors with a religious love. His tragic demise weighed heavily on many hearts.

"She's always the one to unveil the wrong, to have seen it all, heard it all," somebody in the crowd muttered. "She's always the one to discover what the rest of us haven't even noticed. First the qadi's wife, who was said to be as pure as the luminescence of the mosque. Then the incredible blah-blah about the poor Badrah who, to escape opprobrium, threw herself down a well. And the peasant's wife, whose sole crime was that she was too beautiful for the taste of some. And all the others, all the others . . ."

"She's either an infallible seer or an unforgivable shrew."

"The latter name suits her like a caftan."

People talked about Mimouna.

Sid Ali was buried. In the heavy silence that precedes a storm.

"That will not be the end of it!" raged El-Haddi.

El-Haddi was Sid Ali's eldest son. He assembled all his close relations, his brothers, cousins and sons-in-law, in the deceased's house. He sat where the old man had sat when he was alive.

"I have gathered you here today to seek out the truth, the whole truth in all its stark nudity. And if this nudity is indecent, if it risks obsessing us till the end of our days, that's too bad. After all, it is the truth. And who can escape the truth?"

"You propose, we will approve, great brother."

Ed-Haddi rose and invited his people to follow him.

They headed straight for the mosque.

"My children, my children," cried the imam. "I understand and share your distress, but I will not tolerate fighting in our village."

"You see yourself that we're not carrying arms. All we ask is that you call a meeting of the Council of Elders."

An hour later, the entire Council of Elders was in the mosque.

After a brief speech, the Sherif, a high-spirited centenarian, turned the floor over to El-Haddi.

"In the name of Allah the clement and merciful . . . My brothers, first let me start by apologizing for having taken you away from your work, but I am sure that anything to do with the community is close to your hearts. We have assembled in the house of God to learn the truth. Nothing but the truth. For some time now, our village has been living a veritable nightmare. Slander has come into currency. Many of our homes have disintegrated, many of our nearest and dearest have distanced themselves from us. I think the time has come to rediscover peace and harmony. We must now decide the fate of our village. Shall we let doubt and suspicion continue to consume us? Shall we continue to see future scandals in our wives, future orphans in our children? Let us start learning now, today, to confront matters with greater determination and conviction."

There was a rumble of approval.

El-Haddi added: "We shall summon the person who was at the origin of all these anomalies, all this ill feeling. And we shall leave it to the imam to enlighten us. He is not the wisest among you, or the fairest. He has simply promised me to take care of the matter."

Mimouna arrived, her husband and mother at her side.

"My daughter," declared the Sherif, "we are going to unravel an enigma. I ask you to be calm."

"I don't understand."

"Have a little patience. You will answer a few questions. It will be very simple."

He asked her mother and Boudjemaa to join the *djemaa*, then he sat Mimouna on a red carpet and blindfolded her.

The imam appeared, carrying a book. He placed it in front of the woman and whispered to her: "Touch . . . touch . . ."

Hesitant, Mimouna let a nervous hand fall on the thick cover, fingered the pages and fearfully withdrew her hand.

"What is it, my daughter?"

"It's . . . it's a book."

Boudjemaa spent the day in his house where Mimouna would never step foot again. He prepared lunch himself for his two little ones. At dusk, he lay them down on the straw mattress, told them lovely legends about the Brave and the Good, about the Poor who become sultans for having dared to speak the truth, about Truth who was hated by a wicked queen named Lie, because Truth was more beautiful than she. He told them, too, the sad tale of the Innocents who invariably pay for those who are really guilty, and that of a gnome named Justice who always managed to vanquish a cyclops that was as big as a mountain and as strong as destiny, and whose name was Falsity . . .

The two children dropped off into a sleep full of dreams and light.

Boudjemaa prayed.

Then he took down his gun, kissed the little ones who smiled like angels, turned off the oil lamp and went out.

The night was clear and the air soft.

Boudjemaa knew that his weapon was not loaded. He walked knowingly toward a death he deemed to be just. He never even thought of defending himself.

On his way, he came across his wife. She was waiting for him under a cactus. She stood up. With his hand he signaled for her to stay where she was and passed by without stopping.

Mimouna slumped onto the ground, sobbing.

El-Haddi was already waiting for him in the orchard. Only his *gandura* rustled in the evening breeze.

Boudjemaa stopped and lifted his unloaded rifle to his shoulder.

Sid Ali's son did the same with his gun.

A shot roared out and bounced off the mountains before losing itself in infinity.

Not a cry arose.

Boudjemaa lowered his weapon. His chest was burning. Blood flowed from his mouth. He turned on his heels and moved away.

"Allah is the Greatest!" murmured El-Haddi.

His gaze vacant, his legs uncertain, Boudjemaa advanced unsteadily. In the distance a jackal imitated the world and its false dog silhouette was clearly outlined at the top of the rock.

Boudjemaa tried to quicken his step. He hoped to reach his house where his children were afraid of the dark. But his strength was fading quickly. Blood trickled from his wound. He felt no pain. He just seemed to be drowsy. He felt light, very light.

Mimouna rose to her feet upon seeing her husband return. He passed by without noticing her. She held her arms out to the distraught man who was about to die, but she dared not approach him.

Boudjemaa kept walking. Like a blind man. With only his instinct to guide him. He thought he recognized his house. His weapon slipped from his hand. He shivered; he was terribly cold.

Suddenly he fell, the full length of him . . .

Mimouna was rejected by everybody. No one wanted to hear of her anymore. Her children were taken over by their uncles. She lived among the rocks, like a ghost, covered in rags and shame. And the kids learned to pelt her with pebbles, to chase her across the gorge, shouting, "Mimouna, *settoute!* Mimouna, you insult! Mimouna, *settoute!*"

She fled aimlessly from her pain, her body hurting, her head bleeding. In her solitude, she roamed grumbling incomprehensibly, occasionally stopping to pick a herb or an edible root.

I. N. C. A N I E B O

I. N. C. Aniebo was born in 1939 in Nigeria and educated at Government College Umuahia. He joined the army in 1959 and was trained in Cadet Schools in Ghana and England. He then served as an officer in UN Peacekeeping in the Congo (now the Democratic Republic of Congo), and attended the Command & General Staff College at Fort Leavenworth, Kansas. During his country's civil war he fought on the Biafran side, and was discharged from the army in 1971. He is now a senior lecturer at the University of Port Harcourt. He has published the novels *The Anonymity of Sacrifice* and *The Journey Within*, and two collections of short stories, *Wives, Talisman and the Dead* and *Man of the Market*.

FOUR DIMENSIONS

"Hack her to pieces! She must not be born again," cried the Third Priest in a rasping voice.

"Throw her pieces to the four winds. Let them be blown to the ends of the earth so that even her *chi* cannot find them," the Second Priest intoned.

"Who are we that we should sit in final judgment over her?" asked the First Priest, shaking his white head sorrowfully.

"We are the appointed judges of Ajala, our great Mother Earth. This woman sinned against *her* and should not be returned to her," answered the Second Priest contemptuously.

"We were appointed to judge mortals not spirits," countered the First Priest. "Therefore let us be merciful. The woman has sinned, it is true, but her sins have been washed away by her death." His mellow, slow voice calmed the acolytes whose hysterical chanting now became a low dirge.

"You are the First, the anointed head," said the Third Priest. "But let my dissension be recorded. Not all sins can be washed away by death alone, else there would be no evil or tormented spirits and all mortals dying would automatically be washed pure and reborn. But the spirit of sinners must sojourn in Hades, to be tormented and to wander around for some time with hopes of being born again. One of the greatest punishments that can be meted out to a mortal or spirit is to be left wandering without hope. This woman's sin cannot be washed away by death, not even by letting her spirit wander for some time. It is better she be cut to pieces so that she can never be born again and her spirit will wander endlessly."

"So let it be, O First," chanted the Second Priest.

"No! It shall not be. Let it not be said we stretched our mortal hand into a world we know nothing of. Let the spirits judge the spirits and the mortals, mortals. Therefore, let the spirit of the dead woman wander for a while and not endlessly. We will bury her with the honors befitting a noble woman, with chalk and camwood markings on her face and body; with a root of the Iroko and spittle of the tortoise mixed into a potion to anoint her belly and her *okike* stringed across the top of the two tallest palm trees in the village and not untied till it has either been shot down or eight days have elapsed; with the mat woven from the *ute* that grows on the banks of the sacred stream. I, the First, have passed judgment. We will now wait for Mother Ajala to declare her wishes."

There was a hushed silence. Even the acolytes with their heavily chalked faces and foam-specked mouths controlled their moaning.

Presently the rays of the full moon cut through the foliage of the giant age-old trees surrounding Ajala's shrine and fell on the circular sacrificial stone on which lay the naked body of the dead young woman. Ranged round her were the three squatting priests who waited, their closely shaven heads bent, to learn the wishes of their goddess, but their minds could not concentrate on the same thing for a very long time. And as time rolled inexorably by, lengthened by the silence of the surrounding forest, their thoughts veered away to . . .

She had walked into his house that afternoon two years ago, her three multicolored beads sitting becomingly on her slim, dark waist. On her beautiful lips was the smile he knew so well, the teasing smile that could set the muddy blood of an old man on fire. Without touching her breasts, he knew her nipples were hard because of the way they stood out, and round them, as always, were two concentric circles of *uli*.

"Okwomma," she greeted him.

"My child," he answered, controlling, with difficulty, the trembling of the lips and hands that often assailed him in her presence.

She sat down on the opposite *ngidi* (mud bed), not the way women always sat with legs stretched out together in front of them, but in her own exciting way—legs drawn up and hands hugging her knees as if she were cold.

"I just thought I should come by and greet you, Third Priest," she said in her low, husky voice, her eyes modestly lowered.

"You did well, my child. Had your beloved father been alive, he would have approved. But why didn't you go to the Afo Ezinma today?"

"I had nothing to sell, Third Priest. And besides, Mother and the other wives were going, so I decided to stay at home to look after the children and cook dinner."

He grunted and brought out his old black clay pipe and leaf tobacco from his soot-covered raffia bag which had been handed down to him from his grandfather. With superfluous concentration, he began to fill his pipe. He had often discovered that a smoke quieted his blood, and took his mind away from mundane thoughts, particularly the one that bothered him at the moment.

The sound of children praying in the heat haze of the afternoon, the bark of lean, dirty dogs, the occasional squawks of frightened chickens taking cover from the sharp claws of a diving hawk and the bleating of goats emphasized the absence of all the able-bodied men and women in the village who had gone to the Afo market in Ezinma, five miles away.

His pipe lighted, he leaned back on the red mud wall and sucked in a grateful lungful. "Don't you like my staying at home?" asked Maruma.

"Why do you ask, child?"

"Because you grunted after I explained why I stayed."

"I was filling my pipe."

"You hadn't brought out your pipe then." She had dropped the formal manner of addressing the priests of Ajala, and her legs were now curled up under her.

"No, my child," said the Third Priest slowly. "I don't dislike your staying home. In fact, I like it."

"I knew you would, Third Priest."

As if caught unawares, he puffed away nervously at his dying pipe. He had been staring at her for some time, figuring what *it* would be like. Now he bent forward and rearranged the smoldering wood of the fire between them. Deftly, he picked up a glowing charcoal with his fingers and put it into the bowl of his pipe. He drew hard at the pipe, his large Adam's apple moving rhythmically up and down, and now and again he pressed the charcoal in with his index finger. Before long, he was enveloped in pungent smoke.

"I don't like the smell of your tobacco."

"Why, child? It smells good to me."

"Don't call me a child. I'm a full-grown woman."

He removed his pipe and stared at her. Her long slim legs were now stretched out in front of her, thus exposing her wide hips, flat belly and large bosom, and on her lips played that smile—innocent, teasing and inviting, all at the same time.

"Yes, you're right," he said slowly. "I'm sorry . . ."

"It's all right," she hastily assured him. She had begun to feel uneasy and afraid she might not be able to control the emotion she was stirring up. Those looks of his were not the looks of a priest, and she had felt his eyes mauling her. "It's all right, Third Priest," she said, recalling that he was, at a mere thirty-five, the youngest of the three and had become a priest by inheritance, and not by personal achievement or remarkable holiness.

She stood up, tall and straight, luscious and desirable, a woman at eighteen, conscious and proud of her bloom.

"I'm going to prepare lunch for the children." The flesh was strong, but the will weak.

He, too, was standing.

Without looking, she could see the cloth *ugbolo* tied between his legs in the form of pants, striving and straining to contain the stirring of life down there. She could also feel, without touching, the heat radiating from his hard-packed, bare body, and the fire between them accentuating it. She swallowed hard in an effort to clear the impending clogging of her throat, and her other self wondered why she felt as she did, why she had become hypersensitive to every nuance in the environment.

She had been in this situation with him before and had come out of it unscathed, having enjoyed every minute of it, but . . .

"Maruma, look at me." It was the first time ever he had called her by name.

Their eyes met, and she thought she saw lightning flashes crisscrossing between them.

He thought the same too, or willed it, and in one bound, he was by her side and the next carried her into his bedroom. Her cry rent the air as he threw her onto the bamboo bed. He tore at his *ugbolo* with feverish, erratic fingers—but he couldn't undo it!

Her next cry cut across his befogged brain like a whiplash. She had called on the protection of Ajala and she must, therefore, remain inviolate or he would be damned. He wrung his hands in fury, cursing silently the day he was born and his inherent fear of this goddess whom he served and was bonded to serve to the end. With glazed eyes, he watched her get off the bed and walk through the low door to freedom. His bird had flown again, after having walked into his den. Cursed be her *chi!*

And as Maruma stepped into the hot sun she began to shiver as one suffering from the ague.

His son had rushed into the hut that evening holding his stomach, and through his fingers he could see red seeping through, leaving a well-emblazoned trail. His heart sank when he knew instinctively what it was.

"Nwobi, what happened? Who did that to you? Tell me, tell me!"

The boy collapsed on the *ngidi* moaning, his handsome face a picture of pain and wonder. "Maruma, Maruma stabbed me, stabbed me in the stomach." He fainted.

Maruma, that she-devil, thought the Second Priest as he dressed his son's wound. Thanks to Ajala, it was not a very deep one, but still an ugly sight. Nwobi must have jumped back as she struck since his flesh had a "torn" look.

"Oh, Ajala, what shall we do to this vixen before she destroys all our young men?"

With his knowledge of the herbs, the Second Priest brought his son back to the land of the living in four days—one Ibo week—and during that period he often wished he were not Ajala's priest so that he could take vengeance on Maruma, though she was the Chief's daughter and, like everyone in the village, Ajala's child.

The shepherd could not scatter his flock; if he did, he would be many more times damned!

And what was more, no one should ever know that his son had been worsted in a fight with a girl!

It took another three days before the Second Priest could get his son to tell him how it had all happened. Had the boy's mother been alive, he would have known sooner, but then her death had made it possible for him to prepare for the priesthood.

Nwobi had recounted the events in his singsong high tone.

Three days before the incident, Maruma had asked him to escort her to the farm to pull up some cassava tubers. He had accepted with alacrity, for even though he was three years older, she could twist him round her finger. So much did he love her!

The day was hovering between the end of the afternoon and the beginning of the evening when they set out to the cassava farms two miles away. Maruma led, in her loping gait, her body swaying and undulating in a way all her own, and her graceful long neck straight, carrying the head on which balanced an elongated rectangular basket.

"Why do you have to get this cassava tonight?" Nwobi had asked diffidently.

"Because I couldn't do it earlier, and besides we're having many guests on *Nkwo* day."

"What of your other sisters? Surely, they could have escorted you."

"How can the blind lead the blind? They're afraid of the dark as much as I. But with you here . . ."

Pulling up the cassava tubers was easy as they had been planted on slightly sandy soil and soon their basket was full.

In a nearby stream, they washed and chopped the cassava into six-inch lengths and immersed them in a big pot full of water berthed at the edge. By the time they finished they were hot and dirty.

"Let's have a dip before we go," suggested Maruma. They waded to the bathing area downstream. "Do you know that my pots of cassava ferment faster than all those here? Mine take only two days while the others take from three onward."

"It seems you have the devil heating the bottom of your pots."

"Maybe. Father says the devil loves beautiful women!"

They did not dally at the stream, but it became completely dark before they were halfway home.

"Nwobi, may I hold your hand? I can't see well in the dark." In this way they proceeded another hundred yards. "Why don't we wait till the moon comes up?"

"What will your mother say when we come home very late?"

"I'm too old to be lost or kidnapped!"

She put down the basket and he the little hoe and hatchet and they sat close together by the edge of the path. As time passed, she leaned on him more and more, her arms encircling his waist. Once, perhaps to kill an ant, she slapped her right thigh hard and while replacing her hand round his waist, she touched the stirring life. She did not seem shocked but rather fascinated by it, for pushing aside his *ugbolo*, his only article of clothing, she touched it many more times, wonderingly, like a child given a new toy. Sometimes she enclosed it softly in her palm, feeling the urgency, the tautness and the throb of life.

And oh, how hard he tried to get into her! But when he seemed to succeed, she would cry out in pain, withdrawing as if he were a leper, and so he contented himself with touching until his dam burst . . .

He did not see her, even though he constantly patrolled the approaches to her home throughout the next day, till the day of the incident. He had been looking for the holes dug by the *ewi* (big rat) when on parting a shrub . . . she was a few feet away, her back toward him. She was trying to break a small coil of brass bangle and was so engrossed in it—he could see the straining muscles of her back—she did not hear him approach.

He did not disturb her, else she might break the perfect picture she created with the setting sun flooding her naked back with golden tears, and making her beads glint.

She must have succeeded, and with legs placed wide apart, she bent down and began digging up the earth with the broken bangle.

He could stand by no longer, and was soon trying to thrust himself into her, but she was swifter. With a little cry, she swiveled round and . . . the pain . . . the pain and the blood . . .

"The she-devil!" muttered the Second Priest, his lined face a picture of hatred and anger.

"No, Father, she isn't! She is an *angel*. It was my fault . . ."

That was eight years ago, and Nwobi was fifteen then.

The news had spread like an epidemic.

The First Priest was sick, sick unto death. Not even his fellow priests, nor the doctors, could tell what was wrong with him, except that the symptoms were high fever, coughing and lack of appetite. There was no close relative to nurse him, either. He had taken to the priesthood at a very young age, and did not marry, even though he was the only surviving male child of his household. Many times, people had advised him to leave the priesthood and get married but he had refused.

"I was called by Ajala to serve her!" he always answered. "Perhaps if I'm devoted to her, completely and without guile, I may be able to expiate the sins of my family and stop the curse on them spreading to their daughters and their children."

But now it seemed his services to Ajala were coming to an end.

"Ovuegbe," greeted Maruma one afternoon.

"My child," said the First Priest in a barely audible whisper. He was lying on his back and looked very emaciated; one could almost smell death in his smoke-filled room.

"I've come to nurse you back to health."

He managed a thin, wry smile, "My child . . . you talk as if you're Ajala herself. Those who can have tried and failed. I'm resigned to death. Already I can hear the knocking on the wall."

She sat down on the edge of the *ngidi*. "Please don't say that." She brushed away the tears that filled her eyes. "I can't let you die. You're the only person I've got since Father died."

The priest's long silence frightened Maruma. She was about to panic, when he started one of his coughing spasms that often left him exhausted and breathless. After he recovered he said: "Don't bother, my child. Your intention is noble. But it's too late."

"Even if it is, please promise you won't give up hope of being well again. Just promise me that and I'll be satisfied."

His reply took a long time in coming and when it did, she had to bend forward to hear. "Nobody likes to die, my child," and he fell into a coma.

She immediately set to work cleaning the house. She washed the cooking pots and clay plates, swept the compound that was beginning to resemble the abode of a dead man, littered with fallen leaves and refuse of many days. The firewood and water would last her for that day.

From the moment she had entered the First Priest's house, Maruma felt she knew what was really wrong with him, because her father had suffered the same illness at regular intervals, and had allowed only her to prepare his medicine. After restoking the fire in the room where he lay, thus eliminating most of the smoke, she went out in search of herbs. With the optimism of youth, she cut several handfuls of lemon grass, leaves of lime including a few branches, dug up the yellow roots of nkpologwu and picked the kidney-shaped leaves of the *ejeje* shrub. Reaching home, she kindled a fire in the kitchen, and began to boil all that she had collected in a huge wide-mouthed pot. Next, she peeled yams with which to prepare a hot palm oil broth, and as it was getting dark, lit a palm-husk candle.

The First Priest had come out of his coma by the time she finished brewing the medicine and the broth.

"How do you feel, First Priest?" she asked, sitting down on the edge of his bed.

He did not answer but moved his head slowly from side to side.

"Will you be able to stand up?"

Again he moved his head.

Maruma went back to the kitchen and brought out the steaming pot of medicine, placing it as close as possible to the edge of the sick man's bed. She had decided to treat him where he was. From the wooden box on the alcove, she took out a thick cloth that looked like a bedspread. Gently she helped the First Priest to sit up in such a way that the pot of medicine was between his legs and then she covered him and the pot with the cloth. She removed the cloth a few minutes later when the First Priest started gasping for air, and noted with satisfaction his sweat-covered body. She rubbed him down with lukewarm water, fed him some spoonfuls of the broth she had prepared and put him to bed, covering him with every available mat and cloth. For the first time since his illness the First Priest slept through the night like one drugged.

Maruma continued her treatment for another two days making sure, however, that the First Priest drank a potion of the medicine, after she had rubbed him down.

On the morning of the third day, he woke up earlier than she. When she heard her name called in a sonorous voice that reminded her of the echoes of the mother of drums, Maruma was startled. Slowly she sat up, her face a mixture of happiness and relief.

"So you haven't gone yet?" the First Priest asked. She shook her head. She was unable to speak.

"How long have you been here?"

"Three days," her lips formed the words.

"What of your mother? Didn't she look for you? Oh, never mind. But why do you bother yourself with an old man like me?"

And she began to cry, all her pent-up feelings of relief, happiness, irritation and fatigue finding expression at last in a welter of tears.

Six months later, Maruma's husband of one month, Nwobi, died suddenly after a few hours' illness. The rumor was that she poisoned him, but none could prove it. When, however, she went mad a few weeks afterward, the Second and Third Priests said Ajala had punished her for killing her husband. She was immediately ostracized and a hut was built for her at the edge of the bad bush. She lingered on in her madness and at the age of twenty fell off a coconut tree and died.

"I have heard the voice of Ajala," chanted the Third Priest.

In a dreadful crescendo, the acolytes burst into their wild song of the judgment; a song that could be heard miles away, and that warned the villagers of the presence of the great goddess in her shrine.

"I too have heard her command!" The Second Priest could not suppress his joy; at last, at last . . .

"Speak, Third Priest." There was deep sorrow in the First Priest's voice as he added, "And may the goddess hold you to ransom if you speak with a false tongue."

"You cannot scare me, First Priest. I heard the voice of our Mother loud and clear and her message is unmistakable. She said, 'Tell my First Priest I am displeased with his judgment for he has let himself be swayed by sentiments. It is true, this dead daughter of mine saved his life, but then a woman has more than one nature. It is the sum total of her

natures that determines whether she is good or bad, and to know her
natures you have to see her in four dimensions. I have thus listened to
the four winds from the four directions; the winds that saw all her movements during her lifetime and I hereby pass judgment. My dead daughter
was a bad woman! I therefore command that she be thrown into the bad
bush, and a black goat sacrificed to cleanse the people who will take her
there. I also command that on pain of death, none of my children now
and in generations to come be given her name nor told of her.' Thus did
Ajala command, First Priest."

"You have heard rightly, Third Priest. For I, too, heard the same. May
you now seal the judgment, First Priest."

"So be it then, even though I do not think our merciful Mother
would have passed such judgment on a poor girl who suffered greatly.
Third Priest, heat the seal of judgment."

The Third Priest gathered dry leaves and a few sticks and soon made
a fire in the stone hearth twenty yards from the sacrificial stone. The
youngest acolyte, there were thirteen of them, handed him the brass seal
of judgment, shaped in the form of *infinity* with a wooden handle
attached to the center, which he heated until it was hot to the touch. He
was about to pick it up when he heard a rumbling noise from above. He
straightened up, peering into the thick canopy of leaves, but he could
detect nothing.

Meanwhile, the chanting had ceased, and there was a hush and a
chill in the air, and the moon seemed to have lost much of its cold luster.

The rumbling noise increased in volume, and the First Priest, his
voice sounding like a god's, asked, "What is delaying you, Third Priest?
Shall we not seal the judgment you said Ajala passed through you?"

But the Third Priest seemed not to hear. He was intent on the commotion that seemed to be coming from the very heavens. He stood there
petrified, his feet bound to the earth with cords of iron.

Then with a roar and a crash, a huge dead tree fell on him, crushing
him into the earth.

". . . and may the goddess hold you to ransom if you speak with a false
tongue."

Dambudzo Marechera was born in 1952 in Rusape, Southern Rhodesia. He enrolled at the University of Rhodesia in 1972, but was expelled the following year as a result of his involvement with a student movement protesting the wages of black staff members. He was then awarded an Oxford scholarship. While at Oxford he wrote his first book of short stories, *The House of Hunger*, which won the *Guardian* Fiction Prize in 1979. Often homeless during his stint in the United Kingdom, Marechera returned to Zimbabwe in 1981. He died six years later, leaving behind a large body of unpublished work. *The Black Insider*, *Scrapiron Blues*, and *Cemetery of Mind*, a collection of his poems, were released posthumously. His other books include *Black Sunlight* and *Mindblast*.

Thought Tracks in the Snow

The skies had been overcast. My affairs were going badly and I was as gloomy as the great gray clouds that hid the sun from view. I had been ill, a fever, and had had to put up with medicines and a great deal of curious attention from my landlady who had taken the position that my writing was certainly not doing me any good. It snowed heavily that Sunday night and I watched the thick white doves' feathers of it come sailing down and pile up everywhere. I could not sleep. A restless refrain was repeatedly flashing through my mind: "You're crazy, you're crazy, you're crazy." And great armfuls of it were snowing down onto the roofs, onto the roads, onto the pavements, snowing down into everything: "You're crazy, you're crazy, you're crazy."

The week before, I had finished typing out my novel and had sent it off and had thought that I would be free of it. But the thing was oppressing me and I was making the postman nervous and making myself ill all over. I had then pulled myself up sharply and started again, giving lessons to a pimply youth who was certainly not interested in the course he had signed up with me. He came from Nigeria, he said, and what did I think about the Rhodesian crisis and about white girls? And anytime I so much as hinted that we were supposed to be paying attention to his unwritten essay on William Blake he would shake his head in such a way that I felt quite uncomfortable. My sessions with him always turned out to be alcoholic bouts because he brought with him not the essays he ought to have done but bottles of spirit which invariably made us quite jolly and talkative about anything under the sun—as long as it was not anything to do with English literature. He had, he said, read my stories and found them quite indigestible. Why did I not write in my own language? he asked. Was I perhaps one of those Africans who despised their own roots? Shouldn't I be writing within our great tradition of oral literature rather than turning out pseudo-Kafka–Dostoyevsky stories? What did I do with myself when I was not working—did I have a girl? Did I know that I was a shit? No, he said, I did not quite mean that—I meant shit in its good earthy sense.

And outside, the wet snow piled up softly like things which a man has chosen to forget, things sailing down the sky and quietly gathering up inch by inch to bury me. I felt so hot I was unbearably cold. I felt so cold I could not stand the heat of it.

It seemed the teargas fumes were still choking me; the police dogs still biting chunks out of terrified students; the stones still crunching into fat white faces; and from every side the howling of sirens, the grinding run of boots, the upraised truncheon—in the instant before the jarring of bone beneath polished hardwood—arrested by the camera shutter opening and shutting. Thick smoke erupting over the rugby and cricket fields suddenly covered everything; when it cleared armed policemen and soldiers had herded the students onto the old cricket pitch and a long line of wire-meshed vans was taking groups of students to the emergency detention centers. A group of white students were cheering the police and jeering the prisoners; a Rhodesia Television cameraman was carefully recording everything. The huge Alsatians were licking their massive jaws at the long line of prisoners . . .

Thought tracks in the snow—shit!

As the plane burred into the night, leaving the Angolan coast and heading out into the void above the Atlantic, I suddenly remembered that I had, in the rude hurry of it all, left my spectacles behind. I was coming to England literally blind. The blurred shape of the other passengers was grimly glued to the screen where Clint Eastwood was once again shooting the shit out of his troubles. I was on my own, sipping a whiskey, and my head was roaring with a strange emptiness. What was it really that I had left behind me? My youth was a headache burring with the engines of a great hunger that was eating up the huge chunks of empty air. I think I knew then that before me were years of desperate loneliness, and the whiskey would be followed by other whiskeys, other self-destructive poisons; I had nothing but books inside my head, and they were burning me, burring with the engines of hope and illusion into the endless expanse of air. Who was I leaving behind? My own prematurely gray head still sat stubbornly upon my shoulders; my family did not know where I was or whether I was alive or dead. I do not think they would have cared one way or the other had they known that at that moment I was thousands of feet above the earth, hanging as it were in the emptiness which my dabbling with politics had created for me. I felt sick with everything, sick with the self-pity, sick with the Rhodesian crisis, sick!—and the whiskey was followed by other whiskeys and my old young man's face stared back at me from the little window. Would Oxford University be any different—was I so sure of myself then? Dawn broke as we flew over Biscayne Bay; and the fresh white dove's down of breast clouds looked from above like another revelation that would turn out, when eaten, to be stone rather than bread.

"I meant shit in its good earthy sense," the Nigerian repeated.

On the little table between us was the forgotten text of William Blake's *Songs of Innocence and Songs of Experience*.

A sudden knocking saved me from making any reply. I looked at my watch and knew immediately who it was who had come. When she came in and curled herself up on the rug by the fire and muttered something shocking about the weather, I could see the silent accusation in the Nigerian's eye, an accusation that suddenly turned into a challenge. I could see it was going to be one of those days again. My head was burring again with impotent anger, a sickening desperation which for once I dared to crash.

"It's time for my next lesson, so you must excuse me," I said breathlessly.

All my life I had never been able to control my breathing.

The Nigerian looked up sharply. He decided to let things go; and got up and left without another word. Rachel was staring into the fire; the way her shoulders were shaking I knew she had resolved to do something drastic.

"You finished it?"

Her voice was coiled round the steel wire of a taut self-control.

"Yes, I've sent it off to the publishers."

She had not turned round. My glass was unsteady in my hand.

"Aren't you going to say hello to me?"

I had not expected this.

I got up and put my hands on her shoulders but she twisted round suddenly and slapped me hard on my cheek. Good heavens—what was it that had happened to her face? I stood there, with my old man's gray head, and knew that I would always be slightly ridiculous.

She had turned back to the fire. Her shoulders—those small frail shoulders—still shook. I sat down and refilled my glass and remembered quite bitterly the Nigerian's taunts. It was a poisonous comedy the two of them expected me to play.

"Don't you care I've been seeing him? Sleeping with him?" she asked suddenly.

But I was prepared. Though I knew the wound would hurt badly after she left, I was at that moment prepared for the knife thrust. Did she then really think so little of me?

"Rachel, it's your body, not mine, and you can do what you like with it," I said.

"You know what you are—a nigger jackass," she said.

"You don't have to remind me, Rachel," I said.

"A hypocrite."

I felt weak with the heady buzzing inside my head; teargas canisters were exploding around my leaping feet. I hurled a paving stone at an advancing policeman—

My glass had toppled over, spilling my spirit onto the floor.

"I just don't know why I married you," she said.

We had been married for two years but had slept together only for the first five days.

"Perhaps if we had had a child . . ." I hazarded.

She swung round, but the fire was still burning in her eyes. This is it, I thought.

"I am with child," she said softly.

She always lowered her voice when she delivered what she thought was a deadly sword thrust.

"And it's his child," she added.

I refilled my glass; emptied it; refilled it again.

"That Nigerian boy?"

"He isn't a boy," she said. "He's a man, a real man. Not an impotent bastard like you."

"I'd rather you left my mother out of this," I said, "but if you must drag her in, by all means do."

"I want a divorce."

"By all means get one, Rachel. I told you seventeen months ago that . . ."

"You really think you're superior to everybody, don't you?"

"Now, Rachel, you know that's not true."

"Don't Rachel me!"

Her screamed words struck the ceiling and bounced back onto the bookshelves.

I cleared my throat.

"You never really loved me," she said.

The note of self-pity in her voice—I recognized it in that far-off Rachel with whom I had tramped around North Wales and been immeasurably happy for five short days.

I nodded toward the decanter. And she silently, thoughtfully, made a drink for herself.

"Damn it, Charles, why—why?"

She was chewing her lower lip. And then, abruptly, she sat down on the arm of my chair.

"Why?" she repeated.

I said nothing. She was deliberately impulsive—playfully almost—when she chose to be.

"How long have you known?" she asked.

"Long enough not to hurt anymore," I said. The door was opening slowly.

I leaned forward to refill my glass and she circled my shoulders with her arm and with the other turned my face toward hers and kissed me. The door swung wide open and the Nigerian stormed into the room, cursing: "You bitch! You bloody bitch!"

"Charles!"

"Fucking white bitch!"

"Charles, don't just sit there—he's hurting me—your wife!"

I tried to duck but the truncheon struck the side of my head.

"Charles! I'm your wife!"

She was down there on the floor being mauled by an Alsatian. Another canister exploded on the wall behind me. Thick white choking gas engulfed me. I held down my breath and lunged at the uniformed figure. Somewhere in the background, my landlady was hovering about with a rolling pin.

I grappled with the Nigerian. He was still cursing: "Fucking Rhodesians—get independence first, then perhaps you'll learn how to fight!"

He was hurting me badly. I could feel the blood rushing out through my nose. Rachel was somewhere on the floor near the shattered glass case. The landlady cautiously crept up behind him and smashed the rolling pin on his great head. He slumped to the floor, out cold. I was trying to wipe the blood from my face and at the same time trying to congratulate the landlady on her timely appearance when a blinding flash of pain hurled me to the floor. When I regained my senses, the landlady was slapping my face and Rachel was coming in with a dish of steaming water and a towel. The Nigerian was nowhere in sight.

The landlady reached out for the towel, but Rachel said: "You've done quite enough as it is. You could have killed my husband, you know."

The landlady sighed like one who is used to being ill used:

"It's my glasses. I couldn't see which one was the Nigerian and which one was him, you know. And I thought I may as well knock them both down, because I didn't know who it was I knocked down first. You know," said the landlady as she peered down at me.

My lips had stretched out in a tight smile; I was trying not to laugh.

The landlady picked up the dangerous rolling pin and said: "These are very handy, you know. When my husband came home drunk the other day . . ."

"That will be all, Mrs. Sutcliffe-Smith," Rachel said firmly.

The landlady winced and strode out with great dignity.

Rachel stared down at me and—for the first time since those distant five days—looked much older, I mean not much older, than the eighteen-year-old she was.

"It's still not late for an abortion," she said.

She wrung out the towel and wiped the blood streaming out of my nose.

"Did you hear what I said?"

"I'm having dinner with Michael—you remember him, don't you, from when you were training as a nurse?"

"The one with the stammer?"

I nodded.

I corrected myself: "We're having dinner with him tonight. He's the best doctor in Oxford. We'll mention it casually to him.

"Rachel," I added, "welcome home."

Thick white doves' feathers snowed down from the overcast skies. Would my novel be accepted? Would Rachel soon tire of me once again? I was still rather weak; but I knew that deep inside me I had said good-bye to Africa, forever. The illusory down of the white white snow gleamed with a desolate brightness. Christchurch struck four o'clock. Once more I paced up and down in my study and tried vainly to drive away the startling refrain that was, like a stuck record player, repeating itself over and over inside my head. When I looked out through the windows, hoping to retrace my life's footsteps, I saw that fresh armfuls of snow had covered up my thought tracks.

Ken Lipenga was born in southern Malawi. He enrolled at the University of Malawi in 1971, graduated in 1976, and stayed on to teach literature at Chancellor College. In 1981 he published *Waiting for a Turn*, a collection of short stories. He is currently Minister of State in the President's Office for Presidential Affairs in Malawi.

Waiting for a Turn

All roads lead to Sapitwa. All traffic moves toward Sapitwa. Rivers crisscross and point in different directions. But all rivers flow into Sapitwa pool. Tears of laughter and tears of sorrow flow into Sapitwa pool. All enemies meet and shake hands at Sapitwa.

I

There was no question that my Mbambande Tailoring Shop was the most successful in town. Everyone, from platformed young men and bewigged girls to respectable big shots, came to my shop for their clothes. Everyone who wanted the very latest fashion came to Mbambande. Wives refused dresses from their husbands unless they carried the Mbambande label. Girls ignored a young man unless they were convinced that his suit was from Mbambande. Children refused to go to school until *ababa* bought their school uniforms from Mbambande. Anything without the Mbambande label was old-fashioned. Fragile marriages collapsed beneath the weight of the Mbambande label. In short no one was anyone unless they were clothed by Mbambande Tailoring Shop. Such was my success.

All this was a pleasant surprise. There were times, I admit, when I felt genuinely alarmed at my success. For I had not expected anything of the sort when, a few months after leaving the university, I resigned from that insurance job. And here I must give you a little more detail.

I had resigned for two reasons. First, I could not understand why after spending years at the university, I found myself living from day to day, without the slightest sign that I would ever become rich. I am the get-rich-quick type and hadn't the patience to wait till I had crept through all the usual acrobatics that one must perform in order to get raises and rises. I also have a flighty temper, a weakness which wouldn't let me stand being bossed around by someone for the rest of my life.

I saved some money and resigned, planning to start a business of my own where I could boss myself and control the pace of my progress to the top. I chose tailoring. I don't quite know why. It may have to do with the fact that I had always been one for fashions in clothing. But at the time of my decision, I scarcely knew how to operate a sewing machine. I had to take a one-month course at one of the city tailoring shops. Thus I was in every way a novice in the business, and the success which soon came my way was a great surprise.

I think the hunchback appeared at about the time when I was approaching the peak of success and I needed more tailors. He came one morning, and before the day was over we all saw that he was exceptional. Exceptional in his skill and hard work. Give him a piece of cloth to be made into trousers and they would be ready within an hour. Get suspicious and look for faults and you would find none. Customers always went away satisfied. Oh, such a clever, fast tailor I had never seen before.

I was, of course, delighted; not only because his example infected the rest of my staff, but also because I felt his presence would make my business boom. I could already see rival firms withering away as I shot to the top.

Then came the shock. After a week Hunchback came to ask if he could live in the shop, as he could find no accommodation elsewhere. He was serious. But how could I allow this? My shop was on the city's main street, and to allow a hunchback, no matter how skilled and hard-working, to live there would be bad for business. Even without this problem the whole idea was unthinkable. So I said "No," as I am sure any other sane man would have done; but I also told him that I would look into the problem. He said nothing in reply.

The next morning Hunchback came in with his two wives and thirteen children. There was no word of explanation but it was clear that he had decided to move into the shop whether I liked it or not. The arrival of that army of children caused chaos; they roamed everywhere, pulling at the clothing, turning everything upside down, and causing panic and confusion among my tailors. Such rascals I had never seen before. But life is an unpleasant business, and I know such trials ought not surprise anyone. I found it all very painful.

I told Hunchback to leave. But he quietly refused to budge, and generally behaved as though he was only exercising a natural right. Well, I have already confessed that I am not a saint when it comes to keeping my temper on a leash. I kicked the hunchback with a heavy right boot, and, well, I swear I had never thought he was so light. My modest kick sent him clear into the street where he landed on his head, more or less.

I now seemed to be possessed by some evil spirit for I followed him and started clobbering him severely in front of all those people on the street. At this point his thirteen children, all of them very small and apparently of the same age, swarmed over me and started tearing at my clothes. And the people who had quickly gathered in a crowd gasped in amazement. They opened their mouths wide and although they did not say anything in particular I understood the message.

Hunchback, my exceptional tailor, disappeared with his two wives and thirteen children. Where he went, I knew not.

But immediately my business began to decline. It seemed that people generally disapproved of my beating up Hunchback. They also seemed to think that it would have done my business no harm at all to allow the hunchback and his family to live in my shop on Main Street.

I see no harm in begging to differ but, oh, why is life so unpleasant? People stopped coming to Mbambande Tailoring Shop and the ugliest things were said about me. People were earnestly warned off for fear of assault. Some ingenious fellow made the sudden discovery that we were not in fact good tailors at all, that my shop had from the start produced the lousiest tailoring in town. The news spread. Husbands pulled the Mbambande label from the clothes in their households for fear of having them burnt by angry wives. Girls scornfully ignored boys wearing

Mbambande clothes. All around I saw smaller shops booming and growing. My tailors complained that their wives threatened to leave them unless they stopped working for "the murderer." The tailors proved how they loved their wives by dropping out one by one.

Darkness settled on my shop. The sewing machines began to rust; a ghostly silence crept in; spiders built empires in dark corners; lizards played on the walls; grass grew fast outside: Mbambande Tailoring Shop was no more.

My wife, an imaginative woman, began to wonder why there was no bread no margarine no meat no soap no this no that in the house. She then proceeded to conclude that I was squandering my money on other women, and even claimed that she knew I had been doing this all along.

I kicked my wife with my favorite right boot, and I had not thought she was so light. My modest kick sent her flying through the door; I followed and angrily beat her up. My children pulled at my clothes, and the people from the neighborhood, who had quickly gathered in a crowd, opened their mouths wide and although they said nothing specific I could see they were not on my side.

My imaginative wife disappeared with the children, took them to her people. Ah, life is an unpleasant business.

Well, there was no going back now. I went into the kitchen and smashed the china. I came out and smashed all the furniture in the lounge. It didn't help. I piled up all my clothing and blankets and set them on fire. The smoke filled my eyes with tears, I turned on the radio full blast, went into a corner of the bedroom, and cried like a six-year-old. That didn't help either, so I took the radio outside and set it on fire while the crowd watched. They watched me in silence, their mouths agape, and when they were satisfied that I had destroyed all several rushed off in a hurry. I knew where they were going.

But they couldn't make a fool of me, for I had already sized up the situation and made the inevitable decision. None in the crowd dared come near me.

I set out for the mountain.

II

I lifted my bruised limbs and turned round to look back. It had been a great climb. Looking back at the world was like looking down a deep well; everything seemed so infinite. I tried to recall a picture of life down there, to come to terms with it, and mark its place in time. But time vanished and desolation grew. I abandoned the effort and became myself again.

I turned to face my new landscape. So the rocky massif glimmering in heavenly silver before me was Sapitwa. School geography books had merely said this was the highest peak in the area, without suggesting any spiritual power. How thrilling it was! How elevating! What better site could I have chosen? Here on Sapitwa I was at the apex, here on Sapitwa I was (at least physically!) above mortals, and this thought made my blood surge with joy. I kept reminding myself that no other mortal had ever thought of this idea.

Long ago, when I was very young in the village, I asked my grandmother why she held the mountain in such reverence, indeed at times even worshiping it.

"Because, son," she said, "the spirits of the ancestors dwell there."

"Where exactly?"

She had laughed before she realized that I was serious.

"Near the top," she had answered.

"But why not on the very top itself, grandmother?"

"Because on the very top, son, dwell the Great Spirits themselves, guarding the Great Abyss."

Imagine! I had selected for the site of my deed the dwelling place of the Great Spirits themselves! I had not been thinking of the conversation with my grandmother when I made that inevitable decision. I only remembered it on arrival before the peak. I was thrilled at the idea of being received by sacred entities. It added a divine dimension to my plan. And this was what I had wanted: an original kind of departure, not something ready-made which you only had to put on when the time arrived. No, a ready-made life was to be rewarded with an original death.

From the landscape it was easy to guess where it must be, the East. There was something ominously inviting about the East, some mystical spell about this region which was associated with sunrise and the Magi. And that was only proper, for was not the leap itself a step toward spiritual renewal? Would not that simple act let me live in the world of the Great Spirits? I walked on toward the Abyss, oblivious to all but the spiritual ecstasy eating up my inside. Closer and closer to the Abyss I went, and all along I readied myself for the leap.

But from nowhere four hands suddenly grabbed my neck and arms. A dizzy spell pinned my soul to the ground; I felt like a grasshopper under an elephant's foot. I had feared at the start that I was being followed but had never expected anyone to come this far. I sank into delirium.

Hello my exceptional tailor hello my imaginative wife! Glad to see you two again! What can I do for you? I'll do the impossible for you. Just wait here a moment while I fetch the impossible. But why are your friends' mouths gaping? Why doesn't anything come out of those mouths? Why don't they say something?

My captors had given me some time to recover from the shock, for when I came to they were sitting patiently on a rock beside me. I looked at them, two heavy figures in a strange uniform, and my eyes begged for an explanation.

"Sorry, uncle," said one in a voice all its own. "We didn't mean to be rough with you. Only we thought you might need some help."

His voice was a hen's scratch on a healing wound: it provoked a nausea from the distant past which had somehow managed to pocket itself away. I felt insulted, extremely insulted. I mumbled something about privacy; something about rights to my own property; something about Hunchback being a man. But my voice failed, my will vanished when I realized that the two men did not follow what I was saying.

"Sorry, uncle," said the spokesman. "We don't understand what you are saying, but we don't believe we've anything to do with it. We only want to clear up a certain misunderstanding. I . . . er . . . I take it you're on your way to the Abyss?"

I nodded.

"Then please come this way. You must take your place in the queue . . . I take it you're aware of the queue?"

There was something hovering at the doorway of my mind which I struggled to pin down. The man's voice made me feel as if I was cutting a ludicrous figure in a crowd. I felt like a clown. I felt I was being laughed at. Someone had found that I was a clown and spread the news. It seemed that I was about to be the victim of some mysterious force.

"I take it you're aware of the queue?"

All roads lead to Sapitwa. All traffic roars toward Sapitwa. Rivers crisscross and point in different directions. But all rivers flow into the Sapitwa pool. Tears of laughter and tears of sorrow flow into Sapitwa pool. Blood, sweat and tears flow into Sapitwa pool. The wind blows all fires toward Sapitwa. All roads lead to Sapitwa. Deadly enemies seal their mouths with the sap of the *kachere* tree and swear never to talk to each other. But all enemies meet and shake hands at Sapitwa.

In my head, pictures of a clever Hunchback shrouded in smoke.

"I take it you're aware of the queue."

It was a still, multicolored thread which disappeared into the distance on both sides, a silent river made of faces, black faces, brown faces, white faces, yellow faces, young faces, old faces, middle-aged faces, rich and poor faces looking bored, grim faces of businessmen and beggars, faces of red-eyed prostitutes and professors, faces of bus drivers, faces of drunken old women, faces of banana sellers, faces of international politicians, faces of spear-brandishing warriors, faces of mourning mothers side by side with faces of pilots of bomber planes, faces of convicted thieves, tired faces, happy faces, angry faces, frightened faces, faces, faces, faces; faces of all kinds, standing still in that endless line.

"You see," spokesman was saying, "you've to wait for all these people in front of you. They came here before you. You mustn't jump the queue. It isn't proper. Quite against the rules here."

A mystical experience. We walked on.

"These people you see all came here long before you. Er . . . I wouldn't be wrong to assume that you too, uncle, are on the Quest . . . I mean for a . . . er . . . shall we call it a parting of your own?"

The feeling you get is of transparent nakedness, a feeling such as you experience in a dream where, walking around amid a crowd a short distance from your house, you discover that you are going about stark naked.

"In that case, as you can see, you have company. But we believe in being orderly here. Hence the queue. I take it you don't mind?"

Every particle of the experience hovered on the threshold, like a memory struggling to come clear.

"Good. I thought so. You see, uncle, the moment you appeared there, I knew you were one of us. You have company, you have company. I tell you, it used to be all chaos here, before things were organized. People fighting to get a place at the edge to leap to their end. Some even getting killed before they got a chance to die their chosen death. It was survival of the fittest then, crude brute behavior. That's why it was necessary to have a kind of system."

I think we walked, for a year or so. I could not measure the time or distance. But in the end my captor said: "Aha, we're here at last, uncle. This is your place in the queue. Stay here, and wait for your turn."

III

I am still waiting. Been waiting all these years. Gray hairs have raided my head. My front teeth have dropped earthward. Sometimes I feel as if spiders have built empires in the dark corners of my head, and from time to time I think I hear lizards playing hide and seek in my inside. Yesterday I was amazed to see folds on my forehead. These days I avoid making journeys, and when I do I have to rely on my companion the stick. I know that soon I shall have to give up journeys altogether, for my eyes are losing faith.

I am still waiting. My turn has not yet come. They say it will, that we must keep waiting and not lose faith. Last year progress was made: I received The Initiation, and now have a new name. I am at last fit for the Great Abyss. The Great Spirits will receive me! Oh, how I long for the day!

There are many of us here on Sapitwa, and we get new arrivals every day, all on the Quest. If you look over the edge of the peak on the far side, so the young men tell me, you see countless humans clambering to reach the top. Most are young and are on the run for one reason or another. Sometimes I feel the brats ought to be sent back. Their reasons lack depth. But there's no choice, for these youngsters are a force of their own. Only a few months ago, they ganged up and threatened to reintroduce chaos at the Abyss.

I am told that the peaks surrounding Sapitwa are also filled with humans clambering on the Quest. So we are not the only ones after all. It's reassuring, though I don't quite know if the story is true. People can take advantage of your weak eyes and tell you all sorts of lies.

With the growing population here on Sapitwa we had to reorganize ourselves into a kind of community, with leaders and representatives of this and that and the other. Last year came a priest who has been active in establishing a church and school too, because of the many children being born here as we wait our turn. A hospital has also been built and is proving very useful.

I don't know when my turn will come, but I'm certain that more years will pass. While I wait I have found something to fill my time. Over the years it has become necessary to have tailors here on Sapitwa, and my skill was naturally called upon. So, well, I'm not ashamed to say that I have opened a tailoring shop. On the door of my tailoring shop a Sapitwa artist has painted in crude letters: "New Mbambande Tailoring Shop." I have a number of tailors working for me, and among them are two or three who worked for me in the old shop. They came here too. Isn't life a mysterious affair? I have, however, been particularly careful to avoid tailors of the hunchback kind. It is a simple business precaution.

IBRAHIM ABDEL MEGID

Ibrahim Abdel Megid was born in 1946 in Egypt. He published his first novel, *During the 67th Summer*, in 1979. His other books include *The Night of Passion and Blood*, *The Fisherman and the Pigeon*, *The Other Place*, *No One Sleeps in Alexandria*, and the story collection *Small Contemplations Around a Big Wall*.

The Other City

Translated by Alice Copple-Tošić

The door of the aircraft opened and I beheld the silence . . . It is a very rare occasion to feel the freshness of air-conditioning on your back while the sun is already bathing your chest and face and you have not yet passed through the door of the aircraft. A hand pushed me lightly from behind and I had to take the first step.

I had barely let go of the little ladder and brushed the ground when I had the sensation of creating, together with the ground and space, a single and indistinguishable object, empty and hot.

I had to walk the distance that separated me from the airport terminal. The airport was small; one single little dark yellow airplane was parked in the distance. The American flag was drawn on its flank; underneath, I read in English "United States Air Force."

Soldiers with sunburnt faces were standing by the terminal door. One of them yelled, "Men in the line to your right, women to the left." Through the window I noted, in a corner of the terminal, a circular conveyor belt just above the ground and I knew that my suitcase would arrive on it.

"Come forward 'young man,'" yelled one of the soldiers to me.

Those in front of me were already in the terminal . . . I must have fallen asleep on my feet, in the line.

"Have you forgotten me?"

I was confused and almost apologized but I said, "Not at all, I was waiting for you."

"Wait for me, we'll leave the airport together."

The baggage began to arrive . . . I deserted him to approach the conveyor belt. What was it about this young man that put me off?

I picked up my little red suitcase and placed it in front of one of the customs agents, all of whom seemed very young to me; looking at their faces and bodies, they could have scarcely been over eighteen. I opened it rapidly, he searched it just as rapidly. I had barely closed it when he ordered me to open it again.

"What's that, books?"

"That's a medical journal, *Your Doctor.*"

"It's forbidden."

We looked each other in the eye. I could find no rejoinder.

"What is it with these Egyptians, why do they love to read so much?" he asked in a loud voice. I remained silent. Should I say that "Farouk"— the one who'd gotten me the job contract—had asked me to bring him this special issue on "Maternity and Birth," or should I say that I was not familiar with the laws of the country?

"Pass . . ." he said in a nonchalant voice; he closed the suitcase with one hand, leaving the journal inside. I walked away without believing it and saw Farouk smiling at me through the window . . .

"Didn't I say that you'd forgotten me?"

This time I was very embarrassed. It was the second time that Abed had surprised me like this. I was sitting in the car next to Farouk, while he spoke to me through the open window, almost sticking in his long face with narrow eyes and thick eyebrows, clearly knit in the middle. I shook off my confusion and introduced him to Farouk who said, as he started the car, "Hello, Abed. We've already met."

"Yes—is he really a relative of yours? He's awfully shy."

"It's his first trip outside of Egypt, he'll show up at work tomorrow."

Farouk spoke without even bothering to look at Abed who had put his head all the way through the open window. I could almost feel his breath and didn't know which of the two to look at. But Abed left and I said to Farouk: "Why didn't you offer him a ride?"

"He has his own car."

"But he's just come in from Cairo with me!"

"Don't upset yourself about others."

I felt as if I didn't understand a thing and chose to keep quiet. I decided to become a child again, a blank page holding all the colors, a polished mirror reflecting things and making them slide without leaving a trace. The air was hot and stifling . . .

The Japanese Datsun darted onto the long narrow road bordered with endless sand. Farouk drove at a reckless speed. The road was empty, true enough, but I had never been in a car that raced that fast. Farouk put a cassette in the tape deck and I heard the voice of Mohammed Abdo singing "La Turiddin al-Rasail" (You don't answer).

"Here's your enterprise," he said as he caught sight of several shacks scattered on the side of the road. Two children were playing in front of the shacks. A car speeding even faster than ours passed us on the right. I jumped. Farouk smiled and said: "Everyone's wild about speed here and everyone passes on the wrong side . . ."

I retreated into my contemplations and thought about Abed . . . As is usually the case in an airplane, when two people find themselves accidentally sitting in neighboring seats, conversation is inevitable. He worked for the same enterprise that had just employed me and had spent his annual holiday in Cairo. He offered me his place to stay my first night, I answered that I had a relative in the small town, then he told me that lodgings were expensive, that the enterprise had its own residence but that it had been invaded by Asian workers and beds were only available on rare occasions. He questioned me at length about my origins, my previous job, how I had gotten the job contract, my future plans, if I was married or single and many other things besides; his questions really bothered me but I said to myself that perhaps he was only trying to be helpful.

"I see that you were very late at the airport."

"*Your Doctor* . . . They said it was forbidden."

Farouk said: "It's of no more use."

I smiled. "So you've become a father."

He stepped on the gas. "It's more like I became single, I divorced."

The small town appeared and then disappeared again; Farouk had branched off to the right and taken a road that ringed it at some distance. Next to the road I saw a block of low houses, the majority of them single story, unlike most of the residences in town that I had briefly glimpsed which had seemed relatively tall. The car jolted along the poorly paved alleys. Many cars were parked in front of the narrow iron doors of the houses. "In this place, every alley is a real car show," said Farouk, who had certainly noticed how engrossed I was in the different types of cars.

"It's been less than a year since you got married," I remarked.

"She wanted to buy a plot of land in her village," he replied, "and I wanted to buy another in mine."

I didn't understand. The rare times that I had met Farouk, he hadn't appeared nervous or cantankerous. Actually, he was my mother's cousin. Barely five years ago—the year I graduated from the university—he had suddenly appeared in our life, maintaining that he had been posted by the Civil Department of Bridges and Highways as an engineer in Alexandria and that it was an opportunity to come and visit us. My mother mentioned the names of several of her relatives in the village; he told her that they were all dead. He interrupted his visits for a period of one year and then reappeared, reproaching me for not having gone to visit him and my mother had said he was right; I didn't want to say that it was difficult to develop strong ties with a relative who appeared sud-denly when I was already an adolescent, and, in actual fact, I'm not acquainted with our village. I wasn't born there and have never visited it. The strangest thing is that Farouk disappeared again after two or three visits; I don't know how my mother learned that he was in Saudi Arabia or what induced him to write me, offering to help me travel. I hesitated at length, but I had to accept.

I said: "You could have postponed this acquisition."

"Why shouldn't a wife obey her husband?"

I was silent, but he continued.

"I gave her three thousand pounds; that's what the marriage cost me. I'll make up for it and find a much better match." He was quiet for a moment. "Here's my house. A doctor and a teacher lodge with me."

The cold shower is truly a divine invention. I would have preferred to be left alone, to myself, but they insisted that I sit with them and take part in a spirited game of backgammon. I disliked the house at first glance. Two rooms on either side of a large interior courtyard, the bathroom and kitchen at the end. Farouk said that the house had been modeled after Arabic architecture, but in my opinion it was only an arrangement of concrete cubes. Two of the rooms were narrow and their windows looked onto the courtyard and not the street, which was more restful perhaps, but the tiny windows looked like those in a prison cell . . . Under the cold shower, I heard the dice move, the clicking of the counters, the applause and laughs; I thought of sneaking quickly to my room, which Farouk had furnished with a plastic collapsible closet, a single bed and an electric fan, but they surprised me and pronounced in unison, "No one sleeps before midnight here, it's the law of nature . . ." I joined their group. I noted during the short trip from the bathroom to where they sat that my chest and legs were already sweating.

It was almost night and the atmosphere hadn't changed. The air was so heavy and stagnant that it could have been cut into pieces and held in your hand!

"Do you have any rials [Saudi money]?" began the doctor who, I was to learn later, was named Wajih.

The question shocked me, and it was the teacher who replied; I learned later that his name was Said. "We play for money."

I sat at the place they had made for me next to them. Someone knocked at the door. Farouk hurried to answer it. Abed's face appeared behind the door that Farouk held half-open. I got up to greet him.

"One of the beds in the enterprise residence has been vacated, if you want to take it I can reserve it for you!" said Abed.

I would have liked to open the door wider and invite him in, but Farouk held the door ajar and his body almost completely blocked the opening. He spoke before I could say a word: "We'll see about that tomorrow."

"I had quite a time finding your house; I dropped by the enterprise by chance and learned that a Pakistani had died and that his place was free. I thought it was a good opportunity and that I should let you know about it." Abed spoke in a very friendly voice; I stood there, embarrassed.

Farouk said: "Thank you."

Abed answered: "Don't let it slip through your fingers!" and then he left.

Farouk closed the door and returned to his seat. I remained standing for several moments and then followed him.

"I'll lend my cousin five rials," he said.

I made no comment.

"Don't be afraid, whatever you lose you'll win back, that's the rule in this game," said Dr. Wajih.

I did not reply.

"We're just killing time," said Farouk.

I made no remark.

"Each game is worth ten rials; we note the wins and losses in this notebook," said Said, the teacher.

I continued to remain silent.

"At the end of the month, the winner repays the loser the money he's lost, and we start all over again," said the doctor.

We were all silent for several moments and he continued: "You must certainly wonder what is the purpose of all this since each one is certain of recovering his money?"

I didn't reply. He then said enigmatically: "To tell the truth, we don't even know ourselves . . ."

Ndeley Mokoso was born in Cameroon. He has worked as a
journalist, industrialist, and politician, and in 1987 published
Man Pass Man, a collection of stories.

God of Meme

The villagers named the festival the "visitation." A festival
handed down by their grandfathers and great-great-grandfathers
before them. Once a year, they assembled on the banks of the Mungo
River, to pay homage and sing praises to the "god" of the river.

They had trekked for miles, men, women, and children. Among the
throng were members of the man-crocodile cult, identified by woven
strands of crocodile hide worn around their right ankles.

Members of the cult were held in great respect and awe. There were
the stories of the fanatic adherence to the cult by its members; its survival under the ruthlessness of the early German administrators, and its
near demise as a result of the persuasions and organized campaigns by
the Christian missionaries.

The crowd retreated as members of the cult trooped down the riverbank; two of them carrying a bleating he-goat for the sacrifice, another
followed with a machete. The ceremony was brief. The goat was tethered onto a stake driven into the ground. They then surrounded the
goat—all of them. The tallest of them raised the machete high above his
head, then brought it down—one stroke that severed the head from the
body. The blood-spattered carcass was flung deep into the river.

Then the drumming, singing and clapping started, with members of
the cult performing a jig peculiar only to their group. One of their members had worked himself into a frenzy as the tempo of the drumming
increased and dropped heavily on the ground. His colleagues quickly
cordoned off the area, rallying round him as he lay sprawled on the

ground, quite relaxed, his chest heaving slowly. The rest continued in hilarious mood, stamping their feet as the drums throbbed louder and louder.

From the opposite bank of the river came a loud snort, then the snout, the large protruding eyes, the head and the long scaly body.

The crowd yelled in ecstasy and prayed in unison—

Lord of the river
Thy might we acknowledge
Protect us from the evil one
Fill the bellies of our women with babies
And provide the rich harvest to feed them
Long may you reign

The crocodile waddled up the opposite bank and opened its mouth in greeting, displaying two long rows of gleaming white teeth. The crowd roared and cheered hysterically as it later submerged, retrieved the carcass, thrashed its tail and glided slowly downstream and out of sight.

The crocodiles in this river were docile beasts—domesticated, to be more exact. They could be identified, talked to and stroked lovingly. I myself had witnessed a startling and weird incident while taking a trip by canoe to one of the villages. We had come across what appeared to be a log of timber. The canoe man had tried to maneuver his craft on course, when a member of the cult, who happened to be traveling with us, ordered him to drop anchor. He announced, rather jokingly, that a friend of his had blocked our course. He then stood up, waved his hands in salute and called: "Lokindo . . . lokindo . . . Masengo, your colleague, salutes you. Pray let us proceed." A few yams were thrown overboard, and what had appeared to the rest of us as a log of timber turned out to be a live crocodile. It thrashed its tail, submerged and gave us right of way.

Many a time, the crocodiles lay basking in the sun on the muddy bank while men, women, and children swam and bathed with no concern whatsoever regarding their safety. They all knew the animals were harmless—human beings in crocodile form. The story goes, however, that a certain German administrator, named Von Schnieder, had been killed by a crocodile. That he was the only victim seized from a group of five. The rest were unharmed. They said it was a reprisal for his brutality and other acts of callousness against the natives. They said he had caused ten identified members of the man-crocodile cult to be shot.

The natives around had been summoned forcibly at gunpoint to witness what was classified as a punitive measure. In a specially prepared arena, the condemned men were made to climb on trees and a game hunting exercise began. White soldiers armed with rifles brought them down one by one—a spectacle that was intended to shock the natives into submission. Those who showed signs of sympathy or wept for executed relatives or friends were stripped and whipped with horse whips. Von Schnieder's corpse was never found.

But the "god" of the river was now aging. He had lost his youthful skill and speed that had earlier characterized the quick dispatch of his victims. He had been content with lying in wait for forest animals—antelopes and other small game which came down regularly for a drink. Many a time he had succeeded in flailing them with his powerful scaly tail, so powerful that it crushed the victim into a battered shuddering heap. The strong jaws and claws retracted into the body which was then dragged virtually underwater and drowned.

Today, he had watched a small herd of antelopes cropping the grass, anxious for water, but, for some reason he did not know, afraid to approach the river. He moved slowly. Only the tip of the snout and the large bulging eyes above water.

Two young antelopes ventured down the river's edge. They seemed to have sensed the danger, for they suddenly stopped drinking, raised their heads and cocked their ears. Now, he must take his time. A lot depended on this particular kill—he had been some days without food. He made a desperate dash for the nearest antelope. His timing was faulty, and he had just missed his victim by inches. The animals gave the alarm and the whole herd stampeded to the safety of the forest.

Farther up the river, a little footpath zigzagged to the riverbank. The local people simply called the place "Small Beach." Here, everyone to and from the village had to be taken across by canoe. It was market day, a very busy day for the canoe man. Women with baskets of cocoyams and plantains strapped on their backs stood waiting for their turn. Today, they were growing rather impatient and angry—the canoe man had arbitrarily raised the toll by two pence.

The "god" of the river watched these goings and comings with renewed interest. Not that he was doing so for the first time. Today he was hungrier than usual; really hungry and the urge to survive had put him in a different frame of mind. He wondered what human flesh tasted like. "Must be horrible," he thought as he tried to work out how best he would set about it. It was a strange feeling that touched his very heart, but the urge to survive was uppermost.

Five more persons had arrived—three women carrying baskets of cassava on their heads and two petty traders on bicycles. Two of the women were first taken across, the third had emptied her basket of cassava and started peeling them. The two men with the bicycles were ferried across too, and finally the broad-breasted woman, who had by now finished peeling her cassava. After taking her across, the canoe man settled down to his breakfast of koki and plantain. After the meal, he walked down to the river to rinse his mouth and wash his hands.

There was no one in sight. The crocodile moved closer. "Now, I must take my time," he thought. Another false movement meant another day without food. He wanted it to be a clean business. None of his subjects should witness such an atrocity. The "god" of the river was becoming a man-eater.

The man washed his hands, scooped out the water in the boat and checked the mooring rope. Satisfied that all was well, he walked a few paces from the water's edge and sat down for a brief rest before his customers arrived for the return trip.

The crocodile moved stealthily closer. He was not sure whether the man's gaze was fixed on the river. It became clear, as he drew closer, that the man was dozing. Then he struck. It was quick work, delivered with the right timing and precision. Only a sharp, muffled scream. The powerful jaws locked on the man's shoulder like a vise and dragged him to the bottom of the river. The now limp body coughed and kicked desperately until it choked and lay still.

The villagers found the bloody trail. The canoe still lay moored. They could not believe their eyes! It had never happened before! They could not understand it at all, and no one dared accuse the "god" of the river of such an atrocity!

And so the "god" of the river's blood lust continued with unabated fury. The baby left by the mother to wander while she did her laundry had disappeared. Villagers paddling down river in canoes laden with cocoyams and plantains had been chased by the crocodile. At first, the smell of human blood had sickened and frightened him. Now it had a sweetness that caused him pangs of desire to kill again and again.

The next victim was Water-boy, the laborer who carried water from the river to the Estate Manager's house up the hill. Once again, it was a successful operation. Only Water-boy's empty bucket was found. There again were the signs the unseen and merciless enemy had left behind—a bloody trail which ended by the riverbank.

Following this latest incident, David Jones, the Estate Manager, had received a delegation of the Workers' Trade Union. They demanded that some drastic action be taken to safeguard the lives of its members. They had given the Manager ten days to show what was described as some positive measures, failing which the Union would take any action it deemed fit. It was clear to the five-man delegation that the Manager was equally concerned about the recent threat on the peaceful and orderly existence of his little community. He realized that he would have to pay large sums of money under the Workmen's Compensation Ordinance if the crocodile's blood lust continued.

David Jones had discussed the matter with the local Administrative Officer, suggesting that the man-crocodile cult be banned. He had argued that the crocodile was a menace and its continued existence not conducive to public peace and safety. He was aware that crocodiles were protected under the Wildlife Preservation Ordinance, but there was the proviso which stated that if such protected game threatened the peaceful and orderly existence of the community, thereby constituting a danger to life and property, it could be destroyed in the public interest.

This is why David Jones had shot at the beast when it killed his dog before his very eyes. The livid flash and the explosion had brought down groups of scared and angry villagers, all members of the cult, to the riverbank. They had protested vehemently and explained that the recent happenings were the wrath of the "god" of the river. The spokesman pointed out that the tendency had been for certain persons to ignore the laid down taboos with regard to the river. They had continued to shout across the river; they had continued to wash the soot off cooking pots and "bitter leaf" in the river. All these actions were regarded and accepted as gross disrespect for the "god" of the river. His recent attempt

to kill the "god" of the river was an affront and a desecration—an act
which was likely to cause a breach of the peace. They wanted an assurance that the "god" of the river would not be threatened or molested.
"You will be taken away like the other white man before you, if you per-
sist," they warned him.

The meeting ended in uproar. The Manager accused the group of
blackmail, asked them out of his office and threatened to call the police.
That settled it. They shook their fists and cursed as they backed away.
They swore they would "call" the rain. And the rain came a few hours
after the meeting. It rained as it had never rained before. The river
began to rise, and twenty-four hours later the young rubber trees were
standing in three feet of water. Reports soon came in about the two
wooden bridges which had been swept away by the floods. Effective
supervision of the estate was now impossible. The rainmakers too had
joined the vicious circle.

At the meeting convened by the District Officer to agree to a line of
action, the District Clerk, a local man who had made good, sat tight-
lipped throughout the discussions. He looked greatly terrified when
opinion weighed in favor of shooting the crocodile. He had pleaded in
tears that such an act would completely disrupt the communal life of his
people. He expressed the fear that he would be killed by a crocodile if
it was known that he had connived with the administration in making
such a decision. His fears were allayed. He was promised protection
against any possible reprisals or molestation.

But the meeting had not ended when a court messenger arrived with
the sad news of yet another victim—a little girl aged ten. Something
had to be done at once. The man-eater was to be destroyed and the
activities of the cult banned. That was the consensus. Orders were given
for four policemen with crack shots to be issued with four rounds of
ammunition each. They were to report to headquarters for briefing. A
Land Rover equipped with radio communication equipment, tear gas
and handcuffs was requisitioned in case there was mob resistance. The
little force then left, led by the Administrative Officer and the Police
Commissioner.

The road was steep all the way and rugged. There were several
flooded stretches and time and again the auxiliary gears had to be
engaged. After half an hour the Land Rover chugged to a halt. They had

come to the end of the motorable road. The rest of the journey had to be done on foot, through a bush track—a distance of about two miles. The forest was thick, and sometimes it was dark as the dense foliage cut off most of the light.

It was about midday when they arrived at a clearing. The vegetation was less dense. There were plantain and cocoyam farms all over and in the distance there was rising smoke. Another ten minutes' trek brought them to the village. It was like every other village in the district—a tight cluster of bamboo huts covered with thatch. There was a large crowd at one end. People were talking in low tones and over the hum of voices came the traditional wailing so common at village funerals.

The crowd moved back slowly as the group arrived. There, on a rough wooden bed, lay the mangled remains of the ten-year-old girl. The body had been found with the face torn off and the guts scooped.

A slight rustle commenced among the audience as the policemen unshouldered their rifles. Then there was silence as the voice of authority spoke. "This is a very sad thing," the District Officer began. "Very sad, very bad thing," he emphasized, picking his words slowly. "This thing cannot be allowed to go on. People cannot continue to live in fear. Government has an obligation to protect its citizens. This animal is a menace, and it is the Government's determination that it be destroyed." He stopped and watched the reaction of the crowd. Then he went on. "I want three powerful men to pull us up the river in a boat." There was silence. "Are there no volunteers? I will give you three minutes to decide. Thereafter I will take whatever action I deem fit."

The villagers stood their ground. None of them wished to be involved in what they considered a conspiracy against the "god" of the river. The Administrative Officer looked at his watch and raised his hand. "You, you and you," he pointed to three stocky, broad-chested villagers. "March these fellows down the river." The policemen stepped forward, their guns held menacingly. The terrified men meekly and resignedly did a "quick march" as ordered.

One man in the crowd eyed the Administrative Officer owlishly. He began reciting an unintelligible litany of woe, followed by an unending flood of bitter invective. The man was simply known as Tata Maloba, a surly old man aged about sixty. "And what's the meaning of this?" he screamed, his look glowering—contempt mingled with respect. "I've come to shoot the rogue of a crocodile and nothing will stop me. I don't even care if it is your own." He looked determined. The old man threw himself on the ground begging. He would never molest or kill anyone, ever again. He was bluntly told that it was now too late and that his confession could not help him.

Tata Maloba's crocodile lay basking peacefully as a result of the previous day's heavy meal, when the plop-plop of dipping paddles came to him; then the voices of men. His first instinct was to slip away unobserved. But it was too late; the men in the boat had seen him.

Corporal Doh, the man with the best shot, stood up. He withdrew the bolt of his rifle, slid a round into the breech and signed himself. His breathing deepened with nervous excitement as he raised the rifle high in the port, its butt pressing into his armpit. Then he pulled the trigger. He heard the explosion and the short screech of the bullet which smashed into the animal's head. Then followed three other explosions in quick succession as the other men raked him again and again.

The river took on a deeper brown hue as the crocodile in the throes of death thrashed and churned the muddy waters. It took some time to die, making noises that were really human, with eyes full of hate watching the men in the boat as it died.

Back in the village, a small crowd gathered as Tata Maloba collapsed, screaming and clutching at his head, crying: "I've been shot . . . I've been shot . . . I'm dying . . ." And he died soon after. The postmortem indeed proved that he had died from gunshot wounds. The corpse was riddled all over by bullets.

Ken Saro-Wiwa was born in 1941 in Nigeria. He was educated at the University of Obadan and at Government College Umuahia, where he later taught. He began publishing stories as editor of Obadan's student magazine *The Horizon*, and in the mid–1960s became an assistant lecturer at the University of Lagos. His academic career was thwarted by the Biafran War, however, after which he was installed as Civil Commissioner in the Rivers State Government. In 1973 he was dismissed from his post for his opinions on autonomy for the Ogoni people, an ethnic minority occupying Nigeria's oil-rich delta region. He continued to write, and in 1985 his first book, the antiwar *Sozaboy*, was published to widespread acclaim. He gained his largest audience, however, as writer and producer of the children's television show *Basi & Company*. The series was in turn cancelled by Nigeria's military dictatorship in 1992 as a result of Saro-Wiwa's efforts spearheading a campaign against the oil industry's appropriation of tribal lands. In 1994 he was imprisoned for alleged complicity in the murders of four Ogoni chiefs. Despite international protests, he was hanged after a show trial with eight other activists on November 10, 1995.

His books include *Songs in a Time of War*, *A Forest of Flowers*, *Adaku and Other Stories*, *Lemona's Tale*, *Genocide in Nigeria*, and a collection of essays, *Nigeria: The Brink of Disaster*.

Africa Kills Her Sun

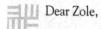 Dear Zole,

You'll be surprised, no doubt, to receive this letter. But I couldn't leave your beautiful world without saying good-bye to you who are condemned to live in it. I know that some might consider my gesture somewhat pathetic, as my colleagues, Sazan and Jimba, do, our finest moments having been achieved two or three weeks ago. However, for me, this letter is a celebration, a final act of love, a quality which, in spite of my career, in spite of tomorrow morning, I do possess in abundance, and cherish. For I've always treasured the many moments of pleasure we spent together in our youth when the world was new and fishes flew in golden ponds. In the love we then shared have I found happiness, a true resting place, a shelter from the many storms that have buffeted my brief life. Whenever I've been most alone, whenever I've been torn by conflict and pain, I've turned to that love for the resolution which has sustained and seen me through. This may surprise you, considering that this love was never consummated and that you may possibly have forgotten me, not having seen me these ten years gone. I still remember you, have always remembered you, and it's logical that in the night before tomorrow, I should write you to ask a small favor of you. But more importantly, the knowledge that I have unburdened myself to you will make tomorrow morning's event as pleasant and desirable to me as to the thousands of spectators who will witness it.

I know this will get to you because the prison guard's been heavily bribed to deliver it. He should rightly be with us before the firing squad tomorrow. But he's condemned, like most others, to live, to play out his assigned role in your hell of a world. I see him burning out his dull, uncomprehending life, doing his menial job for a pittance and a bribe for the next so many years. I pity his ignorance and cannot envy his complacency. Tomorrow morning, with this letter and our bribe in his pocket, he'll call us out, Sazan, Jimba, and I. As usual, he'll have all our names mixed up: he always calls Sazan "Sajim" and Jimba "Samba." But that won't matter. We'll obey him, and as we walk to our death, we'll laugh at his gaucherie, his plain stupidity. As we laughed at that other thief, the High Court Judge.

You must've seen that in the papers too. We saw it, thanks to our bribe-taking friend, the prison guard, who sent us a copy of the newspaper in which it was reported. Were it not in an unfeeling nation, among a people inured to evil and taking sadistic pleasure in the loss of life, some questions might have been asked. No doubt, many will ask the questions, but they will do it in the safety and comfort of their homes, over the interminable bottles of beer, uncomprehendingly watching their boring, cheap television programs, the rejects of Europe and America, imported to fill their vacuity. They will salve their conscience with more bottles of beer, wash the answers down their gullets and pass question, conscience and answer out as waste into their open sewers choking with concentrated filth and murk. And they will forget.

I bet, though, the High Court Judge himself will never forget. He must remember it the rest of his life. Because I watched him closely that first morning. And I can't describe the shock and disbelief which I saw registered on his face. His spectacles fell to his table and it was with difficulty he regained composure. It must have been the first time in all his experience that he found persons arraigned on a charge for which the punishment upon conviction is death, entering a plea of guilty and demanding that they be sentenced and shot without further delay.

Sazan, Jimba, and I had rehearsed it carefully. During the months we'd been remanded in prison custody while the prosecutors prepared their case, we'd agreed we weren't going to allow a long trial, or any possibility that they might impose differing sentences upon us: freeing one, sentencing another to life imprisonment and the third to death by firing squad.

Nor did we want to give the lawyers in their funny, black, funeral robes an opportunity to clown around, making arguments for pleasure, engaging in worthless casuistry. No. We voted for death. After all, we were armed robbers, bandits. We knew it. We didn't want to give the law a chance to prove itself the proverbial ass. We were being honest to ourselves, to our vocation, to our country, and to mankind.

"Sentence us to death immediately and send us before the firing squad without further delay," we yelled in unison. The

Judge, after he had recovered from his initial shock, asked us to
be taken away that day, "for disturbing my court." I suppose he
wanted to see if we'd sleep things over and change our plea. We
didn't. When they brought us back the next day, we said the
same thing in louder voice. We said we had robbed and killed.
We were guilty. Cool. The Judge was bound hand and foot and
did what he had to. We'd forced him to be honest to his vocation, to the laws of the country, and to the course of justice. It
was no mean achievement. The court hall was stunned; our
guards were utterly amazed as we walked out of court, smiling.
"Hardened criminals," "Bandits," I heard them say as we
trooped out of the court. One spectator actually spat at us as we
walked into the waiting Black Maria!

  And now that I've confessed to banditry, you'll ask why I did
it? I'll answer that question by retelling the story of the young,
beautiful prostitute I met in St. Pauli in Hamburg when our
ship berthed there years back. I've told my friends the story several times. I did ask her, after the event, why she was in that
place? She replied that some girls chose to be secretaries in
offices, others to be nurses. She had chosen prostitution as a
career. Cool. I was struck by her candor. And she set me thinking. Was I in the merchant navy by choice or because it was the
first job that presented itself to me when I left school? When
we returned home, I skipped ship, thanks to the prostitute of
St. Pauli, and took a situation as a clerk in the Ministry of
Defense.

  It was there I came face-to-face with the open looting of the
national treasury, the manner of which I cannot describe without arousing in myself the deepest, basest emotions. Everyone
was busy at it and there was no one to complain to. Everyone to
whom I complained said to me: "If you can't beat them, join
them." I was not about to join anyone; I wanted to beat them
and took it upon myself to wage a war against them. In no time
they had gotten rid of me. Dismissed me. I had no option but to
join them then. I had to make a choice. I became an armed robber, a bandit. It was my choice, my answer. And I don't regret it.

  Did I know it was dangerous? Some girls are secretaries, others choose to be prostitutes. Some men choose to be soldiers and policemen, others doctors and lawyers; I chose to be a robber. Every occupation has its hazards. A taxi driver may meet his death on the road; a businessman may die in an air crash; a robber dies before a firing squad. It's no big deal. If you ask me, the death I've chosen is possibly more dramatic, more qualitative, more eloquent than dying in bed of a ruptured liver from overindulgence in alcohol. Yes? But robbery is antisocial, you say? A proven determination to break the law. I don't want to provide an alibi. But just you think of the many men and women who are busy breaking or bending the law in all coasts and climes. Look for a copy of The Guardian of 19th September. That is the edition in which our plea to the Judge was reported. You'll find there the story of the Government official who stole over seven million naira. Seven million. Cool. He was antisocial, right? How many of his type d'you know? And how many more go undetected? I say, if my avocation was antisocial, I'm in good company. And that company consists of Presidents of countries, transnational organizations, public servants high and low, men and women. The only difference is that while I'm prepared to pay the price for it all, the others are not. See?

I'm not asking for your understanding or sympathy. I need neither, not now nor hereafter. I'm saying it as it is. Right? Cool. I expect you'll say that armed robbery should be the special preserve of the scum of society. That no man of my education has any business being a bandit. To that I'll answer that it's about time well-endowed and well-trained people took to it. They'll bring to the profession a romantic quality, a proficiency which will ultimately conduce to the benefit of society. No, I'm not mad. Truly. Time was when the running and ruining of African nations was in the hands of half-literate politicians. Today, well-endowed and better trained people have taken over the task. And look how well they're doing it. So that even upon that score, my conscience sleeps easy. Understand?

Talking about sleep, you should see Sazan and Jimba on the cold, hard prison floor, snoring away as if life itself depends on a good snore. It's impossible, seeing them this way, to believe that they'll be facing the firing squad tomorrow. They're men of courage. Worthy lieutenants. It's a pity their abilities will be lost to society forever, come tomorrow morning. Sazan would have made a good Army General anyday, possibly a President of our country in the mold of Idi Amin or Bokassa. The Europeans and Americans would have found in him a useful ally in the progressive degradation of Africa. Jimba'd have made an excellent Inspector-General of Police, so versed is he in the ways of the Police! You know, of course, that Sazan is a dismissed Sergeant of our nation's proud army. And Jimba was once a Corporal in the Police Force. When we met, we had similar reasons for pooling our talents. And a great team we did make. Now here we all are in the death cell of a maximum security prison and they snoring away the last hours of their lives on the cold, smelly floor. It's exhilarating to find them so disdainful of life. Their style is the stuff of which history is made. In another time and in another country, they'd be Sir Francis Drake, Cortes, or Sir Walter Raleigh. They'd have made empires and earned national honors. But here, our life is one big disaster, an endless tragedy. Heroism is not in our star. We are millipedes crawling on the floor of a dank, wet forest. So Sazan and Jimba will die unsung. See?

One thing, though. We swore never to kill. And we never did. Indeed, we didn't take part in the particular "operation" for which we were held, Sazan, Jimba, and I. That operation would've gone quite well if the Superintendent of Police had fulfilled his part of the bargain. Because he was in it with us. The Police are involved in every single robbery that happens. They know the entire gang, the gangs. We'd not succeed if we didn't collaborate with them. Sazan, Jimba, and I were the bosses. We didn't go out on "operations." The boys normally did. And they were out on that occasion. The Superintendent of Police was supposed to keep away the police escorts from the vehicle carrying workers' salaries that day. For some reason, he failed to do so. And the policeman shot at our boys. The boys responded and shot and killed him and the Security Company guards. The boys got the money alright. But the killing was contrary to our agreement with the Police. We had to pay. The Police won't stand any of their men being killed. They took all the money from us and then they went after the boys. We said no. The boys had acted on orders. We volunteered to take their place. The Police took us in and made a lot of public noises about it. The boys, I know, will make their decisions later. I don't know what will happen to the Superintendent of Police. But he'll have to look to himself. So, if that is any comfort to you, you may rest in the knowledge that I spilt no blood. No, I wouldn't. Nor have I kept the loot. Somehow, whatever we took from people—the rich ones—always was shared by the gang who were almost always on the bread line. Sazan, Jimba, and I are not wealthy.

Many will therefore accuse us of recklessness, or of being careless with our lives. And well they might. I think I speak for my sleeping comrades when I say we went into our career because we didn't see any basic difference between what we were doing and what most others are doing throughout the land today. In every facet of our lives—in politics, in commerce, and in the professions—robbery is the baseline. And it's been so from time immemorial. In the early days, our forebears sold their kinsmen into slavery for minor items such as beads, mirrors, alcohol, and tobacco. These days, the tune is the same, only the articles have changed into cars, transistor radios, and bank accounts. Nothing else has changed, and nothing will change in the foreseeable future. But that's the problem of those of you who will live beyond tomorrow, Zole.

The cock crows now and I know dawn is about to break. I'm not speaking figuratively. In the cell here, the darkness is still all-pervasive, except for the flickering light of the candle by which I write. Sazan and Jimba remain fast asleep. So is the prison guard. He sleeps all night and is no trouble to us. We could, if we wanted, escape from here, so lax are the guards. But we consider that unnecessary, as what is going to happen later this morning is welcome relief from burdens too heavy to bear. It's the guard and you the living who are in prison, the ultimate prison from which you cannot escape because you do not know that you are incarcerated. Your happiness is the happiness of ignorance and your ignorance is it that keeps you in the prison, which is your life. As this night dissolves into day, Sazan, Jimba, and I shall be free. Sazan and Jimba will have left nothing behind. I shall leave at least this letter, which, please, keep for posterity.

Zole, do I rant? Do I pour out myself to you in bitter tones? Do not lay it to the fact that I'm about to be shot by firing squad. On second thoughts, you could, you know. After all, seeing death so clearly before me might possibly have made me more perspicacious? And yet, I've always seen these things clearly in my mind's eye. I never did speak about them, never discussed them. I preferred to let them weigh me down. See?

So, then, in a few hours we shall be called out. We shall clamber with others into the miserable lorry which they still call the Black Maria. Notice how everything miserable is associated with us. Black Sheep. Black Maria. Black Death. Black Leg. The Black Hole of Calcutta. The Black Maria will take us to the Beach or to the Stadium. I bet it will be the Stadium. I'd prefer the Beach. So at least to see the ocean once more. For I've still this fond regard for the sea which dates from my time in the Merchant Navy. I love its wide expanse, its anonymity, its strength, its unfathomable depth. And maybe after shooting us, they might decide to throw our bodies into the ocean. We'd then be eaten up by sharks which would in turn be caught by Japanese and Russian fishermen, be refrigerated, packaged in cartons and sold to Indian merchants and then for a handsome profit to our people. That way, I'd have helped keep people alive a bit longer. But they won't do us that favor. I'm sure they'll take us to the Stadium. To provide a true spectacle for the fun-loving unemployed. To keep them out of trouble. To keep them from thinking. To keep them laughing. And dancing.

We'll be there in the dirty clothes which we now wear. We've not had any of our things washed this past month. They will tie us to the stakes, as though that were necessary. For even if we were minded to escape, where'd we run to? I expect they'll also want to blindfold us. Sazan and Jimba have said they'll not allow themselves to be blindfolded. I agree with them. I should want to see my executors, stare the nozzles of their guns bravely in the face, see the open sky, the sun, daylight. See and hear my countrymen as they cheer us to our death. To liberation and freedom.

The Stadium will fill to capacity. And many will not find a place. They will climb trees and hang about the balconies of surrounding houses to get a clear view of us. To enjoy the free show. Cool.

And then the priest will come to us, either to pray or to ask if we have any last wishes. Sazan says he will ask for a cigarette. I'm sure they'll give it to him. I can see him puffing hard at it before the bullets cut him down. He says he's going to enjoy that cigarette more than anything he's had in life. Jimba says he'll maintain a sullen silence as a mark of his contempt. I'm going to yell at the priest. I will say, "Go to hell, you hypocrite, fornicator, and adulterer." I will yell at the top of my voice in the hope that the spectators will hear me. How I wish there'd be a microphone that will reverberate through the Stadium, nay, through the country as a whole! Then the laugh should be on the priest and those who sent him!

The priest will pray for our souls. But it's not us he should be praying for. He should pray for the living, for those whose lives are a daily torment. Between his prayer and when the shots ring out, there will be dead silence. The silence of the grave-yard. The transition between life and death. And it shall be seen that the distinction between them both is narrow, as the neck of a calabash. The divide between us breathing like every-one else in the Stadium and us as meat for worms is, oh, so slim, it makes life a walking death! But I should be glad to be rid of the world, of a meaningless existence that grows more dreary by the day. I should miss Sazan and Jimba, though. It'll be a shame to see these elegant gentlemen cut down and destroyed. And I'll miss you, too, my dear girl. But that will be of no conse-quence to the spectators.

They will troop out of the Stadium, clamber down the trees and the balconies of the houses, as though they'd just returned

from another football match. They will march to their ratholes
on empty stomachs, with tales enough to fill a Saturday evening. Miserable wretches!

The men who shall have eased us out of life will then untie
our bodies and dump them into a lorry and thence to some
open general grave. That must be a most distasteful task. I'd not
do it for a million dollars. Yet some miserable fellows will do it
for a miserable salary at the end of the month. A salary which
will not feed them and their families till the next payday. A
salary which they will have to augment with a bribe, if they are
to keep body and soul together. I say, I do feel sorry for them.
See?

The newspapers will faithfully record the fact of our shooting. If they have space, they'll probably carry a photograph of
us to garnish your breakfasts.

I remember once long ago reading in a newspaper of a man
whose one request to the priest was that he be buried along
with his walking stick—his faithful companion over the years.
He was pictured slumping in death, devotedly clutching his
beloved walking stick. True friendship, that. Well, Zole, if ever
you see such a photograph of me, make a cutting. Give it to a
sculptor and ask him to make a stone sculpture of me as I
appear in the photograph. He must make as faithful a represen-
tation of me as possible. I must be hard of feature and relentless
in aspect. I have a small sum of money in the bank and have
already instructed the bank to pay it to you for the purpose of
the sculpture I have spoken about . . .

Time is running out, Zole. Sazan and Jimba are awake now.
And they're surprised I haven't slept all night. Sazan says I
ought at least to have done myself the favor of sound sleep on
my last night on earth. I ask him if I'm not going to sleep
soundly, eternally, in a few hours? This, I argue, should be our
most wakeful night. Sazan doesn't appreciate that. Nor does
Jimba. They stand up, yawn, stretch, and rub their eyes. Then
they sit down, crowding round me. They ask me to read out to
them what I've written. I can't do that, I tell them. It's a love

letter. And they burst out laughing. A love letter! And at the
point of death! Sazan says I'm gone crazy. Jimba says he's sure
I'm afraid of death and looks hard and long at me to justify his
suspicion. I say I'm neither crazy nor afraid of death. I'm just
telling my childhood girlfriend how I feel this special night.
And sending her on an important errand. Jimba says I never
told them I had a girlfriend. I reply that she was not important
before this moment.

I haven't even seen her in ten years, I repeat. The really
compelling need to write her is that on this very special night, I
have felt a need to be close to a living being, someone who can
relate to others why we did what we did in and out of court.

Sazan says he agrees completely with me. He says he too
would like to write his thoughts down. Do I have some paper to
lend him? I say no. Besides, time is up. Day has dawned and I
haven't even finished my letter. Do they mind leaving me to
myself for a few minutes? I'd very much like to end the letter,
envelope it and pass it on to the prison guard before he rouses
himself fully from sleep and remembers to assume his official,
harsh role.

They're nice chaps, are Jimba and Sazan. Sazan says to tell
my girl not to bear any children because it's pointless bringing
new life into the harsh life of her world. Jimba says to ask my
girl to shed him a tear if she can so honor a complete stranger.
They both chuckle and withdraw to a corner of the cell and I'm
left alone to end my letter.

Now, I was telling you about my statue. My corpse will not
be available to you. You will make a grave for me, nonetheless.
And place the statue on the gravestone. And now I come to
what I consider the most important part of this letter. My epitaph.

I have thought a lot about it, you know. Really. What d'you
say about a robber shot in a stadium before a cheering crowd?
That he was a good man who strayed? That he deserved his
end? That he was a scallywag? A ragamuffin? A murderer whose
punishment was not heavy enough? "Here lies X who was shot

in public by firing squad for robbing a van and shooting the guards in broad daylight. He serves as an example to all thieves and would-be thieves!"

Who'd care for such an epitaph? They'd probably think it was a joke. No. That wouldn't carry. I'll settle for something different. Something plain and commonsensical. Or something truly cryptic and worthy of a man shot by choice in public by firing squad.

Not that I care. To die the way I'm going to die in the next hour or two is really nothing to worry about. I'm in excellent company. I should find myself recorded in the annals of our history. A history of violence, of murder, of disregard for life. Pleasure in inflicting pain—sadism. Is that the word for it? It's a world I should be pleased to leave. But not without an epitaph.

I recall, many years ago as a young child, reading in a newspaper of an African leader who stood on the grave of a dead lieutenant and through his tears said: "Africa kills her sons." I don't know what he meant by that, and though I've thought about it long enough, I've not been able to unravel the full mystery of those words. Now, today, this moment, they come flooding back to me. And I want to borrow from him. I'd like you to put this on my gravestone, as my epitaph: "Africa Kills Her Sun." A good epitaph, eh? Cryptic. Definite. A stroke of genius, I should say. I'm sure you'll agree with me. "Africa Kills Her Sun!" That's why she's been described as the Dark Continent? Yes?

So, now, dear girl. I'm done. My heart is light as the daylight which seeps stealthily into our dark cell. I hear the prison guard jangle his keys, put them into the keyhole. Soon he'll turn it and call us out. Our time is up. My time here expires and I must send you all my love. Good-bye.

Yours forever,
Bana

Alifa Rifaat was born in Egypt in 1930. Although she showed
promise as a writer and artist from a young age, her family did
not allow her to attend university. She continued to write while
raising three children, and much of her work concerns the
problems of women living in a society with strictly defined gen-
der roles. Many of her stories remained unpublished until the
death of her husband in 1974. She is most well-known for *Distant View of a Minaret*, translated from Arabic and published in
English in 1983.

At the Time of the Jasmine

Translated by Denys Johnson-Davies

He leaned his head against the backrest of the seat as the all-
station train to Upper Egypt took him joltingly along, producing
a doleful rhythm on the rails.

With his handkerchief he wiped his face, removing the specks of
sand. Even so the view before his eyes remained blurred, the telegraph
poles intermingling with the spectral forms of date palms that broke up
into misty phantoms that were soon erased, leaving the yellow surface of
sky to others which no sooner made their appearance than they vanished with the same speed.

He caught sight of some young boys plunging naked into the long
winding cleft of the Ibrahimiyya Canal, cooling themselves in its shal-
low waters, while the sun's heat grew stronger, carrying with it what little breeze there was and turning it into a scorching inferno.

Time was at a standstill, stifling his breathing. He began toying
wearily with his black tie as he glanced distractedly at the platforms of
the small stations the train was passing by, amused at seeing the hefty
men proudly clasping their guns slung on their shoulders, and the
women spread out on the platform, their children carried close to them,

while alongside them lay the cages of chickens they would be trading in the markets.

The cable he had received that morning lay in his jacket pocket.

"Your father Hagg Aballah Shalabi has died. Respect for the dead demands speedy burial."

The words fell heavy as gravel in his throat, despite the fact that for a long time his father had, for him, been like someone already dead—ever since the day he had sent him away to the English school in Maadi some time after his mother's death.

Every morning his mother would place the silver ewer before him and he would rush off to where his father would be sitting at the edge of the prayer mat, his sleeves rolled up and his hands stretched out above the little silver basin, and he would pour the water over them slowly and carefully, in his eyes an expression of admiration for his father as he made his ablutions; then he would pour the water over his feet from which he had removed his socks. He couldn't remember ever having opposed his father in anything, not even when he had carried him out to where the men were and had put him on Antar's back, laughing and boasting jubilantly: "My son Hassan's a real man, a bold horseman—riding's in his blood."

He hadn't been scared that day and hadn't looked up toward the window from which his mother surreptitiously gazed down on him, the kohl mixing in her eyes with tears of pity. He had merely let his short legs hang down the warm flanks and, taking the end of his galabia between his teeth, had clung with both hands to the long hair of the mane. Antar had rushed off with him, crossing the intersecting banked-up tracks round the village, and had brought him back, prancing about amid the admiring cries of the men.

Even when Muntaha, the sweet, shy girl with the thick black pigtails, had come to the house with her red box in her howdah on top of the camel from the neighboring hamlet, and his father had carried her and put her into his bed where his mother used previously to sleep, even Muntaha he had loved. He would cling to her bright-colored, scented dress as she went about the house, finding companionship in her from the loneliness he suffered after his mother had left him.

During the time away from home spent with foreign tutors his childhood quickly died, his love for his father froze and he himself became a sophisticated man not greatly concerned with emotions, subordinating everything to rational standards and to convention. The nostalgia within himself for his village Behbesheen was lost with the passing of the days, and the nights erased from his mind the memory of its rich pastures.

When he grew up he did his duty by visiting the place whenever his father was blessed with another child lest it be said of him that he was annoyed about brothers and sisters sharing with him his father's lands. Once he had opened his own accountancy office his visits grew less owing to his being taken up with business and then came to an end when he married his Turkish colleague Louga Hanem Toubchi. That day he had sent his father a cable reading: "Am getting married tonight."

His father received the news with silence, and when he was blessed with a daughter he again informed his father of the good news. The father contented himself by replying with a cable which said: "Call her Jasmine."

As the days passed his wife turned into a person who was always grumbling, afflicted by the arrogance of her countrymen. He bore her patiently until the day when she shouted at him: "I am Louga Hanem Toubchi—is my name to become Madame Shalabi?"

"Go back to them," he told her with frightening calm.

Taking her daughter, she had gone to the Toubchi household in Zamalek and he had stayed on in his flat in the center of Cairo, not worried about being on his own. He let her be, thinking to break her obstinacy, but she only grew more stubborn and did not return. After this he did not think of visiting the village owing to his having become wrapped up in his work. Today, after the death of his father, his link with the rest of his relations would no doubt be cut and he would remain without roots.

The train stopped at Boush, his village's main township, so he took up his suitcase in which he had, together with his pajamas, thrust the shroud he had bought before leaving Cairo. Duty demanded that he should bring with him a shroud that was in keeping with his father's position in the village. People would think badly of him if he didn't bring some white and green silk and a cashmere shawl and lay on a fine funeral night. In his pocket was a large sum he had drawn out from his savings at the bank to be spent on doing what was expected of him.

As he got down from the train he was seized by the hands of men come to convey their condolences. Faraghalli, who used as a child to steal with a fishhook the chickens of Madame Carmel, wife of the Health clerk, and who had now become a spokesman for the peasants, wrapped him round in an embrace inside his rich *aba* as he muttered: "May God give you strength to bear this loss, Mr. Hassan."

He muttered some vague words in answer, then his hand was seized by the strong grasp of Sheikh Hammad, his father's overseer, as he passed him Antar's reins with the words: "It's very hot, men, and it would be wrong of us to leave the dead man till midday."

Hassan jumped onto Antar's back, proudly sitting upright in order to assure Sheikh Hammad that a soft hand had nothing to do with being a real man. The sun was sending down its scorching vertical shafts onto his bare head. The men were pressing their mounts forward, having let down the ends of their turbans to protect them from the blazing heat. He himself lifted up the morning newspaper over his head as he used to do in Cairo, then lowered it again to his side when he saw the line of girls from the jasmine factory standing and staring at him as he passed between them.

The blast of hot air brought with it the aroma of jasmine, whose pervasive smell clung to the flying specks of sand, penetrating deeply into men's chests so that, in time, all the people of the district suffered from a chronic cough—and no sooner had things quieted down than the next season had made its appearance.

By staying in Cairo he had escaped the malady but now, breathing in the aroma, he began to cough badly. With the coughing his eyes watered, until they became reddened and puffy, while Antar took him along the banked-up tracks between the fields and then came to a stop in front of the stone wall surrounding the house.

"The burial permit is ready," said Sheikh Hammad, "and the sheikhs are here."

As soon as he entered voices were raised in wailing from the women seated on the ground, who were covering their heads with earth.

His young brother came forward carrying the silver basin and ewer for him to make his ablutions, his face bearing the same dull dismay he himself had been afflicted with the day his mother had died.

He patted his shoulder consolingly, then made his ablutions and entered the dead man's room. His legs began shaking suddenly as he advanced toward the brass bed where his father's body lay. He drew back the end of the sheet covering the face and the flies buzzed, then settled again. Staring at his father's face, he muttered through dry lips: "Peace be upon you and the mercy of Allah."

Then he pressed them to the cold forehead. Though incapable of returning the salutation, the dead man had certainly heard him. Crystal tears glinted in his eyes, putting the walls out of focus and setting dancing before his eyes the framed Qur'anic verse in large Kufic calligraphy that stood over the bed: "Make ready for them such force and tethered horses as you are able—Allah the Great has spoken aright."

The voices of the sheikhs grew louder as they recited the most beautiful names of Allah. Sheikh Abdul Maqsoud the corpse-washer came forward and drew off the white galabia and undid, from round the waist, the black snakeskin belt that the Hagg used to wear, a snake he had shot after it had for long struck terror in Behbesheen.

Sheikh Abdul Maqsoud turned the belt over in his hands, his deep-set eyes gleaming with joy; he then took hold of the dead man's hand and pulled the large gold ring off it: all this had now become his, a contribution of alms made to him by the family in memory of the dead man. He then raised the rigid body with his assistant and laid it down on the wooden plank set over the large brass bowl.

He handed the brass cup to Hassan and advanced the container of pure water toward him, saying: "Take hold of yourself, my son, otherwise your tears will make the water impure." With steady hand Hassan poured the water over the head and body which Sheikh Abdul Maqsoud was rubbing down with soap.

When the voices began reciting the Qur'an they performed the rites of ablution on the dead man, then dried the body. They tore the winding sheets with a shrill screech that jolted Hassan's nerves. He took control of himself as they stitched up the pieces of cloth and wrapped them round the body, tying them securely at the legs and on top of the head. They spread the bed covering in the wooden bier and laid the body on it, then covered it over with the cashmere shawl.

Sheikh Hammad entered and took the brass bedstead to pieces, while the women's voices rose loud with wailing. The brass bedstead had been set up ever since Hagg Aballah's first marriage; Hassan's mother had breathed her last in it, and to it he had brought Muntaha in marriage and in it she had had his other children. But with the death of the master of the house the bedstead must be done away with and not set up again till after the period of mourning.

Hassan gave a sharp cough as the aroma of incense inflamed the sensitivity of his nose and the tears flowed copiously from his eyes. Stolidly, he passed the handkerchief over his face and went forward to take up one of the front shafts of the bier with Sheikh Hammad, who took the other, the rear ones being taken by two faithful retainers. Resting it on their shoulders, they went out into the courtyard.

Owais, the man in charge of the livestock, threw a young water buffalo to the ground in front of the bier and ran Hamid the butcher's knife over its throat and the blood spilt out on the hot, burning sands in a sacrifice to the dead man.

The men trod across the pool of blood as they bore the bier to the other side of the stone wall and the funeral cortege arranged itself in ranks behind them.

They hurried along with the bier as they fervently uttered, in hoarse voices, the formula of the unity of Allah: there is no god but Allah. The women hastened behind them, clad in the shagga that hung down over their bodies like a tent, allowing nothing to show but the gleam of their eyes.

The sun had passed the center point in the sky but still sent down its searing rays into the sands so that its heat penetrated stingingly through their sandals.

They passed along the winding village lanes till they came down to where the only mosque stood, in the middle of the road that led to the other hill where the ruins of graves lay in ranks at the foot of the mountain.

Casting off their sandals, they took the dead man in and placed him in the mihrab. Seven times they uttered the words "Allah is greatest," then said the funeral prayers, after which they again took up the bier and hurried along with it to the cemetery. The gravedigger had prepared the grave, opening the mouth and removing the earth from the entrance and collecting up the bones of the former inhabitants and tying them up in their decaying shrouds and placing them against the inner wall painted with lime; then he scattered the soft sand mixed with henna, in preparation for laying down the new corpse.

The coffin grew heavier on its bearers as they hurried along, panting hard, their shoulders almost twisted from their bodies; it was as though the dead man was resisting the grave in terror, so that, as they advanced, the front of the bier turned them in the direction of the houses and they progressed with sideways steps. The stalks of maize in the basins of culti-vated land gave out, behind red sparks discharged from the sharp blade of the sun, a white vapor that made their eyes smart. Having reached the opening, they put down the bier in front of it.

Sheikh Hammad placed a small pair of scissors in Hassan's hand, say-ing between his teeth: "Come along, man, do your duty. Snip the shroud or it will be stolen by those dirty thieves of gravediggers. I swear by the Almighty if one of them falls into my hands I'll hang him on the tree alongside the mosque."

Then he spat on the ground to show his disgust.

Hassan took the scissors and went down behind the corpse into the darkness of the grave.

The sound of the Qur'an reciters grew louder, speeding up their recitation, as though they had another appointment.

A lizard passed between his feet, then disappeared into the darkness. He squatted down on his knees alongside his father and stretched out his hand with the scissors and began cutting the shroud, careful not to touch the dead flesh. The gravedigger patted him on the shoulder as he muttered: "Come along, man—may the Lord give him protection."

He got to his feet and walked backward behind him, as he gave his salutations to the dead man and then came out into the sunlight. He stood among the men till the gravedigger had completed his task and had piled the earth against the entrance and poured water over it, then watered the nearby cactus with what was left.

The sun was now suspended over the peak of the mountain, and it cast forth red shafts of light that made long shadows, depicting vague specters. The tombs looked similar to the scattered houses in the dusky light of sunset.

Someone called out: "Say that Allah is One!"

In a deep voice they all muttered fervently: "There is no god but Allah."

"Everyone thereon passes away," quoted the gravedigger, "and there remains your Lord's face possessed of majesty and splendor."

"That which Allah has said is the truth," they all called out.

Stealthily Hassan passed some money to the gravedigger and set about returning, with the crowd following him, to the courtyard of the house.

The men seated themselves on the cane chairs that had been set out in rows with the kerosene lamps above their heads; each time the Qur'an reciter finished a chapter, cups of coffee were handed round. They would listen fervently, rocking to the rhythm, until the reciter concluded by reciting the Fatiha. By this time it was midnight, and the men spread out the palms of their hands, then passed them over their faces in supplication.

Giving Hassan a sideways look, Sheikh Hammad said: "May Allah have mercy upon him, he was a loving father to everybody, and the greatest horseman in the whole district."

Faraghalli answered him: "There are plenty of horsemen about, man. What was special about him was that he could put his ear to the ground and say 'So-and-so's going along such-and-such a track and he'll be arriving after such-and-such a time,' and his words would ring true as a gold guinea."

Hassan lowered his head in silence. Perhaps these men knew his father better than he did. Was it in fact he himself who was responsible for the estrangement between himself and his father? He took out a wad of notes from his pocket and thrust them into Sheikh Hammad's hand.

"Spend them on what's required—tonight's at my expense."

Confused by Hassan's generosity, Sheikh Hammad exclaimed: "What nobility—May the Lord bless you."

Trays with bowls of broth ranged round with pieces of boiled meat were set up on the low tables, and Hassan rose to invite the men, while he himself ate a little with difficulty, waiting till everyone had dispersed and the pressure lamps had been put out.

Entering the house, he walked in loneliness through its rooms, passing among the women squatting on the mats, clad in black. From the ground there rose a black tent that moved toward him; from two tiny slits there looked out at him two eyes which he recognized as those of Muntaha, his father's wife. She held out her hand with a key, muttering in a voice choked by weeping: "The Hagg Aballah handed over to me the key of the cupboard in trust for me to give to you."

"Be strong," he muttered, taking the key from her.

"Strength is with Allah."

He went to the cupboard he had known since childhood. As he did so his eyes fell for an instant on the glistening water on the floor, left over after the dead man had been washed.

His hand came across a large bundle of notes, also a piece of paper on which was recorded the names of those who were to benefit from the sum of money. His gaze came to rest on the name of his daughter Jasmine mentioned among those to inherit. The words became blurred and he sat down on the edge of the mattress that had been laid out on the ground for him to sleep on instead of the bed that had been dismantled and some of whose pieces were leaning in the corner against the wall. He placed his head between his hands and the papers between his out-stretched legs. The smell of the jasmine whose flowers were opening in the night like white stars was wafted in to him by the breeze. He had said "Call her Jasmine." He had loved her and had mentioned her among his own children in his will. He had no doubt thought about her and had perhaps sometimes longed to see her. Why had he not asked to meet her? More than once he'd said to Louga Hanem, before the final break: "We must take a train to the country so my father can see my child." She would put her elegant nose in the air and he would keep silent. Too often he kept silent. Once, during one of the rare times they met, his father had said: "Next year, my son, we'll make the pilgrimage together," and he had burst into childish laughter.

The years had passed and a life had come to an end and the wish had not been fulfilled. He smiled sadly at the memory, beset by a feeling of bafflement. The days had robbed the two of them and they had not gone. They hadn't even seen enough of each other, and a sensation of yearning for his father exploded suddenly in his breast. Which of them was to blame?

He woke up from his thoughts to the echoing howling of the mountain wolves. Had the grave robber done it? Had he left the opening of the grave unclosed after him?

The blood rose up into his neck, as he choked with grief and anger and he let his body fall back as though struck by a blow from the Hagg's famous staff. He had never in fact suffered it. When he was young it was enough for Hagg Aballah to wave it in his face and shout "The rod's for the insubordinate," for his weak body to tremble under the imaginary blows.

"Father, you gave me a real beating tonight."

The winds whistled forlornly through the branches of the date palms, then silence reigned while the jasmine buds carefully folded themselves against the rapidly spreading rays of the sun. The cooing of pigeons rose from the dovecotes on top of the houses.

Sheikh Hammad's voice called from outside: "Mr. Hassan, the commissioner has sent the Jeep to take you to the station—there's half an hour till the train goes."

Awwad entered carrying the basin and ewer, and in his wake Muntaha, her hair disheveled and in her nightgown, carrying a tray of breakfast.

He went out to the car. As he got into it he waved at the men who had gathered, then it moved off, leaving behind it a whirlpool of dust that enveloped the children who had risen from sleep and collected at the sound of the car and were now trying to catch up as, with the ends of their galabias in their teeth, they ran along on their thin brown legs.

Leila Aboulela, born in Cairo in 1964, is half-Egyptian, half-Sudanese. She graduated from the University of Khartoum in 1985, later studying statistics at the London School of Economics. She has written stories for BBC Radio, and is the author of *Coloured Lights* and *The Translator*, which was long-listed for the Orange Prize and the IMPAC Dublin Award, and short-listed for the Saltire Prize. She lives in Aberdeen with her husband and family.

The Museum

At first Shadia was afraid to ask him for his notes. The earring made her afraid; the straight long hair that he tied up with a rubber band. She had never seen a man with an earring and such long hair. But then she had never known such cold, so much rain. His silver earring was the strangeness of the West, another culture shock. She stared at it during classes, her eyes straying from the white scribbles on the board. Most times she could hardly understand anything. Only the notation was familiar. But how did it all fit together? How did *this* formula lead to *this*? Her ignorance and the impending exams were horrors she wanted to escape. His long hair was a dull color between yellow and brown. It reminded her of a doll she had when she was young. She had spent hours combing that doll's hair, stroking it. She had longed for such straight hair. When she went to Paradise she would have hair like that. When she ran it would fly behind her; if she bent her head down it would fall over her like silk and sweep the flowers on the grass. She watched his ponytail move as he wrote and then looked up at the board. She pictured her doll, vivid suddenly, after years, and felt sick that she was daydreaming in class, not learning a thing.

The first days of term, when the classes started for the M.Sc. in Statistics, she was like someone tossed around by monstrous waves—battered, as she lost her way to the different lecture rooms, fumbled with the photocopying machine, could not find anything in the library. She could scarcely hear or eat or see. Her eyes bulged with fright, watered from the cold. The course required a certain background, a background she didn't have. So she floundered, she and the other African students, the two Turkish girls, and the men from Brunei. Asafa, the short, round-faced Ethiopian, said, in his grave voice—as this collection from the Third World whispered their anxieties in grim Scottish corridors, the girls in nervous giggles—"Last year, last year a Nigerian on this very same course committed suicide. *Cut his wrists.*"

Us and them, she thought. The ones who would do well, the ones who would crawl and sweat and barely pass. Two predetermined groups. Asafa, generous and wise (he was the oldest), leaned over and whispered to Shadia: "The Spanish girl is good. Very good." His eyes bulged redder than Shadia's. He cushioned his fears every night in the university pub; she only cried. Their countries were next-door neighbors but he had never been to Sudan, and Shadia had never been to Ethiopia. "But we meet in Aberdeen!" she had shrieked when this information was exchanged, giggling furiously. Collective fear had its euphoria.

"That boy Bryan," said Asafa, "is excellent."

"The one with the earring?"

Asafa laughed and touched his own unadorned ear. "The earring doesn't mean anything. He'll get the Distinction. He was an undergraduate here; got First Class Honors. That gives him an advantage. He knows all the lecturers, he knows the system."

So the idea occurred to her of asking Bryan for the notes of his graduate year. If she strengthened her background in stochastic processes and time series, she would be better able to cope with the new material they were bombarded with every day. She watched him to judge if he was approachable. Next to the courteous Malaysian students, he was devoid of manners. He mumbled and slouched and did not speak with respect to the lecturers. He spoke to them as if they were his equals. And he did silly things. When he wanted to throw a piece of paper in the bin, he squashed it into a ball and aimed it at the bin. If he missed, he muttered under his breath. She thought that he was immature. But he was the only one who was sailing through the course.

The glossy handbook for overseas students had explained about the "famous British reserve" and hinted that they should be grateful, things were worse farther south, less "hospitable." In the cafeteria, drinking coffee with Asafa and the others, the picture of "hospitable Scotland" was something different. Badr, the Malaysian, blinked and whispered, "Yesterday our windows got smashed; my wife today is afraid to go out."

"Thieves?" asked Shadia, her eyes wider than anyone else's.

"Racists," said the Turkish girl, her lipstick chic, the word tripping out like silver, like ice.

Wisdom from Asafa, muted, before the collective silence: "These people think they own the world . . ." and around them the aura of the dead Nigerian student. They were ashamed of that brother they had never seen. He had weakened, caved in. In the cafeteria, Bryan never sat with them. They never sat with him. He sat alone, sometimes reading the local paper. When Shadia walked in front of him he didn't smile. "These people are strange . . . One day they greet you, the next day they don't . . ."

On Friday afternoon, as everyone was ready to leave the room after Linear Models, she gathered her courage and spoke to Bryan. He had spots on his chin and forehead, was taller than her, restless, as if he was in a hurry to go somewhere else. He put his calculator back in its case, his pen in his pocket. She asked him for his notes, and his blue eyes behind his glasses took on the blankest look she had ever seen in her life. What was all the surprise for? Did he think she was an insect? Was he surprised that she could speak?

A mumble for a reply, words strung together. So taken aback, he was. He pushed his chair back under the table with his foot.

"Pardon."

He slowed down, separated each word, "Ah'll have them for ye on Monday."

"Thank you." She spoke English better than he did! How pathetic. The whole of him was pathetic. He wore the same shirt every blessed day. Grey and white stripe.

On the weekends, Shadia never went out of the halls and, unless someone telephoned long-distance from home, she spoke to no one. There was time to remember Thursday nights in Khartoum: a wedding to go to with Fareed, driving in his red Mercedes. Or the club with her sisters. Sitting by the pool drinking lemonade with ice, the waiters all dressed in white. Sometimes people swam at night, dived in the water—dark like the sky above. Here, in this country's weekend of Saturday and Sunday, Shadia washed her clothes and her hair. Her hair depressed her. The damp weather made it frizz up after she straightened it with hot tongs. So she had given up and now wore it in a bun all the time, tightly pulled back away from her face, the curls held down by pins and Vaseline Tonic. She didn't like this style, her corrugated hair, and in the mirror her eyes looked too large. The mirror in the public bathroom, at the end of the corridor to her room, had printed on it: "This is the face of someone with HIV." She had written about this mirror to her sister, something foreign and sensational like hail, and cars driving on the left. But she hadn't written that the mirror made her feel as if she had left her looks behind in Khartoum.

On the weekends, she made a list of the money she had spent: the sterling enough to keep a family alive back home. Yet she might fail her exams after all that expense, go back home empty-handed without a degree. Guilt was cold like the fog of this city. It came from everywhere. One day she forgot to pray in the morning. She reached the bus stop and then realized that she hadn't prayed. That morning folded out like the nightmare she sometimes had of discovering that she had gone out into the street without any clothes.

In the evening, when she was staring at multidimensional scaling, the telephone in the hall rang. She ran to answer it. Fareed's cheerful greeting, "Here, Shadia, Mama and the girls want to speak to you." His mother's endearments: "They say it's so cold where you are . . ."

Shadia was engaged to Fareed. Fareed was a package that came with the 7-Up franchise, the paper factory, the big house he was building, his sisters and widowed mother. Shadia was going to marry them all. She was going to be happy and make her mother happy. Her mother deserved happiness after the misfortunes of her life. A husband who left her for another woman. Six girls to bring up. People felt sorry for her mother. Six girls to educate and marry off. But your Lord is generous: each of the girls, it was often said, was lovelier than the other. They were clever too: dentist, pharmacist, architect, and all with the best of manners.

"We are just back from looking at the house," Fareed's turn again to talk. "It's coming along fine, they're putting the tiles down . . ."

"That's good, that's good," her voice strange from not talking to anyone all day.

"The bathroom suites. If I get them all the same color for us and the girls and Mama, I could get them on a discount. Blue, the girls are in favor of blue," his voice echoed from one continent to another. Miles and miles.

"Blue is nice. Yes, better get them all the same color."

He was building a block of flats, not a house. The ground-floor flat for his mother and the girls until they married, the first floor for him and Shadia. When Shadia had first got engaged to Fareed, he was the son of a rich man. A man with the franchise for 7-Up and the paper factory which had a monopoly in ladies' sanitary towels. Fareed's sisters never had to buy sanitary towels, their house was abundant with boxes of *Pinky*, fresh from the production line. But Fareed's father died of an unexpected heart attack soon after the engagement party (five hundred guests at the Hilton). Now Shadia was going to marry the rich man himself. "You are a lucky, lucky girl," her mother had said, and Shadia had rubbed soap in her eyes so that Fareed would think she was weeping about his father's death.

There was no time to talk about her course on the telephone, no space for her anxieties. Fareed was not interested in her studies. He had said, "I am very broad-minded to allow you to study abroad. Other men would not have put up with this . . ." It was her mother who was keen for her to study, to get a postgraduate degree from Britain and then have a career after she got married. "This way," her mother had said, "you will have your in-laws' respect. They have money but you will have a degree. Don't end up like me. I left my education to marry your father and now . . ." Many conversations ended with her mother bitter; with her mother saying, "No one suffers like I suffer," and making Shadia droop. At night her mother sobbed in her sleep, noises that woke Shadia and her sisters.

No, on the long-distance line, there was no space for her worries. Talk about the Scottish weather. Picture Fareed, generously perspiring, his stomach straining the buttons of his shirt. Often she had nagged him to lose weight, without success. His mother's food was too good; his sisters were both overweight. On the long-distance line, listen to the Khartoum gossip as if listening to a radio play.

On Monday, without saying anything, Bryan slid two folders across the table towards her as if he did not want to come near her, did not want to talk to her. She wanted to say, "I won't take them till you hand them to me politely." But smarting, she said, "Thank you very much." *She* had manners. *She* was well brought up.

Back in her room, at her desk, the clearest handwriting she had ever seen. Sparse on the pages, clean. Clear and rounded like a child's, the tidiest notes. She cried over them, wept for no reason. She cried until she wetted one of the pages, smudged the ink, blurred one of the formulas. She dabbed at it with a tissue but the paper flaked and became transparent. Should she apologize about the stain, say that she was drinking water, say that it was rain? Or should she just keep quiet, hope he wouldn't notice? She chided herself for all that concern. *He* wasn't concerned about wearing the same shirt every day. She was giving him too much attention thinking about him. He was just an immature and closed-in sort of character. He probably came from a small town, his parents were probably poor, low-class. In Khartoum, she never mixed with people like that. Her mother liked her to be friends with people who were higher up. How else were she and her sisters going to marry well? She must study the notes and stop crying over this boy's handwriting. His handwriting had nothing to do with her, nothing to do with her at all.

Understanding after not understanding is fog lifting, pictures swinging into focus, missing pieces slotting into place. It is fragments gelling, a sound vivid whole, a basis to build on. His notes were the knowledge she needed, the gap filled. She struggled through them, not skimming them with the carelessness of incomprehension, but taking them in, making them a part of her, until in the depth of concentration, in the late hours of the nights, she lost awareness of time and place, and at last, when she slept she became epsilon and gamma, and she became a variable, making her way through discrete space from state "i" to state "j."

It felt natural to talk to him. As if now that she had spent hours and days with his handwriting, she knew him in some way. She forgot the offense she had taken when he had slid his folders across the table to her, all the times he didn't say hello.

In the computer room, at the end of the Statistical Packages class, she went to him and said: "Thanks for the notes. They are really good. I think I might not fail, after all. I might have a chance to pass." Her eyes were dry from all the nights she had stayed up. She was tired and grateful.

He nodded and they spoke a little about the Poisson distribution, queuing theory. Everything was clear in his mind, his brain was a clear pane of glass where all the concepts were written out boldly and neatly. Today, he seemed more at ease talking to her, though he still shifted about from foot to foot, avoiding her eyes.

He said, " Do ye want to go for a coffee?"

She looked up at him. He was tall and she was not used to speaking to people with blue eyes. Then she made a mistake. Perhaps because she had been up late last night, she made that mistake. Perhaps there were other reasons for that mistake. The mistake of shifting from one level to another.

She said, "I don't like your earring."

The expression in his eyes, a focusing, no longer shifting away. He lifted his hand to his ear and tugged the earring off. His earlobe without the silver looked red and scarred.

She giggled because she was afraid, because he wasn't smiling, wasn't saying anything. She covered her mouth with her hand then wiped her forehead and eyes. A mistake had been made and it was too late to go back. She plunged ahead, careless now, reckless, "I don't like your long hair."

He turned and walked away.

The next morning, Multivariate Analysis, and she came in late, disheveled from running and the rain. The professor, whose name she wasn't sure of (there were three who were Mc-something), smiled, unperturbed. All the lecturers were relaxed and urbane, in tweed jackets and polished shoes. Sometimes she wondered how the incoherent Bryan, if he did pursue an academic career, was going to transform himself into a professor like that. But it was none of her business.

Like most of the other students, she sat in the same seat in every class. Bryan sat a row ahead which was why she could always look at his hair. But he had cut it, there was no ponytail today! Just his neck and the collar of the grey and white striped shirt.

Notes to take down. *In discriminant analysis, a linear combination of variables serves as the basis for assigning cases to groups*.

She was made up of layers. Somewhere inside, deep inside, under the crust of vanity, in the untampered-with essence, she would glow and be in awe, and be humble and think, This is just for me, he cut his hair for me. But there were other layers, bolder, more to the surface. Giggling. Wanting to catch hold of a friend. Guess what? You wouldn't *believe* what this idiot did!

Find a weighted average of variables . . . The weights are estimated so that they result in the best separation between the groups.

After the class he came over and said very seriously, without a smile, "Ah've cut my hair."

A part of her hollered with laughter, sang: "You stupid boy, you stupid boy, I can see that, can't I?"

She said, "It looks nice." She said the wrong thing and her face felt hot and she made herself look away so that she would not know his reaction. It was true though, he did look nice; he looked decent now.

She should have said to Bryan, when they first held their coffee mugs in their hands and were searching for an empty table, "Let's sit with Asafa and the others." Mistakes follow mistakes. Across the cafeteria, the Turkish girl saw them together and raised her perfect eyebrows. Badr met Shadia's eyes and quickly looked away. Shadia looked at Bryan and he was different, different without the earring and the ponytail, transformed in some way. If he would put lemon juice on his spots . . . but it was none of her business. Maybe the boys who smashed Badr's windows looked like Bryan, but with fiercer eyes, no glasses. She must push him away from her. She must make him dislike her.

He asked her where she came from and when she replied, he said, "Where's that?"

"Africa," with sarcasm. "Do you know where *that* is?"

His nose and cheeks under the rims of his glasses went red. Good, she thought, good. He will leave me now in peace.

He said, "Ah know Sudan is in Africa, I meant where exactly in Africa."

"Northeast, south of Egypt. Where are *you* from?"

"Peterhead. It's north of here. By the sea."

It was hard to believe that there was anything north of Aberdeen. It seemed to her that they were on the northernmost corner of the world. She knew better now than to imagine suntanning and sandy beaches for his "by the sea." More likely dismal skies, pale, bad-tempered people shivering on the rocky shore.

"Your father works in Peterhead?"

"Aye, he does."

She had grown up listening to the proper English of the BBC World Service only to come to Britain and find people saying "yes" like it was said back home in Arabic: "aye."

"What does he do, your father?"

He looked surprised, his blue eyes surprised, "Ma dad's a joiner."

Fareed hired people like that to work on the house. Ordered them about.

"And your mother?" she asked.

He paused a little, stirred sugar in his coffee with a plastic spoon. "She's a lollipop lady."

Shadia smirked into her coffee, took a sip.

"My father," she said proudly, "is a doctor, a specialist." Her father was a gynecologist. The woman who was now his wife had been one of his patients. Before that, Shadia's friends had teased her about her father's job, crude jokes that made her laugh. It was all so sordid now.

"And my mother," she blew the truth up out of proportion, "comes from a very big family. A ruling family. If you British hadn't colonized us, my mother would have been a princess now."

"Ye walk like a princess," he said.

What a gullible, silly boy! She wiped her forehead with her hand and said, "You mean I am conceited and proud?"

"No, Ah didnae mean that, no . . ." The packet of sugar he was tearing open tipped from his hand, its contents scattered over the table. "Ah shit . . . sorry . . ." He tried to scoop up the sugar and knocked against his coffee mug, spilling a little on the table.

She took out a tissue from her bag, reached over and mopped up the stain. It was easy to pick up all the bits of sugar with the damp tissue.

"Thanks," he mumbled and they were silent. The cafeteria was busy, full of the humming, buzzing sound of people talking to each other, trays and dishes. In Khartoum, she avoided being alone with Fareed. She preferred it when they were with others: their families, their many mutual friends. If they were ever alone, she imagined that her mother or her sister was with them, could hear them, and she spoke to Fareed with that audience in mind.

Bryan was speaking to her, saying something about rowing on the River Dee. He went rowing on the weekends, he belonged to a rowing club.

To make herself pleasing to people was a skill Shadia was trained in. It was not difficult to please people. Agree with them, never dominate the conversation, be economical with the truth. Now, here was someone to whom all these rules needn't apply.

She said to him, "The Nile is superior to the Dee. I saw your Dee, it is nothing, it is like a stream. There are two Niles, the Blue and the White, named after their colors. They come from the south, from two different places. They travel for miles over countries with different names, never knowing they will meet. I think they get tired of running alone, it is such a long way to the sea. They want to reach the sea so that they can rest, stop running. There is a bridge in Khartoum, and under this bridge the two Niles meet. If you stand on the bridge and look down you can see the two waters mixing together."

"Do ye get homesick?" he asked. She felt tired now, all this talk of the river running to rest in the sea. She had never talked like this before. Luxury words, and this question he asked.

"Things I should miss I don't miss. Instead I miss things I didn't think I would miss. The azan, the Muslim call to prayer from the mosque. I don't know if you know about it. I miss that. At dawn it used to wake me up. I would hear 'prayer is better than sleep' and just go back to sleep. I never got up to pray." She looked down at her hands on the table. There was no relief in confessions, only his smile, young, and something like wonder in his eyes.

"We did Islam in school," he said. "Ah went on a trip to Mecca." He opened out his palms on the table.

"What!"

"In a book."

"Oh."

The coffee was finished. They should go now. She should go to the library before the next lecture and photocopy previous exam papers. Asafa, full of helpful advice, had shown her where to find them.

"What is your religion?" she asked.

"Dunno, nothing I suppose."

"That's terrible! That's really terrible!" Her voice was too loud, concerned.

His face went red again and he tapped his spoon against the empty mug.

Waive all politeness, make him dislike her. Badr had said, even before his windows got smashed, that here in the West they hate Islam. Standing up to go, she said flippantly, "Why don't you become a Muslim then?"

He shrugged, "Ah wouldnae mind travelling to Mecca, I was keen on that book."

Her eyes filled with tears. They blurred his face when he stood up. In the West they hate Islam and he . . . She said, "Thanks for the coffee," and walked away, but he followed her.

"Shadiya, Shadiya," he pronounced her name wrongly, three syllables instead of two, "there's this museum about Africa. I've never been before. If you'd care to go, tomorrow . . ."

No sleep for the guilty, no rest, she should have said No, I can't go, no I have too much catching up to do. No sleep for the guilty, the memories come from another continent. Her father's new wife, happier than her mother, fewer worries. When Shadia visits she offers fruit in a glass bowl, icy oranges and guavas, soothing in the heat. Shadia's father hadn't wanted a divorce, hadn't wanted to leave them, he wanted two wives not a divorce. But her mother had too much pride, she came from fading money, a family with a "name." Of the new wife her mother says, Bitch, whore, the dregs of the earth, a nobody.

Tomorrow she need not show up at the museum, even though she said that she would. She should have told Bryan she was engaged to be married, mentioned it casually. What did he expect from her? Europeans had different rules, reduced, abrupt customs. If Fareed knew about this . . . her secret thoughts like snakes . . . Perhaps she was like her father, a traitor. Her mother said that her father was devious. Sometimes Shadia was devious. With Fareed in the car, she would deliberately say, "I need to stop at the grocer, we need things at home." At the grocer he would pay for all her shopping and she would say, "No, you shouldn't do that, no, you are too generous, you are embarrassing me." With the money she saved, she would buy a blouse for her mother, nail varnish for her mother, a magazine, imported apples.

It was strange to leave her desk, lock her room, and go out on a Saturday. In the hall the telephone rang. It was Fareed. If he knew where she was going now . . . Guilt was like a hard-boiled egg stuck in her chest. A large cold egg.

"Shadia, I want you to buy some of the fixtures for the bathrooms. Taps and towel hangers. I'm going to send you a list of what I want exactly and the money . . ."

"I can't, I can't."

"What do you mean you can't? If you go into any large department store . . ."

"I can't, I wouldn't know where to put these things, how to send them."

There was a rustle on the line and she could hear someone whispering, Fareed distracted a little. He would be at work this time in the day, glass bottles filling up with clear effervescent, the words 7-Up written in English and Arabic, white against the dark green.

"You can get good things, things that aren't available here. Gold would be good. It would match . . ."

Gold. Gold toilet seats!

"People are going to burn in hell for eating out of gold dishes, you want to sit on gold!"

He laughed. He was used to getting his own way, not easily threatened. "Are you joking with me?"

"No."

In a quieter voice, " This call is costing . . ."

She knew, she knew. He shouldn't have let her go away. She was not coping with the whole thing, she was not handling the stress. Like the Nigerian student.

"Shadia, gold-colored, not gold. It's smart."

"Allah is going to punish us for this, it's not right . . ."

"Since when have you become so religious!"

Bryan was waiting for her on the steps of the museum, familiar-looking against the strange grey of the city streets where cars had their head-lamps on in the middle of the afternoon. He wore a different shirt, a navy-blue jacket. He said, not looking at her, "Ah was beginning to think you wouldnae turn up."

There was no entry fee to the museum, no attendant handing out tickets. Bryan and Shadia walked on soft carpets, thick blue carpets that made Shadia want to take off her shoes. The first thing they saw was a Scottish man from Victorian times. He sat on a chair surrounded by pos-sessions from Africa: overflowing trunks, an ancient map strewn on the floor of the glass cabinet. All the light in the room came from this and other glass cabinets and gleamed on the waxed floors. Shadia turned away; there was an ugliness in the lifelike wispiness of his hair, his deter-mined expression, the way he sat. A hero who had gone away and come back, laden, ready to report.

Bryan began to conscientiously study every display cabinet, to read the posters on the wall. She followed him around and thought that he was studious, careful; that was why he did so well in his degree. She watched the intent expression on his face as he looked at everything. For her the posters were an effort to read, the information difficult to take in. It had been so long since she had read anything outside the requirements of the course. But she persevered, saying the words to her-self, moving her lips . . ."*During the 18th and 19th centuries, northeast Scotland made a disproportionate impact on the world at large by contributing so many skilled and committed individuals. In serving an empire they gave and received, changed others and were themselves changed and often returned home with tangible reminders of their experiences.*"

The tangible reminders were there to see, preserved in spite of the years. Her eyes skimmed over the disconnected objects out of place and time. Iron and copper, little statues. Nothing was of her, nothing belonged to her life at home, what she missed. Here was Europe's vision, the cliches about Africa, cold and old.

She had not expected the dim light and the hushed silence. Apart from Shadia and Bryan, there was only a man with a briefcase, a lady who took down notes, unless there were others out of sight on the second floor. Something electrical, the heating or the lights, gave out a humming sound like that of an air conditioner. It made Shadia feel as if they were in an airplane without windows, detached from the world outside.

"He looks like you, don't you think?" she said to Bryan. They stood in front of a portrait of a soldier who died in the first year of the twentieth century. It was the color of his eyes and his hair. But Bryan did not answer her, did not agree with her. He was preoccupied with reading the caption. When she looked at the portrait again, she saw that she was mistaken. That strength in the eyes, the purpose, was something Bryan didn't have. They had strong faith in those days long ago.

Biographies of explorers who were educated in Edinburgh; they knew what to take to Africa: doctors, courage, Christianity, commerce, civilization. They knew what they wanted to bring back: cotton—watered by the Blue Nile, the Zambezi River. She walked after Bryan, felt his concentration, his interest in what was before him and thought, "In a photograph we would not look nice together."

She touched the glass of a cabinet showing papyrus rolls, copper pots. She pressed her forehead and nose against the cool glass. If she could enter the cabinet, she would not make a good exhibit. She wasn't right, she was too modern, too full of mathematics.

Only the carpet, its petroleum blue, pleased her. She had come to this museum expecting sunlight and photographs of the Nile, something to relieve her homesickness: a comfort, a message. But the messages were not for her, not for anyone like her. A letter from West Africa, 1762, an employee to his employer in Scotland. An employee trading European goods for African curiosities. *It was difficult to make the natives understand my meaning, even by an interpreter, it being a thing so seldom asked of them, but they have all undertaken to bring something and laughed heartily at me and said, I was a good man to love their country so much . . .*

Love my country so much. She should not be here, there was nothing for her here. She wanted to see minarets, boats fragile on the Nile, people. People like her father. The times she had sat in the waiting room of his clinic, among pregnant women, a pain in her heart because she was going to see him in a few minutes. His room, the air conditioner and the smell of his pipe, his white coat. When she hugged him, he smelled of Listerine mouthwash. He could never remember how old she was, what she was studying; six daughters, how could he keep track. In his confusion, there was freedom for her, games to play, a lot of teasing. She visited his clinic in secret, telling lies to her mother. She loved him more than she loved her mother. Her mother who did everything for her, tidied her room, sewed her clothes from *Burda* magazine. Shadia was twenty-five and her mother washed everything for her by hand, even her pants and bras.

"I know why they went away," said Bryan, "I understand why they traveled." At last he was talking. She had not seen him intense before. He spoke in a low voice. "They had to get away, to leave here . . ."

"To escape from the horrible weather . . ." she was making fun of him. She wanted to put him down. The imperialists who had humiliated her history were heroes in his eyes.

He looked at her. "To escape . . ." he repeated.

"They went to benefit themselves," she said, "people go away because they benefit in some way."

"I want to get away," he said.

She remembered when he had opened his palms on the table and said, "I went on a trip to Mecca." There had been pride in his voice.

"I should have gone somewhere else for the course," he went on. "A new place, somewhere down south."

He was on a plateau, not like her. She was fighting and struggling for a piece of paper that would say she was awarded an M.Sc. from a British university. For him, the course was a continuation.

"Come and see," he said, and he held her arm. No one had touched her before, not since she had hugged her mother goodbye. Months now in this country and no one had touched her.

She pulled her arm away. She walked away, quickly up the stairs. Metal steps rattled under her feet. She ran up the stairs to the next floor. Guns, a row of guns aiming at her. They had been waiting to blow her away. Scottish arms of centuries ago, gunfire in service of the empire.

Silver muzzles, a dirty grey now. They must have shone prettily once, under a sun far away. If they blew her away now, where would she fly and fall? A window that looked out at the hostile sky. She shivered in spite of the wool she was wearing, layers of clothes. Hell is not only blazing fire, a part of it is freezing cold, torturous ice and snow. In Scotland's winter you have a glimpse of this unseen world, feel the breath of it in your bones.

There was a bench and she sat down. There was no one here on this floor. She was alone with sketches of jungle animals, words on the wall. A diplomat away from home, in Ethiopia in 1903, Asafa's country long before Asafa was born. *It is difficult to imagine anything more satisfactory or better worth taking part in than a lion drive. We rode back to camp feeling very well indeed. Archie was quite right when he said that this was the first time since we have started that we have really been in Africa—the real Africa of jungle inhabited only by game, and plains where herds of antelope meet your eye in every direction.*

"Shadiya, don't cry." He still pronounced her name wrongly because she had not told him how to say it properly.

He sat next to her on the bench, the blur of his navy jacket blocking the guns, the wall-length pattern of antelope herds. She should explain that she cried easily, there was no need for the alarm on his face. His awkward voice: "Why are ye crying?"

He didn't know, he didn't understand. He was all wrong, not a substitute . . .

"They are telling lies in this museum," she said. "Don't believe them. It's all wrong. It's not jungles and antelopes, it's people. We have things like computers and cars. We have 7-Up in Africa, and some people, a few people, have bathrooms with golden taps . . . I shouldn't be here with you. You shouldn't talk to me . . ."

He said, "Museums change, I can change . . ."

He didn't know it was a steep path she had no strength for. He didn't understand. Many things, years and landscapes, gulfs. If she had been strong she would have explained, and not tired of explaining. She would have patiently taught him another language, letters curved like the epsilon and gamma he knew from mathematics. She would have shown him that words could be read from right to left. If she had not been small in the museum, if she had been really strong, she would have made his trip to Mecca real, not only in a book.

Milly Jafta was born in Namibia. In addition to writing short stories, she is also the coauthor of the screenplay based on *The Home-Coming*. Trained as a social worker, she works at the Legal Assistance Centre, a nonprofit public interest group, in Windhoek.

The Home-Coming

The bus came to a standstill and all the passengers spilled out as soon as they could. It was Friday, end of the week, end of the month, end of the year, and the trip from Windhoek to the north was hot and unending. Unlike previous times, I remained in my seat until the bus was empty. Then I gathered my belongings and moved to the door. Through the window I could see Maria scrambling to claim my two suitcases.

The heat of the late afternoon sun hit me as I alighted from the bus. The warmth outside was different from the human heat that I felt inside the bus. Now the smell of sweat and over-spiced fast food seemed like a distant memory. The welcome smell of meat overexposed to the sun filled my nostrils. I could even hear the buzzing of the metallic-green colored flies as they circled and landed on the meat hanging from the tree branches and the makeshift stalls. Circled and landed, circled and landed . . . Hawkers and buyers were busy closing the last deals of the day. The air was filled with expectancy.

Maria bent down and kissed me on the lips—a dry and unemotive gesture. She smiled, picked up the larger of the two suitcases and placed it on her head. Then she started walking ahead of me. I picked up the other case, placed it on my head and put both my hands in the small of my back to steady myself. Then I followed her. I looked at Maria's straight back, the proud way she held her head and the determination with which she walked. How beautiful is the unbroken human spirit. I tried desperately to think of something to say, but could not find the words. Thoughts were spinning in my head, but my mouth remained closed and empty. So we continued in silence, this stranger—my daughter—and I.

So this was it. My home-coming. What did I expect? The village to come out in celebration of a long-lost daughter who had come home? How long had it been? Forty years? It must have been about forty years. How I have lost track of the time. How could I be expected to keep track of the time, when I could only measure it against myself in a foreign land? When I planted seeds but never had the chance to see them grow, bore children but never watched them grow . . . when I had to make myself understood in a foreign tongue . . . had to learn how an electric kettle works, how and when to put the stove off, that doors are not opened to strangers, and that you do not greet everyone you meet with a handshake.

I tried not to look at the long dusty road ahead of us. In any case there was nothing in particular to look at. Everything seemed barren and empty. No trees, no grass, just the sprawling brown and orange ground all around us. The last rays of the sun seemed to lighten it to a golden glow. I am sure this would make a beautiful color picture: the two of us walking behind each other in the narrow path with my luggage on our heads, silhouetted against the setting sun. One December I saw a large picture like that, only it was of giraffe. I remember standing there, looking at it and for a moment longing to smell the fields after the rain. But I was in Swakopmund with my *Miesies** and her family as she needed the rest. It was holiday time, family time, but I was without my own family, just as I was for the rest of the year and for most of my adult life.

Now all that has changed. I am on my way home. I am walking the same path as I walked many years ago. Only then I was seventeen and my eyes looked forward. A young girl has left and now—after forty years, three children, and a couple of visits to the village—an old woman is on her way back home. An old woman who has her eyes fixed to the ground.

My daughter, the stranger, stopped suddenly. Turned around and

* Mistress of a household.

looked inquiringly at me. I realized that she must have been waiting for an answer or a reaction of some sort. I was so lost in my thoughts that I had no idea what she was waiting for. But then, I never had any idea what my children's actual needs were. In her calm voice she repeated the question, asking whether she was walking too fast for me. Oh dear God, what kindness. Someone was actually asking me whether I could keep up. Not telling me to walk faster, to have no males in my room, to get up earlier, to pay more attention, to wash the dog . . . I was overcome. Tears filled my eyes. My throat tightened, but my spirit soared. The stranger, my daughter, took the case from her head and put it on the ground next to her. Then she helped me to take my case down from my head and placed it next to hers.

"Let us rest for a while," she said gently. After we sat down on the cases next to each other she said: "It is so good to have you home."

We sat there in complete silence, with only the sound of some crickets filling the air. I never felt more content, more at peace. I looked at the stranger and saw my daughter. Then I knew I had come home. I did matter. I was together with the fruit of my womb. I had grown fruit. I looked down at my wasted, abused body and thought of the earth from which such beautiful flowers burst forth.

"We must go now. Everybody is waiting for you," Maria said, standing up. "You walk in front. You set the pace, I will follow you."

I walked ahead of Maria in the narrow path, my back straight and my eyes looking forward. I was in a hurry to reach home.

Ben Okri was born in Lagos, Nigeria, in 1959. At the age of eighteen he went to England where his first novel, *Flowers and Shadows*, was published in 1980. *The Landscape Within*, *Incidents at the Shrine*, and *Stars of the New Curfew* followed. He was awarded the Booker Prize in 1991 for his novel *The Famished Road*. Among the other awards he has received include the *Paris Review* Aga Khan prize for fiction, the Commonwealth Writers' Prize for Africa, the Chianti Rufino-Antico Fattore International Literary Prize, and the Premio Grinzane Cavour. He has been a visiting writer-in-residence at Trinity College, Cambridge. He lives in London.

What the Tapster Saw

There was once an excellent tapster who enjoyed climbing palm trees as much as the tapping of their wines. One night he dreamt that while tapping for palm wine he fell from the tree and died. He was so troubled by the dream that late as it was he went to visit his friend, Tabasco, who was a renowned herbalist. But that night Tabasco was too busy to pay much attention to what the tapster was saying. Harassed by the demands of his many wives, the herbalist kept chewing bundles of alligator pepper seeds and dousing his mouth with palm wine. When the tapster was about to leave, the herbalist drew him aside and, with curious irrelevance, said:

"I used to know a hunter who, one day while hunting, saw a strange antelope. He followed the antelope till it came to an anthill. To his surprise the antelope turned into a woman and then disappeared. The hunter waited near the anthill for the woman to reappear. He fell asleep and when he woke up the ground was full of red water. He looked up and found himself surrounded by nine spirits. He went mad, of course. It took me three weeks to recover after I went inside his head to cure him. A little of his madness entered me. Tomorrow if you bring me three turtles and a big lobe of Lola nut I will do something about your dream. But tonight I am very busy."

The tapster agreed and, disappointed, went back home and drank his way through a gourd of palm wine. He managed to forget his dream by the time he fell asleep.

In the morning, he gathered his ropes and magic potions, tied three empty gourds to his bicycle, and rode out into the forest to begin his day's work. He had been riding for some time when he came to a signboard which read: DELTA OIL COMPANY: THIS AREA IS BEING DRILLED. TRESPASSERS IN DANGER. The tapster stared at the signboard without comprehension. Farther along he noticed a strange cluster of palm trees. He rode through thick cobwebs in order to reach them. The smell of their red-green bark intoxicated him. He immediately tied his magic potions to one of the tree trunks, brought out his rope, and proceeded to climb. Pressing his feet on both sides of the tree, switching the rope high up the rough rungs of the bark, he pulled himself up rapidly, till his chest began to ache. The morning sun, striking him with an oblique glare, blinded him. As the golden lights exploded in his eyes the branches of the palm tree receded from him. It was the first time he had fallen in thirty years.

When he woke up he was surprised that he felt no pain. He even had the curious feeling that the fall had done him some good. He felt unbelievably light and airy. He walked through spangles of glittering cobwebs without the faintest idea of where he was going. Fireflies darted into his nose and ears and reemerged from his eyes with their lights undimmed. He walked for a long time. Then he saw another signboard which read: DELTA OIL COMPANY: TRESPASSERS WILL BE PROSECUTED. Around him were earth mounds, gravestones, a single palm tree, and flickering mangrove roots. He made a mark on the tree trunk. Suddenly it became a fully festered wound. As he passed the twisting roots, troubled by the whitish ichors of the wound, they clasped him round the ankles. They held him down and tickled him. When he began to laugh they let him go.

He came to a river whose water was viscous and didn't seem to move. Near the river there was a borehole. Three turtles lazed on the edge of the borehole, watching him. One of the turtles had Tabasco's face. The tapster was about to say something when a multicolored snake emerged from the borehole and slithered past him. When the snake slid into the river the color of the water changed, and it became transparent and luminous. The snake's skin burned with a roseate flame. While the tapster looked on a voice behind him said:

"Don't turn round."

The tapster stayed still. The three turtles gazed at him with eyes of glass. Then the turtle that had Tabasco's face urinated in the tapster's direction. The turtle seemed to enjoy the act. The ecstasy on its face made it look positively fiendish. The tapster laughed and a heavy object hit him on the head from behind. He turned round swiftly and saw nothing. He laughed again and was whacked even harder. He felt the substance of his being dissolve. The river seemed to heave during the long silence which followed.

"Where am I?" the tapster asked.

There was another silence. The snake, glittering, slid back out of the river. When the snake passed him it lifted its head and spat at him. The snake went on into the borehole, dazzling with the colors of the sun. The tapster began to tremble. After the trembling ceased a curious serenity spread through him. When he looked around he saw that he had multiplied. He was not sure whether it was his mind or his body which flowed in and out of him.

"Where am I?"

The voice did not answer. Then he heard footsteps moving away. He could not even sleep, for he heard other voices talking over him, talking about him, as if he were not there.

In that world the sun did not set, nor did it rise. It was a single unmoving eye. In the evenings the sun was like a large crystal. In the mornings it was incandescent. The tapster was never allowed to shut his eyes. After a day's wandering, when he lay by the borehole, hallucinating about palm wine, a foul-smelling creature would come and stuff his eyes with cobwebs. This made his eyes itch and seemed a curious preparation for a vision. When the tapster tried to sleep, with his eyes open, he saw the world he knew revolving in red lights. He saw women going to the distant marketplaces, followed by sounds which they didn't hear. He saw that the signboards of the world were getting bigger. He saw the employees of the oil company as they tried to level the forests. When he was hungry another creature, which he couldn't see, would come and feed him a mess of pulped chameleons, millepedes, and bark. When he was thirsty the creature gave him a leaking calabash of green liquid. And then later at night another creature, which smelt of rotting agapanthus, crept above him, copulated with him, and left him the grotesque eggs of their nights together.

Then one day he dared to count the eggs. They were seven. He screamed. The river heaved. The snake stuck its head out from the bore-hole and the laughter of death roared from the sun. The laughter found him, crashed on him, shook him, and left large empty spaces in his head.

That night he fled. Everything fled with him. Then, after a while, he stopped. He abused the place, its terrible inhabitants, its unchanging landscape. Unable to escape, he cursed it ferociously. He was rewarded with several knocks. Then, as the eggs tormented him with the grating noises within them, as if a horrible birth were cranking away inside their monstrous shapes, he learned patience. He learned to watch the sky, and he saw that it wasn't so different from the skies of his drunkenness. He learned not to listen to the birth groaning within the eggs. He also learned that when he kept still everything else around him reflected his stillness.

And then, on another day, the voice came to him and said:

"Everything in your world has endless counterparts in other worlds. There is no shape, no madness, no ecstasy or revolution which does not have its shadow somewhere else. I could tell you stories which would drive you mad. You humans are so slow—you walk two thousand years behind yourselves."

The voice was soon gone.

Another voice said to him:

"You have been dead for two days. Wake up."

A creature came and stuffed his eyes with cobwebs. His eyes itched again and he saw that the wars were not yet over. Bombs which had not detonated for freak reasons, and which had lain hidden in farms, suddenly exploded. And some of those who lived as if the original war was over were blown up while they struggled with poverty. He saw the collapse of bridges that were being repaired. He saw roads that spanned

wild tracts of forests and malarial swamps, creeks without names, hills
without measurements. He saw the mouth of the roads lined with
human skeletons, victims of mindless accidents. He saw dogs that followed people up and down the bushpaths and brooding night-tracks. As
soon as the dogs vanished they turned into ghommids that swallowed up
lonely and unfortified travellers.

Then he saw the unsuccessful attempts to level the forest area and
drill for oil. He saw the witch doctors that had been brought in to drive
away the spirits from the forest. They also tried to prevent the torrential
rains from falling and attempted to delay the setting of the sun. When
all this failed the company hired an expatriate who flew in with explo-
sives left over from the last war. The tapster saw the expatriate plant
dynamite round the forest area. After the explosion the tapster saw a
thick pall of green smoke. When the smoke cleared the tapster watched a
weird spewing up of oil and animal limbs from the ground. The site was
eventually abandoned. Agapanthus grew there like blood on a battlefield.

The tapster saw people being shot in coups, in secret executions, in
armed robberies. He noticed that those who died were felled by bullets
which had their names on them. When his eyes stopped itching the tapster wandered beneath the copper bursts of the sky. He noticed that
there were no birds around. Streamers of cobweb membranes weaved
over the wounded palm tree.

And then one day, fired by memories of ancient heroes, he pursued a
course into the borehole. In the strange environment he saw the multicolored snake twisted round a soapstone image. He saw alligators in a
lake of bubbling green water. He saw an old man who had died in a sitting position while reading a bible upside down. Everything seemed on
fire, but there was no smoke. Thick slimes of oil seeped down the walls.
Roseate flames burned everywhere without consuming anything. He
heard a noise behind him. He turned and a creature forced a plate containing a messy substance of food into his hands. The creature then indicated that he should eat. The multicolored snake uncoiled itself from
the soapstone image. While the tapster ate the snake slid over and began
to tell him bad jokes. The snake told him stories of how they hang black
men in quiet western towns across the great seas, and of how it was possible to strip the skin off a baby without it uttering a sound. The snake

laughed. Partly because the snake looked so ridiculous, the tapster laughed as well. Several sharp whacks, as from a steel edge, drummed on his head, and put him out for what could have been eons of time.

When he recovered he traced his way out of the place. As he passed the man who had died reading the bible upside down he saw that the man looked exactly like him. He fled from the borehole.

His impatience reached new proportions. He counted the rocks on the ground. He counted the cobwebs, the colors of the sun, the heavings of the river. He counted the number of times the wind blew. He told himself stories. But he found that whatever he told himself that was sub-versive was simultaneously censored by the knocks. He counted the knocks: He grew used to them.

Then the voice came to him again. It sounded more brutal than usual. The voice said:

"Do you like it here?"

"No."

The tapster waited for a knock. It didn't arrive.

"Do you want to leave?"

"Yes."

"What's stopping you?"

"I don't know how."

The voice was silent.

Another voice said:

"You have been dead for three days."

The tapster, who had seen the sky and earth from many angles, who knew the secrets of wine, had learned the most important lesson. He listened without thinking.

"If you want to leave," the voice said, "we will have to beat you out."

"Why?"

"Because you humans only understand pain."

"We don't."

There was another pause. He waited for a knock. It came. His thoughts floated around like cobwebs on the wind. The tapster stayed like that, still, through the purple phases of the sun. After a long while the voice said:

"Here are some thoughts to replace the ones that have been knocked away. Do you want to hear them?"

"Yes."

The voice coughed and began:

"Even the good things in life eventually poison you. There are three kinds of sounds, two kinds of shadows, one gourd for every cracked head, and seven boreholes for those that climb too high. There is an acid in the feel of things. There is a fire which does not burn, but which dissolves the flesh like common salt. The bigger mouth eats the smaller head. The wind blows back to us what we have blown away. There are several ways to burn in your own fire. There is a particular sound which indicates trouble is coming. And your thoughts are merely the footsteps of you tramping round the disaster area of your own mind."

"Thank you," the tapster said.

The voice left. The tapster fell asleep.

When he woke up he saw the three turtles lazing again at the edge of the borehole. The turtle with Tabasco's face had on a pair of horn-rimmed glasses and a stethoscope round his neck. The turtles broke a kola nut, divided it amongst themselves, and discussed gravely like scholars without a test. The multicolored snake came out of the borehole and made for the river. It paused when it neared the turtles. The tapster was fascinated by its opal eyes.

"There are six moons tonight," said the turtle with Tabasco's face.

"Yes, there are six moons tonight," agreed the other turtles.

The snake, lifting up its head, its eyes glittering at the firmament, said:

"There are seven moons tonight."

The turtles were silent. The snake moved on towards the river. The turtle with Tabasco's face picked up a little rock and threw it at the snake. The other turtles laughed.

"There are no snakes tonight," said the turtle with Tabasco's face.

As if it were a cue, the other turtles set upon the snake. Tabasco the turtle grabbed it by the neck and began to strangle it with the stethoscope. The other turtles beat its head with rocks. The snake lashed out with its tail. Tabasco and the snake rolled over and fell into the borehole. Noises were heard below. After a while Tabasco the turtle emerged without his glasses and stethoscope. He took up his place amongst the others. They broke another kola nut. Then Tabasco the turtle began to prepare a pipe. Instead of tobacco, he used alligator pepper seeds. He lit the pipe and motioned to the tapster to come closer. The tapster went

and sat amongst the turtles on the edge of the borehole. Tabasco the turtle blew black ticklish smoke into the tapster's face and said:

"You have been dead for six days."

The tapster didn't understand. The turtles gravely resumed their discussions on the numbers of heavenly bodies in the sky.

After some time the smoke had the effect of making the tapster float
into a familiar world. A tickling sensation began in his nose. He floated
to a moment in his childhood, when his mother carried him on her back
on the day of the Masquerades. It was a hot day. The Masquerades thundered past, billowing plumes of red smoke everywhere so that ordinary
mortals would be confused about their awesome ritual aspects. All
through that day his nose was on fire. And that night he dreamt that all
sorts of mythical figures competed as to who could keep his nose on his
face. He relived the dream. The mythical figures included the famous
blacksmith, who could turn water into metal; the notorious tortoise,
with his simple madness for complex situations; and the witch doctors,
who did not have the key to mysteries. As they competed his mother
came along, drove them away by scattering a plate full of ground hot
pepper, worsening the problem of his nose.

And while the tapster floated in that familiar world the voice came
and bore down on him. Another voice said:

"It's getting too late. Wake up."

Invisible knocks fell on him. It was the most unusual moment of the
sun, when it changed from purple to the darkness of the inward eye.
After the knocks had stopped the tapster relieved himself of the mighty
sneeze which had been gathering. When he sneezed the monstrous eggs
exploded, the snake lost its opal eyes, and the voice fissioned into the
sounds of several mosquitoes dying for a conversation. Green liquids
spewed out from the borehole and blew away the snake, the signboard,
and the turtles. When the tapster recovered from the upheaval he
looked around. A blue cloud passed before his eyes. Tabasco the herbalist stood over him waving a crude censer, from which issued the most
irritating smoke. As soon as their eyes met, Tabasco gave a cry of joy and
went to pour a libation on the soapstone image of his shrine. The image
had two green glass eyes. At the foot of the shrine there were two turtles
in a green basin.

"Where am I?" asked the tapster.

"I'm sorry I didn't pay attention to your dream in the first place," said the herbalist.

"But where am I?"

"You fell from a palm tree and you have been dead for seven days. We were going to bury you in the morning. I have been trying to reach you all this time. I won't charge you for my services; in fact I'd rather pay you, because all these years as a herbalist I have never had a more interesting case, nor a better conversation."

London, June 1987

Funso Aiyejina was born circa 1949 in Ososo, southwestern Nigeria. He obtained a B.A. in English in 1974 at the University of Ife (now Obafemi Awolowo University), and completed his postgraduate studies in Nova Scotia and Trinidad. His poetry collection, A *Letter to Lynda and Other Poems*, won the Association of Nigerian Authors' Prize in 1989. He is also the author of *The Legend of the Rockhills*, which was short-listed for the Commonwealth Best First Book Prize. He has been a Fulbright Scholar-in-Residence in Creative Writing at Lincoln University in Missouri, and now lectures at the University of the West Indies in Trinidad, where he lives with his wife and family.

The One-Handed Hero

When, after the war with dissidents, Arije returned to Egwure, wearing a faded army uniform, his left hand amputated just above the wrist, and his mouth teeming with war stories, nobody was surprised.

Arije was one villager about whom there was a consensus. Everyone said something was bound to happen to him; failing that, he was bound to happen to something. He hated farmwork with a passion but he always had one scheme or another going to ensure that he stayed robust and well fed. Whenever he was teased about his more than generous girth and asked how he managed to keep it so well fed, he quipped that the source of the egret's whiteness would always remain a secret beyond the reach of the brown-feathered guinea fowl. His, he boasted, was a charmed life. Let no one attempt to compare their head with his. It was not his fault that they did not choose better heads from Sokoti, the head-molder in heaven.

He didn't have to tell them. The villagers knew better than to compare somebody else's head with theirs. What if that somebody was the tail-less cow whose flies God chased away with strong gales? No, they would never compare their heads with his. Everyone with his own head. Some heads got a break. Others got broken. The villagers prayed for a break for their heads and let Arije be with his.

One day, Arije disappeared from the village. His disappearance coincided with the visit of a recruitment team to solicit volunteers for the war. The recruitment officer had told the villagers that his visit was their golden opportunity to demonstrate their love for their country. The government, he revealed, was so anxious to give all able-bodied men the opportunity to demonstrate their love of country that it had abolished the minimum educational requirement for entering the army. Once you could press your thumb on an ink pad and make an impression with it on paper, you were good enough to serve the nation and be paid for it. To shoot a gun, you pulled its trigger with your finger. To claim your salary, you made a mark with your thumb. It was that simple. He went on to paint a picture-perfect image of the army: free food, free housing, free medical care, and, yes, free women.

His promises notwithstanding, not a single villager had volunteered. It was that time of year when all they cared about was the impending harvest of their cocoa crops. Who did he think he was going to get to abandon their preharvest cocoa farms to go and fight in a war they knew nothing about? Did he think they were all freeloaders like Arije or what?

But then, not even Arije had volunteered. At least, nobody in the village remembered his stepping forward to be counted as a lover of the nation, as the recruitment officer had challenged them to do. When, however, he had gone missing from the village on the same day the recruitment team visited, the villagers said they should have known better than to think that Arije could resist the recruitment officer's chant of free this and free that. He must, they concluded, have sneaked off, behind all the free things, after the meeting in the village square. Were they worried that he was gone? Why should they? What use was he when he was around? The village promptly rearranged him into the back room of its consciousness and left him there to mold, until that afternoon when he returned, after the war, bearing his badges of courage.

Arije returned to the village about two months after the leader of the dissidents abandoned his people, taking with him, according to the many tales that soon took root, items ranging from a Mercedes car to concubines in his executive jet, to go in search of peace, leaving his trusting deputy with the short end of the stick: the task of surrendering to the federal forces and facing prosecution for treason.

In addition to Arije's badges of courage, he returned with an order that he should no longer be called Arije.

Really? What should they call him?

OC.

What did that mean?

Officer-in-Charge. However, since he did not want them to bite their uneducated tongues trying to pronounce all of Officer-in-Charge, OC would do. Seeing how he would be the only one with that kind of a name around, he would know they were addressing him.

How did he come about this new name, this *Offisher-in-Sharge*?

Not *Offisher-in-Sharge*. Officer-in-Charge. Exactly why he told them to keep it simple and call him OC. Anyway, it meant a big soldier.

How did he get such a big soldier's name?

It was a long story; someday, when he had the time and the urge, he would tell them. But, in the meantime, did they hear the good news?

No, what was it? Had they finally raised the price of cocoa?

Cocoa, was that all they ever thought of? There was a life before and after cocoa. No, it was not about cocoa. It was about him. OC.

What was it?

The Federal Military Government, in recognition of his contribution to the war, was going to declare him a national hero. Did they know what that meant?

The villagers confessed their ignorance. Would he be kind enough to forgive them, seeing how there was no school around when they were growing up, and make them wiser, educate them with his knowledge and heroism?

Why not? Someone had to start it someday. When you were named a national hero, you were invited to the capital, decorated by the General, the biggest soldier in the country, and presented with a *thousand* anila.

Whaoo. A *thousand* anila? How much was that?

Ten in ten places in ten places. More money than they had ever seen.

When would this great event take place?

First, his name would be announced on the radio; then, a *signal* would be sent from the capital, directing him to report there *on the double*, to be decorated and presented with one thousand anila.

From that day on, at seven o'clock in the evening, the villagers congregated at the home of Mr. A. A. Akinyemi, HM—headmaster and sole teacher at the local authority one-room primary school which served all the villages in the area. They did so to listen to the national news and instructions, on his radio, the only radio within a twenty-mile radius. In the course of the news, every day, except on Fridays and Sundays—out of respect for Allah and Yahweh—one national hero was named.

There were two categories of heroes—the living and the dead. The living were summoned to the capital to collect their medals and cash rewards, while the dead, having no need for either, were directed, by the decree which set up the awards, to pass on both medal and money to a next of kin, designated by the government (the person didn't have to be a legal or a blood relative).

There was no way of knowing in advance whether the sole hero for the day was going to be living or dead. The list was neither alphabetic nor geographic. And there was no telling at what point in the thirty-minute bulletin the name of the hero for the day would be announced. It varied from day to day. So, if you fought in the war and survived or if you knew someone who fought in it and you wanted to know whether or not they had qualified for hero status, you just had to keep tuning in at seven o'clock and stay tuned until seven-thirty, until you heard the anticipated or got tired waiting for it. It was that simple.

But the villagers had their evenings to spare. Their work was in the day. They waited with bated breath for the momentous announcement, barely concealing their vicarious identification with Arije's future importance. At last, they were going to have their own big man, someone to plead their case before the government. At last, they would have an elephant killer and the terror of dissidents to plead with the authorities for an increase in the price of cocoa and a proper road for the transportation of their goods out of the forest. No longer the nine-mile trek to get a *bolekaja* wagon to take them to the big market at Akoda.

By the way, which name would be announced on radio? The old or the new?

Arije assured them that he would be addressed by all of his names: OC Arije Abolonjeku.

What about his praise song: *Oko Iya Alamala*? And would they, by any chance, indicate that he was an illustrious son of Egwure?

There was no space on the enlistment form for praise names. As for being the illustrious son of Egwure, he was not sure. Not likely though. He did not put down Egwure as one of his names. Although he indicated that he was from Egwure, he did not make it a part of his names like those big officers who called themselves So-and-So *dan* This or *dan* That. Did they know that the *This* and the *That* in those names were the towns the officers were from?

No, they didn't.

Yes. And if you saw how many of them were big officers in the army.

But why were so many of them big officers in the army?

Simple; an officer who was a *dan* This saw a recruit who was a *dan* That, *fiam*, he promoted him to the rank of officer. But, not to worry, in the next war, God willing, he would be Arije Abolonjeku *dan* Egwure.

May God forbid a next war, but should there be one, would they accept him back in the army with only one hand?

What did they mean, "would they accept him back in the army with only one hand"? If they didn't know, a hero was a hero, with or without hands. Did they hear him? A hero was a hero. He didn't blame them, ignorant villagers that they were. If only they knew how he lost his hand of courage in the service of the nation, they would not be asking such a stupid question.

Without even the courtesy of an *"alo o?*—may I tell a story?"—Arije launched into the story of how he lost his hand of courage. The villagers listened to this story, which invested him with the status of a hero and gave him the right to the now famous words "When-I-become-a-national-hero," with which he prefaced his long list of what he would and would not do once he was crowned a national hero. If OC asked for food and you were slow in offering him some, he would remind you of what he would do or not do to the likes of you once he was anointed a national hero; if he asked you for two things and you only had one to give, he would promise to show you how not to be mean to a future national hero; if he owed money to you and you made the mistake of reminding him that payment was long overdue, he would ask you what money you thought you had that you were allowing it to get to your head, just wait until he got his one thousand anila and you would see what was called money; if you met him on one of the village's narrow footpaths and you were slow in yielding the right of way to him, he would remind you how, as a national hero, his outriders would run over arrogant fools like you before his official car finished you off. Arije, also known as OC, soon became known as When-I-become-a-national-hero, and, in no time, was shortened to When-I.

The villagers listened to the story of the missing hand, a story they had always wanted to ask When-I to tell, but had not because they did not want to be accused of pointing their questions at the invisible.

When-I launched into his daring, single-handed (no pun intended) capture of the dissident leader.

Were they aware that he, OC Arije, the son of Abolonjeku, single-handedly captured the leader of the dissidents?

No, they were not. Didn't he vanish into thin air before the victorious federal soldiers could arrest him at the end of the war?

Vanish into what thin air? Nonsense. He did not vanish anywhere. He fled like the coward that he was, with his tail tucked between his legs.

But didn't he just single-handedly capture him?

Look at trouble. If only they would keep quiet just long enough for him to put the two feet of his story on the ground before they lawyered him! Was that too much for a national-hero-in-waiting to ask of a group of ignorant villagers?

Not at all. They were sorry: it wouldn't happen again.

Did they hear of the big wedding?

No. What big wedding?

The General's wedding?

No, they did not.

While the war was on, the General decided that war or no war, a man had to do what a man had to do. He was tired of not having an official First Lady in the State House. Even the dissidents had a First Lady. Just imagine that. Never mind that their so-called leader sent his so-called First Lady and their children out of the country before he declared his dissent. At least he had a First Lady. You must first have one before you could ship or fly her and the nation's First Children out for safekeeping.

Didn't you? So it was that the General decided to get married in the middle of the war.

When the General asked the First-Lady-to-be what she most desired for a wedding gift, she said she would like a mini-zoo on the grounds of the State House for their First-Child-in-the-making. The General asked if that was all she wanted. She said yes. In that case, it would be ready in twenty-four hours. What manner of animals did she want in her mini-zoo? Only one. Only one? Yes, only one: the leader of the dissidents.

That was how a signal came to be sent to all the commanding officers on the battlefield: Anyone who delivered Colonel Big Beard before the eve of the General's wedding would be promoted to the rank of General. Yes. General. A rank higher than that of any commanding officer. The signal was signed and sealed by the Head of State, Commander-in-Chief of the Armed Forces, the Groom-in-waiting, and the only General in the country.

What did I do? What kind of a question is that? What did I do? Of course, I did what every man who did not want God to leave him behind would do: kept pace with God by visiting the most powerful priest in Osomorika and spreading my life before him.

"Father of all mysteries, I humble myself before you. Fix my future for me."

Homage to those Osomorika priests. The man took one look at the three miserable stripes on the sleeves of my uniform and, before I could open my mouth to tell him what kind of a future I wanted, he saw it, right there on his divination tray. He told me that I was after a promotion, a rapid one.

"Yes, father. I want to become a General. And the only thing standing between me and General is Colonel Big Beard. With your help, I want to capture Colonel Big Beard as a present for the First-Lady-in-waiting so the General can give the order to change my three miserable stripes into the bright stars of a General."

He named his fees and my mouth let out a loud *So much?* Did I want his help or did I not? There were others waiting and willing to pay more for less. I begged his forgiveness. It was my poverty that spoke without thinking. I had a pricker buried in my foot; he was the only one who could root it out. Not to worry, I had his fee on me.

Armed with my newly acquired spells, I went back to the battle front, ready to go after my future as a General. I made myself invisible, crossed over to the *tactical headquarters* of the dissidents, and made straight for the *bunker* where their leader was living it up. You should have seen me marching about the camp as if I was in my living room. I even allowed one or two soldiers to bump into me just to watch the confusion on their faces on bumping into something solid in an empty place.

You know what I saw as I walked into Colonel Big Beard's *bunker*? The bastard was busy splitting a beautiful log of wood. Let me not lie, I stood there salivating. But I quickly remembered that I had a job to do and that after that job, once I became a General, I would be able to get all the mammy-water queens in all the oceans of the world.

How was I going to get the Colonel out of the *bunker* since he was not invisible like me? Well, the priest had taken care of that. He had given me another spell to put the camp to sleep. Once they were all snoring, in whatever position they were caught by the spell, I made myself visible and woke up the Colonel. He jumped up from on top of his snoring mammy-water, grasped his pants, and held them up to protect his now limp third leg before diving for the gun under his pillow. He took aim and fired. But nothing happened. Of course, I had emptied it of its bullets before I woke him up. I smiled. He wanted to know how I got through his security? What did I do to his guards? How much did I pay them? It was one question after another. He wouldn't even pause to let me answer one before asking a next one. When he finally stopped long enough for me to get in an answer, I told him I had done to his guards the same thing I did to his queen. That was when he noticed that she was fast asleep and completely uncovered. He quickly pulled the sheets over her. He realized that I was now the officer and he the recruit. What did I want? I told him. He said I was mad to think that he would follow me to be exhibited in a zoo. He would rather die first.

I was the wind. He was the leaf. Wherever the wind directed the leaf, there it went. I commanded him to get dressed. He did, unable to resist my spell. I handcuffed his right wrist to my left wrist as an additional insurance and led him, like a sheep, out of his headquarters.

What didn't he do? He begged, he pleaded, he tried bribery, he tried corruption; he would make me a Major if I set him free and joined his army. What did he take me for, a fool? He must really have underestimated his own worth. I was going to be made a General for bringing him in, and there he was, offering to make me a Major if I set him free and joined his ragged-soon-to-be-vanquished army. Foolish man. No wonder his army was losing the war.

We had just cleared the outer boundary of his headquarters, making our way across to the federal side, when a federal plane roared over the camp on a bombing mission. Maybe it was the sound of the plane, or maybe the spell was not designed to last that long. Whatever the reason, the dissident soldiers woke up from the spell and started to shoot at anything that moved. We were still within their shooting range, so I ducked, pulling the Colonel and his beard into the nearest bush. There was shooting from the soldiers on the ground and there was bombing from the plane above. It was chaos and pandemonium everywhere. That was when it happened.

What happened?

When I handcuffed Colonel Big Beard's right hand to my left hand, I was under the assumption that he was right-handed. Unfortunately for me, he was not. So, while I was struggling to pull us under cover, he got hold of my side dagger with his left hand, slashed through my wrist in one deft, powerful motion, set himself free, and made a dash for freedom, leaving what was my left hand jumping up and down on the battlefield.

Nobody would have believed my story had Colonel Big Beard not dropped his cap, the one with the parrot plumage, in his haste to regain his freedom. On realizing that I had lost him, I made myself invisible again and got out of there as fast as possible, clutching my bleeding wrist and his cap—my only proof of how close I came to delivering Colonel Big Beard to the General on my road to becoming a General.

The villagers commiserated with him, advised him to thank his head, and announced that it could have been worse. The loss of a hand was bad, but it was not as bad as the loss of one's life. After that story, their anticipation doubled. Their hero would soon become a national hero. They were willing to wait as long as it took to hear his name on the radio.

But, after months of feting Arije in anticipation of his future importance, when the radio had not yet named him a hero, the villagers began to despair. Some said it was because they had nobody with contacts in the government to put in a good word for him. Some said that it was because HM's transistor radio was too small; it could not bring everything the government sent it to bring. A few, while still keeping hope alive, wondered: How much salt, pepper, and locust bean had When-I seasoned his story with? What would be left of his pot of war tales if these condiments were removed? Such was the range of the villagers' thoughts about When-I, when HM was invited to attend a conference of headmasters of the Akoda Local Government area primary schools, in Akoda.

The villagers said, Yes, their time had finally come.

How come?

Wasn't it true that there were big radios in Akoda?

Yes. It was true.

In that case, could HM listen for OC's name on one such radio while in Akoda? In addition, if it was also true that they had another kind of radio which displayed both voices and pictures, could he seek out one of such and see if that was where OC's name would be announced? Seeing that OC alone had dared to attempt the capture of Colonel Big Beard, didn't it make sense that his heroism would be acknowledged in a special way?

HM heard them out, offered neither encouragement nor discouragement, and promised to do whatever they wanted.

He was away in Akoda for one week. The question everyone was waiting to ask, even before he dismounted from his Raleigh bicycle, was whether or not the big or the special radios in Akoda had announced OC's name.

No. But he brought something even more convincing than a name on the radio. Could they congregate at his place at news time that evening as usual?

Of course. Why not? What kind of question was that? What did he think they had been waiting for all these months? Even if they had to be carried on their sick beds, there was no way they were going to miss this confirmation of the heroism of their hero.

By six-thirty that evening, there was no standing room in front of HM's place. Men, women, and even the children, who treated When-I only as a comic relief and were not caught up in the euphoria of his past courage or his future wealth, were all there. Everyone, except the hero himself. Those who had passed by his house, now overgrown with weeds since he had time only for dreaming of the future, said he was not at home. They knew it: he had not given up on his selfishness. He had sneaked off again, this time to go and collect one thousand anila. He didn't want the village to go with him, to share in his glory and his wealth. They would show him when he returned. But for now, they were not going to let anything distract from their celebration of their hero's heroism.

At seven o'clock, HM came out to the crowd, this time, without his transistor radio. Instead, he was holding a sheet of newspaper. As soon as the crowd noticed that he had come out, everyone fell silent in anticipation. He thanked them for coming as he had requested. A man whose invitation had been answered must remember to be grateful.

In case they had not noticed, the anticipation of the news of Arije's national award had united the village more than anything he could remember since his arrival among them.

Nodding heads affirmed the truth of his position.

Thenceforth, he hoped, the village would continue to approach the future with the same collective strength.

Thank you. But the proof? Show us the proof.

HM unfolded the sheet of newspaper to reveal a picture of three men, the one in the middle in military uniform. They stood erect like house-posts, hands behind their backs, each wearing an unsmiling face. HM passed it around. The first group of villagers to recognize the man in the middle let out a chorus of It is him, it is him and were answered by several It is who? from different sections of the anxious crowd. Their Arije, the son of Abolonjeku, was a hero. Look, his picture, on a piece of paper. Others pressed forward to see for themselves that the man in the middle was actually their own Arije. The page of newspaper went from hand to hand followed by various versions of It is him, it's really him and loud admonitions to the children, who were tugging and pulling, to be careful and not tear it.

How did HM get it?

Through one of the many miracles of big towns.

Could he be more specific?

Of course. In big towns like Akoda, you walked into important pieces of information, such as top secret government documents, on the streets every day.

How was that possible?

To make ends meet, some civil servants stole old newspapers and government documents which they sold to groundnut sellers.

What for?

To be used to wrap groundnut for sale. He had bought groundnut to supplement the breakfast, something they called *saladi*, more grass than food, which they had been fed at the University of Akoda where the conference was held. He was about to crumple the piece of newspaper in which the groundnut had been wrapped, before throwing it into the dustbin, when a face called out to him. He took a closer look and his eyes made four with those of Arije, the son of Abolonjeku.

Akika! And to think they had been there waiting, every day, to hear his name and he had been in a paper for the rest of the world to see. Look at how HM just went to Akoda and brought back the evidence, just so. He must buy a bigger radio. There was no other solution. Otherwise, they would be there in that village and the whole world would go and leave them behind. That radio of his was too small. Wasn't it the case that the size of a tongue was determined by the size of the mouth in which it was housed? How did he expect that small radio to bring all the many things the government sent out to the people?

"The fault was not with my radio or its size. The fault was with our hero."

What was HM saying? After they had seen the evidence with their own naked eyes? Did he think that they had borrowed their neighbors' eyes to see with or what? This was plain to see; it was a disease of the eye, not of the stomach. By the way, where was their hero? Had anybody seen him?

"He left, as soon as I showed him that picture."

Why did he do such a thing?

"Very simple. He did not fight in any war."

The uniform, what about his uniform?

"According to the story on that piece of paper in your hands, he worked as a cleaner in one of the military barracks in the North, many miles from the battlefield in the East. He must have got himself someone's discarded uniform."

The hand, what about the hand?

"Oh yes, the hand. Send up the picture to the front."

When the picture finally made it to him, he called on one of his star pupils to come forward, read, and translate the caption under the picture for the benefit of the villagers.

The boy turned the words around in his mouth, sounded them out through barely moving lips, and proceeded slowly to release them to the attentive villagers. It was important that he took his time: he did not want to let down his headmaster.

"A-b-o-v-e a-r-e t-h-e f-i-r-s-t v-i-c-t-i-m-s o-f s-h-a- . . . ," he stumbled. HM gave him a congratulatory pat on his head and told him the word was *sharia*, it was not English, it was Arabic.

What did it all mean? The village wanted to know.

"Arije and the two men in the picture had been caught stealing. They were taken before a *sharia* court, the new legal system in the North, and were found guilty. The court, in accordance with Islamic laws, ruled that they should have their left hands chopped off."

As they dispersed, someone was heard muttering: "I knew it. I knew he would bring nothing but shame on us."

Farida Karodia was born and raised in South Africa. She emigrated to Canada in 1969, having lived and taught in Johannesburg and Zambia. She is the author of *Daughters of The Twilight*, *Coming Home and Other Stories*, *Against an African Sky*, and *A Shattering of Silence*. She has also written several radio dramas for the BBC. She divides her time between South Africa and Canada.

The Woman In Green

I was awakened from a deep sleep by a confusion of sounds. For a while I listened to the noise and the chatter of passengers hurrying by my window, then I sat up and drowsily peered at my watch. It was a few minutes before midnight. I rolled over in my bunk to squint through the slit between the wooden shutters. The sign at the railway station read "Bloemfontein."

The hissing and clanking of couplings, the screeching of wheels, the shrilling of a whistle, and the mist-shrouded lights on the platform lent an air of eeriness to the scene outside.

I remained by the darkened window caught up in the atmosphere but then the whistle shrilled, rudely jolting me back to reality. The train jerked forward and just as I thought we were on our way, it abruptly screeched to a halt again. I noticed a commotion at the far end of the platform and inquisitively lowered the blind a few inches, craning my neck to see. A couple hurried into view. They appeared to be VIPs of some sort. I watched the woman who paused beneath the light standard. Her bearing and the atmosphere seemed to give her a quality of dislocation. Ensconced in the comfort of my bed, I felt a twinge of sympathy for the latecomers. I watched for a while longer until the group and their entourage passed beyond my line of vision.

———————

Later the next morning, I saw the woman again, for the second time, at Park Station in Johannesburg, where the Cape Town Special sat on a branch-line awaiting a diesel engine. Eventually the engine arrived, reversed, grabbed the connection and jerked the carriages forward. The train heaved, the sudden motion throwing its unsuspecting passengers back against their seats.

I groped for my shoes, found them, but couldn't get them onto my swollen feet. I, obviously, was not going anywhere. I leaned back, propped my feet up on the radiator and, absorbed in thought, stared out. Suddenly I heard high-pitched, girlish laughter. I thought I recognized the laugh and glanced up quickly. It was her, the same woman from the previous night dressed in a gorgeous lime-green outfit. She hurried towards the train from the small bookstall where she had been browsing.

Last night too, they had almost missed the train at Bloemfontein. Some people were like that, I reflected wryly, always missing the boat or as in this case, the train. I watched as the man straightened his tie and buttoned his jacket, following a few steps behind her.

"Hurry, dear!" she called in Afrikaans, "or we'll be left behind."

The train continued its slide along the track. Suddenly it braked with that screech of steel on steel that set one's teeth on edge. Although hampered by high heels, the woman broke into a run. Out of breath she stopped beneath my window in the second-class nonwhite carriage.

She had not yet noticed that she was being observed by me and placed one hand to her chest; with the other she pressed down her hat, a matching lime-green cloche. She was an attractive woman: tall, slim, and elegant looking. She was close enough for me to notice details, like the way her blouse was draped a bit daringly and pinned with a cameo. Even though I admired the simple elegance of her outfit, I knew that with my extra weight, the style would be quite unsuitable on me. I couldn't take my eyes off her. There was something so familiar about her. But for the life of me, I couldn't place her.

At that moment, while I was thinking about all this, she turned round, still wearing her smile. As she did so, her eye caught mine. She glanced at me, and there was a flicker of emotion in that look that I couldn't quite identify. At the same time the blood just seemed to drain right out of her face. It all happened very quickly. Her pallor, our glances meeting, her frozen smile. Then she hurried by. But in those split seconds my brain had registered her expression and I was perplexed. I cursed my bad memory for faces. Did I know her or did she merely remind me of someone I once knew?

For the next little while I could not shake her image from my mind. It haunted me. I was baffled. Who was this white woman in a green dress with dark brown hair and a laugh so distinctive and familiar that it had stirred a deep, subconscious memory? It was like having a word poised on the tip of the tongue and not being able to spit it out.

She and her husband hurried to the first-class carriage at the head of the train. I followed the green hat as it forged a path through the crowd. When they got to the carriage the man solicitously took her arm to assist her up but before she took that last step onto the train, she hesitated, turned and glanced again in my direction.

The train shunted back onto the main line. A warning whistle shrilled, followed by a general scramble as the passengers who were strolling about on the platform hurried back. The conductor waited, green flag poised. He dropped his arm and the train heaved and jerked. The string of carriages lumbered forward, then jolted back on each other like an uncoordinated caterpillar. Finally we eased out of the station and gathered speed.

My carriage was near the tail section and I could see the engine and front carriages snaking around a curve. Preoccupied as I was, I hardly noticed the steepled churches and big houses which streamed past the smoke-blackened windows.

It was a hot summer's day and the train racketing and swaying along the tracks to Pretoria was crowded with students on their way home for the holidays. We left the city behind, passing twisted tree trunks ripped by lightning and covered with weeds, then sped along miles of open *veld* before the bottles, rusted skeletons of old cars and smouldering rubbish heralded the arrival of yet another township.

At Irene where the train stopped for fifteen minutes, passengers leaned out of their windows to fling fruit and sandwiches to children who were begging alongside the tracks. I remained comfortably seated beside the window, nodding off in the sun.

I heard the quiet knock and thought that I had imagined it. It came again, louder this time. A little irritated at being disturbed, I got up to open the door. To my astonishment, standing in the doorway was the woman in green.

"Alice, thank goodness, I found you," she said, slipping by me. Astounded, I automatically slid the door shut behind her.

"Henny Marais," I gasped.

"*Ja*. It's me," she laughed.

That laugh. How could I have forgotten? "Henrika Marais," I said again. "I thought there was something familiar about you. It's been driving me mad." I stepped back to get a better look at her. "My God, you've changed so much." No wonder I couldn't make the connection. "What a surprise," I cried, hugging her. "It's been years . . . years."

"Twenty-five years," she added.

"Sit down." I patted the seat beside me.

"Listen Alice. I can't stay long. I'd love nothing better than to catch up with all the news, but I've got to get back to my husband." She pulled a wry face and sat down anyway.

"For heaven's sake. What's the rush?"

"Are you still in Pretoria?" she asked.

I nodded.

"Alice I really can't stay," she said. "Give me your phone number, I'll get in touch with you when we get to Pretoria."

I was still astonished at meeting her so unexpectedly. Then I remembered the white man with her and it all became crystal clear.

"I recognized you the moment I saw you at Park Station, but I couldn't come over." She sensed that I had guessed the truth.

"I see." I nodded slowly.

"Look, don't judge me until you've heard the whole story."

She had tiny flecks of hazel in the grey of her irises. I remembered them from the time when we were little girls growing up in the Bazaar which was the colloquial term for the township then. "It's not up to me to judge you." I dropped my glance before replying.

"We'll catch up on everything. How about tomorrow? Are you busy?"

I shook my head.

"I'd better get going or my husband might come looking for me. Give me your phone number. I'll ring you in the morning."

I rummaged through my handbag for a scrap of paper. All I could find was my checkbook. I ripped off the corner of a blank check and scribbled my name, address, and phone number. "Where's home now, Henny?" I asked.

"Kroonstad," she said.

"Good Lord, don't tell me you're living in the Free State?"

"*Ja.* I married an Afrikaner."

"I see," I muttered.

"I thought that might surprise you. I am the wife of Deputy Minister Johan Mulder."

I glanced at her in disbelief.

She nodded. "We've been married for nineteen years . . . and they've been the happiest years of my life," she added. "I have two grown sons."

I was still incredulous.

"My past is dead, Alice. No one knows, not even Johan."

"I see," I muttered. "I thought you had gone overseas."

She raised a delicate shoulder. With the movement, the cameo caught my eye. I remembered now that it had once belonged to her mother. As a young girl I was always admiring and coveting it. Her mother used to tease me saying that one day when she was dead, I could have it.

"For how long will you be staying in Pretoria?" I asked.

"A week or so. My husband is here for a briefing before Parliament closes for the holidays."

She got up to go. We hugged, promising to get together the next day. I let her out and locked the door behind her.

The train lurched and started to move out of Irene. The African children shouted, waving and running alongside the train. A sandwich flew by the window. The wax wrapping opened, spilling its contents into the dust. The children scrambled after it. A half-eaten apple followed the path of the sandwich.

The warmth and the rhythmic sway of the train soon dispelled all thoughts, including those of Henny, lulling me to sleep. I dreamed I was a child again, spending a Sunday morning at the zoo with my parents. We were walking along the shaded pathways towards the ravine where the big cats were housed. My father held my hand as we started out, but when we got to the ravine a stranger had taken his place.

I cried out for Daddy, thrashing and kicking, but the man lifted me over his shoulder like a sack of potatoes and carried me towards the ravine. I was still screaming for my father as I flew through the air into the lion's enclosure. Before I hit the ground, I awakened with a jolt. My heart pounding, I sat bolt upright and covered my face. It all came back to me. The woman in green and everything.

I sat up gathering my scattered wits and gazed out of the window, marveling at how easily a dream is able to turn into a nightmare. A grove of pepper trees flashed by and in the distance the Voortrekker Monument came into view.

We had almost arrived and I collected my belongings. I thought it best under the circumstances to delay disembarking in order to avoid Henny and the possibility of embarrassing her. I waited until most of the passengers had left the front carriages and then got off.

Amidst the noise and commotion I heard a page for Mr. Mulder. He was a tall man and I saw his head moving towards the information booth. There was something very possessive in the way he held Henny's elbow and ushered her towards the rotunda. She saw me and gave a small nervous smile. I smiled back at her and walked by.

When I got home I told Aunty Dorothy about my unexpected encounter with Henny.

"What a coincidence," Aunty Dorothy cried. "Cousin Betty was telling me the other day that she had met her father, Piet Dimbaza, in O.K. Bazaars."

"You're joking!"

"No. Cousin Betty said he came right up to her, tapped her on the shoulder and said, 'Do you remember me Ousies?' She said she almost died of fright. Then she recognized him. She says he's still a striking man. He told her he was living in Mamelodi and that he had a nice job in some government office."

I listened in silence.

"What does she look like? I mean her hair . . . her father's a little backward in that respect. I was trying to remember what she was like as a child but I've forgotten."

"She's the image of her mother."

"What about her hair?"

"It's not as wild as it used to be. It's dark brown, it's not *kroes* just curly. Lots of curls like a perm I would say. When I saw her she had it tied back."

"Good thing she didn't get his hair," Aunty Dorothy said.

"She's got some of her father's looks. He was quite good-looking, but she definitely has her mother's eyes. They're grey with little flecks in them."

"Oh, I remember now," Aunty Dorothy said. "What's her husband like?" she asked, settling down with her cup of tea, relishing the opportunity for a good bit of gossip.

"I didn't really get a good look at him, but from the little I saw, I think he's difficult and very possessive about her. He could be a real hard case. Oh yes, I almost forgot the most important bit. Do you know who he is?" I asked.

She shook her head, her eyes glinting eagerly.

"Johan Mulder."

She stared back blankly.

"Deputy Minister Johan Mulder," I said.

Aunty Dorothy's eyes opened wide. "You mean . . . ?" she breathed.

Aunty Dorothy wanted to know every little detail. I told her all that I knew.

"Better not say anything to anyone," I urged her when she left.

"Don't worry." The look in her eyes, however, left me skeptical about this assurance.

"Whatever you do, stay away from Mrs. Simons, you know what she's like, the old *skinderbek*."

"Stop worrying about it. I know when to open my mouth and when to keep it shut," she said.

When I looked out an hour later, I saw Aunty Dorothy heading down the road in the general direction of Mrs. Simons, and I knew by the end of the day it would be all over the township.

Henny rang around noon. We talked on the phone for a while and I offered to pick her up the following day.

"Are you sure it won't be any trouble?" she asked.

"No trouble at all," I replied.

"Okay I'll meet you in the lobby of my hotel." She gave me the name and the address.

"Do you know where it is?" she asked.

"Yes, I drive by there quite often."

The hotel was a small, unpretentious but chic establishment near the university campus. I had no trouble finding her, even in the dimly lit lobby. She was the type of woman who stood out in any crowd. She was wearing a print dress, simple but elegant, with low-heeled pumps. Her hair was drawn back into a bun. It occurred to me then that she didn't look at all like a typical Afrikaner woman. It seemed incongruous that she could have buried herself in the heart of Afrikanerdom. I suspected that a woman like her would be painfully conspicuous and out of place in a right-wing Afrikaner community like Kroonstad. She had a straw hat in her hand and hurried over the moment she saw me.

"My car is outside." I pointed to the slightly beaten-up Volkswagen across the street.

"Oh, good." She dropped the sunglasses over her eyes. "I was wondering whether you'd have transportation."

"I call her 'Old Faithful'; she hasn't let me down yet." I laughed as we hurried across the street at the crossing.

I opened the door and threw some of the clutter onto the backseat. "When were you last in Pretoria?" I asked.

"Not since I left here and went to Boxburg."

"Not once?"

She shook her head. And when she saw my expression of surprise she said, "When you hear the whole story, you'll understand."

I started the car and we eased into the traffic. The jacaranda trees were in full bloom and it was truly a sight to behold. This was one time of the year when the city was exquisitely beautiful. The avenues of trees and the manicured gardens gave it an atmosphere of elegance that made one forget the harsh ugliness of the townships located miles out of the city. We passed the university campus and then took the road which passed by the zoo. I recalled the nightmare I had had on the train.

"Remember the zoo?" I asked.

"I was just thinking how much Nicholas and Ben would enjoy it."

"Your children?"

She nodded. "Nicholas has just turned eighteen and will be attending Stellenbosch University. My youngest is Ben. He's fourteen and he's at school in Bloemfontein."

I listened as she talked about her boys.

"What about you?" she asked suddenly.

"I don't have any children. I was married for four years. David, my husband, was killed in a car accident. We'd postponed having children because of our careers. He was a doctor and I had just started teaching." I hurried through this explanation not wanting to dwell on it.

"I'm sorry," she said.

I shrugged. "That's life."

"You never got married again?"

"No."

She stared out of the window in silence as we headed for the Bazaar. I saw her face reflected in the window, bright and alert with anticipation. At the corner where the Indian market used to be, I turned left. I still remember the distinctive morning smells of boiled mealies and peanuts, or frying meat.

"The market used to be here!" She was surprised that it wasn't where she had expected to find it. "What happened to it?" she asked.

But before I could respond, it dawned on her. "How stupid of me, I forgot everyone was moved out years ago."

I slowed to a crawl and she looked about eagerly, trying to identify landmarks. Ahead of us the Imperial Bioscope rose from amidst the ruins like a shrine.

"It's hard to believe that it's all gone."

"People were dispersed—the Indians to Laudium and the Coloreds to Eersterust." We bumped over potholes and past a few remaining stores in the main street. "They'll he moving those too," I added.

We turned around in a large field. "Our school used to be there . . . and right here where we're parked is where Moosa's Cafe used to be. Remember the mango chutney and thick slices of bread?"

"What happened to Moosa?"

"The old man died soon after they tore his shop down."

I turned back into the main street. "This is Third Street." I turned into an empty lot overgrown with grass and weeds. "This is about where your house used to be."

"It was further down," she argued.

"No. That's where the Pillays lived."

"Of course, the Pillays and their ten children. I used to be beaten up regularly by the three older girls."

"Because they thought you were Miss High-and-Mighty," I reminded her.

"That wasn't true though." She denied this with an expression of such serious indignation that it brought a smile to my face. "I was shy, but not high and mighty."

"You were okay," I replied. She had always been quiet and aloof, almost standoffish. The other children had mistaken this aloofness for weakness and had nicknamed her "Mousy." I always thought that her quietness had to do with the fact that her mother was white and her father black. They had got married in the early forties, long before laws were introduced prohibiting interracial marriages. Rumor had it then that her mother had fallen in love with him when he was still working on the farm for them as a laborer. He was a good-looking man who looked more colored than African.

"I heard that after your mother died, you went to live in Boxburg with her sister. Your father just disappeared from the scene after Aunty Sophie died. Have you ever heard from him?"

"No." She shook her head. "The last I heard was that he was living with a black woman in one of the townships. But that was twenty years ago. He may be dead now for all I know."

I didn't say anything. This was not the time to tell her that her father was alive and living in Mamelodi. I turned the car and we headed out of the Bazaar, past Mohammed's Furniture Emporium and A.B. Bazaars. "I've arranged for us to have lunch at my place," I said.

"That would be lovely. But are you sure I'm not putting you out?"

"Definitely not," I assured her. "My Aunty Dorothy prepared lunch. Remember her?"

She shook her head.

"She's a nurse. Actually a matron at the hospital now. She's a bright and efficient lady who has traveled all over. In fact she's just come back from Australia." I went on and on about Aunty Dorothy. I wanted her to shine forth. I wanted desperately for Henny to see that we, too, had done something with our lives. We had not stagnated despite adversity.

The pale sky shimmered through a veil of heat. I rolled down the window and a blast of air caught her hat. I rolled the window up again.

"I'll take this off," she said, placing her straw hat on the seat beside her.

"Aren't you going to tell me about your family? What happened after you left for Boxburg?"

She had lapsed into a comfortable silence and I waited impatiently to hear the rest of her story. Finally she said: "Living with my white family, I became white. I went to a white school in Boxburg. It wasn't difficult. My mother had registered me as white on my birth certificate." The practice of having children from mixed marriages registered under the name and race of the white parent was a fairly common one.

"I did well at school, passed my matric and went to the University of Stellenbosch on a scholarship. I met Johan in my first year there. We got married and that was the end of my studies."

There was a strange note in her voice and I couldn't quite decide whether it was regret or not. She lapsed again into a contemplative silence.

"That's it?" I asked.

"That's it."

"Does your husband know . . . ?"

"Of course not." She shook her head emphatically. "At times I've wanted to tell him, but how could I? If anyone ever found out that I had been fathered by a black man, his career and everything I hold dear would be destroyed: my marriage, my children." She stared straight ahead, her face pale and pinched.

"Perhaps he loves you enough to accept it?" I suggested. "Think of the peace of mind you'll have if it's all out in the open."

"The scandal would destroy him."

We stared at the road in silence. What a mess, I thought. Her worst nightmare would be being recognized by one of her old school friends while accompanying her husband. It wasn't that improbable; after all, I had recognized her . . . well, in a way, I conceded.

At Derdepoort the traffic increased. Most of the vehicles were loaded to the hilt with passengers. "Pirate taxis from Mamelodi," I explained.

She chuckled. "I remember how they used to pack people in, some of us sitting on the laps of others—complete strangers."

"*Ja*, and when the police were spotted, we all had to duck," I laughed.

"Beneath the surface things haven't changed much, have they?"

I shook my head.

"The only difference is that we've grown older," she added.

We passed a service station and turned left at the next intersection into Eersterust. It was a barren dusty township with rows of houses all having the same basic design. "So this is Eersterust." She looked around. "I often think back to my childhood and the good times we had growing up. Life was quite different for me in Boxburg. Auntie was determined to turn me into a lady," she smiled wryly. "Johan believes that I was orphaned. I actually began to believe that myself. Do you know what I mean?"

I nodded. "It's partly true anyway," I remarked.

She glanced at me and then looked away, not quite sure what to make of my comment.

We stopped at a store to buy milk, then went home.

Home was two rooms in Aunty Dorothy's backyard. I had fixed them up as best I could, turning them into a comfortable little bed-sitter.

Aunty Dorothy had set the table and a small casserole stood on the warmer above the stove. There was a note from her to say that she hoped I didn't mind her coming in and doing a few things for me.

After lunch Henny and I looked through my old photograph album. We laughed and reminisced about old times. We argued a bit about politics, but nothing serious.

"Johan and I try not to discuss politics at home," she said.

I wondered about her husband, wondered what sort of man he actually was. Somehow from what she said, I sensed a gap between them that had nothing to do with love, but more with a difference in perspective. She seemed almost intimidated by him.

She glanced at her watch.

"I'd like you to meet my aunty," I said.

A look of alarm crossed her face.

"It'll only take a moment. I told her about you."

"Okay," she agreed.

"I would never have recognized you," Aunty Dorothy said to Henny. "Except your hair, maybe. I remember how wild it used to be when you were a child. Your mother used to sit out on the *stoep* combing your hair, and we could tell when this was happening because of your crying and screaming. Oh goodness, it was terrible. Your hair was so thick, it used to be a real paradise for lice," she laughed. "Now look how beautiful it is. My goodness. Come sit down here by me." Aunty Dorothy patted the chesterfield beside her. She was a big woman and getting in and out of a chair was no easy task.

We stayed for quite a while and Aunty Dorothy told her all about her father.

She asked many questions and in the end she asked me, "Did you know about this?"

"*Ja*, but I thought it would be best for Aunty Dorothy to tell you."

"Aunty Dorothy, thank you," she said gravely. "I'm glad you told me."

Eventually Henny caught my eye. I could see that she was anxious to get back.

"Are you ready to go back?" I asked.

She nodded. "It's getting late. Johan will be wondering what's happened to me."

Aunty Dorothy nodded.

"I'll get my keys." I hurried to my own quarters.

When I got back the two women were waiting for me at the car.

"Goodbye Henny," said Aunty Dorothy. "I hope that things work out for you."

Henny stepped forward and hugged Aunty Dorothy. I could see a tear gathering in the corner of Henny's eye. On the way back to the hotel, she was quiet.

"So now you know about your father," I said.

We drove most of the way back in silence, except for the odd comment she made about something that caught her attention.

"How would you like to come to a barbecue at the weekend?" she asked as I pulled up in front of her hotel.

"I don't think so."

"I wish you'd come. It's at a Professor Malherbe's home. I'd like you to meet my husband."

I shook my head. "I don't think that's such a good idea, Henny."

"Why not? You're a friend of mine."

"Don't you think my presence would require awkward explanations?"

"Nonsense. Besides you don't look much different from any of them. Remember how we sometimes used to pass ourselves off as sisters?"

"You want me to play white," I said bluntly.

"No. I just want you to come with me and be yourself."

"Henny, please."

"I need your support, Alice. I need a friend."

"You must have lots of friends."

"Will you stop arguing," she cried.

I laughed. It was all so outrageous.

"If you change your mind, let me know. Here's my number. The barbecue is on Saturday."

"You'll be going with your husband anyway," I said.

"No, I won't. He has a Saturday meeting. He'll meet me there of course, but much later in the afternoon."

"Don't you know anyone there?"

"No."

"What about this professor?"

"Never heard of him. The invitation is really for Johan, I'm just baggage," she said dryly. "I make a point of not accompanying him on business trips. This has been the one exception."

I thought of her often in the days that followed, and on Saturday afternoon I met her at her hotel.

"I'm so glad you decided to come," she told me.

"I won't stay long. I just want to see how the other half lives," I teased her. "Your husband will be joining you anyway."

The sprawling Malherbe home was located against the side of the mountain in a very select area, and from the driveway one could see all the way down to the manicured grounds of the Union Buildings.

There were at least a dozen cars parked in the driveway. I eased the Volkswagen in between a Lincoln Continental and a Mercedes.

We got out. I felt very awkward. She seemed oblivious to my discomfort. When we got to the door she hesitated, glanced at her reflection in the glass panel beside the door, and adjusted her hair.

I fumbled in my bag, patting for my purse and keys to make sure that they were all there, and looked about uneasily while Henny placed her finger on the doorbell. I could hear it echoing through the house.

We waited, but there was no answer.

"Let's go around the side."

We heard the sound of splashing water and loud laughter and came upon a group of golden-limbed sun-worshippers splayed in wide-legged ecstasy around the brilliant aquamarine of the pool.

I hesitated for a moment, intimidated by the large crowd. Henny stood looking around trying to find a familiar face.

"Yoo hoo!" Someone waved and called.

I directed Henny's attention to the far end of the terrace.

"Oh, there's Rebecca." Her face lit up. "She's Johan's secretary."

"You told me that you didn't know anyone here," I reproached her.

"Oh, come on," she said gaily. "I'm glad she's here. She's very nice. You'll like her." Henny briskly started out to where a woman sat cross-legged on the grass amidst the purple blossoms shed by the Grandaddy of Jacaranda trees, its branches so gnarled and overgrown that it covered most of the terrace.

It was late afternoon and sizzling on the spit for the evening's barbecue was the carcass of a lamb. The delicious aroma of scorched meat wafted on the air. I walked by the spit, glancing at the carcass slowly and lusciously rotating over the coals. The servant in a stiffly starched white jacket was basting the lamb. I slowed down and arranged a smile on my face for his benefit. Somehow I felt like a fellow conspirator. Neither of us belonged.

I lagged behind and Henny waited for me. We joined Rebecca. "I suppose Johan is still in a meeting. My God, you look fresh," she remarked, dabbing at her brow with a handkerchief.

"I'm so glad you're here," Henny said to Rebecca and then introduced me. For a moment, attention was focused on me and I nodded and muttered my acknowledgement, wishing that I were somewhere other than here.

Fortunately, the conversation revolved around Henny. Questions were asked about her husband and I had a chance to collect my thoughts.

"What are you doing tomorrow?" Rebecca demanded, including me in her smile.

I had been introduced as a friend and so far there had been no awkward questions.

"She might have other plans," Rebecca's husband interrupted.

"Of course. I'm sorry if I appear forward. My weakness you know," Rebecca laughed.

I smiled distractedly.

"Sit down here," Rebecca said. We squatted in the shade of the tree, and were soon joined by others.

I was hot and uncomfortable and edged away, finding a spot on the grass against the trunk of the tree.

"Something wrong?" Rebecca called.

I shook my head. "I'll be all right in a minute."

I must have dozed off for I awakened to the sound of voices raised in argument. I sat up with a start and realized that there was a heated discussion going on. I leaned back against the tree trunk, reflecting that people weren't all that different. The same thing happened whenever we got together at a picnic too. I listened to parts of the conversation, my mind drifting around aimlessly.

"Give them the franchise and we'll drown in a sea of black vengeance. You mark my word," a freckle-faced young man said, adjusting his glasses and glaring at the faces around him.

I wondered what these self-righteous people would say if they knew that I was an interloper.

"It'd be a lot better for us to sit back and let them kill each other off," the freckle-faced youth continued. "I am a second-generation Rhodesian and look what happened to us. On the other hand we could wait until the country falls apart. When it's in a shambles they'll be begging us to recolonize them."

"Don't hold your breath," someone chipped in dryly.

"Oh God, not another social history of the colonial inferiority complex," groaned one of the girls who had just come out of the pool, as she bent forward and toweled her long blond hair.

There was a sprinkling of derisive laughter.

"You're just a bunch of hypocrites," the girl said, tossing her long mane like a colt and striding back to the pool. Then turning to scowl at them she stepped onto the diving board. Her body arched like that of a graceful dancer while she stood poised on the edge. Then, aware of the interest in her, she jackknifed, cleanly cutting through the water.

"Nice dive," someone called.

"Could've been an Olympic hopeful if we hadn't been kicked out of the bloody Olympics," said a fellow who was built like a rugby player.

"I think the whole bloody world's gone crazy," one of the girls of the flat-chest-firm-thigh variety added, leaping to her feet. She was a pretty girl, about twenty, darkly tanned with dark hair and brown eyes. "You'd think that other countries would have their hands too full with their own problems to still worry about us."

There was a surprised pause and all eyes turned to her.

"What more do they want us to do? In this country the blacks live well; they have the highest standard of living in Africa," she continued, her face red with indignation. "I think it's just a small bunch of communists going around making trouble. I say keep them in their place. I don't want to mix with blacks and I sure as hell don't want to marry one of them. I'm proud that I don't have any black blood in me."

Her outburst was followed by a startled silence.

"But my dear we all have," Henny said sarcastically.

"Not me. My ancestors are all direct descendants of the voortrekkers," she snapped with comic pique.

A baby-faced boy laughed. "They were the worst offenders."

"You bloody liberals have screwed up our country," someone complained.

"Things are going from bad to worse. Few of us sleep soundly at night anymore. My father sleeps with a revolver under his pillow," the freckle-faced youth added.

I enjoyed a good vantage point and I could see their expressions. I was watching Henny. Her lip curled contemptuously, her eyes like flints of steel. The argument continued but I wasn't listening anymore. The words merely splashed against my consciousness.

Henny got to her feet, picked up her hat, and inclined her head towards me. I got up too, dusting the grass from my dress.

"I think it's time for me to go," she said. "I'll give you a call," she told Rebecca, who watched her in dismay.

"You've just got here," she complained. "Aren't you waiting for Johan?"

"Please tell him that I've returned to the hotel."

"God, I couldn't stand any more of that," she groaned as we got into the car. "I'm not in the mood for it. You know what I'd really like to do?" she asked.

"What?"

"I'd like to see my father."

I didn't say anything, merely concentrated on the road back to the hotel, thinking about the conversation and wondering how she was going to get hold of her father. I sensed that something was going to happen. I left her at the hotel with a feeling of disquiet. Something was going to happen. I could sense the tension, like the building up of a storm.

I waited all the next day for her to call, and when she didn't I started worrying about her. Finally I gathered my courage and telephoned. Her husband answered the phone and said that she wasn't in. From his aloof tone I suspected that this was a problem. I asked him to give her a message, but she never called. That was it. I never heard a word about her again. Occasionally her husband was mentioned in a news report; once I even thought of phoning her, but changed my mind, reluctant about intruding. If she wanted to get hold of me, she had my number, I reasoned.

Two years later, I was walking down the main street with Aunty Dorothy when a man stopped us with a: *"My goodness is that Dorothy?"*

Aunty Dorothy came to an abrupt halt and gave the man one of her "looks." Then her expression softened with recognition. She looked quite taken aback as the man grasped her hand, shaking it energetically. "I would never have recognized you," she cried, and turning to me said: "And remember Uncle Piet . . . Henny's father?"

There were the usual exchanges. I told him that I had seen Henny two years ago, and described some of the circumstances of this meeting.

"Ja, I saw her too. She telephoned me and came to see me. I was so surprised, but my heart was really glad that she hadn't forgotten me altogether." He shook his head as if he still could not believe it.

"I didn't see her again after the barbecue at Professor Malherbe's house. I waited and waited for her to call, but I think there was some trouble with her husband," I said.

He shook his head sadly.

"Ja, I know. She told me." He glanced away.

"Where is she now?" I asked.

"Don't you know?" he asked, surprised.

"No."

"She's dead."

"What!" I gasped.

He nodded. "I got a card from her husband. She went off her head and died in the asylum."

"I didn't read anything about it in the papers," I said, still shocked by the news.

"You know how these white people are, surely. If they want you to know they tell you, if they don't they keep it quiet," Uncle Piet said. "She had a nervous breakdown or something." He shook his head, sighed, and kicked the toe of his shoe against the pavement.

I could see in that gesture a lifetime of regret.

"Too bad things didn't turn out for her," he continued.

"What about her husband?" I asked.

"He married again. I read something about *that* in the newspaper," he said.

Aunty Dorothy gave me a rueful smile.

"Anyway, I got to go," he said. "Maybe one of these days I'll visit you. I know where you are in Eersterust."

"*Ja*, okay," Aunty Dorothy said.

I mumbled a good-bye and watched the old man crossing the street, expertly weaving his way through the traffic.

Salwa Bakr was born in 1949 in Cairo. She received degrees in
literature and business administration before embarking on a
career in journalism. She emerged on the literary scene in 1986
with the self-published story collection *Zeinat at the President's
Funeral*. She has worked as a rationing inspector for the Ministry of Supply, as a journalist in Beirut and Cyprus, and has
spent time in prison for her political activities. Her other books
include *The Golden Chariot That Does Not Ascend to Heaven*
and *The Wiles of Men*.

Thirty-one Beautiful Green Trees

Before telling the story let me say, right at the start, why it is I
decided to write it and set it down precisely as it happened to me,
just as I have lived it and felt it moment by moment until they brought
me to this terrible place. So isolated am I from the world that I have
become wholly convinced there is no hope of ever being released, unless
it be to go to the world of the dead. Thus it was that I said to myself:
Write it, my girl. Kareema Fahmi, write your story in detail and hide it
away in some safe place, perhaps in the mattress, having scooped out a
little hole in one of its sides, so that maybe one day someone will find
the pages you've written and will feel pity for you, realizing how
wretched you were when, wrongly and by force, they put you in this
place merely because you preferred silence, everlasting silence, that day
when you decided to cut off your little tongue, that simple lump of flesh
with which you were always giving vent to words and thoughts.

I shan't speak of this hellish place in which I am now living; I shan't
describe my feelings about the filthy grey walls which keep me from
sleeping, keep me staring up at the ceiling the whole night through,
frightened they'll close in so tightly on me that they'll fall onto my body

and shut off my breathing. I go on watching them drawing nearer and nearer, craftily stealing up on me until they are right close by me, at which I scream with all my strength, and then they move away from me and return again to their original positions. I shan't talk about that, nor about the fat lady with ugly little hairs scattered about under a chin rounded like the small egg of a serpent, as she bears down upon me and plunges her horrible injection in my backside, which, despite all the pain and the hatred, makes me laugh and guffaw so much that I make her enraged by having triumphed over her. I shan't speak of the filthy poisoned food they put before me every day and against which I have no right to protest. Once I wept long and bitterly when I saw a sparrow slip through the window and eat a few crumbs of it; I ran towards it to frighten it away but it had already picked up a small piece in its beak before flying away, a small piece of the poisoned food I eat. This made me weep bitterly for the whole day as I thought about the kind of miserable end that unfortunate sparrow would meet.

I shan't speak about all that, nor about many other things I have seen in this place, because thinking about such things makes me feel as though I have been tied to some enormous bomb that is about to blow up or, to be more exact, that is about to blow me up and scatter my brains and body into endlessly small fragments. I shall therefore confine myself to writing about what happened to me before I was forced into living in this place, when, one day some years ago, I began to feel there were things that were changing around me, had also in fact changed within myself, for ever since I graduated from the university and was appointed as an employee at the Water Company, a few drops from the flood had already made their appearance on the horizon, affecting both people and things, and even animals and plants.

This was the flood that came and which I saw sweeping over everything, everything of beauty in my beautiful city, so that on the very day they brought me to live in this frightful place, I was smiling tenderly and looking at the tall buildings scattered here and there, with the van passing through the streets at a crazy speed. I was smiling and saying: Farewell, farewell, my beautiful city, the flood has once again swept you away.

I first noticed signs of the flood in the street which I used to walk along on my daily journey from home to my job at the Water Company, that street I loved so much, was so proud of, and about which I felt so strongly because of being an inhabitant of the city in which it lay. Even at this moment as I sit down to write, a feeling of joy flashes through me and my heart is filled with yearning as I imagine the pictures made by the bright, laughing colors of the shop awnings, bright orange and sparkling blue, and that marvelous awning I used to gaze at so long while the vendor handed me the paper cone of monkey nuts, the awning of the "Freedom Star" shop that sold chickpeas and all types of salted melon seeds and other things to munch and chew.

When the advance of the flood started, the street I had been familiar with since childhood, and along which I had walked so many times, began to change and little by little started to lose its landmarks. The glass of the clean bright shop windows in which, so brilliantly did they shine, one could of a morning see one's face, had begun to lose their lustre and grow dull, and the well-laid pavement damp with water during the hot hours of summer had come to be pitted with holes in which dirty water had collected, and I would notice that these holes were becoming larger day by day till they formed what looked like stagnant pools spread around the pavement. Making my way along the street daily, coming and going to work on foot, I would generally amuse myself by gazing at the street's beautiful little trees, and I would count them. I would know that after the blue gum tree there would be the casuarina, then the Indian fig, and some ten meters before arriving at the door of the Water Company there would be a beautiful tree whose name I never got to know, a tree with spreading branches almost all of whose leaves would fall at the coming of spring when it would be resplendent with a vast quantity of large purple flowers; it would look magnificent, a unique spectacle among the other trees. I knew by heart the number of trees along the way: thirty-one green-leafed trees adorning the street and bringing joy to my heart whenever I looked at them.

Then one day I counted them and found there were thirty. I was amazed and imagined I had miscounted because of being preoccupied with something else as I had been walking. But when I counted them again on my return from the Water Company at midday, I discovered that one of the nine Indian fig trees had disappeared from its place; it had been uprooted and thrown down on the pavement amidst the rubble from the old building they were pulling down. It looked to me like the dead body of some harmless bird that had been treacherously done to death without having committed any crime. I found myself weeping bitterly, for nothing but tears was of any use with that terrible lump stuck in my throat that made me feel I was about to be throttled. From that moment I began to sense changes taking place inside me: there were slight pains in my insides and I would constantly have frightful headaches. To begin with I didn't give the matter much thought, but things continued like this for days and weeks, and after a while the headache changed into ghastly pains in my head, crazy pains that accompanied every breath I took.

It was then that I went to the doctor, who began giving me sedatives and tranquilizers, though these had no effect. Eventually they diagnosed my condition as being a chronic inflammation of the large intestine brought about by nervous tension. When there were only three trees along the whole of the road, a mere three trees out of the thirty-one, I didn't know exactly what had come over me, nor what calamity had befallen my city or the people in it. All I remember about that period is that my weight went up enormously so that I was regarded as being obese, and that I had lost the capacity to be cheerful. No longer did I have any desire to go to the cinema or to converse with my women friends on any of the topics I used to talk about. I even made up my mind not to think about marriage at all, despite my getting on in years— though I might say that I was by no means ugly. Even after putting on weight as mentioned, I was still regarded by some people as possessing a certain beauty, maybe because of my good complexion, large eyes, and soft hair. The truth was that during this period I was always thinking about one thing: how could I one day get married and bear children who would live in this city? What misery they would experience when they looked around them and found nothing but a vast jungle planted with concrete and colors of grey and brown! Also, I won't conceal the fact that I was even more afraid for my grandchildren, when I thought about what it would be like for them when they came out into the world and lived in this city, without seeing a flower or knowing the meaning of the word. Besides, those who presented themselves as possible husbands did not appeal to me in the least, maybe because I would have liked a young man who was completely different from all the men I had come across in my life, a young man who loved this city as I did and who wouldn't get bored counting its trees on warm summer evenings when the sky is clear and the moon shines down on the world from on high. I would let my gaze wander far away and would dream of my unknown young man who would accompany me as we walked hand in hand in the city's streets, chatting away as we ate monkey nuts.

Nevertheless, I won't deny that I did go out one day with a colleague of mine from work. There was a certain simple affection between us that prompted us to do this. On that day, the day I went out with him, he asked me to sit with him at a riverside café and have a lemonade or some other cold drink. I refused and said that I preferred to sit right at the river's edge and watch the water as it made its way aimlessly to the sea. I also said that I didn't like lemonade. When I saw his dark eyes under the arched eyebrows gleaming because of the golden rays of sunset, making him look so handsome and gentle, at that moment my heart missed a beat and, leaning over, I kissed him on the lips. At this he got to his feet angrily, scolding me harshly and asking why I had been so forward as to do such a thing in a public place. At the time there was no one there but an aged vendor of lupin seeds. I too became angry; so we got up and parted in the large square, and from that moment on I haven't talked to him.

What brought me to their notice and led to their putting me here in this loathsome place, and what made me utterly convinced that I was on one side and they on another, had its beginnings in a day when I slept late because of a beautiful dream in which I had seen that the trees of my beloved street had all returned to where they had been; in fact they were all in leaf and flower and they had produced wonderful, fantastically shaped fruits of exquisite colors the like of which I had never seen before. Waking from my dream to the heat of the sun's rays falling on my forehead, I discovered that I would be very late for work. I therefore got up and dressed hurriedly, without having any food or drinking my usual glass of tea, and rushed along the street which I had now become used to seeing so dirty and crammed with cars and people. Suddenly, as I ran, I discovered that I had forgotten to put on my brassiere. I felt embarrassed and upset and said to myself: How stupid of me! Fancy forgetting such a thing! I thought of returning home to put on the brassiere, but this would have meant arriving too late to be able to sign in at the Water Company. So I continued on my way, saying that maybe no one would notice. It seemed to me that my not going back home that day confirmed everything that was said of me at the Company about being eccentric and not caring about my work.

I stopped for a while in front of a store which had put a large mirror behind the shoes it was displaying in the window, and I gazed at myself and found that my breasts seemed to be hanging rather loosely. I said to myself: And what's the harm in that? and I went on my way again thinking about brassieres and who had invented them and what was the significance or the point of them. And when I had thought and thought I came to the conclusion that it was a funny piece of clothing, really funny, and that women were stupid to insist on putting their breasts into them every day. Also, what was so shameful about a woman's breasts?

When I got to work, and after about an hour of doing some of the routine accountancy work, I went to the chief's office for him to sign some papers. I noticed that when he stretched out his hand to take them from me he was overcome by a sudden fit of embarrassment and that the tips of his ears began to go a bright red, after which he started to sweat profusely. As this was the end of autumn and it was early morning, I was afraid the man might be ill. "Anything wrong with you, Mr. Aziz?" I said. "Shall I bring you a glass of water?" He answered me with a brusqueness I had not known in him, I who had been accustomed to being treated by him with such kindness and gentleness, for I am, as he always used to say, very sensitive. He asked me to leave and to return to my office and said that he would summon me in a little while.

However, after a while, he called for my colleague Nadia, who is senior to me in both age and rank. No sooner had she left his office than she came towards me, with flushed face, and asked me, as she scrutinized me, to follow her as she would like to have a word with me in the corridor by the toilets. Once there she glared at me and began rebuking me: "How dare you," she said, "come to work without a brassiere?" and she informed me that this behavior had greatly upset Mr. Aziz and that he regarded it as a dangerous precedent in the company which he could not pass over in silence and that he would punish me for behaving in an indecent manner. I became quite frantic and almost slapped her heavily made-up face.

I then ran off to Mr. Aziz's room and said to him, trembling with rage and exasperation, that I had in fact forgotten to put on a brassiere, determined as I was to arrive at the Water Company at the time laid down. I also informed him that I had decided from now on to turn up at the Water Company without a brassiere because I had given a lot of thought to brassieres and had found that there was no need for such a piece of clothing, in the same way that there was absolutely no sense to the necktie he was wearing. There was a large number of male and female colleagues gathered in Mr. Aziz's room and for the first time I heard such whisperings as: "She's not normal! She's mad!"

Before the mishap mentioned there had been various other small incidents, but in none of them did I clash with a boss or colleague. I used to avoid all of them and would converse with them only within the most narrow limits and on matters relating solely to my work. I would save up the thoughts and opinions I had formed about the streets and people for one of the most pleasurable times of the day: those minutes before going to sleep during which I would always feel a clarity of mind and cleanliness of spirit that made me think about my own life and the lives of the people in this city. Once the thought came to me: Why is there all this filth at the Water Company? Why is the color of the desks always a gloomy grey? Also, why is it that so many files and heaps of papers are stacked up in corners to form a nightly playground for insects and rats? An idea came to me which I expected would be a happy surprise for everyone: having saved up several pounds from my salary, I bought a beautiful desk and asked the man I'd bought it from to paint it a bright red and to send it addressed to me at the Water Company.

I went to work early on the day the desk was to be delivered and began cleaning up the accounts room in which I sat with six of my colleagues: I swept it and polished it and cleaned the windows, then placed on the desk of each employee a pretty bunch of flowers in a glass of water. At noon the man came to the Company to deliver my red desk, but the security officer who was in charge of who was allowed in and out refused to let in the man with my red desk. However, after the man had shown him the bill with my name written on it, he contacted the company manager, who immediately summoned me. He asked me what it was about and I said to him: "Why do we have to have grey desks? What would be wrong if one employee were to be seated at a red desk, another at a green desk, and a third at a yellow desk, and so on? Wouldn't this make everyone feel jolly?" He looked at me in amazement, at which I said to him: "I bought the desk out of my own money and when I've saved some more money I'll buy some simple pieces of furniture for the accounts room."

The man, whom I still dislike right up to this very day, looked at me scornfully and said: "Go back to your office." Then he ordered the security officer not to allow the desk to be brought in. At this the blood boiled in my veins and I began shouting: "This isn't fair! Why do you think in this way? What's wrong with a red-colored desk?" and I was so upset that I had a slight fainting fit, after which they took me home.

Until now I have been speaking of trifling matters. I have spoken about some things but not about all of them. Now I shall tell exactly how it was that they brought me, wrongly and by force, to this place. It was on the day they decided to hold general elections in the city. I went along to cast my vote, for, as a citizen of full legal age, I had to make a point of exercising my constitutional right. However, the problem that kept worrying me, as I was on my way to vote, was purely and simply that I did not know exactly who was the proper candidate to vote for. I went on turning the matter over in my mind. The fact was that, being quite interested in public affairs, I used to attend several discussion groups held here and there that dealt with such matters, and once, when I was still at school, I marched in a demonstration acclaiming the Algerian Revolution and Jamila Buhairid,* and every day I used to devote myself to assiduously reading the newspaper, but none of this led me to the candidate for my vote.

As I was walking along one of the streets leading to the elementary school where the election committee was to be found, I noticed a weasel warily sticking its head out from the doorway of one of the closed shops, then scurrying across the street in the direction of the school. I stopped for a while and thought about the scene I had witnessed a few minutes ago. What did it mean? What was it all about? A weasel in the full light of day?! I couldn't control my feelings as I thought about it, for this was not the first time I had seen this small animal with the dejected face and soft, lithe body roaming through the streets of the city. I had seen it many times before crossing the streets, coolly going wherever it pleased. My violent headache had me in its grip and the chronic pains I used to

* A heroine of the Algerian Revolution who was arrested and tortured by the French.

suffer from played their mad tunes in my stomach, a stomach that had become as inflated as that of a pregnant woman. I sat down on the edge of the pavement in a state of semicollapse, crying bitterly.

Some people came along and began to calm me down. An old woman said, "There is no power or strength except through Allah," as she patted me on the shoulder, while I answered their enquiries as to what was wrong. All I could say was, "Nothing . . . nothing." Then I got up, stopped crying, and continued on my way until I reached the elementary school.

What happened after that? I don't know exactly. There were many people there and one of them gave me some papers which I read without understanding anything. Someone else was hanging up various pictures and patterns, such as a palm tree, a dog, a camel, a watch, and other such things.* It seems one of them noticed I was reading the pieces of paper with interest, so he came up to me and began a conversation. Then he indicated that I should vote for the candidate to whose party he belonged, so I enquired: "Does your party do anything about planting trees in the city instead of concrete? Has it formed a well-equipped army to deal seriously with the weasels? Does it possess some medicine that can restore my good spirits?" The discussion circle began to grow as some people joined in, and after a lot of talking and arguing I said to them: "It's quite futile what you're all doing, with your bodies as flabby as they are, for a healthy mind is in a healthy body. Apart from which, most of our ministers are ugly and they have such fat necks one doubts their ability to do anything useful." Then in a loud voice I enquired: "Where are the women? I see no women around me. Why have you not sought out the reasons for the sparrows having fled from our city and why is it so full of flies and mosquitoes?" They began guffawing with laughter and some of them moved away. One man, however, asked me in a commanding tone to go inside the building with him for a while. When I asked him why, he scowled at me. I paid him no attention, and when he demanded to see my identity and voting cards, I produced them in all good faith. He took them from me and refused to give them back. I cursed him and started to hit him, at which I suddenly found some of the people attacking me. I called out for the police and for those in charge, after which I was aware of nothing until I found myself back home.

* To help illiterate voters, candidates are given such symbols.

On the following day they brought me here, where I am now. How did this happen? I had come to at the beginning of the night to find myself in my bed, with a terrible headache and feeling exhausted. I found my mother giving me anxious, angry looks and saying to me, "Have things come to such a state with you? Have you reached the stage when you'll ruin the future of your brother? Do you not know that he is an officer and that this behavior of yours may force him to leave his work? Won't you ever stop your silliness and keep silent? By Allah, you deserve to have your tongue cut out." Then she began crying and left the room.

After that I stayed for a while staring up at the ceiling thinking about what she'd said. I went over it word by word and felt that I was truly in the wrong, that it was criminal of me. How could I have done such a thing without taking into account how it might affect my brother's sensitive position in his job? How could I heedlessly have done something to harm him? Suddenly there came into my mind an image of myself when small and of my mother threatening to cut off my tongue with a pair of scissors because I had divulged a secret to my father, directly on his return from work, which was that my brother had broken a china vase in the sitting room while playing with a ball. My mother had taken up the scissors after my father had gone out to the café at sunset, and she had trapped me in a corner of the room. She had then opened them wide and had approached me menacingly, asking me to put my tongue right out so she could cut it off and stop it from divulging any more secrets. I was screaming with terror and pleading with her not to do it. Then I expressed my regret and apologies for what I had done, while my young brother stood watching me and laughing.

I was remembering this as I continued staring up at the ceiling. What, I thought, would have happened if my tongue had actually been cut off? Would not all my difficulties have ended there and then? Would I not have kept silent forever? I would have contented myself with watching what went on around me without expressing any opinion or saying anything. Is not this less dire than suicide? Previously I had often thought about committing suicide, and on one occasion I had tried to cut a vein in my hand with a razor blade, but at the last moment I had drawn back, firstly because I had been afraid of dying, and secondly because I was afraid of dying an unbeliever and never being accepted into heaven. At the time, though, I was more afraid of the pain and so had changed my mind. But one's tongue is a different matter; cutting it off did not mean I would die, I would merely be losing the ability to articulate. I was in a state of great tension and agitation as I arrived at that point in my thinking. So I got out of bed and stood in front of the mirror, then gazed at the strange image of my face which now constantly had dark circles round the eyes. I looked at the yellowness of my complexion, then put my tongue so far out that I could see my uvula. I found it to be long and wide and a deep red color. I said: "Fear nothing, dear tongue, you are but a small piece of flesh. There will be a little blood and, of necessity, some pain, then all your pains will be over forever"—and I remembered my circumcision operation when I was nine and I said to myself: Never mind! I stretched out my hand to the scissors lying on the dressing table below the mirror and opened them out wide, as my mother had done one day in the past, and placed my tongue between the blades.

Where in the Devil's name did my mother appear from at that moment to snatch the scissors away from me? I don't know exactly, only that I suddenly found her in front of me, bearing down and snatching them from me, then screaming and wailing so that the neighbors and people from the street gathered. After a while they took me off to this place. I do not know how long has gone by since I was first lodged here, maybe many years. But my mother, who used to visit me a lot and who would talk to me without my replying to her, no longer comes at all. As for my brother, who has been visiting me at infrequent intervals, he says nothing. I have told my story without avail to all the nurses and doctors around me who merely smile and pat me on the back; I tried to make them understand that I was thinking of cutting off my tongue so that I might stop talking and avoid trouble, but this has been of no use.

And here I am now writing these words. Perhaps some person will read them and learn the truth about me, the truth about my being unfairly treated and put in this place, wrongly and by force. I am writing this because of my growing feeling that I am at the point of death, for my body has withered, my hair gone white and my legs are no longer able to carry me. Yet I hope to get out of this place, be it even for a single hour, that I may see my city and the road so dear to my heart, which I have so often walked along and in which at such time I would so hope to see thirty-one beautiful green trees.

Gaele Sobott-Mogwe was born in Australia in 1956, and emigrated to Botswana in 1978. *Colour Me Blue*, her first collection of short stories, was published in 1985. She is also a writer of children's books, having won the 1993 Zimbabwe Literary Award for Children's Literature. She currently teaches in the English Department at the University of Botswana.

Smile of Fortune

His parents had long passed away. Khumo had friends in high places who made sure he qualified in England. They arranged the scholarship and he came home with an M.Sc. in Economics. He was a happy, friendly type. Always willing to please. If he did disagree with the opinions of his superiors or elders, he never showed his opposition. He would politely murmur or loudly voice his agreement with the viewpoints of those who mattered. He laughed boisterously at their jokes and dressed for the occasion. Dinner parties, cocktails, roof wettings, turning the sod, sports and charity events—he could be seen, a beer in hand, chatting to the right people, smiling amicably.

He married the daughter of a wealthy farmer, an established family. His friends in high places suggested the match. Khumo didn't mind. She was beautiful, quiet, suitably subservient, sweet—his idea of an ideal wife. The wedding was all that could be expected of a society affair. The yellow and white striped marquees stood fresh and crisp against the manicured green of the lawns. Children, dressed as miniature adults, pastel frills, high-heeled patent leather shoes, and three-piece suits, wove excited patterns through the guests. The guests, all relieved to have received their gold embossed invitation cards, exchanged niceties and switched on standard facial expressions. Their senses worked with keen simultaneity through strained ears and corners of eyes, sieving vital tidbits peripheral to their conversations. Fiercely fashion-conscious, money-conscious appraisals were hidden behind polite geniality. Who was talking to whom? Saying what? Matching hats and shoes competed with the colorful extravagance of expensive dresses, lavish hairstyles, suits, and ties.

Men congregated around the bar. Some people filed past the VIP tent, bending respectfully, silently clapping their hands in greeting. Aunts, uncles, first, second, and third cousins giggled, gossiped, and worked to make the day a success. They had slaughtered beasts, prepared food, and made ginger beer. Some took the wedding presents and put them in a safe place. The array of duties stretched into exhausting infinity.

Six white Mercedes carried the wedding party to and from the church. The bride and groom looked cheerfully self-conscious as their arrival at the house was announced by loud ululations. The guests rallied around the beaming couple and their entourage of bridesmaids and attendants. They took a closer look at the bride's dress, the fine satin, the trillions of sequins hand-sewn into flower shapes, and the lace. Women began to ululate again and dance. Some stooped, pretending to sweep the path. Some carried straw brooms. Men and children joined the women. Bodies swung and shook to the songs, to the joyous beat of stamping feet and clapping, as the procession meandered around the yard, through the trees, tables, and chairs to the main table where the bride and groom finally sat down.

One by one the guests approached the couple, shaking their hands, kissing them, whispering, joking, and congratulating them. Queues of people wound their way towards the long food tables. They helped themselves to large portions of seswaa, chicken curry, bogobe, samp, and salads. Women wearing aprons ran from table to table carrying cham-pagne and clearing away the empty glasses and dirty plates.

Khumo kept a picture of his wife on his office desk. He studied her smooth, dark brown skin. Her shiny black hair was pulled back into a tight knot. Her mouth turned up cheekily on one side in a secret, Mona Lisa half smile. He tried to remember who had taken the photo. It wasn't him. He didn't know one end of a camera from the other. He had never loved her. He had collected her in the same way he collected cars and houses. She was a status symbol, an organizer, a hostess. She should have been a mother. The mother of his children. The mother of his son. They had been married six years now and he resented the fact that she hadn't produced an heir. He ran his finger over the grain of his antique oak desk. The secretary interrupted his thoughts.

"I'm sorry, Sir, but Mr. Smith is here to see you."

Khumo felt a little annoyed that Mr. Smith hadn't bothered to make an appointment.

"Give me five minutes, then show him in," he said brusquely and breathed in the movement of the secretary's plumpish buttocks as she walked towards the door. His personal assistant was on maternity leave. She would have put Mr. Smith in his place. She was expecting Khumo's child. He paid. He always did. He looked after his children financially and kept their mothers happy. It was tidier that way. Mr. Smith was here about the tannery project. He checked through the list of contenders. Smith's company didn't really qualify. He would probably put it to the board next week.

The secretary escorted the grey-haired, slightly balding Englishman into the room. Khumo rose from his seat to shake the limp hand that was offered to him. His eyes slipped down the secretary's skirt to the soft, inside thigh that showed just above her knees and quickly back to Mr. Smith who was apologizing for not having made an appointment. The Englishman lisped as he spoke.

"Actually, thith ith jutht a courtethy call and I would like to take the opportunity to invite you and your lovely wife out for dinner thith evening, that ith, if you are free."

Khumo stood up and walked slowly to the window. He studied the view for a moment, his hands in his pockets and his back to Mr. Smith.

"Yes, dinner would be nice."

Mr. Smith jumped up from his seat. "Good, good, shall we thay theven at the Peacock Lounge?"

They shook hands again and the Englishman left.

Sitting in his leather chair, Khumo spun round slowly, looking at the ceiling. The phone rang. It was his politician friend.

"Listen, I want to talk to you about United. I think they're the best people for the job. I'll see you at five at home."

Khumo fiddled with the telephone cord. Obviously Smith's company had more going for it than he had been able to assess. It did not have a good reputation for keeping to schedules and it was the most expensive. It would be one of those deals. Khumo smiled. His friend the politician filled him in. There was nothing more to be said. It wouldn't go to the board after all. Not this time.

Khumo argued with his wife that evening. She said she didn't feel well. That was another thing that frustrated him lately. She was always finding reasons not to accompany him to dinners and parties. He sat through the dinner with Mr. Smith who talked about his days in the British Army in Kenya and the "Mau Mau." He claimed to have spent most of his life in Africa and to identify with the continent more than he did with his own Britain. He placed his thin hands on the white tablecloth and said in a whiny voice, "But between you and me thingth have really gone to the dogth."

Khumo smiled and nodded. He thought of the holiday he had been offered in London. He might just take that secretary along. He thought of his percentage.

One percent of total contract price amounted to a lot of money. He had collected on some hefty projects. That was after his friends had taken their share. It was a network of influence. It wouldn't work without trust and reward. It was still a lot of money. He had to put it somewhere. Do something with it. The excitement of holidays had long worn thin. He had to spend some time in the office. Wine and women, shopping, nightclubs were fine in small doses. He wanted property. Solid assets. He bought more houses, land. State-of-the-art stereo equipment, television sets, furniture for the mothers of his children, for his women. Swimming pools, BMWs, and a Range Rover. Life was good. He put money in foreign bank accounts, started up new companies, and bought houses in his wife's name. What did she know? She just signed obediently on the dotted line. She had to be good for something. She was obviously incapable of continuing his family line. He had been through the pros and cons of divorce with his lawyers. It was still a possibility.

His wife was in bed asleep when he got home. He poured a whisky, put a jazz fusion CD in the system, and lay on the couch. He thought of the secretary. It would probably be the first time she had traveled overseas. The dogs started barking. He ignored them. The front gate bell rang. He didn't move, hoping whoever it was would just go away. The bell rang again. He swore. The bell rang for the third time.

"All right, all right. I'm coming. I'm coming," he muttered.

Three of his friends were at the gate. These were men who had helped him in life. His friends in high places. Police, army, politics, the church. He had friends where it mattered. It was a network and a good one. He poured them drinks. They asked how his wife was and discussed the weather. They jokingly remarked that he was putting on weight.

"Life must be treating you well, Khumo. You've got a public opinion."

Khumo laughed and patted his stomach proudly. "I'm playing squash these days, gents. Trying to keep fit."

The politician stood near the fireplace and fiddled with the ornaments on the mantelpiece.

"Talking of public opinion, Khumo, there's a problem."

Khumo waited. His friend the policeman continued, "It's the journalists. Some bleeding heart, do-gooder journalist has got hold of the Intercity Consultants story. It will be out in tomorrow's newspapers. They don't know much but they know enough. We've got to have a fall guy. A kind of red herring that will divert the whole thing. You know we can't afford an investigation."

Khumo remained silent, a powerful sense of dread growing within him. They explained the principle of the domino effect to him. They didn't want the main players unmasked. They didn't want the other deals exposed. There was that recently signed contract worth millions to all of them. They could not afford protracted public scrutiny, not at this point. The politician patted him on the back.

"I know you won't allow that to happen will you, brother?"

Khumo tried to smile. He didn't want to take the rap. He had to find a way out. They promised him money. They talked of sacrifice. How it was a vital component of life. How sacrifices were made to the ancestors to ensure that families now living on earth received protection, bountiful harvests, good rains. The healthier those on earth, the more children there would be. The larger and happier the population, the more the living would worship those who had passed before them and eventually when it came to dying, add to the ancestor pool. It was a replenishing, reciprocating, and everlasting circle. Khumo suddenly saw himself as a tiny thread in an invisible, suffocating web. He had to shoulder the blame, absorb and deflect the heat. He had to sacrifice. He had to be the sacrifice.

They left. Khumo locked the gate, went back inside, and slumped onto the couch. He couldn't do it. Almost a year had gone by since he had awarded Intercity Consultants the pipeline. He had put it before the board and as Intercity was the cheapest, it hadn't been difficult to convince them. Their price was low. Everybody was happy. Nobody suspected anything. The network had siphoned off millions in false claims over and above the original price. It wasn't the consultants' fault that the contractors didn't turn up on time. It was only fair that the company charge standby time and that the client pay.

Then there were the extensions. What was initially a thirty million job ended up at sixty million. It was Khumo who approved the claims and the requests for extensions. It was a lucrative setup. He sighed. He was in a tight spot. He wondered how much the journalists knew. Surely they couldn't have traced the link between the consultants and the contractors?

There was something else bothering him. It had been nagging him the whole day but he hadn't been able to put his finger on it. That South African company. The one he had given the infrastructure contract to. They had paid him handsomely. Now they wanted the northern road job. They were insistent. He wasn't sure if he could swing it. One of the directors had phoned him that morning. He reflected for a while over what the man had said. He hadn't realized it at the time but it was clear now that he had been issued with a subtle threat. He held his head in his hands, thinking, looking for a way out. It was too much. He was scared.

Sun was streaming in through the window when he woke. His neck was stiff. He had fallen asleep in an awkward position. Fear ate at his being like some kind of persistent hangover. There was a note in the kitchen from his wife. She had gone to her parents for the weekend. The dogs barked and the front gate bell rang. He stumbled out. His friends were already in the yard.

"You look terrible, Khumo man," the politician laughed. "What did you get up to after we left last night?"

His squash partner was with them.

"Remember you promised me a game this weekend."

Khumo couldn't remember but went and changed into his track suit all the same. They played squash and had a few drinks at the clubhouse. They showered and changed, finished the beers in Khumo's refrigerator, and drove to a wedding just out of town.

The wedding was just what he needed. The secretary was there. He danced with her, pulling her close for the slow songs. She didn't seem to mind. It was three o'clock in the morning. His friends persuaded him to go home. The secretary had already left. Khumo got into his car. He felt alone. The monotony of the road encouraged him to increase his speed. The headlights flickered through the dry grass and illuminated the occasional thorn tree that fringed the road. There were two ghostly donkeys grazing. Dangerous these beasts. He had to keep an eye out for them.

A car pulled out in front of him. He almost welcomed the relief this brought to his loneliness. If he sat behind this car he wouldn't have to concentrate so hard. Let someone else look out for cattle. He laughed to himself. Blinding lights penetrated the muscles behind his eyes. His reflexes reacted, knocking the offending rearview mirror into crooked submission.

The car in front was slow. Too slow. It rose from the road like some ominous, hunchbacked animal. He slammed his foot down on the brake. His neck snapped forward. His head hurtled towards the windscreen. Grinding teeth gnashed the back of his vehicle. He tried to straighten his neck. He tried to accelerate. The engine roared with pain, caught in the vicelike grip of two metallic maniacs. They let up for a while and then pounced with renewed fury. The car behind began to overtake. It bashed into the side of his car. Again. Again. Again. Pulverizing, grating. He howled in terror. Searing, tearing, hot spasms ripped through his shoulder as he lost control. Thick, white iridescent rails loomed ahead. Noise. So much harsh, jarring noise. The car was rolling. It felt like eight or ten times. He tasted sand and blood. Grit coated his hair and skin. He crawled. Dragging himself over shattered glass like a newborn puppy. Twitching. Heavy footsteps registered somewhere in his conscious mind. The cold steel barrel sucked in his taut temple and released it in a brutal explosion.

"Ya, my brother," the knife bent over his already lifeless throat. It couldn't resist. "This is the last time you will smile." They were laughing as they drove off.

It was an accident, they said. A tragic accident. He was driving home late at night and lost control. He had been drinking. Some suggested suicide. There was that scandal in the newspapers. They went to prayers at his house. They went to the vigil and burial. They paid for a magnificent, ornate coffin. His wife behaved in the dignified manner expected of her. No vulgar public displays of grief at the funeral, her face hidden behind dark sunglasses and a veil.

She bore her widowhood bravely, mourning the full year, celibate, attired in traditional black. Her aunts and other female relatives were there at the end of the one-year term, by her side for the ritual discarding of the black clothing. They admired her strength and composure.

There was no one with her when she went to the doctor to have the small copper tee removed from the mouth of her womb. It didn't hurt. She booked first class for her trip overseas. She carried a briefcase full of documents with her signature on them. As the plane took off she smiled, a secret, Mona Lisa half smile.

Makuchi was born in Cameroon and educated at the University of Yaounde and McGill University in Canada. Her collection of stories *Your Madness, Not Mine* was published in the United States in 1999. She is now associate professor of English at the University of Southern Mississippi in Hattiesburg.

Slow Poison

Manoji was lying on the bamboo bed his mother had placed in the parlor, positioned in a strategic corner where he could see the sunlight, if and when he was able to turn his head to face the nsaa. Yes, the nsaa, the sun; the two who now watched obsessively over him ever since the people stopped coming, ever since the relatives fled. Manoji painstakingly turned his head, each movement an effort that could kill him. His neck was rigid, the bones in his back creaked, his arms refused to follow directions meted out by an equally numb mind. The bones in his feet seemed to crackle, his knees knocked against each other, and he let out a quiet moan. He thought it might take him an entire day to turn his head, at least he hoped it was daylight. He had long lost the ability to stay in focus, to synchronize his being with trivial things like day or night. But he had to see the sun, that much he was certain of. He wanted to stare at the golden streaks slashing through the foliage of huge trees, burning through the eyelids of children who mocked its power, defied its scorching manhood, and played to the tunes of juvenile dreams. He wanted to feel those dreams again and again . . . He wanted to see the sun, no, he wanted to feel the rays burn through his brown (or was it rosy pink?) parched skin. He wanted to feel the sun on his estranged epidermis, toasting his emaciated, lifeless body and to taste the stench of burning fat in his mouth, in his nostrils, in his belly. He turned. One more inch, he told himself. He knew that inch would cost him. He shut his eyes, and just as he was about to make the move, called one memory to his rescue. Each memory lent him the support he needed to move his head an inch. Rememorying took over, fighting the aches in his head, in his neck, in his body, with the fierceness of a hen protecting her young ones from the penetrating gaze of a very patient but hungry hawk. Rememorying numbed the pain and, inch by inch, Manoji's face came into full view of the sun.

He gazes at the sun, his eyes wide open, blinking with the curiosity of a newborn discovering and pondering the world of humans. He suddenly feels an urge to stand, to lift his body, to stand up and walk—no, to float towards the sun. The hunger of a curious child who will not be daunted by vain threats is burning in him, through him. He has to stand up. He has to. He speaks to his legs. "Have I ever eaten and not shared with you?" he asks them. "Never," they reply. He doesn't know why, but his legs actually move. He is pulling his knees up and they are saying, Yes, go ahead, let's hit the floor, let's stand. He is dreaming, yes, but a good dream. He can feel his body swinging precariously upright. He is nause-ated and has to place his bony hands on his knees to steel himself. Every effort, every single effort costs him. A lot. But he refuses to be paralyzed by the fear that threatens to glue his body to his bed. He has to fight the invisible paws that are forcing him to the ground. He lifts his hands from his knees and places them on the bamboo bed. He can feel the softness of the foam mattress his mother bought for him, the one she spent her savings on to give his bones some temporary relief. Most times, he couldn't notice the mattress was there. But sometimes he was grateful for her sacrifice. He moves his fingers and clutches its softness. His fin-gers say they are alive. He thinks he is alive. He awakens to being alive and smiles, in spite of himself. The mattress smells so much of death, how could he be alive?

He raises his head, holds firmly onto the exposed bamboo and con-centrates on the brightness advancing through the open door, almost sucking him into its vortex. He grinds his teeth, lifts his torso and he is in the air. He can feel his feet on the floor. The house is quiet and he can hear the silence buzzing through his head. He begins to feel dizzy but knows he cannot afford to give in to the spasm moving like a wave through his bowels. And so he fixes his gaze on the receding shadow of the door and stares. He concentrates on the rays of the sun and stares. He moves towards them, gliding through space. He feels he is falling. He thinks he is falling and desperately grabs at anything he can touch. His hands can feel the firmness of wood. He clings to it, braces himself, and opens his eyes. He recognizes the door frame. He runs his fingers, a few inches, up and down the mahogany as if scratching a lover's back. He desires its firmness. He longs for its ageless demeanor of defiance. He is about to take a step forward when something catches his eyes. The image is bleary. He has to still himself and focus. An image is reflected back at him. It seems to be projected from within the far reaches of the closet, of the mirror hanging on the brick wall. He stills himself and waits. The image is moving closer, zooming in. He is struck dumb, startled by the old man staring back blankly at him. The face looks curiously familiar. It displays marks and features peculiar to his family. The prominent forehead, like his uncle's; the prominent, high cheekbones, like his mother's; the full head of kinky hair, the protruding, stubborn chin, like his father's. But the eyes, the haunting, scared eyes of a caged animal, whose eyes are these? Eyes like those of an owl. Eyes that look too big for his face; eyes that seem to be popping out of their sockets; eyes whose whiteness is frightening, a whiteness that seems to spread, overpowering the blackness of the face, highlighting two deep, dark pupils, spinning like a whirlpool at the bottom of a well. Manoji cannot place these eyes. He cannot place this bony face. He makes a supreme effort to lift his hands and feel the bones sticking through the cheeks. What is left of them. But the hands divert his attention from the face. The thin, long fingers with their overgrown nails look like claws. They are skeletal and remind him of the hands of the scarecrows he used to make with his father when he was a young boy and proudly display in his mother's farms. He tries to imitate the movement of the scarecrow's hands, agitating, stirring excitedly with the force of the wind, but the hands remain hanging in midair. They are refusing to follow his command. He cannot bear to look at those fingers. His hands slowly drop by his side. He can hear his clavicles creak. His gaze follows the clavicles down his bare torso. Manoji stares at his scrawny, wasted body. The brownness of his skin seems to have been bleached away, leaving behind an almost transparent pinkish surface. The dermis is disrobed, ugly in its nakedness. He traces the long lines carefully designed and left bare by exposed ribs. They are nothing like the tiger's, nothing like the zebra's. He can see the thin layer of flesh clinging desperately to the bones as he struggles to breathe in and out. Caught between the hollow lines are spots, huge dark spots. They are nothing like the leopard's. Some of the spots look like scars that leave an imprint on the skin after a bout of yaws. They are competing with shingles and scabies for space. He is thankful for the hard, dark crusts of the shingles that taunt him with a semblance of blackness. He knows these spots are bearing witness to the poison that has slowly but tenaciously been devouring his body, eating away his life. He has become a bag of bones. He has become a scarecrow. He fidgets with the wrappa wrapped around his waist. What is left of it. The wrappa falls to the ground. He doesn't hear a sound. He looks with bitterness at the two straight sticks that used to be thighs; he wants to knock on the protruding, round knees. He tries to make a fist but his fingers will not indulge him. He suddenly realizes he has missed something. He can't tell what it is. He has to think. What am I forgetting? he is desperately asking himself. He needs a memory, right now. He needs a memory to ignite his brain again. He is feeling dizzy. He wants to throw up, but there is nothing to throw up. He clutches the firmness of the mahogany, stills himself and the old man in the mirror comes back in focus. The man is missing something, something between his bony thighs. Where is his manhood? What is this shriveled up, almost unnoticeable appendage, clinging ferociously to the pubis? Or what is left of it? It looks almost like a stamp, affixed on an envelope. Manoji is feeling dizzy; he is choking; he is coughing; he cannot hold his sides, he cannot hold onto the mahogany. Its firmness is letting him go. He feels his hands gliding off the wood. He is falling. Falling. Floating backwards to the ground. He feels as light as a wisp of smoke. He wants to see the sun. He wants to wrap his body in the folds of its golden warmth. He wants to remain suspended in its splendor. But he is falling. Falling. The last thing he glimpses in the mirror is the familiar face of his mother. She is standing, silently, right behind him. Their eyes meet. He can feel the heat. The sun is right there with him. He can feel its warmth enveloping his body, seeping through his bag of bones, melting the marrow, taking over his memories. He knows they will be kept in a safe place for him. He lets himself fall. Her arms are open. He is grateful he is falling into her waiting arms.

Manoji died the way he had lived: in the arms of a woman. At least that was the one thing, the one ounce of consolation he grasped firmly in the palms of his bony hands, in the wiry folds of his shriveled-up heart, when his spirit quietly and calmly abandoned his body, or what was left of it. My son passed away in my arms. I was sitting on the floor, holding him firmly to my chest, oblivious to the silence, the loneliness, the abandon that was threatening to sweep me away. I sat there, the hard floor beneath me, the only thing that reminded me I was still alive. Even as I held my son's lifeless body, I adamantly refused to accept his death. He is still alive, I kept saying to myself. It's not possible. He can't be gone, I kept consoling myself. But then, his usual paper-light body began slowly to weigh down on me like a basin of water. I began to wonder how this had all happened. How had this little baby I carried just a few months ago on my back as I cleaned the house, as I cooked food, as I worked on the farm, as I went to the market, how had this baby come to this? When did this all begin? When? How had this happened to us? To our lives? I couldn't think straight. I knew I needed his memories. I needed to rememory his life in order to do the right thing for my son, in order to set him free. There was no time for tears. There was no place for tears. I held him firmly to my chest and his memories took over. I needed them to consume me the way they had consumed his body.

A few years ago, Manoji started going out with young women unusually bigger than the ones I had always seen him with. It isn't that he hadn't had big women friends before. This time was different. He stuck to big women only. I pointed this new preference out to him. "My son, why are you going out with all these fat women? What's wrong with you? Is this the new craze?" I asked him. Humm, Manoji smiled and reminded me that the women were just "bigger." They are true African women, he enthused. True African women with flesh on their bones, he parroted. But I was not to be fooled and I kept on teasing him. One day, as he was about to walk away after one such conversation (I called them conversations, he called them unnecessary snooping on my part), he changed his mind and walked back into my house. He pulled up a chair, sat down by the fire, put those long hands calmly on his knees, and asked me an embarrassing question.

"Mother," he said.

"Yes, my son. What is it?"

"Have you heard about this thing they call AIDS?"

"What's that my son?"

"Come on mother, you know what it is. Stop pretending not to know."

"No, I don't know what it is. What is it?"

"Mother, you know it's an illness."

"An illness. What kind of illness?"

"Mother, you know what illness it is. You know it's that terrible disease people call 'slow poison.'"

"Slow poison? Are you talking to me about those lies those people from the Ministry of Health are spreading around the country?"

"Mother, they're not lies. You heard what that doctor said the other day at the community meeting."

"I know what he was saying. He was talking about a disease that eats people away, slowly, as if they had taken slow poison. But my son, only people struck with witchcraft can suffer such a disease. This is not something the white people and those strangers from the Ministry of Health should come here and talk to us about. What do they know about our witchcraft? What do they know about esotericism? Nothing. Absolutely nothing. I tell you they know nothing about our abilities to manipulate the natural and the supernatural, how can they know about slow poison? . . ."

"But mother, this is serious . . ."

"Say what you want my son, but let me tell you something. If those liars keep on coming here and talking about this so-called new disease that kills people slowly like the slow poison we cast on our enemies, then they will all suffer the same fate . . ."

"But mother, they say this slow poison is different from our own. It is different because you get it by having sexual relations with a man or a woman who already has the poison in them."

"So, why sleep with a woman who has been poisoned, my son?"

"You don't know she is."

"Impossible. How can you not know when a woman has been poisoned? If you can't, then you are not my son . . ."

"That's why my women are all plump . . . they have good blood, unlike thin women. You can't be sure of their blood . . ."

I knew what my son meant when he talked about bad blood. It had to do with our neighbor, a father who for three years had consistently given blood for his sickle-cell anemic child. But things never used to be like that. Over the years, his eight-year-old son had been given blood by almost every relative or friend living in this neighborhood. Previously, when the child got ill, three, four, or five of us would go to the blood bank with the father and they would systematically collect our blood, test it, and then give the right blood to the child. And then things changed. They claimed the government had run out of money. That testing of blood from many people had become too expensive. They even started charging five thousand francs to cover the cost of each blood bag. If you have four people with you, that means twenty thousand. Imagine that. Who can afford that? People couldn't afford to give blood anymore. So now they pretest a sample and only collect the blood if the donor's blood is the right one. That's how our neighbor ended up as sole donor for his son. He gave his blood, gave his blood, gave his blood, and then one day the doctor said his blood was bad and could not be given to his son. "How is that possible?" he asked the doctor. "Your blood isn't good anymore," the doctor said.

"What do you mean, anymore? . . . I've been giving blood for three years and suddenly my blood isn't good? How? Has my blood group changed?"

"No, your blood group is still the same. But your blood now has a disease. Have you heard about AIDS? . . . Your blood is HIV-positive. That means your blood has a disease and I can't give your blood . . . I can't give the disease in your blood to your child . . ."

"I do not understand . . . I don't understand . . ."

"I understand . . ."

"No doctor, you don't understand. You know my son has sickle-cell anemia . . . He needs my blood or he'll die . . . Who's going to give my child blood? Who? . . . And now you're telling me I must stop. You're telling me I'm going to kill my child. You're telling me I'm going to die. You're sitting here and issuing death warrants . . ."

"Well, it's not that simple. True-true, you are HIV-positive. But it might take a while before the real illness . . . AIDS—you get from this bad blood—manifests itself. Having HIV is not the end of your life . . ."

"How long?"

"It could be a few months, it could be years . . . this disease works like slow poison . . ."

"So it watches from the shadows of the bushes as its messengers eat you up, step by step, is that it?"

"Yes, something like that . . . When the time comes, you might begin to cough a lot. You might have big craw-craw all over your body. You will have diarrhea. You will pass out a lot of water and fluids from your body. Then your body will begin to waste away because it is losing so much water, because of the slow poison in your body . . ."

Our neighbor broke down in the doctor's office and cried and cried and cried. He came to the complete realization of the magnitude of this illness when the doctor referred him to the Presbyterian Mission Hospital. The doctor asked him to come and see Dr. Peter at your mission hospital. Our neighbor was devastated. He came home a broken man. We couldn't believe it when we heard the news. How does a father deal with such news? It's always easier to deal with this illness when you don't know the person. You hear someone has this disease and you say, "oh!" or "sorry ooh" or "na which kana baluck dis now?" and that's it. There is a safe distance between you and that person. You express your sorrow because that's the right thing to do and life goes on. But when you know someone, like we knew our neighbor, someone for whose child we had all, at one time or another, given blood . . . when you know someone that intimately, and you hear they have AIDS, you are totally in shock. Shock. Pure and simple. You feel as if someone has divulged a terrible secret that should have remained concealed. You can't bear the weight of the bad news you are now carrying. You know they've been sentenced to death. You know they cannot reverse the verdict. You are conscious of their certain death. You withdraw your tears. Your tears desert you. Your tear glands dry up like the Sahara. You deny the illness, you banish it from your mind, but it won't leave. You begin to have nightmares about it. You get angry. You want to scream, you want to cry, but you can't. You think about the meaning of the illness, the ramifications: is his wife infected? What will happen to the children? You begin to think of them as orphans—and that, while their father is still alive. But then, that is nothing when you haven't come face to face with the person. It is worse when you come face to face with someone you know, someone you love who has AIDS. When I met my neighbor for the first time after that fateful trip to the hospital, I didn't even have the courage to extend my hand . . . I . . . I . . . I couldn't extend my hand. What's a greeting? Something we offer freely, every day, to everybody—friends, family, and enemies alike. But there I was, standing in front of Pa Ambrose, and I couldn't offer my hand. I found it difficult to extend my hand. It seemed to weigh ten tons. It couldn't move. Later, only later, did I realize that I had unconsciously moved my hands towards my back. I had pretended to scratch my back. I had fidgeted with the ends of my wrappa and had pretended to wrap it more firmly round my waist. I had done everything so as not to offer my hand. I had even looked at the floor, searching my toes for jiggas that were not there. I couldn't look him straight in the eyes. This man, with whom I had joked and laughed so often in the past . . . this man, whose children have sat down and eaten food with me in my house . . . who call me mother. Our conversation was mono-syllabic, monotonous: Hello. Hello. Morning. Morning. Bright day. Yes. Are these your eyes? Yes. Yours? Yes. How are you? Fine. How have you been? Sick. Your son? Fine. You see what I mean? A stupid conversation like that. Taking us nowhere. Although I was on my way to the market, I turned around and went back home. I remember thinking to myself on the way home: at least the child is safe, for now. Ambrose should count himself lucky. He will not be branded a wizard for eating his own son. What about mothers who kill the babies in their wombs with this dis-ease without knowing it? Tegheh kwu! Ambrose is lucky indeed. He will be fine, I kept saying to myself. I didn't eat all day. I was so disgusted with myself. I was overwhelmed with sadness. I had never known such sad-ness. I had never known the day would come when I couldn't bring myself to greet my own neighbor, my own friend, my own blood. How do things like these happen? How?

It was about then that my son became the "fat virgin" man. Virgins and fat women seem to be in demand these days! Apparently, fat women do not have AIDS, or so Manoji claimed. He said fat women were less likely to have slow poison. I know our culture has always placed value on the shine of a woman's skin, on the plumpness of her curves, and especially on what these curves say about her husband's ability to take care of her, but this new craze about fat women and no AIDS was simply beyond me. Who can blame him or all the men who began to think like him? When people have AIDS, they lose weight so fast you can't even recognize someone you knew. They might have to call out to you and say, it's me, so and so. Manoji was certain he had found the way to conquer this new ulcer that was quietly eating through the nervous system of our people. Then the time came and that fateful day came knocking on our door. My sister got ill and was wilting like a leaf in sun, before our eyes. I didn't believe the diviner who said her ex-husband was bewitching her. So I took her to the hospital to get her checked for worms. I knew it had to be worms or something easy to treat. They tested for worms. They said she had worms. But they also said she was anemic. They said she needed a blood transfusion, and only after that could she go home and pursue her treatment by eating a lot of vegetables and liver. Manoji offered to give his aunt the blood she needed. But first, they had to pretest his blood. And the nurse said she had to tell us first why they had to test it.

"So you were given some pretest counseling by the hospital staff? That's good."

"Yes, even though I didn't see any need for the lecture." Anyway, that woman reminded me that we should be grateful someone was taking the time to talk to us before taking our blood. She made it clear that pretest counseling for HIV wasn't done systematically in most hospitals. She told us that doctors had difficulty explaining to people why the blood they were giving for relatives and friends had to be tested for AIDS. They had problems with donors who would refuse to give their blood for such a test or who would refuse to see or accept the results. She was relieved that wasn't the case with us. Manoji was prepared to do anything for his aunt, so he gave a blood sample and we waited. Waiting for the results was excruciating. Those six minutes we spent waiting for the rapid test are the longest six minutes I have ever spent in my entire life. Manoji, especially, made it feel like a lifetime. He paced up and down the hospital corridor. He bit on his nails. He stuck and removed his hands from his pockets more times than I could count. He was a nervous wreck. Anxiety was drumming tunes all over his face. The look in his eyes kept saying, What if? . . . what if I am? . . . what if I am HIV-positive? My worried look reflected back the same at him. What if the result is positive? we kept asking ourselves. The question kept pounding through my head. The feeling was oppressive, overwhelming. The waiting was killing me. My palms were sweaty, my skin was aching. My blood pressure kept rising. My heart would not stop pounding. We were so nervous I wanted to open my mouth and scream, but my throat was completely dry. The wetness in my mouth seemed to have evaporated into thin air. Minutes felt like hours. You try to relax but you can't. You try to relax, you close your eyes but your eyelids are heavy and feel like rocks. Manoji paced up and down. Six minutes felt like six hours. Manoji paced up and down. Manoji bit on his nails. Six hours felt like six days. Manoji paced up and down. Manoji repeatedly stuck his hands in and out of his pockets. Six days felt like six years . . .

"Please sit down," the nurse said softly, almost too kindly. "I am sorry, I have bad news . . ."

" . . ."

"I am sorry to tell you that we cannot take your blood . . ."

" . . ."

"Mr. Manoji . . . you are HIV-positive, so we cannot collect your blood . . . we cannot give your blood to your aunt . . ."

" . . ."

"Please do not take this the wrong way. Being HIV-positive isn't the end of one's life, as most people think . . ."

" . . ."

"I understand how difficult this is, but . . . It's okay Mami. Hold him. Let him cry . . . it's alright."

"Sister, so what do we do now?" I heard a voice that sounded like mine ask the nurse.

Manoji's head was resting on my lap, his entire body convulsing as if fighting a bout of malaria fever, his hot tears leaving wet patches on my wrappa. I placed my hands on his shoulders, bent down, and rested my face on the back of his head. Our hearts were breaking like the sea waves that drenched our faces. After what seemed like an eternity, I felt the nurse's hand on my cheek, wiping away the tears.

"Mami Manoji, I am truly sorry . . . but I have to ask you . . . would you like me to test your blood . . . ?"

" . . ."

"Is it possible to ask someone else . . . another family member to give blood? . . ."

I have to tell you that in all this tragedy, what hurts most is what happens to families when a family member is HIV-positive or has AIDS—the breakdown of the family as we know it. I didn't mind the furtive looks, the whispering, the gossip, when it came from strangers; after all, they didn't know me. They didn't know my son personally. I came to a point where I cared even less when people withdrew their hands in midair from a greeting or stepped back when it dawned on them my son had AIDS. I was only his caretaker . . . why wouldn't they shake my hand? Why wouldn't they hug me? They withdrew their hands, their smiles, their words, as if I were the plague. I erected a wall in my heart and shut out their callousness as we navigated from one hospital to the next, and between hospitals. I forgave them their ignorance. But how could I forgive my own family for slandering and deserting me and my son? They called my son a womanizer who had inherited his philandering ways from his mother. My son a philanderer and I a prostitute! Imagine that. They all fled. The cowards. They deserted me. They were scared of me, as if I were a witch . . . as if I would curse them with slow poison and watch them die faster than my son. The cowards! They watched me from the bushes, as I shouldered his illness and his ailments; they watched as I cooked his food, cleaned his wounds, cleaned his body, removed the feces from incessant diarrheal bouts that threatened every day to kill him. I watched my son hurt as he coughed. I watched my son hurt as he drank water. I watched my son hurt as fluids drained out of his body like water disappearing in the sand. I watched my son waste away on the bed as friends and relatives stood safely in my nsaa and talked at me through the open door.

"Take him to the native doctor," they'd say. "I know so and so. I hear he cures people who have slow poison in their blood. Take your son to him. He has a good reputation. He's the best in the land. Take your son to him. He'll cure your son . . ."

The hospitals had said over and over that there was no cure for AIDS and I had believed them, but when you have gone through what I have gone through, you begin to believe that they must be lying. You begin to say to yourself that there must be a treatment for the whiteman's slow poison, just as there is a treatment for our slow poison. At least with our slow poison, all you need is to know who cursed you in the first place, and that person can be persuaded to lift the curse and let you live. In the case of the whiteman's slow poison, you don't know who poisoned your blood, so how can your blood be treated? Some people even warned me that my son did not have the whiteman's slow poison but had been bewitched by one of my own relatives—my paternal granduncle, to be exact. Traditional medicine was the only cure my son needed, they insisted. Why was I wasting my time with whiteman medicine, they queried. I wanted the death of my son, they accused. Those frightened dogs, with their tails tucked between their legs, accused me of eating my own son! And without realizing it, I was moving my son from one medicine man's compound to another.

"Did the native doctors help?"

"No."

"So you decided to come back home?"

"Yes. I came back because I couldn't afford it anymore. They had taken all I have: the liters of palm oil, the bundles of salt, the goats, the fowls, the money—those vultures! And they were killing my son with all sorts of concoctions that made him weaker day by day instead of purging and cleansing him of the poison, as they claimed. I had to come back. I came back because I wanted my son to die at home. To die at home with dignity. To die at home among his people, his ancestors. His people might have forsaken him but his ancestors would not. Never."

"I hear you."

"But I also came back home because I heard of your services. I heard about the charity work that the Presbyterian Mission was doing around the village for people who are dying from slow poison like my son . . . Sister, it is a great thing that your mission, your people are doing for us . . . It is a shame that your mission charity has taken on the responsibility of our government and our own families. Help, concern, kindness are things we do and offer each other because we're family. Now, other people . . . total strangers, have replaced our family . . . It's a terrible thing that's happening to us. This monster is threatening the very foundation on which our family institution is built. What are we going to do? What are we going to do . . . ?"

"Oh, Mami Manoji, I didn't know you still had tears in your eyes . . . Here, let me dry your face . . . You look like a little girl who's getting married when you cry like that . . ."

"Sister, you know I lost the desire to laugh. Why are you making me laugh? . . . I tell you, family is dead. Family isn't what it used to be. Not when it comes to AIDS. No, not when it comes to AIDS . . ."

" . . ."

"Can I ask you something, Sister?"

"Weh, Mami Manoji, you know you can ask me anything."

"Why doesn't your hospital keep people there, I mean, in the hospital itself?"

"It wasn't always like this. We used to hospitalize our AIDS patients. But as you know, ours is a small hospital and we don't have as many beds as we'd like to. Our AIDS patients used to take up beds . . ."

"So? I thought those beds are meant for patients."

"Yes, but they were taking up beds for months. Some, for long, long periods of time—years. And besides, they were . . ."

"Certain to die anyway . . ."

"Yes. We had to face the fact that they were all going to die and so instead of keeping the patients in the hospital, we decided to send them home. We created the association of nurses who would run an outreach program so that we could visit them weekly and provide them with care at home. Even though the hospital funds the outreach program, the program actually cuts costs . . ."

"Sister, I have to thank all of you. Every day, I invoke the gods to come to our aid. I pray to the ancestors each night before I go to bed, that they bless us with more programs like yours. Your outreach program has done more for me than my own government, than my own family. Manoji and I both looked forward to the weekly visits your AIDS teams paid us. Your visits put a rare ray of hope and anticipation in our lives. We couldn't have survived without the drugs you provided weekly for his diarrhea, the vitamins, the painkillers . . . We couldn't have survived it without the weekly counselling, the attention, the encouragement, the strength you gave us to move forward. Your visits were a moral booster that helped my son more than anything else. Those visits helped a mother deal with her grief. They helped my son and I watch him pass away in dignity. Sister, you should have seen him. When the time came, he wasn't afraid to go. He made peace with himself. He said good-bye in my arms . . . My son died. My son is dead, and still, I have to carry the stigma of what killed him like a badge. AIDS has claimed my son. AIDS has branded and banished me from my people. Do you know some fled before his body was even in the ground? They were disrespectful of their own blood. Fewer people attended and participated in the death celebrations. Death—life—we all celebrate, an event we all flock to, to cry, laugh, sing, dance, eat, and drink until we get drunk, whether we're connected by blood or not. They shunned him, even in death. Death! Life! . . . What kind of a disease is this that, like leprosy, is amputating our families, extremity by extremity, limb by limb? What kind of a disease is this that is taking away our words, cloaking us with silence, numbing us with fear? Eeh, Sister, you tell me."

Hama Tuma was born in Addis Ababa in 1950. He studied law at Haile Selassie University, and spent years actively opposing the Mengistu regime in Ethiopia. He has published a poetry collection in English, *Of Spades and Ethiopians*, and a collection of stories, *The Case of the Socialist Witchdoctor*.

The Waldiba Story

The old man smiled, his brown eyes sad. "Tell me I am going to die and I will bless you," he said.

I knew he was dying. Though I was not a qualified doctor, never having finished my medical studies at the University, I had practiced medicine in the jungle for more than six years, had seen really sick people, dying people, wounds and ailments of all sorts, and I could tell that the old man was going to die. Weak and anemic he was, and probably had leukemia but there was no way I could tell. He needed a laboratory examination, extensive tests beyond my capacity as a guerrilla doctor. The chances were also that even if I had known his ailment, I would probably lack the necessary medicine.

"You will get over it," I lied.

"You are kind," he said tactfully, knowing full well I was not telling him the truth. "But I feel the end is near; anyway it's time I met my Creator and got my judgment. Don't waste your precious pills on me," he added. "Give them to your sick or wounded friends. They need it more, poor boys."

The priests in the famous and remote monastery of Waldiba always spoke with sadness when they talked about us guerrillas: "Young people so brimming with life and yet about to die" was the way many of them put it. Some cried whenever they saw us, some shook their heads sadly, some just turned away not wanting to look at us.

A famous monastery, this Waldiba monastery. Centuries old, no women allowed, with its own hierarchy and strict rules. Anyone who has had enough of the temporal world can join it. The new arrivals begin with a year or two of service for the monastery, tending cattle, farming the land, bringing water, taking care of the banana garden with its own irrigation system. After this period of service, the promotion comes, each "priest" or recluse given his own hut. Days and nights of prayer, much of the time spent in the huts—this being the reason for the pallid or "white" color of the monks. Life is Spartan: no alcoholic drinks, the food made up of only mashed bananas mixed with honey or noug. No meat or *injera* and many of the monks usually undergo the "subae"— long periods in which they stay in isolation in their huts without seeing or meeting any other person and coming out only in the dead of the night to relieve themselves.

"I called you not to ask you to treat me," said the old monk. "I wanted to ask you a favor."

"I will do it if it is in my power," I said readily.

"I want you to hear my confession," said the old man calmly, catching me totally unawares.

Hear my confession! The confession of a monk! My face must have shown my surprise for he smiled again, his eyes still sad, and motioned me to come nearer. I picked the three-legged stool, *birchuma*, and sat near his bed. He smelt of incense just like the narrow hut in which our conversation was taking place.

"Perhaps you wonder why I should confess to you and not to the priests?" he began rhetorically. I nodded. "The reason is simple," he went on. "You are a guerrilla who has given his life to save others. You are a doctor, you care for the poor. Many times you have come here to treat me and others, always kind, always polite. The main thing is that you have decided to serve others, to die for others. You have followed Christ more than me. Don't protest for it is true. What have I done? I have closed myself behind these walls, shut off the outside world which refuses to go away, and taken steps only to save myself. I know of the injustice in the outside world but what I have done to combat it is slight. I ran away instead and hid in this monastery. Who takes care of the aggrieved? Who cries justice when the rulers trample upon the poor? Who dries the tears of the mothers whose sons and daughters get killed every day? Who consoles your mother when she worries about you? Not me. Of course, I pray for better times, for an end to these years of agony. But prayer is not enough. He Himself came down to earth to die for our sins. We need to emulate Him. I haven't."

I wanted to say some words of protest, wanted to tell him that he was praying for all of us, helping us in his own way. But no words came. In silence I looked at him and he picked up his tale. And what a strange tale it was to be.

"Many of us here in Waldiba, we were not priests originally," he said. "You know, of course, that here there are nonpriests like me who have come from the cities, others from the rural areas. We all came here to seek atonement for our sins; some had killed, others had committed other sins. Some succeed in atoning for their sins, others get weak and become even more sinful right here in this monastery. Intrigues, evil thoughts, backbiting, petty and selfish acts—in Waldiba they exist too."

I knew that Waldiba was so austere that singing was forbidden. There is a common saying alluding to the impossible happening: "Even in Waldiba a song is sometimes heard." I had also come to know that the monks had internal squabbles—power struggles to be the keepers and dispensers of the monastery's wealth. Politics had also intruded into the monastery with some supporting the government, others sympathizing with us guerrillas.

"My confession would show you the truth of my statement," the monk went on in his whispering voice, born of years of practice as no one is allowed to talk out loud in the monastery. "I came to Waldiba some six years ago from Addis Ababa. In my other life, I was a retired policeman. I see it surprises you, but Waldiba is full of strange people. Thirty years I served in the police force; I even became a sergeant. I never went into any battle and I never killed a human being. Guard duty, catching thieves, night patrols, I did it all.

"In 1974, when havoc erupted, I had already retired. Poor but happy. My two sons were in school and I was proud of them, having raised them correctly by myself. Their mother, a good woman, died young leaving them to me. I loved them both, never remarried, and worked hard for them. I had a good life really, bless the Lord. When one of the boys finished high school, he got himself a job and we managed to open a small shop which I ran after I went on pension. He then had the luck to get a scholarship and go to the land of the *ferenjis*. America, I think it was. The younger boy entered the University in Addis and lived with me. When the chaos began, the young boy was involved like other students in the demonstrations and all the troubles. At first I tried to stop him from engaging in such activities but I found out that his mind was set and that the more I insisted on him leaving politics, the more estranged he became from me. You know the problem there was between parents and their children at the time. No agreement. I never understood what got hold of the young in those days. Why do I say those days? I still don't know what fires you all up.

"Anyway, I let him be. Let God take care of him, I said. After all, only He decides our fate, doesn't He? The whole year he was right in the middle of the turmoil, sometimes days passed before he came home and I could see him. All parents in the area had the same problem and we used to meet in church, share our sorrow, and pray to Him to protect our children from harm.

"The king was overthrown and the soldiers came. Good days were promised. I told you I was a policeman and I had seen much injustice in my days. Still, the king was not the evil man my son made him out to be. I was sad to see soldiers who had been serving the king suddenly cursing him to the skies. Some applauded and said things have changed for the better, but I kept my counsel. I was a soldier and I knew soldiers. I knew we had no ability to rule a country, no patience, no respect for the unarmed, no tact. I suspected many would die in the hands of those same soldiers they had hailed. Surprisingly, my son had the same idea. He told me that the soldiers had stolen the *abyot*, the Revolution, that the people had to rule themselves though I never knew how this was to be realized. As you know, within a short time, the troubles began anew, this time between the soldiers and the likes of my son.

"Again, I tried to talk to my son. Give them time, I said to him, though I knew the problem with the Derg was not time. Time does not turn a serpent's egg into a pigeon's, he replied. This I understood; other things which were being said at the time were beyond me. Too many words, new words, so much hate, so little patience. But the soldiers had guns, my son and his friends had none. I could see that this led to massacres. But who can stop the wheel of God? What had to be had to be, what is written had to pass, all is in His will. Here and there people were

being killed by the new rulers, the radio was busy with its announce-
ments of executions . . . Many of the old regime were killed, many
youngsters who called for their downfall were also killed. And many of
us missed the meaning of what you all called Revolution, change.

"My other son came back from abroad. I was both happy and wary.
But he proved to be unlike his young brother. He was calm and I
thought at the time apolitical. He got himself a good job and stayed out
of politics as far as I could tell. At dinnertime, he took my side and
advised the young one to leave politics and concentrate on his studies.
Advice the young one never accepted. Relations between them were
not good and I used to blame the younger one for this.

"Then the shooting started. You people started it, for all I know you
may have been there. My son must have been involved, he never told
me but I suspected when he left his house and disappeared. I thought he
was dead but he used to come unannounced late at night, talk to me and
then go again for weeks. And then one day, I found out he had been
arrested and shot at night. No burial, just thrown into a ditch no one
knows where and forgotten. The kebele officials told me the news since I
knew some of them quite well. I couldn't cry in public or sit in mourning
since all this was forbidden by the Derg.

"What I did was go to the house of a longtime friend, someone called
Woizero Askalu. She was a nice lady whose husband had died a long
time ago and she had raised her only son and sent him to the University
by working as a maid, selling *tella* and *tej*. She had never remarried but
she was not like other *tella* sellers and did not indulge in prostitution.
You could say she was my very best friend for years, we shared worries
and sadness and occasional joy. We did not spoil our friendship by tum-
bling into bed, though we loved one another. Her son was a friend of my
son, a good student, very gentle, he loved his mother and took good care
of her by working in the evenings. You could say she lived for him.

"When my son died I went to their house and mourned there in private for a week. She shared my sorrow and her son was also sad as if he
was guilty of being alive when my own had died. Neighbors and others
in the district quietly shared my sorrow, secretly expressing their condolences. I was to do the same for them in a short while as more and more
sons and daughters started to die. Every night the sound of gunfire, every
night we parents died a little. Many joined their sons and daughters,

helping them fight the Derg, many others stood by bewildered, caught in a storm which was incomprehensible. No one listened to reason, no one asked for advice, everyone was busy shooting, fighting, arguing. I prayed, we prayed. But even in church there was no peace. How could there be when thousands were dying, when children were being fed to hyenas? Some of the priests raised this in their sermons, some directly, some by examples and allegories. But we all knew. Fear was everywhere. Am I boring you with a story you know perhaps better than me?"

"No, no," I replied. I had been there at the time but the old man's story enthralled me. The view of the observer, the anxiety of the parent—these were things I had no direct experience of.

"I will not bore you long," the old man said. "One day during those days of tears and death, my friend Askalu came to my house and once inside she broke down and wailed and cried. It took me some time to learn that what I had feared when I saw her tear-stained eyes as I opened the door was true. Her one and only son had been killed. Worse still, his body had been thrown for all to see in a street nearby. Someone had seen the corpse and broken the news to her. Bad times breed bad manners. We should have been told first so as to break the news to her gently. I calmed her and after calling on a neighbor to watch over her and to restrain her in case her cries got loud and attracted the attention of the Derg guards, I went and saw the corpse for myself. It was mutilated as if a hyena had been playing with it. I stood there for a long time, looking at the remains of a gentle boy, the reason for the suffering of a beloved woman. I looked at the guard standing near the corpse, watching the onlookers in case somebody cried and thus committed a crime.

"I fought back my tears with difficulty. And I tell you that right there I committed a grave sin in my heart by calling on the Lord in anger: 'Where are You?' I asked in rage. 'Where are You when Your children are being killed? Wasn't my son and thousands others enough? Do You have to take her only son?'

"I was angry beyond words and anger leads to sin. I sinned. I came back to my house, back to the broken life of the poor woman who had been my friend for so many years. What do you say to a woman like her? Be brave? Trust in God? All words were empty and inadequate. I simply cried with her. She stayed in my house for a week just like I had stayed in hers. We shared our grief but it did not decrease because of this. We cried together.

"My elder son, I forgot to tell you, had got into the habit of staying out for a week or so. He told me he had an exacting job and he had to work at night and with the curfew and shooting he said it was better if he slept at the office. But he came to visit me every Sunday night. And left early in the morning. I did not pay undue attention to all this.

"Woizero Askalu returned to her house but she had changed. I visited her every day but it was like visiting a dead person. She hardly talked, ate very little, and cried all the time. I feared for her and started to stay long hours in her house. I talked with other people and without letting her know we also passed the night in her house as well, in a shift, taking turns. Left to herself, I was afraid she would kill herself. How mistaken I was! How could she kill herself when she was not alive even though she moved and breathed? This was a woman I loved and I died with her. I hated the world, the government. I hated seeing the armed guards swaggering proudly, their hands drenched in blood. Ashamed they should have been but there they were parading themselves arrogantly. Killers of children and old men and women. Criminals all.

"My taste of hell came one afternoon. I was at home reading the Psalms of David when an old friend came to visit me. He had been with me in the police force but unlike me he hadn't retired. We talked for a while of the old days and the new brutal ones. He expressed his sorrow for the death of my son.

"'And how is Askalu?' he asked me. I told him she was more dead than alive. 'Poor woman,' he said in sorrow. 'Poor you,' he added suddenly. And I asked him why he had said that. He fidgeted a little and then, when I insisted, he came out with it and I cursed the day he had come to see me."

The old man stopped his story and asked me to give him water. After drinking, he continued with his tale.

"He told me that my elder son had been responsible for the death of Askalu's son. What a shock he gave me. I was totally numb. I couldn't believe my ears and I even shouted at my friend angrily, refusing to believe, though deep down I was already beginning to doubt. 'I am sorry,' my friend said. 'I thought you knew.' But I knew nothing. And I had to

calm myself and beg him to tell me the truth. And he told me. He told
me that my son belonged to one of the groups which supported the Derg
and participated in the killings. He told me that my son had fingered
Askalu's son as an 'anarchist.' He told me that as a result Askalu's son
had been arrested and that my son had, with others, interrogated him
and tortured him. He told me that this was God's own truth, that my son
spends his nights in a nearby kebele prison run by his friends and that
each night they torture and kill many youngsters. How could I not know
all this, he wondered, since, he said, many in my district knew of my
son's activities.

"What could I say? I had to work at night, my son had said. The Sunday visits at night, the early departures, the silence about his work, the
silence about his work . . . It all fitted in and in my sorrow I also remembered that he was not that aggrieved when his young brother had died.
In my sorrow I also realized the reason why Askalu broke down in tears
every time she saw me. I had thought she was sorry for the loss of her son
while she was actually crying for me."

Tears were now beginning to run down the old man's cheeks. "I
should have died with my wife, with my son! I was ashamed, destroyed,
an accursed old man. The fruit of my loins bringing agony to the woman
I loved, my own son a murderer. I felt dirty, reeking of blood, soiled to
the core. I stopped going to church. But, reluctant as I was I forced
myself to go to Askalu. She cried when she saw me. I cried silently and
before I left her I told her simply: 'I know. I am sorry.' And the kind
woman grasped my hands and with tears in her eyes said: 'It's not your
fault. It's not his fault, it is the times. God knows.' And this increased my
grief even more. Maybe I had wanted her to curse me, to make me angry
and thereby to reduce my guilt by being angry at her. But there she was
crying for me, absolving me of my sins. I am his father and how could I
not be responsible for the crimes of my son?

"I waited for the Sunday calmly. No, that is not entirely true. I was in
turmoil. Should I leave the house and not ever see his face? Or should I
confront him? What would have been his mother's feelings had she been
alive? What would have been my dead son's advice had he been alive?
What would Askalu say if I asked her? What about her dead son if he
could talk to me from beyond the grave? I heard no voices, saw no
dreams. But I waited.

"Sunday night came and my son arrived. He was his usual self and did not even notice me watching him closely as if he was a stranger with weird habits and actions. And finally, what had to be said had to be said and there was no use wasting time or words. 'Are you working for the kebeles?' I asked him directly.

"He did not reply outright but his eyes told me. I promised not to bore you but let me say he admitted it finally and even tried to convince me that 'enemies of the people like Askalu's son had to be killed if they refused to change their views.' The more he talked the more he sounded like the radio and the more I saw a stranger in front of me. No tears came to me, I was dry, spent, barren. A man without children you could say.

"In the morning he left promising to come back next Sunday. It was a long week. Askalu came once or twice as if I was to be pitied more than her. Seeing her increased my guilt and in a way strengthened my resolve. One has to do one's duty, I believed. My son was my responsibility. I had brought him into this world, he was my burden. And yet I could not make the decision to do what I felt I had to do. I was a coward or perhaps a father. Just a father. I knew a boy in our area whom I suspected was secretly working with your friends. I went to him and we talked. Nothing direct. I let him know that I knew about him and he neither denied it nor confirmed it since nothing was stated openly. I told him that my son usually came to visit me every Sunday night and left early in the morning. I said this and no more. As I was about to leave, the boy asked: 'Why?' I looked at him and said: 'For Askalu's son. For my dead son. For you. For himself.' And I left. I did not say 'for me' though I have thought since that I should have said that as well.

"Sunday came and my killer son also came to visit. It was a quiet night. I looked at him for a long time, saying farewell to him in my heart. I did not cry. I heard him leave early in the morning, right after curfew time. After a few minutes, I heard some shots. I knew what had happened. I did not go out to see him. They later brought his corpse into the house but I avoided seeing his dead body. I did not cry and they thought I was a tough old man ready to sacrifice his own son for the Revolution. His name was published in the newspapers and officials came to his funeral. I heard later on that some prisoners were killed in reprisal for his death. Even dead he had caused more deaths. A cursed son, a cursed father.

"Some time later I got the kebele pass to come to these parts but before I left I went to Askalu and told her that I had decided to leave the temporal world and become a recluse. She bade me good-bye and told me that she was also going to become a nun in the Debre Libanos monastery.

"And this," the old man said, "is my confession. I caused the death of my own son. It is fitting you should hear it since it involved your struggle and for the reasons I told you before. This is why," he continued with a smile, "I want to die. Your pills will be wasted since I want to die and I will die."

"You burden me with a heavy responsibility," I said to the old man.

"I am educating you about the sins of man," the old man stated. "I seek no absolution from you. I await God's judgment. But by telling you my story I am advising you to continue to do good. The world is full of evil but it is also full of good. You suffer for the good of others, isn't that good? Too many deaths still continuing . . . it is so saddening. Killing, killing, killing . . . when will it stop? When will God hear our cry and save us from agony? When will He take pity on the living who have to suffer for every day they live? I will ask Him when I meet Him soon," said the old man without a smile.

"I think He will understand you," I said lamely. What else could I say? As a fighter, I believed that what he had done was commendable. Still, I also felt the anguish that tore at his heart. Does one congratulate a father for having his son killed? Does one sympathize with a son who resorts to murder and breaks his own father's heart? Pity the unfortunate parents whose offsprings become killers of innocent people.

I bade the old man good-bye, aware that I would never see him again. I gave him no pills, none would have served to reduce his pain for his real agony was beyond the curative capabilities of science, let alone of a poorly supplied guerrilla doctor like me.

Waldiba was eerily quiet as usual. Monastery of the living dead, keeper of tormented souls. Guardian of agonizing secrets behind the doors of closed huts. One whispers in Waldiba and never talks out loud, the terrible tales of Ethiopia paralyze the tongue and deafen the ears.

I had a life to lead, a struggle left unfinished. I left the old man and went to join my guerrilla friends. More battles, more painful tales, some to be whispered, some to be told aloud. Guerrillas confess to guerrillas if they ever get the time to do so before dying.

Ossie O. Enekwe was born in 1942 in Nigeria. He received his
Ph.D. from Columbia University in 1982. He is the author of
Broken Pots, a collection of poems, and the novel *Come Thun-
der*. He has also written several books of nonfiction, including
Igbo Masks: The Oneness of Ritual and Theatre and *Theories of
Dance in Nigeria*. A member of the editorial board of *Okike*
since 1978, he teaches dramatic arts and creative writing at the
University of Nigeria.

The Last Battle

It was about 7:30 P.M. in Uzolla sector.

Noise of battle completely swallowed the whole front. The
battle line was one vast furnace as Federal and Secessionist guns roared
and thundered like a thousand wounded monsters. Flashes of fire lit the
jungle as shells burst into fragments, swept away in all directions, carrying with them dust and rocks, branches torn from trees and pieces of
flesh and bone.

It was in this circumstance that young Lt. Joseph Umeh, formerly of
the Suicide Squad, arrived at the 30th Brigade Camp at Emele-uzo. He
was angry to be sent there. His request to be transferred to the rear had
been rejected and he was now being sent to another hot sector.

"To another hot sector," he murmured, biting his lower lip with his
front teeth, "I must be told whether I alone caused this war. How can I
be moving from sector to sector like an armored car, whereas other officers, those that have godfathers, remain at the rear attending parties."

He had felt like this, disillusioned and angry, since he received the
deployment signal. He had almost gone mad. Something would have
happened to him if he had not been restrained by some of his fellow officers. He had wanted to march to his C.O. and tell him to "go to blazes."

He would have ripped open his fading battle shirt and shown him the scar of a ferret wound spreading from his navel down to his groin. He would have shown him his buttocks too. And then said to him: Sir, have you ever heard the whistling of a bullet? But his fellow officers had restrained him. No doubt he would have ended up in a court-martial which might have cost him his life.

And to top it all, he had also to carry his kit on his head and hitch-hike a distance of about fifteen miles to Uzolla sector. What an affront! His C.O. had refused to assign a vehicle to him because he was no longer his "responsibility." They would not even allow him to take his batman with him because of "scarcity of men." So he had to carry his kit on his head to the front.

So, Lt. Joe Umeh was like a battered old pugilist. He had joined the Rebel Army because he wanted to cut a figure. His bravery in battle was not all as a result of his belief, but something inside him, a capacity for hard labor and an obsessive desire to excel. Many of his kind had kissed the dust and rotted in hundreds of fields. But he was lucky. Since the start of the shooting, he had taken part in twenty battles. There were some he knew who got killed in their first battles. Before every battle he never expected to return alive, but God was very kind to him.

It seemed he would never die. After each battle, he came out full of praises. Once he had single-handedly wrecked a ferret car which he had trapped in a ditch. The proper name for him should have been the "forest fox." But his mates and followers called him "Attila." He was tall and heavy, but his face and manners were gentle. He smiled often, even when he was angry.

God was kind to Lt. Umeh, but his fellow human beings were hostile. In spite of all his exploits, he had been passed over again and again for promotion. Maybe it was because he was a stammerer or because he did not curry favor with his superiors. It could have been both. It could also be because his face was ugly (not from nature, but from the handiwork of a bullet which had hit him between his right eye and his nose). He was lucky though. The bullet had traveled very far before it hit him and buried itself two inches deep. The doctors had pulled it off quickly. So within four weeks he was again battle-worthy.

The 30 Brigade Camp in which he found himself was dark and cold as a mortuary. There was a tiny arrow of light sticking out of someplace. So he walked toward it. It turned out to be a batcher. He halted and listened and then tapped on the bamboo door. After about ten seconds, he heard boots approaching the door. When the door swung open, the light of a lamp hit his face and he was looking up at a soldier. Lt. Umeh said, "Good evening. I am Lt. Umeh recently deployed here. Can I see the Adjutant?"

The soldier stepped back into the room and said, "Come in . . . I am Captain Ofili, the Adjutant. I am pleased to meet you."

"Thank you."

"How did you come?"

"On foot."

"Hah, you must be tired."

"Yes, I am really exhausted."

Captain Ofili led the way to the end of the hall. Lt. Umeh noticed that he had a slight limp. He was happy to see a man who had got a battle scar, like himself.

Captain Ofili said, "Lt. Umeh, we have no food in the camp. But we have some palm wine. Let me get you some."

"It's okay, sir."

Captain Ofili indicated a low bench by the corner and asked Umeh to sit down. There was a cupboard full of files by the corner, too. Ofili opened it and brought out a bottle of palm wine and a tumbler which he handed over to Umeh. Umeh filled the glass, drank half of it, and, looking up at Ofili, asked, "When do I meet the C.O.?"

"Not this night. He lives five miles away. But he will be here tomorrow morning."

Umeh sighed. "When did the present operation begin?"

"Exactly at 18:00 hours. It has always been like that here. We have lost over eighty men since the present ops. Over ten officers have died since the last twenty days."

"This is a disastrous war," said Umeh, full of premonition. "We are doing the impossible, like throwing pebbles at a man armed with a spear."

"And on top of that, hunger," added Ofili.

There was a long pause during which the two men reflected. Presently, Ofili said, "Umeh, come along, let me take you to my room. I suppose you want to sleep?"

"Yes," said Umeh, "I need to sleep. I am dog tired." Ofili limped along, leading the way, across the dark field of the camp. Soon they approached a collection of batchers. Ofili tapped on the door of one of them. A young private opened the door.

When he was seated Ofili said, "Umeh, we are glad to have you here." But Umeh kept mum. "We have heard of your exploits."

Umeh sighed and said, "But you have not heard of my problems."

"Everybody has problems."

But Umeh said, getting a trifle angry, "I don't care about other people's problems."

Ofili was surprised. He asked, "What is wrong?"

"I have two fat bullets inside my buttocks, but that doesn't qualify me for a transfer to the rear. I am among those who have to die so that the mighty lords may live and enjoy."

"Yes, I understand. I too have a crippled knee. But couldn't the doctors remove your bullets?"

"How could they? No. The bullets went into corners where they cannot be tampered with. They won't come out unless my bones are split like firewood. And yet I do not deserve to be given rear duty." Lt. Umeh was getting more infuriated as he spoke.

"Now look," he said, unbuttoning his khaki shirt and loosening his belt, "this is a ferret wound I got at Onitsha sector."

Captain Ofili shrugged his shoulders when he saw the scar. He did not say anything. It was amazing that somebody could have had such a wound and remain alive.

Umeh continued: "So you can see . . . I have been moving from sector to sector collecting bullet wounds and being stitched all the time like a punching bag."

Captain Ofili sighed and said, "Hah, if one were to worry about the injustices inflicted on us little men, the war would have ended a long time ago."

There was silence for about five minutes. Captain Ofili indicated the bed and said, "Umeh, you better sleep. I go back to the office. I'll remain there until I hear reports from the battle."

Umeh asked, "What of the other officers?"

"They are all taking part in the ops. And if we lose them, only two officers will be left in the Brigade—you and me."

"Why?" asked Umeh in amazement.

"We have been expecting several officers from the DHQ. But none has arrived. Good night."

Captain Ofili wanted to get away fast. His conversation with Umeh did not cheer him. When a hero loses faith, his admirers go dumb.

Later in the night, remnants of the attackers from the 32 Brigade staggered back into the camp. Of the one hundred and twenty attacking force only forty returned. The two officers who led them had been torn to pieces trying to charge a Federal position. The report, though shocking, was not altogether disheartening for there were several reports of cold-blooded bravery. There was the story of a young private who charged a machine-gun crew with an empty rifle. It was only the lack of ammunition that brought them defeat, claimed the survivors.

The next morning, during parade, the C.O. drove up in his Land Rover. There was a hush as the six soldiers on escort jumped out onto the field and spread out, brandishing automatic rifles. It was as if the whole camp was full of enemy troops. The escorts stood in a horseshoe formation behind him. The Adjutant limped toward him and saluted. The C.O. got the report of the last operation and asked, "Have the Infantry officers deployed here arrived?"

"Only one, sir."

"His name?"

"Lt. Joe Umeh, sir."

"Dismiss the parade and bring him to me."

In the office, the C.O. congratulated Lt. Umeh on his previous exploits and explained his plans, one of which was to launch an attack on the Federal positions the same night. He told him, "As soon as the objective is secured, at least five hundred troops will arrive from other sectors to help. Lt. Umeh . . . I'll allow you to draw your plans and choose your men. You have ample ammo."

"Yessir."

"Any questions?"

"Yessir. Please, can I have some automatic rifles for my men?"

"There are no automatic rifles . . . As you were."

"Yessir."

Lt. Umeh walked across the wide school field toward the old school hall where the privates were being rested. Some of them were sitting on the grass in front of the building and breaking palm kernels which they chewed and swallowed hurriedly in order to numb the hunger which was gnawing their maws all the time.

Some of them were naked, stark naked. Some had tattered rags around their hips. The outlines of their ribs were clearly discernible on the dark skins.

When they saw him striding toward them, they got to their feet like tired dogs and began to scuttle back into the hall. Lt. Umeh smiled—a wan, painful smile. He was not surprised. These boys were like waifs waiting for extermination. These boys were afraid of the world. The world had treated them badly. They were full of bitterness: an inexpressible feeling was eating deep into their hearts. They were the boys who won and lost battles. When they were well led by good officers, they fought. If not, they ran. They were used to being kept at a camp for rest which was meant to keep them available for new attacks. And so they were afraid of new officers, new signals, and new movements.

Lt. Umeh walked on as if he was not interested in them. He strode into the hall and saw many of them lying on the bare floor among little heaps of kernel husks. They stood up with great effort and saluted, "Mon sarp."

"Good evening, my brothers," he said. "Wey the sergeant?"

"Here, sir," said a tall boy who had no visible sign of his rank.

"Okay, I want everybody outside immediately."

"Yessum."

Lt. Umeh stood there and watched them shuffle along like people who had never drilled before. Only two or three of them had boots on. But those boots were worn to the sole.

Outside, they stood in lines and waited for him. Lt. Umeh marched forward and said, "I be Lt. Umeh. I don fight for every sector, but I never die. And I no go die. Those wey follow me, no go die. I don come make I come help you people here. Make you no fear. Everything go be alright. You go get plenty wakis. Stand by . . . Rest and sleep. Biafra, Kwenu! . . . Biafra Kwenu! . . ."

There were only fragmentary sounds of "yah."

Lt. Umeh said, "Make una sing me one song."

There was silence for about thirty seconds. Then the sergeant began,

"*Enyi Biafra le le, Enyi Biafra le le le,*" expecting the boys to reecho the second line. There were only tired responses but he kept on singing. Singing painfully.

Remember nu Chuma Nzeogwu
Chuma Nzeogwu bu nwa Biafra, Enyi.
Remember nu Willie Archibong
Willie Archibong bu nwa Biafra, Enyi.

The singing continued for a few more minutes and died.

Lt. Umeh was now incredibly downhearted. His head was full of voices speaking to him at the same time. He went back and lay on the bed till midnight.

At 5 A.M. Lt. Umeh was at the battle line with the boys. With the light they would see the Federal positions and attack immediately. That was the plan. The Federal side would not be expecting them so soon after the previous day's disaster. It was going to be a surprise attack.

The boys were armed with bolt-action rifles which they called "cock-and-shoot." They had six bullets apiece. Lt. Umeh, since his last encounter with the C.O., had been very taciturn. But these boys had never fought under him and so could not tell that he had changed.

His position was about five hundred yards to the enemy trenches. He was looking up at them from a valley. He said to the boys, "You no go fire until I command." "Yessir," they murmured with fear in their hearts. At six, he said, "Advance."

When they marched about a hundred yards he pulled a dirty white handkerchief from his pocket, stuck it to his bayonet and said, "Make una drop your guns. Raise your hands. We are surrounded." They obeyed easily enough.

From where they lay with their guns at the ready, Federal troops watched in amazement as the platoon marched toward them with their hands raised over their heads.

ADEWALE MAJA-PEARCE

Adewale Maja-Pearce was born in 1953. He is the author of *Loyalties and Other Stories*, *In My Father's Country*, *A Mask Dancing: Nigerian Novelists of the Eighties*, *How Many Miles to Babylon?*, and *Who's Afraid of Wole Soyinka?* He also edited *The Heinemann Book of African Poetry in English* and now serves as the editor of the journal *Index on Censorship*.

Civil War I–VII

I

We were split up into groups of two and assigned a hut each. Our Commander said: "Be ready at 05:30 hours," and with that we turned in.

In our hut a woman lay on a mat and an old man squatted on the ground beside her. He stopped talking and stood up to meet us. His skin seemed to be stretched across his bones.

"Welcome, gentlemen, welcome," he said. He turned to the woman, who had not stirred.

"Can't you see that we have guests? Stand up and attend to them," he said. The woman, who was young, got up silently and backed into a corner. She watched us with frightened eyes. She was clutching a bundle.

The old man raised his hands: "It is little enough, gentlemen, but it is yours. Will you take tea?"

"Don't bother," I said.

"Old man, where are your troops hiding?" my companion said.

"Troops?"

"Yes, your troops. Where are they hiding?"

The old man laughed.

"Do you think I am joking?" my companion said. He removed his revolver from the holster and held it in his palm. "Where are they?" he asked.

"Gone," the old man said, "those of them that are alive."

"I don't believe you. I think they are hiding in the forest. They are waiting for us to sleep."

The woman made a sound.

"They are waiting for us, I can feel it," my companion said. "Light a candle, I know that you want to trick us."

"But . . ." the old man began.

"Light a candle I say, don't you hear me?" He waved the revolver in the old man's direction. The woman began whimpering and would have screamed but I looked at her and shook my head.

When the candle was lit I went over to my companion. "Take it easy," I whispered. "Remember that we have sentries posted all around. If anything happens they will alert us. Let's get some sleep, we've been marching all day, and tomorrow it'll be the same." He looked at me mistrustfully. "You can take the mat," I said.

He looked at the woman, who had not moved.

"Come here," he said. She opened her mouth to say something but no words came. Only her eyes expressed her terror.

"Are you deaf?" the old man said to her. She got to her feet.

"Show me," my companion demanded, indicating the bundle. She began whimpering as before and tightened her hold on it. He slapped her hand across the face and snatched it from her. Wrapped in the cloth was a tiny child.

"It's dead," he said. "Doesn't she know?"

The old man shrugged. I went out.

When I returned my companion and the woman were lying together on the mat. The old man was squatting against the far wall. I stretched out across the entrance and fell asleep.

I woke up when it was still dark. I heard a noise from the mat. As my eyes became accustomed to the darkness I peered over to where the old man was. He was in the same position, staring at the couple. I closed my eyes.

In the morning we marched out. We were a pathetic bunch. We had been fighting continually for weeks and we were exhausted. All day long the insects swarmed around us and the sun beat down on us. What little food we had would not last us much longer.

Those who were wounded had to take care of themselves. By evening time some of them had fallen behind. We did not expect to see them again.

When we finally camped our Commander said: "According to my calculations we should be near the town of O___. With any luck we will be there the day after tomorrow. Try and get as much rest as you can. I myself will take the first watch."

Suddenly my companion shouted: "I don't believe you, Captain, it is all lies you are telling us." I ran toward him as he started to unbuckle his revolver but before I could reach him I heard a single shot and he fell. When I got to him he was already dead. The bullet had entered his skull and lodged in his brain.

I waited until everyone was asleep and then started out. When I thought I had traveled far enough I switched on the flashlight. The forest was full of sounds, and every moment I expected to be my last.

When I reached the village I sought out the hut. At the entrance I paused. I heard the familiar voice of the old man. He was speaking in a low voice in a language I couldn't understand. I entered.

"Who is there?" he asked, turning to me. I shone the flashlight on my face and then back at them. The woman was lying on the mat, clutching her bundle.

"You've come back," he said.

"To . . . to see if I could do anything for you," I said.

"Have you any food?" he asked.

"No, but I have some money." I held out some notes; it was all I had. He spat on the ground.

"What will that do for us?" he said.

"I don't know," I said.

"Then go back to your people, you can do nothing for us," he said. He turned his back on me and bent over the woman and continued his monologue in his unfamiliar language. I stood there for a while before I left.

II

For three days we had been wandering about in the bush, tired, hungry, and sick. Outside the town of O___ we had been surprised by a patrol of Federal troops and only a handful of us had managed to escape. Now we were without supplies, and if we did not soon find food and shelter we would perish.

There were a dozen of us, with half as many rifles between us and hardly any ammunition. We had no choice but to press on and hope.

It was the nights that were the worst. After a long day's march we would be exhausted but unable to sleep. The wounded among us would begin to moan, low and steady at first but, as the night wore on, louder and more insistent, the only sound in that vast tropical stillness. And as if that wasn't enough we would be assailed by mosquitoes, thousands of them, attracted no doubt by the smell of human blood. By the morning of the fourth day I knew something had to be done.

There was only one man I fully trusted. He was the only other with some experience of warfare. I called him over.

"Joshua, we must go west, back to the town of O___," I said.

He nodded.

"Can we do it in a day, do you think?"

"Only if we get rid of the sick," he said.

He had understood me perfectly. The war had knocked all the sentimentality out of him, which is why I liked him.

"Round up the fit ones and take them away," I said. "I will do what must be done and catch up with you." He made as if to go, but hesitated. "What's the matter?" I asked.

"Let me be the one to do it, Captain. They are my people, it will make it easier for them."

I agreed. There were four who would be left. One was a boy of fourteen. He had been shot in the leg and gangrene had set in. Without medical help he would have died anyway.

So I set off with the remainder. Although no one spoke I knew what they were thinking, but I also knew they were relieved not to have been the ones to have had to make the choice.

That night we arrived back at the town. We split up into groups of two and made for a house where we knew we would be welcome. The Federal troops were all over but we managed to make it without incident.

The house we gathered at was owned by an old man whose sons had fought under my command, and he was pleased to see us. While his daughter served us he gave us a rundown of the movement, size, and distribution of the enemy.

In the morning I was the first to wake. Dawn was only just breaking but I felt refreshed. Somewhere in the depths of a dream an idea had presented itself to me and I went off in search of Joshua. He was stretched out on a mat in the corner of the living room. His throat had been cut with a sharp instrument and the blood had congealed without spilling. Which of my men had done it? Or had they all conspired? Had they been called upon to avenge the blood of their brothers?

III

After six months' heavy fighting they liberated the city of N___ from the rebels. Death and disease had cut their original force by half and they had almost run out of ammunition. A relief force was on its way to take over and they were recalled to barracks, a journey of almost six hundred miles.

The last night in the city they spent celebrating. Oluwaju lost count of how many beers he'd had after the first couple of hours. He went from one bar to the next until, sometime after midnight, he found himself in a nightclub with three companions.

Because he had money in his pocket he was immediately surrounded by women. He ordered drinks all round and danced. This went on until he passed out. When he woke up it was morning and he was in bed with a young woman.

"Where are we?" he asked.

"In my room, don't you remember?"

"Did you drag me all the way here yourself?"

"How could I? You walked."

His head was throbbing. He saw his trousers hanging from a nail on the back of the door.

"Where is my money?" he demanded, searching through the pockets.

"I didn't touch your money," she said.

"You lie," he said. "I couldn't have spent it all."

She shrugged. "As you like," she said, and began to dress. Furious, he grabbed her shoulder and slapped her face.

"You are a liar," he repeated.

She looked at him without fear. "Are you happy now?" she said and went out.

When she returned she handed him a cup of tea and sat on the bed. Her mouth was sore from where he had hit her because she drank hesitantly, the rim of the cup barely touching her lips. Then there was a knock on the door and an old woman entered. She was lame in one leg and carried a stick.

"You have a visitor," she said when she saw him.

"Yes, Mama."

The old woman went away.

"Does she live with you?" Oluwaju asked.

"Yes."

"Tell her to come back, I have to be going," he said.

"Wait," she said suddenly, clutching his arm. "I want to go with you."

"How do you know where I'm going?"

"You and your friends were talking."

He laughed. "How can I take you and your mother? You're crazy. And what will you do in Lagos? Do you know anybody there?"

"I am young, I know how to survive. I can't stay here any longer. Please, take me. If I stay here I don't know what will happen to me. Before this war started I had a good job and I lived in a house with my family. Just look at me now," she said.

"I'm sorry," he said, "but it's out of the question. Even if I wanted to my Captain wouldn't allow it. And then there's your mother, she's an old lady . . ."

"My mother would stay here," she said.

"You would leave her here!"

"Of course," she said, and added: "The journey alone would kill her."

"And what will become of her?"

"She hasn't long to live," she said. When she saw the look he gave her she said: "So you think it is bad of me, eh? What do you know of my suffering? Did I ask for this stupid war? Did I? The things I have to do to eat . . ."

"I'm sorry," he repeated.

"Now it's you who lie," she said. "If you were really sorry you would help me." She was working herself up; in a moment she would be hysterical. He grabbed his shirt and fled, and as he emerged into the street he heard her calling after him.

IV

Look, let me tell you at once: he was not a bad man. In the three years I spent fighting I saw worse men, believe me. If I tell you some of the things our men did you will call me a liar to my face.

The day before it happened he saved my life. If it wasn't for him I wouldn't be here today. You think I'm joking? Let me tell you. It was like this. We were advancing on the village of O___. It was nearly dark and we were tired and hungry. All I wanted was to lie down and go to sleep, even in that bush. I didn't care about the war or anything, I just wanted to be left in peace, you understand me?

Okay, so our Captain told us that we had to capture the village that night. Well, what could we do? We had to obey. Orders were orders: let me see the man who would have said otherwise. As I told you, night was approaching. He and I and two others were told to go on ahead and scout around. All of a sudden there was a shot and I was hit. Then you know what happened? The other two ran away. Only he remained. He placed himself in front of me and opened fire in the direction from which the shot had come. There was a scream and then silence.

Time passed. We heard our men some distance behind us. The next thing I knew he lifted me up on his shoulder, and then I passed out.

When I woke up I was lying on a mat in a hut. There was a candle beside me and he was bending over me.

"How are you feeling?" he asked.

"I'm fine," I said.

"Good," he said, then, in a whisper: "Listen, I saw a woman. You know how it is. If you think you will be alright here by yourself I won't be more than an hour at most."

"Go ahead," I said.

I fell asleep. I was woken by a sound while it was still dark. It was him: he had returned. I waited for him to settle down before I spoke.

"Was it good?" I asked him.

"Not bad," he said and lit a cigarette. There was something wrong with the way he said it, but I did not press him: after all, it was his own business.

When I woke in the morning he was not there. I heard a commotion outside. People were shouting. I could not make out what they were saying and I was too weak to go and see for myself.

Later in the day our Captain came to see how I was. I asked him what was happening.

"There was a murder here last night. One of the men from the village was killed, and his wife says one of our own men did it. She has identified him."

He didn't have to tell me; I knew who it was.

"What are you going to do with him?" I asked. He shrugged and turned to go. At that moment I felt sorry for him: I could see how troubled he was.

"Listen and you will hear," he said, and left.

I waited. An hour later I heard the order and half a dozen rifles go off in unison.

Well, such is war. It changes a man. As you see me so I am not the same person I was before this wretched business started: in those days I was only a kid. But bear witness now: never again will I do it. You can trust me on that.

V

The boy hid behind the old shed and watched the soldiers march into the village, and when the last of them had gone past he ran across the yard and into his hut.

"Mama," he called, excited. The woman looked up from the stove before which she was squatting. There was a baby tied on her back.

"Come and eat your food," she said.

"Mama, the soldiers have come," the boy said.

"Sit down and eat, I say," the woman said. The baby started crying. She untied it, sat on the bed, and gave it her breast.

"And when you have finished don't let me hear that you were playing among them," she said.

"Yes, Mama."

"They are not good people. They are the ones who killed your father and they wouldn't mind to kill us. How many were they?"

"Plenty," he said, "about a hundred. And they all carried rifles."

"You better not go out at all," she said.

"But . . ."

"But nothing. Do as I say. You want to get yourself killed? Don't you know that they take small boys like you into the bush?"

"Yes, Mama."

The day grew hotter until the heat was almost intolerable. The boy read some of his old schoolbooks and listened to the shouting and laughter of the soldiers. In the middle of the afternoon two of them came. One sat down while the other searched the room. It was the work of two minutes: after he had looked under the bed and inside the wardrobe there was nowhere else.

"Nothing, Captain."

"Where is your husband?" the Captain asked his mother.

"He's dead."

"How do you know?"

"I was told."

"By whom?"

"A friend whose husband was killed with him."

"How long ago was this?"

"About six months."

"Are there no men left in the village?"

"Only the old and wounded."

"Where have they all gone?"

"They are all dead."

"I don't believe you," he said. The boy saw how frightened his mother was, and he pitied and hated her for it.

"But it is true," she said.

"We have had reports that rebel troops were seen here less than a week ago."

"Who told you, it's a lie."

"So you say, but we were told about it from several of your own people."

"They only told you that to please you."

The Captain suddenly banged his clenched fist on the table. The boy saw his mother jump, and then try desperately to regain her composure.

"You know what we do to people who lie to us?" he shouted. His mother hung her head. Her hands were shaking by her side, and he saw that the Captain noticed it.

"Hey, you, come with me," the Captain said and stood up. His mother swung round and pulled him to her.

"Leave him, he is only a child," she pleaded. The Captain laughed.

"Do you think we are going to harm him?" He signaled to the other, who had all the while been standing to attention.

"I just want to have a little chat with him, that's all," he said.

The Captain took him around the village, all the while watching everything.

"It's women who bring all the trouble in this world," he said. "We men know how to speak the truth and get it over with, not so?"

"Yessah."

"Don't call me sir, my name is Baba. What is yours?"

"Christopher."

"Well, Christopher, won't you level with me, man to man, eh?" He stopped and looked at him and smiled. "Now, tell me, is it true that your father is dead?"

"Yes."

"You saw his body for yourself?"

"No, I was told."

The Captain put his hand on his shoulder. "Don't let it worry you, I can see that you are somebody who will go far in life. It's this wretched war that messes up our plans. Perhaps when it's over I'll see what I can

364

do to arrange for you to get out of here and make something of yourself in the world."

The boy nodded. They resumed walking. Still the Captain never ceased his watching.

"How many of your troops were here last week?" he asked abruptly, peering toward the distant bushes.

"About thirty," the boy answered without thinking, and then he knew he had done wrong. The Captain stopped and looked at him. The smile had gone from his face. The boy felt fear.

"Were they armed?"

"I . . . I . . ."

"Answer me, boy!" he shouted. Terrified, the boy nodded.

"All of them?"

"Yes."

VI

There were ways in which he was absolutely fearless. The men under his command had the greatest respect for him, and there were many who thoughtlessly risked death at his word. He was the only Commander who lived like his men, and more. He took privileges for himself and always headed the scouting parties into enemy territory.

One day he walked straight into a contingent of Federal troops. It was not an ambush and they were as surprised as we, and only managed to get the better of us because there were more of them than there were of us. And they were better armed. At some points the fighting was literally hand-to-hand, but I knew we were done for.

"Let's get out of here," he shouted to me at the first opportunity and we fled. We lost ourselves in the jungle and never paused to look back. By the time we finally stopped our clothes were torn and we were bleeding all over.

"We'll rest here for a while," he said.

"Do you know where we are?" I asked.

"I think so, but I'm not sure." He looked up. Through the tops of the trees the sun dipped to the west.

"If we go that way we should come to the village of O___ by night-fall," he said, pointing in the opposite direction. "Let's hope the Federal troops don't get there before us."

"Are we the only survivors?" I asked.

"I suppose so. There was nothing we could have done. It's my fault, I made the mistake of underestimating their advance. I knew they were in the area but I didn't think they would have moved so fast."

"There's no point blaming yourself," I said.

"I know, I know, but I was responsible for the lives of those men and it weighs heavy on me. The usual precaution and it may not have happened," he said and stood up. "Anyway, first thing tomorrow we better try and find Okafor's men and join up with them until we get fresh orders."

We started off, traveling slower to keep up our strength. Several detours were necessary to avoid the worst of the undergrowth. Once I nearly stepped on a boa constrictor; as for the mosquitoes, our sweat and blood seemed to attract them from miles around. At last, as the sun was starting to set, we came in sight of the village, just as he had predicted.

We approached with caution. About a hundred yards away, concealed by the bushes, we lay down and waited for darkness. A few women, children, and old men wandered about talking in low voices.

"That is the hut we will spend the night in," he said, pointing to one near us.

"Who does it belong to?"

"A woman I used to know when I was a child. We grew up in the same neighborhood and then she married a man from here."

"Do you know her husband?"

"Yes. He's a good soldier."

"Where is he now?"

"Who knows? Fighting somewhere most probably." From his shirt pocket he produced a crumpled cigarette and a match. He broke the cigarette in half and we smoked in silence.

"What were you doing before this war started?" he asked afterward.

"I was studying at the University."

"One of the lucky ones, eh? When I was fifteen I was supporting my family. I had six younger brothers and sisters and my father was a drunk. One day he disappeared and we were all a lot happier," he said.

The sun was now an orange glow on the horizon. In a moment it would be out of sight.

"Where is your family?" he asked.

"In Lagos. My father didn't waste any time. When he saw what was happening he packed up and took them all to safety."

"Why didn't you go with them?"

I shrugged. "It's not so easy to say. I was idealistic enough in those days to think that it was my duty to fight for what I believed in."

"And now?"

"I'm not sure any longer whether it's worth believing in anything. I've seen too much death and misery to think anything can be worth it."

He laughed. "You know what your trouble is," he said.

"What?"

"You think too much. Life has always given you a choice whereas I have always had to survive from day to day the best way that I could."

The darkness was falling rapidly. A few stars had appeared in the sky.

"War is a peculiar thing," he said.

"How do you mean?"

"For example, it is only because of it that you and I met."

"We might have otherwise, you never know. The world is altogether a very strange place indeed. Sometimes, if I think about it long enough, I find it hard to believe that it's real, do you understand me? It's as if the whole thing is just a dream, a bad joke, and nothing really exists. I'm not saying it very well but do you see what I'm getting at?" I said, half-ashamed at my outburst.

"I already told you, you think too much," he said and laughed.

It was completely dark now. We had to wait until the moon had risen to give us enough light.

"All my family are dead," he suddenly said after what seemed like a long time.

"I'm sorry."

"They were traveling to my mother's town and the bus was blown up. There were no survivors. I heard about it many months later."

"I'm sorry," I said again.

After about an hour we decided to move. As we neared the village we heard voices but saw no one. We reached the hut and entered quickly.

"Who is there?" a woman's voice called.

"It is I, Chike. I have a friend with me."

"Wait," she said. I heard the rustle of clothes, and then she struck a match.

"Sit down," she said, indicating two chairs. By the light of the candle I saw that she was young. Her head was bare and she was wearing a faded cotton housecoat. She drew a curtain across the doorway. Then she gave us some bread and margarine and sat down on the bed.

When we finished eating she said: "There is a rumor that the Federal troops will be here by morning."

"I thought as much," he said. "We left them not twelve hours ago. Don't worry about them. What of you, how are you keeping?"

"Obi was killed, did you hear?"

"No, I didn't. When did it happen?"

"About six months ago. Thank God he saw his son before he died."

For the first time I noticed the child on the bed.

"Are they treating you well here?"

"As well as I can expect, but you know how it is. I married one of their sons but I am not one of them."

"Our people!" he said and shook his head.

"It's better if I blow the candle out so as not to attract attention," she said. She got up and took a mat from under the bed and handed it to me.

"Can you manage with this?" she asked me.

"Thank you," I said. I rolled it out in a corner and lay down and then realized how tired I was. Before I knew it I had dozed off.

The war had made me into a light sleeper. While it was still dark I was woken by voices from the bed.

"I am afraid to die," he was saying.

"We must all die when our time has come," she said.

"I don't have your faith. I don't believe in God anymore."

"You're suffering from strain, you don't know what you are saying. Try and sleep, it will be better in the morning."

"It won't be better in the morning, it will be the same . . . and the next day and the next."

There was a desperate quality to his voice. I had heard it so many times before. In most cases it turned out to be a premonition of death, but perhaps someone in that state just becomes careless. The baby stirred and began whimpering.

"Wait, I must feed it," she said. There was a movement and then I heard it suckling with short, greedy noises.

"Obi was strong, that is why you married him. I am weak," he said.

"No, you mustn't talk like that. You are only human."

I heard him sit up. And then I heard him crying.

"Come," she said, "come."

As the time passed he grew calmer. By now I could make out their forms, three shapes crouched together on the bed. She was sitting up, her back to the wall, while the baby suckled at one breast and the man at the other. And then I heard her own weeping, quieter, more restrained than his, and then I fell asleep again.

VII

What could I have done? There were five of them, and they were armed, and there was just her and me, tired, hungry, and demoralized. We were at their mercy, and they knew it. At best I could have gone for one of them, but that would only have been misplaced heroism, surely you can see that. Just look at the facts and tell me what you would have done. One move and they would have cut me down without a thought. As it was I could see that two of them had half a mind to put a bullet through me and have done with it. Who would have known? I would have just been another dead Biafran, so much the better!

It was like this. In the middle of the night our town was attacked. Our own soldiers ran away and we civilians were herded into the hotel. Sure I had listened to their propaganda, their promises that no genocide would be committed, but would you have believed them? Those Nigerian soldiers were wild, let me tell you, and to make matters worse they had uncovered a stash of palm wine and they were getting drunk. There was no telling what they would do. So I escaped. I ran into the forest and just kept on running until I dropped from exhaustion.

Toward morning I fell asleep. When I woke up there she was squatting on the ground beside me.

"What are you? How did you find me?" I asked her.

"I followed you," she said.

"I didn't hear you. Why didn't you call out to me?" I asked.

"I did not want to frighten you. Anyway, you would have told me to go back because I am a woman," she said.

"Who are your people?" I asked her.

"I am not from your town," she said. "I am from N___, but after we were attacked I and my family left with the others."

"Where is your family now?"

"I left them behind. They did not want to come with me. They said that they were tired of running," she said.

We started off. If we followed the sun I knew that we would reach the main road by nightfall, and from there we could follow it to the new capital. If we moved quickly the journey would take us about five days.

All that day we pushed forward. We were lucky that the rainy season was late, otherwise it would have been impossible. As it was, without a machete, we had a tough time getting through the worst of the undergrowth. I was surprised that she was able to keep up with me and did not once complain. My annoyance at her presence gradually gave way to pity, and then admiration. In the end I was grateful to have company.

Just before dark I called a halt. We found a clearing about half a mile from the road.

"The Red Cross people use that road," I said. "We may be lucky tomorrow and meet one of their trucks."

"And if we don't?"

"Then we will have to beg. There is a village about twenty miles farther on, they cannot refuse us."

We set about collecting wood, and when we had enough I set fire to it. I hoped there were no troops about, but I was more afraid of being attacked by animals. I could hear hyenas in the distance, and I knew it was our presence that they could smell.

I smoked my last cigarette, but on an empty stomach it made me dizzy.

"What is your name?" I asked her.

"Charity."

"Are your people Christians?"

"Yes."

"I don't believe in the white man's God," I said. She did not answer. She just squatted there and gazed at the fire.

"How old are you?" I asked.

"Eighteen," she said. A bat flew by overhead. It looked black against the purple sky.

"What were you doing before the war began?" I asked. She threw some more sticks on the fire. They crackled and sparked and lit up her face.

"Nothing. We were poor farmers. I helped my mother in the house," she said.

I put out my hand and touched her arm. "Come and lie down with me," I said. She did so. I held her to me, and then made love to her. She was a virgin.

We slept fitfully that night. Every now and then she would get up and feed the fire, but it was the mosquitoes that kept us awake. They buzzed round our ears and by the sound of them they must have been monsters.

When day broke we set off again. The going was easier but we had to remain on the alert all the while. In the middle of the afternoon we heard a truck approach. We hid in the bushes but when it passed us I saw that it was our own troops. We went back on the road to listen for others. I was certain they were heading for the capital and they might see their way to giving us a ride. Sure enough another approached. I waved it down but it wasn't until a Nigerian soldier jumped down that I realized I had made a mistake.

So you see. You can't say that once I had hailed them down we could have escaped. We were at their mercy. They took us into the back of their truck and then one by one they raped her while I was forced to watch. She screamed and fought and begged, but what could she have done against them? And let me tell you, I made myself deaf to her suffering, I did nothing, and worse. When the ringleader had finished with her he looked at me and smiled. Yes, he smiled at me, and I smiled back. I knew he despised me, that he was saying, "Look at what I can do to your woman in your presence and there is nothing you can do about it"; and I was saying, "Do what you like with her, what is she to me? She is only a woman, but please spare me." He knew what I was thinking and he despised me even more. To him I was less than a dog. When they finished they drove off and left us there.

Now I ask you: Would you have done otherwise? Would anybody else have done different? Only a fool would have tried to stop them. Put yourself in my place for a moment and think about it. It was a time of war, normal feelings and behavior no longer applied. For the next eighteen months I forgot all about it. When you are fighting for survival you forget everything except what concerns you at the present time. But it couldn't last forever, and sooner or later it had to end. I began to dream about her, and then I could think of nothing else. I remembered how I had smiled at the soldier and what had gone through my mind. Gradually I lost interest in everything. Women no longer attracted me and I did not care about my work or anything. Life seemed pointless and the struggle for survival a waste of time. I know now that it would have been better for me to have died then. Life has become pointless, do you understand what I am saying?

ACKNOWLEDGMENTS

Grateful acknowledgment is made to the following for permission to reprint previously published material.

"The Museum" by Leila Aboulela from *Coloured Lights*. Copyright 1997. Reprinted by permission of Polygon.

"The One-Handed Hero" by Funso Aiyejina, from *The Legend of the Rockhill and Other Stories*. Copyright 2000. Reprinted by the permission of TSAR.

"Four Dimensions" by I. N. C. Aniebo, from *Of Wives, Talismans and the Dead*. Copyright © 1983 by I. N. C. Aniebo. Reprinted by permission of the author.

"Thirty-one Beautiful Green Trees" by Salwa Bakr, from *The Wiles of Men*. Copyright of the English Translation by D. Johnson-Davies 1992. Reprinted by permission of Danys Johnson-Davies.

"A Life in Detail" by Mohammed Berrada, from the periodical *Lotus*, Afro-Asian Writings, Journal of Afro-Asian Writers Association, No. 59, 1988. Not copyrighted. (Translation by Alice Copple-Tošić.)

"A Child in the Bush of Ghosts" by Olympe Bhely-Quenum, from the Nigerian literary periodical *Okike*. Copyright © 1980 by *Okike*. Reprinted by permission of O. O. Enekwe, editor, on behalf of the author.

"The Three-Piece Suit" by Ali Deb, from the periodical *Lotus*, Afro-Asian Writings, Journal of Afro-Asian Writers Association, No. 59, 1988. Not copyrighted. (Translation by Alice Copple-Tošić.)

"The Last Battle" by O. O. Enekwe. Published by permission of the author.

"Bossy" by Abdulrazak Gurnah, from the Nigerian literary periodical *Okike*, January 1979. Copyright © 1979 by *Okike*. Reprinted by permission of O. O. Enekwe, editor, on behalf of the author.

"Papa, Snake & I" by L. B. Honwana, from *We Killed Mangy Dog and Other*

Mozambique Stories. Copyright © 1969 by Luis Bernardo Honwana. Reprinted by permission of AP Watt Ltd., literary agent, on behalf of the author.

"Hot Days, Long Nights" by Nnadozie F. Inyama, from the Nigerian literary periodical, *Okike*. Copyright © 1989 by *Okike*. Reprinted by permission of O. O. Enekwe, editor, on behalf of the author.

"The Home-Coming" by Milly Jafta, from *Coming on Strong: Writing by Namibian Women*, Copyright 1996. Reprinted by permission of Gamsberg Mcmillan Publishers.

"The Woman in Green" by Farida Karodia, from *Coming Home*. Copyright 1988. Reprinted by permission of Heinemann Educational Publishers.

"Waiting for a Turn" by Ken Lipenga, from *Waiting for a Turn*. Copyright © 1981 by Popular Publications. Reprinted by permission of Popular Publications, Malawi.

"The Advance" by Henri Lopès, from the book *Tribaliks*, *Contemporary Congolese Stories*. Copyright © 1971 by Editions Cle, Yaounde. English language translation copyright © 1987 by Andrea Leskes. First published by Heinemann Educational Books Ltd. in the African Writers Series in 1987. Reprinted by permission of Andrea Leskes.

"It Was Easter Sunday the Day I Went to Netreg" by Sindiwe Magona, from *Living, Loving and Lying Awake at Night*. Copyright © 1991 by Sindiwe Magona. Reprinted by permission of the author.

"Civil War I–VII" by Adewale Maja-Pearce, from *Loyalties*. Copyright © 1986 by Adewale Maja-Pearce. Reprinted by permission of Longman Group Ltd., UK.

"Slow Poison" by Makuchi, from *Open Spaces*. Copyright 1999. Reprinted by permission of the author.

"Thought Tracks in the Snow" by Dambudzo Marechera, from *The House of Hunger*. Copyright © 1978 by Dambudzo Marechera. Reprinted by permission of Zimbabwe Publishing House (PVT) Ltd., Zimbabwe.

"The Other City" by Ibrahim Abdel Megid, from the periodical *Lotus*, Afro-Asian Writings, Journal of Afro-Asian Writers Association. No. 59, 1988. Not copyrighted. (Translation by Alice Copple-Tošić.)

"The Dignity of Begging" by William (Bloke) Modisane, from *Hungry Flames*, ed. by M. Mzamane. Copyright © 1986 by Mbulelo Mzamane. Reprinted by permission of Ingeborg Modisane.

"God of Meme" by Ndeley Mokoso, from *Man Pass Man and Other Stories*.